Flaunting It!

"The liberation of homosexuals
can only be the work
of homosexuals themselves"
— Kurt Hiller, 1921

Vancouver
Pulp Theatre Press,
Canada
1992

Flaunting It!

**A decade
of gay journalism
from
The Body Politic**

An anthology
edited by Ed Jackson
and Stan Persky

New Star Books
Vancouver
Pink Triangle Press
Toronto
1982

First printing July 1982
5   4   3   2   1

Canadian Cataloguing in Publication Data

Flaunting It!

Includes index.
ISBN 0-919888-32-1 (bound)
ISBN 0-919888-31-3 (pbk)

1. Gay liberation movement — Canada — Addresses,
essays, lectures.   2. Homosexuality — Canada —
Addresses, essays, lectures.   3. Homosexuality —
Addresses, essays, lectures.

I. Jackson, Edward 1945-   II. Persky, Stan,
1941-   III. The Body Politic

HQ76.8.C2F43   306.7'66'0971   C82-091112-7

Book design by Kirk Kelly
Cover design by Rick Bébout / Tony Trask
Production by Victor Bardawill, Jr
Typesetting by volunteer labour at Pinktype, Toronto
Printed and bound in Canada

This book was published with the assistance of the Canada Council

New Star Books Ltd   Pink Triangle Press
2504 York Avenue   Box 639, Station A
Vancouver, BC   Toronto, ON
Canada V6K 1E3   Canada M5W 1G2

Contents

In the courts, on the hustings, in the streets
The Seventies
Into the Eighties

List of illustrations

Introduction

For as long as homosexuals have been visible and faintly vocal, they have been accused of being *too* visible and *too* vocal. They have been told that they are acting too flamboyantly, going too far, shoving it down people's throats. Journalists quip that the love that dared not speak its name now won't shut up. And so on. In a 1928 column in the London *Sunday Express* attacking Radclyffe Hall's lesbian novel *The Well of Loneliness*, an editor said of homosexuals, "They flaunt themselves in public places with increasing effrontery and more insolently provocative bravado." In 1981 Peter Worthington, the editor of the *Toronto Sun*, wrote, "Every literate person should know that 'flaunt' is what some homosexuals do with their preferences."

The Body Politic, as one of the most visible gay institutions in Canada, has often been subjected to this predictable and increasingly gay-specific accusation. *Our very existence* has been interpreted as shaking an irreverent lavender fist under the noses of an affronted citizenry. Outrage, simulated or otherwise, has been the standard response of the morality-watchers.

"When a heterosexual shows a picture of his family, it's called sharing," observes lesbian comic Robin Tyler elsewhere in this book. "When we show them a picture of our lover, it's called flaunting. Isn't it time we shared?"

The discrepancy between what *The Body Politic* has actually done or written and what the ignorant, the fearful and the cynical accuse us of doing is so wide that it becomes a significant phenomenon in itself. Given how simple it is to earn the "flaunting" brickbat, it seemed time to transform it into a sweet-smelling bouquet for the world of willing readers.

Survival

Gay pride took a quantum leap forward throughout North America in 1969, the year the gay liberation movement marks as its symbolic birth. It was the year that street queens and other bar-goers responded in an unexpected way to an harassment visit by New York policemen to a Greenwich Village bar on Christopher Street called the Stonewall Inn. The customers fought back, demonstrated, threw things at the police, distributed flyers and experienced, for the first time, the astonishing sensation of resistance.

The match, once struck, ignited a movement. The next four years saw the burgeoning of a gay press, irrepressible, irreverent, militant, lively. Social change movements, sociologist Laud Humphreys has said, "must find a common language, develop an ideology, counter the propaganda control exercised by the state and communicate both warnings and hope.... The role of the gay press becomes a central and decisive one in the movement for gay freedom."

One by one the journals bloomed: *Gay Sunshine* in San Francisco (August 1970), *Gay Liberator* in Detroit (April 1970), *Fag Rag* in Boston (Summer 1971), *The Body Politic* in Toronto (November 1971), *Gay News* in London, England (June 1972) and *Gay Community News* in Boston (June 1973). Suddenly so much had to be written, so much had to be said, and finally there was an audience hungry to read and eager to listen.

The Body Politic began as a radical tabloid born of political conviction and a hunger for change. None of its founders paused to consider the risks. No one thought of conducting a market survey to determine if there was a readership that could sustain a gay liberation magazine in Canada. Since 1971, *The Body Politic* has evolved gradually into a Toronto-centred community service newspaper with a strong national outreach, concerned with discrimination, rights and community as the immediate and practical aspects of liberation, oppression and the gay movement. Increasingly, it is also concerned with investigating the real lives of gay people, the everyday aspects of their sexuality, loves and lives.

The Body Politic has made many changes over the years. It discovered, for example, that it was necessary to accept display advertising in order to maintain financial solvency and that it didn't hurt to learn a few simple techniques of traditional magazine management. It learned that serving its community also meant providing basic features like classified ads and entertainment and community event listings. That functioning in the Canadian magazine world made it useful to join in common cause with other struggling periodicals. That to maintain the right to publish a magazine for sexual liberation requires an ongoing legal defence fund and increasing familiarity with the meatgrinder of the legal system.

The Body Politic is a testament to survival rather than a Canadian publishing success story (or are they the same thing?).

Tomorrow's pocket
Issue 1 of *The Body Politic* tumbled off the presses in November 1971. Hawked on the streets and inside gay bars in Toronto and sold for the modest sum of twenty-five cents, it is very much a document of a particular time and place.

A lead article called "Unmasquerade" contained musings about gender roles and self-oppression. It was followed by an article on coming out ("Closet door, closet door, I don't need you any more") and an article on "The power of zapping," which discussed the early gay liberation tactic of gay couples entering straight clubs to "liberate" the dance floor. Reviews of the film *Sunday, Bloody Sunday* and E M Forster's early gay novel *Maurice* presaged *The Body Politic*'s persistent concern with the cultural image of the homosexual. The first Community Page contained a brave little list of all of the known gay organizations in the country. One feature was called "Sweeping statements, or the ambivalence of the universe," in which the author earnestly proclaimed, "The path to self-actualization and to a life-affirmative unity of our species must begin by seeing through the reality games which alienate and divide us." We used to say things like that. A lot.

In 1971, to have produced this twenty-page folded newsprint tabloid with its quirky counter-cultural layout and typewritten text was the most exciting activity imaginable to the little band of pioneers who called themselves the editorial collective. Over the years, hundreds of contributors and volunteers have come and gone, some have stayed longer than others, but most of them would echo the words of long-time collective member Gerald Hannon:

"I got hooked, I guess, on empowerment, the transformation of The Helpless Queer with no history and an unlikely future into Someone, into a *group* of Someones, who uncovered a history, who found heroes, who grabbed today and shook it till tomorrow fell out of its pocket and there was a place there in it for us."

The personal voice, the political act
The personal is political. Sexual politics matter. These are two fundamental principles that the gay liberation movement has learned from the women's movement. After 1969, homosexuals found an entirely new way to view their place in the world. The gay movement provided, in the words of Gerald Hannon, "that quick, sharp snap with the past that lifted people out of their frightened, reflex hesitations about their sexuality." That gay is good has always been one of the shiningly simple messages of the gay movement, especially to homosexuals needlessly handicapped by doubt and shame. It is a message that *The Body Politic* has tried to communicate over and over again, for it continues to be a fresh revelation to new generations of young lesbians and gay men emerging from the prison of social condemnation. Affirming the validity of a homosexual identity is a political act and challenging the social and institutional control of our sexual lives is a political struggle.

The personal is political. Sexual politics matter. Stan Persky and I have kept these ideas in mind while making the final selections for this anthology, which is intended for the general gay and lesbian reader as well as for anyone else interested in learning more about gay people and the gay movement in Canada. As editors, we gave preference, where possible, to the personal voice and the concrete experience. We chose, for example, an article by a lesbian describing her coming out in the teen years over a theoretical article on the political importance and social significance of coming out.

Flaunting It! is neither the authorized version nor the official history of *The Body Politic*. It is not the product of a correct political committee. It will inevitably reveal some of the personal biases of the individual editors. *Flaunting It!* cannot take the place of a history of the Canadian gay movement.

Readers who are familiar with *The Body Politic* will notice immediately that we have made no attempt to translate the look of the magazine into book form. The cartoons of Gary Ostrom and Paul Aboud are the only visual leavening in this book because words, finally, are our medium. Many of these words have come from writers who are not professional in any traditional sense. Some writers first found their voice in *The Body Politic*. Some have gone on to write elsewhere. Some have written nothing else since. It is a source of pride that we have helped to penetrate the silence of decades and provided a medium for the articulation of previously unspoken emotions and ideas of gay people.

The pink triangle

"Part of the oppression of gay people lies in the denial of our history," wrote gay historian James Steakley in 1973. "The veiled allusions, isolated anecdotes and embarrassed admissions which occasionally crop up in standard works of history provide ample evidence of this mode of oppression, which functions by silence and distortion."

Steakley was introducing his pioneering history of the early German homosexual emancipation movement, published as a three-part series in *The Body Politic*. The series was the first discussion in English of a movement which had flourished in Germany until crushed by the Nazis in the 1930s. Steakley's account was sobering: what had once been a significant force for change for homosexuals had virtually disappeared from memory. How could it have happened? Could it happen again? That series whetted our appetite for more knowledge of the past.

The Body Politic has long understood the importance of history in creating a sense of gay identity, and its editors and writers have actively pursued articles which popularized an understanding of our past and highlighted the lessons from earlier movements. In 1975 *The Body Politic* organized itself legally as a non-profit corporation and chose the name Pink Triangle Press. The pink triangle was used by the Nazis to identify homosexuals in concentration camps. *The Body Politic* helped to popularize the pink triangle both as a symbol of hope and as a reminder of oppression. We placed the words of an early German gay activist on our masthead as a guide to present and future actions: "The liberation of homosexuals can only be the work of homosexuals themselves."

"We'll take this place apart"

They came on a Friday afternoon before a long New Year's Eve weekend. They even sent out for chicken sandwiches and coffee. That was when I realized they were going to stay for awhile.

It was December 30, 1977, and "they" were five burly members of Operation P, a special joint Toronto/provincial police unit set up to investigate pornography. Operation P had arrived at *The Body Politic* office armed with a search warrant to collect information in preparation for laying charges.

I happened to be in the office during that raid. When, on the advice of our lawyer Clayton Ruby, I refused to help the policemen find certain records, the sergeant in charge said, with a menacing grade-B-movie cop stare, "All right. We'll take this place apart." Nearly four hours later, twelve cartons of office documents and material were disappearing slowly down the service elevator.

On January 5, 1978 a charge was laid, under Section 164 of the Criminal Code ("use of the mails to transmit immoral, indecent and scurrilous material"), referring to an article called "Men loving boys loving men" in the current issue of The Body Politic.

With the police raid and the laying of charges, the life of The Body Politic changed abruptly and forever. When once the worst we could expect was low-level media harassment and a bland refusal to acknowledge our existence, we now faced palpable risks. Our right to publish had become an issue. The Body Politic was transformed into a legal case.

The newspaper found itself fighting for its life. In order to pay legal expenses we organized a defence fund which, before the legal battle was over, had raised more than eighty thousand dollars from a generous community. We worked to turn around the frightened reaction which caused some individuals to say to us, "You deserve everything you get." We helped people to re-think their views on pedophilia and to understand that the central issue was the freedom of a community's press. We went to court in 1979 and were acquitted in the flashiest trial the gay community had ever experienced. Despite the Crown's successful appeal of this decision, the long process gained us the support of many people, both gay and straight. And we continued to publish.

Now obscene

Even as this introduction was being written, The Body Politic was confronted with a fresh legal challenge. In early May, 1982 plainclothes officers from Metro Toronto Police's Morality Squad appeared at TBP's offices armed with a search warrant. Although they took nothing during the raid, on May 12 they charged all nine members of The Body Politic editorial collective with "publishing obscene material." The charge referred to an article in the April issue on the etiquette of fist-fucking entitled "Lust with a very proper stranger." At the time, a retrial on the January 1978 charges of sending immoral, indecent and scurrilous material through the mails was less than three weeks away.

That retrial turned out to be a shorter, much saner version of the first event. The social climate appeared to be less hysterical, the media did not sensationalize its coverage, the Crown attorney showed little relish for his appointed task. On June 15 a provincial court judge acquitted Pink Triangle Press and its officers of the same charges a second time.

The founders of The Body Politic could never have foreseen that the magazine would be forced constantly into challenging the limits of press freedom in Canada. But laws which classify and criminalize writing with antiquated and vague terms like "immoral," "indecent," "scurrilous" and "obscene" are clearly a threat to our ability to talk about our lives as gay people in the language of our own choosing. Likewise, laws that define and stigmatize our sexual practices as "gross indecency" and "indecent acts," and label our sexual and social meeting places, even our homes, as "common bawdyhouses" are a threat to our ability to live and love on our own terms.

Having found our voice a mere ten years ago, The Body Politic is not about to shut up now. Our task couldn't be clearer: keep warning, keep hoping, keep talking, keep visible.

Acknowledgements
The production of this book depended upon a remarkable number of people who have given freely of their time and expertise. Their generosity is typical of the consistent support of friends and readers which lies at the core of *The Body Politic*'s will to survive.

I am especially indebted to the thirty-six contributors to this anthology. My exchanges with them have been never less than a pleasure.

The members of the Body Politic editorial collective have been more than patient with me while the book was in production. I'm grateful to them for temporarily exempting me from some of the never-ending demands of the office routine.

I am indebted to the following people for assistance in production and advance promotion of the book: John Allec, Carol Auld, Paul Bartlet, Gay Bell, Richard Brail, Allan Chewinsky, Rachel Epstein, Pam Godfree, Gerry Hunt, David Kidd, Michael Petty, Sister Opiate of the Masses and Sister Intelligentsia, OPI, David Smith, Stephen Stuckey and Tony Trask. Thanks also to Rhinotype for donating its services.

Other people deserve particular mention. George Akrigg and Lionel Morton provided indispensible proofreading. Kirk Kelly was responsible for inside book design and Rick Bébout for cover design. Rick was always available with advice and assistance on a hundred other design problems. Herb Spiers compiled the index in record time. James Fraser, Dana Rice and Michael Pearl did the preliminary indexing of news pages in *The Body Politic*'s back issues which made it possible to assemble the chronology in chapter five. Bert Hansen is probably used to having his name mentioned in lists of acknowledgements, but he may be surprised to see it here. His criticisms and suggestions were particularly useful to me.

I am pleased to acknowledge Michael Riordon's role in helping me choose the title. His popular column by the same name in *The Body Politic* provided the initial inspiration.

The folks at New Star Books have been unfailingly helpful during the long gestation period of this anthology. It was Stan Persky's idea in the first place, and his enthusiasm and perceptions were very important to the final shaping of the collection. Without the generous cooperation of New Star Books, in fact, the economics of publishing would have made the project virtually impossible for a modest operation like *The Body Politic*. My special thanks to Lynda Yanz and Lanny Beckman for their refusal to panic as deadlines came and went.

Finally, I wish to record the large debt I owe to Victor Bardawill, Jr for his assistance. Without his tireless attention to detail and his long hours at the video display terminal, this book could never have been completed.
Ed Jackson
June 16, 1982

Chapter one
Risks

"She still knows very few people, feels lonely and afraid much of the time, but about a month ago she lifted a copy of *Rubyfruit Jungle* from the public library. She'll return it: she wasn't ready to use her card."

*

"In a small voice he said to the attackers, 'Leave him alone.' Either they didn't hear him or they weren't impressed. He breathed deeply and ordered in a loud voice: 'Stop! Leave him alone!' The three men looked at him in astonishment."

*

"The rest of the evening was like a nightmare. We were taken to police headquarters on Jarvis Street and then up to the offices of the Morality Squad. Then we were taken downstairs, photographed and fingerprinted. I was struck by the matter-of-factness of the policemen.

"We were simply two of the night's quota of faggots."

*

Throat-ramming
Gerald Hannon

Issue 18, May/June 1975

We went to the movies that afternoon. It was a bright day, it was a movie we had been waiting to see, and being a creature of small enthusiasms, I took his hand as we wandered with the crowd through the lobby towards our seats. It was abruptly shaken off, and we had to smoulder through a feature, two trailers and a National Film Board short on British Columbia before we could continue the quarrel. It struck me very sharply and keenly that afternoon that we were arguing about *holding hands*—that two people who loved each other very deeply, who had been in a relationship for almost two years, were arguing not about frenching on the subway or blow jobs in the park, but about a caress so casual as to be invisible among heterosexuals.

You will want to know about us—about Robert and me. I am thirty, he is twenty-six. We are both middle-class white males with decent educations and the sort of background that promised comfortable suburbia. This is the first gay relationship for both of us, and it came as something of a surprise to two people who had more or less resigned themselves (and not uncontentedly) to a life without a significant relationship of this sort. We reacted to the wonder and delight of it all by behaving in a fashion more frequently associated with a teeny-bopper pash than with two mature people who had stumbled into a love affair. We were extravagant and silly, we were very happy and obviously so, we loved touching each other and we did. And scarcely noticing what we were doing, we began to walk about holding hands.

It didn't take us long to realize we had power. Want to see smart Toronto blow its cool? Just saunter down Yonge Street hand in hand. Want half the sidewalk to yourself? Ditto. Interested in the anatomy of disbelief? Just link those digits. And it was fun and a part of our being in love then, and at first it was only amusing when the hard, ugly shouts of "faggot" followed us down the street, or erupted out of the streetcar we had just left....

But it never stopped. And it followed us home. Our street became a gauntlet. They'd get tired of it, we thought; how can anyone, even teenage boys be *endlessly* titillated by two men holding hands? The catcalls, the hoots, the "hi, girls" continued all summer. It seemed to make no difference that we talked to them about our being gay, and our pride in it — our little gay-lib-enlightenment raps just weren't working. What did work, to our shame, was an out-and-out street brawl (broken up, deliciously enough, by the neighbourhood mothers), and that initiated an uneasy peace which lasted until we left that house a few months later.

By that time the damage had been done. Fear had had its slow, corrosive effect: spontaneous affection in public was no longer possible in our relationship. If we held hands it was because I insisted. The occasional kiss was grudg-ingly, reluctantly received—but his eyes were not on mine. They were shifting from side to side, and they were looking for danger.

I realize this paints a less than flattering picture of Robert and a very flatter-ing one of me. The facts of the matter: what frequently constitutes my cour-age is a mixture of obliviousness and a desire to shock. What some might call cowardice in him is a loathing—emotional and intellectual and purer than anything I shall attain to—of violence in any form and all of its macho varia-tions. But whatever the personal dynamics involved, something very impor-tant had come to an end.

I define myself as gay. I know life is broader than that, I know sexuality isn't everything, I *know* I'll spend only a minute fraction of my life making love: I've heard all the arguments. And yes, I read novels, I go to movies, enjoy photography but, damn it, it's because I'm gay that those novels, for all their "universality," say less and less to me, because I'm gay that movies only infuri-ate me now with their endless variations on the same drab heterosexual themes, because I'm gay that much of my life is spent struggling for what so many take for granted. The corollary, of course, is that I am invisible.

To the extent that you define yourself as gay, you define yourself as invis-ible. There is no accent, no colour, no shared system of beliefs to make you whole and visible. There is only a mirror which we have had to place where *we* ought to be and which presents to other people, with varying degrees of suc-cess, the woman or man they can most easily deal with. Most of us have begun the process of breaking that mirror—the process of becoming visible. Not surprisingly, most of us begin by telling our families and our closest friends—people we think may have suspected anyway, people we are sure have enough emotional investment in the relationship not to reject us out of hand. Nine times out of ten they are shocked and hurt, eight times out of ten they accept and try to understand, ten times out of ten *you* experience a sense of exhilara-tion / relief which, I am convinced, must be outside the realm of straight ex-perience. And almost as often, that's where it all stops.

So now Mom and Dad know, so do sister and brother (but not the grand-parents—it would just kill them / they wouldn't understand), and a small cir-cle of close friends are discreetly dropping fag jokes from their repertoire. The tragedy: we will settle for *that much* visibility. We have cherished invisi-bility for so long (and it *does* have its moments of bittersweet, ironic delight) that we can feed for years off the fact that we actually *told* someone—not that they will ever bring it up again after the original confessions are over. Further-more, we spend eight hours a day at a job where no one knows. Acquaintan-ces don't know. Lovers are introduced as friends. Has anything changed...?

I have some close straight friends. They know I spend a great deal of time working in the "movement," yet they never ask, even jokingly, how the battle is going, or what my feelings are on gay-related news events. They make no comment on *The Body Politic*, though they are aware I have been involved with it almost since its inception. One of them—a teacher—quite shocked me recently by remarking that she had concluded that one of her male students was gay because she had met his parents and mother was very dominant and the father very passive!

Visibility must be our own choice. It is also a daily choice. My experience has taught me that most people, vis-à-vis homosexuality, are quite eager to forgive and *forget*. They seem incapable of realizing that my sexual orientation has molded me in ways which were not open to them, that my present situation is not defined simply by the fact that I have sex with men. And it is so *easy* for us to coast. Why bring it up? They're not always ramming their heterosexuality down *my* throat (but they are, even when they aren't). Why make a social situation tense? Why risk being tedious?

Simply because the only other alternative is the slow drift back into invisibility. And I am too well acquainted with the thousand tiny compromises that that entails to ever endure it again. Each compromise is tiny, and each one is easy, and each one edges the mirror a little further back into place. The new closetry: being "out" to family and friends but never hearing the word "gay" from them again after the original cathartic revelation.

Robert and I holding hands at the movies. A public display of affection. More than that—it is the aggressive statement of what I am and what I am fighting for. It is part of my refusal to be invisible. And I will do it even when I don't feel like doing it, when we're hustling through crowds and it's inconvenient, when it's hot and our palms are glued together like molasses sandwiches. And I won't be doing it because I'm naive enough to think that we're going to win over the hets (not many are going to come out with an "isn't that cute why it's just love after all isn't it?"), but I *am* hopeful enough to think that young gay people seeing us—seeing public and casual gay affection for the first time—might gain some of the courage they need to come out, or just begin thinking about coming out. At least they'd know they weren't the only ones.

A public display of affection. One step to put gay people vibrantly and visibly where they belong: in the streets, the parks (by day as well), the plazas, the offices, the schools, the factories of our country. We're there now, of course. But not so's you'd notice. And can we expect—do we deserve—consideration in union contracts, inclusion in human rights legislation, full acceptance (on our terms) in society if our very existence comes as a surprise to the majority of people?

I seem to be hoping for a great deal from two men (or women) expressing affection in public. Yet I do not feel that it can replace gay people working together in a systematic, public way for the eventual achievement of certain political goals. The latter, however, brings us before the public only occasionally for demonstrations and you soon realize that except for your working hours (when you're probably not out) your time is spent completely with gay people, and a small number of gay people at that. One more road to invisibility.

Throat-ramming. It must become the social extension of our public struggle for civil rights. "Having it rammed down my throat" is a fairly common straight reaction to one's insistence on one's visibility as a gay person. They find it difficult to admit that every as ect of culture today is one violent heterosexual thrust down everyone's throat. Throat-ramming. It means never

"Dear Mom and Dad,
  Miguel and I like to put our dicks
into each other's bums and mouths.
       Love,
         Gary"

Gary Ostrom, Issue 35, July/August 1977

hearing a fag joke or seeing a limp wrist parody without protesting the insult. (I was in a bookstore a few weeks ago. Two girls were beside me leafing through *After Dark*. One of them said "forget it, they're just a bunch of god-damned fags." I said nothing. I hated myself for it, but I couldn't face the prospect of a scene in that bookstore. As I said, it won't be easy.) It means bringing it up at work whenever it seems remotely natural to do so—and it will be natural to do so far more often than you think. People ask about one's private life after all, people chat about news events, people go to movies.... Throat-ramming. It means *never* appearing in public with another gay person (or persons) unless it will be obvious that you are gay people. The easiest way to do that is to hold hands. It means never appearing in public *alone* unless it is as obvious as you can make it that you are a gay person. The easiest way to do that is to wear a button saying you are.

It seems I am asking a great deal. Indeed I am. I have my own failures as a throat-rammer to cite as proof of that. But unless you're a twenty-four-hour-a-day gay you can expect the following to continue: (1) legislators will continue to see our demands for equal rights as the hysteria of a few exotics —"If there are so many of you, how is it I've never met one?" is a common question; (2) the myth of gay people as sex-crazed child molesters or harmless nellies or lesbians too plain to get a man will remain firmly fixed in the public consciousness; (3) young gay people will continue to grow up feeling that they are the only one, feeling alone and hopeless. Remember?

Make the move. Make it in a small way at first—not alone but with a number of friends. But make it. Alone if you have to. It's amazing how hooked you can get on feeling visible. And human.

*

Postscript: Robert and I? We're working on it. Together. And with the participation and encouragement of our friends in our house. We go everywhere arm-in-arm now. Not quite as rammy as hand-holding, but it's what looks comfortable and easy on us.

Last week we wandered past a schoolyard. The usual chorus of hoots. But not from everyone—one boy, about thirteen or so, was a little apart from the others. I caught his eye: disbelief—perhaps distrust?—at first, but the face slowly blossomed into an open and winning smile. And though we'd never seen each other before, it was a smile of recognition.

Under the clock
Michael Riordon

Issue 31, March 1977

A man (heterosexual) said to a woman friend of mine, they were discussing Homosexuals: "I have nothing against them. I think it's only right they finally have their own places to go." Finally? We've always had our own places, at least the Bedrooms of the Nation, whether the government is in there with us or not. But beyond that you always knew where to go, you knew or you stumbled into certain caves, tents, antechambers, storage rooms in barracks, cellar corners in seminaries, the city gates, the great fountain, across from the equestrian statue, under the clock. Until recently most of our history was told in these places, a particular indistinguishable house, our own beach, the Impressionist Room in the art gallery—everybody who needs them eventually comes to know them. Best of all: *we* know but *they* don't. (The police often know, some of them even indulge, but they can always beat it out of one of us.) There are other risks, some of us get killed, but what can you do? You can find these places faster with the right kind of guidebook, but two hours or two days in a new town, depending on how aggressive or how determined you are, you'll know them, anywhere on earth. There's this sauna at the South Pole... (am I joking?).

Night is ours. Some of us function from 10 pm to somewhere in the dawn, like owls. (We develop special vision, and keep black glasses for excursions into day.) We share night, the underside of the buying, selling city, with water trucks slicking down streets, bored and cruising cops, garbage collectors, thieves, spent or unwanted prostitutes, loners drifting in and out of all-night restaurants, weary, sleepless, drunk, hurt, guttering lives, unimportant people waiting to die. The Normal people are at home.

Know that we're here on sufferance, only. We maintain a token presence, a few of us wound-tight, heads whirring and singing on a fix of one kind or another, skin yellow-lit, ignoring poison from passing goons, punched sick in the cops' 52 Division (do I commit libel?), falling into strange beds. Wait for the next night to come, if ever, and one day you're old. At worst, all these wonders will be taken from us in a flash, they'll notice us and hound us back into the cellars, back under the city gates. Even where we have them, we could lose the Bedrooms of the Nation with or without the stroke of a pen. So we may as well enjoy.

The "gay ghetto." A contradiction in terms if there ever was one, the expression is bandied about by gay liberation people, with a certain amount of lip-curling. But just what is being named, or described? In smaller places, is the ghetto that certain booth in the bus station washroom plus the requisite percentage of private dwellings? In the Big City is it the several bars and baths huddling together for protection or for easier cruising, plus the adjacent overpriced bachelorette highrises containing such numbers of gay people that political candidates actually begin to notice them, as Votes if nothing else? Is it strictly geographical, could a wall be thrown up around it, Warsaw 1944, and the occupants systematically wiped out? Or a state of mind? Does it matter where it is?

Blessed are the deviates: a post-therapy check-up on my ex-psychiatrist
Michael Riordon

Issue 21, December 1975

He turned up at a gay dance. If it was him.

It was the same face, weak and inert, a bit more collapsed (from the inside; the outside is preserved with something), the same all-year expensive tan. Could I mistake him? Cruel mouth. Teeth. A mask hanging over a black desk. My ex-psychiatrist. He treated me to aversion therapy, electric shocks three times a week, an all-out assault for a year, to straighten me out, to kill the homosexual. My stomach clenched. I could not mistake *him*, he was too much part of my memory. But here, at a gay dance (I was taking tickets at the door), at a gay *liberation* dance?? He gave no sign of recognition, entering with four other men. I was dreaming.

"Excuse me, do you remember me?" I shouted over the music.

"Yes, Michael, I do." I wasn't dreaming. That plush voice, like rotting fruit. Still I thought it was a trick, an illusion, a double. That warrior, that saviour of homosexuals wouldn't come to a gay dance unarmed, without his electric shocks. I was trembling, I think. Why was he here?? I wanted to tell everyone: that man, the one I told you about, the electric shock one, he's *here*, among us, the enemy is behind our lines! He was drunk. The other four men were dancing together. He sat beside me, staring at the crowd, bleery, sagging. Off-guard, opened a little by alcohol, momentarily unable to do his psychiatrist act. Open to attack. A glorious moment for an ex-patient, an ex-victim, the wildest fantasy come true, the shoe on the other foot, the worm turned, this sloppy wreck my executioner, *triumph* — but I felt like crying.

"Are you here on business or pleasure?"

"Pleasure." Slurring. An awful smile.

"Do you still practise aversion therapy?"

"Yes."

I felt burning. "You *can't*. Did you read 'Capital punishment'?" (I'd written an article about him for *The Body Politic*.)

"Yes. It was beautifully written, very well written."

"But you haven't stopped —"

"It's good money." Leering.

"I don't believe you!"

"No, no. I'm not doing it anymore." Edgy laughter. I couldn't read him at all, I never could. You aren't supposed to, of course. Even more foppish and ornamented than I remembered him. Was he mocking me? Was the eerie tinge of despair feigned, or my invention? The music, so loud, people wanting tickets, his four friends watching me. One came over with a beer for him: "Here's your beer, darling." The friend gave an unpleasant sidelong glance, and left. I couldn't make sense.

"Michael, what are you doing here with these *people*?" He groaned, gestured at the dancing crowd. The place was full, steamy hot, clothes were coming off.

"They're my people." A bit pretentious perhaps, but I felt giddy, strong. "They're handsome, aren't they?"

"They're *trash*." He almost spat. Then he grinned. "They're perverts, *perverts*!" Carefully managed, the word, not an easy one. "Why have you compromised, Michael, why are you slumming?"

"What do you mean by 'compromised'?" He shrugged. Of course. I was an aversion therapy failure. "Would you like me to introduce you to anyone, do you see anyone you like? Look at him, he's lovely, isn't he?" A beauty, curly hair, muscles, tank top, tiny shorts, drowsy half-smile.

Again: "They're *trash*."

"Are you afraid of them?" Why didn't I ask what I wanted to ask? My stifling good manners.

"Oh yes, terribly." Mocking. Not mocking. If only he were sober, or less drunk. As much as it reveals, it disguises. He leaned his head on my shoulder, as if he were falling asleep. I couldn't sell tickets like that, he would have to go.

"By the way, how's your wife?" He was married while I was in therapy. He answered something I couldn't hear. He wouldn't repeat it.

"It's been lovely!" he shouted in my ear, and moved away to join his friends. He turned on me a strange look, bleak, hopeless, I thought. And he shrugged, to say—what??

Other people knew he was here by then, I couldn't help telling. For the first time in my life perhaps, I felt a sense of community, I felt I had allies, and because of it I felt dangerously strong, and potentially cruel. The others were angrier than I was (other people always were, about my aversion therapy. I must have believed I deserved to be punished.) "The bastard—how dare he come here?—let's hitch electrodes to his ass—he should be shot—you feel *sorry* for that creep??" Yes. I don't know. The thing is so dark. I know the power and hurt of self-hate. He's trying to kill in others what he most fears in himself—no, that's too much like a textbook to be possible!

Soon he left, with the friend who called him "darling." I wish I'd thought of asking him to dance, my ex-psychiatrist.

The next few days I wavered between a frightening desire for revenge—or did I already *have* that, was he in the midst of a breakdown that I'd already survived?—and a saintly mist of forgiveness. He is only a victim himself, I thought. (But Camus's idea: I must be neither victim or executioner.) This man is both. As a victim he must be pitied, but as an executioner he must be stopped. He can't abandon psychiatry, he's too greedy, and he probably doesn't know how to do anything else, certainly not anything that pays $30-40 an hour. He hasn't the character to be a good human therapist, an artist instead of a pseudo-scientist—or could it be there, locked? Anyway, how do I know he's a victim at all, maybe he's only an executioner. But his victims....

At the dance, I told him I must write a follow-up story for *The Body Politic*, after "Capital punishment." He said: "Michael, give me a *break*!"—a confusion of sarcasm and whining. Friends cautioned me: he might sue, don't use his name. Why—because I wrote his face is still weak and inert? A public confrontation might be interesting. Would he risk it? His career depends on a facade of solid respectability—mine doesn't, I'm a deviate—his patients have to think they can trust him. How strange—the psychiatrist-priest always assures his anxious patient that he won't reveal any shameful secrets, but what is he to think, or do, when the axis tips, and a patient, or an ex-patient talks? What happens to the world when the sheep become more bold than the shepherd?

I telephoned, four days in a row. Each time, I shivered—he frightens me still. On the fourth he returned my call.

"Hello, Michael. How are you?" Perfect calm, oiled voice. Nothing had happened. The dance—a fantasy. He was back in his fortress. I knocked at the gates.

"Why were you at the dance?"

"Why not?" A silvery casual laugh.

"Were your friends gay?"

"Two of them." The other two were dancing together for exercise....

"Are you?" Finally.

"What does that matter?" Echoes from the empty courtyard within. No admittance. But he agreed to see me three weeks hence, at his office, of course.

He told me once that I had come to defend myself by charm, by fooling people, and that I lived in perpetual terror of being seen through, and found empty. He was talking to a mirror. Physician, heal thyself.

"If this is some kind of witch-hunt, I won't answer any questions."

"It isn't. I want to know what you think and feel about homosexuality, as a person and as a therapist." I'd prepared that, to be as concise and unequivocal as I could. He must not fool me again.

His office was more opulent than I remembered it, heavy drooping black curtains, brass pots, one manila file folder lying conspicuously on the desk, closed. He was a picture from *Gentleman's Quarterly*, creamy three-piece suit —he removed the jacket for our "chat." He sat and crossed his legs in one smoothly choreographed glide.

"Am I being taped?" he asked.

"I was going to ask the same question!" We both laughed, but the ice between us was too thick to crack.

"I want you to understand that I will not answer any question about my personal life—who I go to bed with has nothing to do with my functioning as a therapist." A moat, a castle wall, *and* a suit of mail. I couldn't hold his eyes, they flitted like grey moths. What were mine doing? Therapists watch your hands for signs of anxiety; I kept mine quite still, but not clenched.

He no longer practises aversion therapy, he said; I had demanded it, threatening to destroy myself if I weren't cured of homosexuality. After me, despite an apparent extinction of my homosexual impulses (along with almost every other impulse; therapy isn't subtle), he lost faith in its efficacy. "No reputable behaviour therapist uses it any more." Was he lying, or ignorant? Either was dangerous. "If a homosexual comes to me now, I try to get him to accept his homosexuality; if he insists on aversion therapy, I won't treat him, I send him to the Clarke (Institute of Psychiatry, in Toronto)." I wondered idly whether his electric bill had risen too much; this was no miraculous conversion.

"They still do it? I thought you said no reputable—"

"The Clarke isn't a behaviour therapy clinic." Like saying the electric chair doesn't run off batteries.

"The person who described people at the gay dance as 'perverts' and 'trash' doesn't seem to me very well suited to help homosexuals accept themselves."

"I was overdrawn, we'd been out drinking."

"Your friends weren't drunk, only you. Are you a drunk, or was this a special night?" I knew I had him at every point of logic, but logic wasn't about this man.

"I was upset, political groups irritate me—gay liberation and women's liberation only increase society's resistance. To me they're just angry people over-reacting. One of my patients who was at the dance overheard people talking about me. (His presence *had* caused quite a stir, like a shark in a school of fish.) He said to me afterwards: 'I was ashamed to be a homosexual! If they claim to be supportive of gay people, and they thought you were one, why were they being so nasty?' Do you see what I mean?" Ashamed to be a homosexual—what would happen to that man in this one's hands?

"They weren't attacking you—*we* weren't attacking you as a homosexual, you still haven't admitted to being one, we were attacking you as a therapist who mangles the lives of other people!

"But did I ever hurt *you*?" His voice pained at the thought. He went behind the desk, opened the file. Memories, photographs, electric shocks, suffocating, drowning. "You insisted on aversion therapy." He pointed to his notes by way of evidence. I suppose I did. But do you drown someone if he asks you to?

"When I came to you I was drowning, pleading to be saved. The only thing I knew to *ask* for was aversion therapy. Instead of saving me, you held me under until I wasn't moving anymore. It's taken me four years just to *begin* to —(to what? How do you describe flying to someone who hates the sky?) How many others have you done that to?" It came in a molten rush, I caught myself, afraid of anger. "You can't do *me* any harm now, and I don't care what you do to yourself, but I *do* care what you do to other people like me."

"Are you happy, Michael?"

"Happy? What kind of question is that?"

"From reading 'Capital punishment,' I got the impression you were very bitter, not happy at all." The psychiatrist's indictment, his secret weapon: you aren't happy, *you need me.*

"I'm angry sometimes, that was an angry person you were reading, someone who'd been cheated and brutalized. What do you expect? I'm happy— sometimes."

"I think you still have the same problem."

"What would that be?" Don't play his game, you fool!

"The inability to get close to people—to anyone."

"Of course I still have it, it took twenty-five years to build it. This is the first year in my life I've been able to recognize the separate *existence* of other people, to distinguish their orbits independent of mine. But what help did I get from you? Do *you* honour the autonomy of anyone else?" Can the blind lead the blind? He was trying to lure me back into an abandoned role, or an escaped one. My "therapy" was incidental to this, gloomy history, part of the wasteland—*he* is the defendant now. I wondered: if I were candid, would he be? Not as long as he was locked in his fortress. I sought openings, darting here and there, pressing, pressing. Who he goes to bed with has *everything* to do with his functioning as a therapist. Groin and head are in the same person, separated only by a nerve. But where in this man is the nerve?

"If you're so interested in how I treat my patients, you should be asking me how I relate to the world around me."

"Yes! First question on how you relate to the world: *are you attracted to men?*"

Silence. The grey moths fluttered here and there. He folded his hands together.

"Some." Soft and slow.

"If I ask the same question about women, I'll get the same answer?"

"Yes. I told you, where I put my cock has nothing to do with therapy."

"What *has* to do with therapy? Do you have so many watertight compartments? What's the *object* of therapy with you?" He is supposed to say: the patient's goal is my goal.

"To help my patients adjust to the prevailing values of their society. They are happier that way, much less threatened. I don't want them to suffer as outsiders." Outsiders, deviates, perverts. Not average, that is.

"Your society's prevailing values include the *destruction* of gay people by any means possible—just get rid of them, keep them out of sight, keep them quiet—that's what you want us to adjust to!!" I railed. "Haven't you any values of your own? Haven't your patients any values worth respecting, or even —unholy thought—*protecting*?"

He smiled. "Michael, you're out of date. The new generation of psychiatrists has changed all that—the American Psychiatric Association no longer considers homosexuality a mental illness!" He almost trumpeted, declaring a new era. Now the APA calls it a "sexual orientation disturbance"—some revolution....

"Are *you* the new generation of psychiatrist? You called us 'perverts' and 'trash'."

"I was upset, I told you...."

"We're not getting anywhere, are we? (That had happened once before between us.) Since you won't answer my questions, I have to tell you how you appear to me." He looked fatuous—I hoped it meant he was afraid. "I think you're so threatened by doubts about yourself that you aren't equipped to counsel *anyone*, least of all homosexuals. Either you adjust to the values of society or you fight them, there's nothing in between. I think you live off other people in the worst way, without giving them anything in return. You suck their blood. You're a parasite." So much for polite conversation.

My ex-psychiatrist smiled. There was more, but I don't remember what else was said. I was drained, I'd worked too hard dancing with this ghost. Under the glossy surface, the mannerisms, the creamy suit, the training, the layers and layers of "prevailing values," I couldn't find anything. People cry out to this man and others like him—to help them let go, to grow, or to express their natures against huge odds, and he can't even help *himself*. My wish to see him collapse, or be suddenly thrilled by a vision of freedom, has faded, I'm not a real revolutionary or an evangelist. I suppose a guerilla fighter might have killed him and settled the matter on the spot. But how do you kill a ghost? I just wanted to be away from there. Ghosts, I think, chill the space around them, with murderous effect.

Out on the street—sudden noise, cars, diesel fumes, people walking, trees in the park, pink clouds, dusk. The world hadn't frozen. Which way to walk?

How do you become a ghost? Was he always one, a tiny wraith in a tomb-cradle? Did he sell his substance later, or just give it away? Whatever happened to him, now he wanders lost in the awesome power, the righteousness, the tyrannical smugness of the fabulous, legendary *majority*.

It has legions and generations of victims. It masquerades as many things, most cunningly as love. It sings to you to celebrate your birth, sweet songs that never leave you. "*We* understand, but others won't. We love you, we don't want to see you hurt." (We don't want to *see* you hurt. Go away if you must get hurt.)

It acts through its emissaries, neighbours, moms and teachers, priests, psychiatrists, dads, policemen, buddies, personnel directors, kids — anyone who wants the job. With a kind word, a look, a punch, an occasional execution, it imposes its blank, lifeless rule.

My ex-psychiatrist said: "I encourage homosexuals to accept their homosexuality"— a hopeless contradiction, because it isn't one of the prevailing values. It irritates him when two women or two men hold hands on the street, kissing at the bus station isn't love, it's childish defiance! He isn't lying exactly, he's speaking-in-tongues, saying what comes to him from psychiatric drift, intoning the majority funeral chant: Conform or deviate. Conform or deviate. Conform or deviate.

He said: Adjust to the prevailing values of society, and people will be happier, less threatened, they won't suffer as outsiders. The emissary's song is so beguiling:

Happiness is security.

Security is the absence of pain and suffering.

To avoid suffering, you must play the game, join the team, adjust. You have your models, heroines and heroes. Made in Hollywood, Moscow, Washington, (Ottawa?), Peking and Rome.

There's nothing to it.
Now do it.
No!

Their rewards have too many strings with nooses attached; the more they let you have, the deeper your investment, the more they can take away—and they will, at the first sign of deviation. Why give them the satisfaction, or the power?

I cannot believe both in them *and* in me, they won't allow it. So I choose me. Their direction of life is a failure. Now it's my turn, and they'll never have it back.

I choose to deviate.

For what rewards? What about security? Am I strong enough? I don't know. I know this: security is an illusion, a sneaky trick, an aspirin always just out of reach.

I am a deviate. As an outsider I suffer, and will always suffer, the indecent pressing of the majority. Having rejected its models as impossible to emulate in real life, and having found or invented none of my own, I have nothing to hold onto, nothing in fact to lose. I am nowhere, balancing (at best) on grains of quicksand.

I can imagine nothing in this universe more dangerous, or more beautiful. I am blessed.

Coming out... at seventeen
Lilith Finkler

Issue 44, June/July 1978

Silence. Shhhh. Pupils' eyes like cameras focus on teacher and discussion begins.

"Can homosexuals have children?"

Boys giggle, tease: "Hey, how come we gotta talk about faggots?"

"Let's learn about regular screws."

Teacher shakes head: "Shhh. I think it's important to know about different kinds of sex. Not everybody is the same. Well, class, what answers did you come up with in your groups?"

"I think it's OK. There's these two guys and they're gay, but...."

"Queers are cool so long as they're far away...."

I sit still. My mind is filled with jumping jellybeans.

Am I a woman faggot? Or a queeress?

I do not know.

I cannot know.

II.
I am. I am a woman. I may be a lez-bian.
  Me? A lezzbian? *No!!*
  In the change room in gym class.
  There was Sandy, my close friend and present heart murmur. Strong muscular legs draw tight while swimming. Wisps of blond caress widow's peak. Her eyes meet mine. "Shh... You do not feel. You cannot feel," she whispers. "It is simply not allowed."
  Ten shun — lez bian?
  Sandy runs quickly and undresses in a cubicle. Only clothes thrown hastily appear on floor. Hidden body, silent soul.

III.
I rant, rave, scream. Adolescent anger commands me. My enemy, Frank the faggot, childcare worker in group home. Tall, dominating, authority figure.
  Con/fron/tae/shun.
  "I like you not. I like you not."
  Guardian of house, office, refrigerator supplies — and sometime father. "*You fucking homosexual*," I yell. "*You bastard.*"
  "Disturbed youth;" together we laugh at worker and lover: "Happy Birthday, Dear Queers. Happy Birthday, Queer Dears."
  Hah! Hah! Hah!

IV.
Neighbourhood girlfriend plays ball, laughs and "a gay time was had by all."
  My friend asks, "Do lezzies live in this house?"
  Sally, another worker, answers, "What do you mean?"
  "But are loving women always lesbians?"
  Silence of a dreaded kind. The answer wilts like a flower in late autumn; untouched.
  My friend bends her head and dashes out the door.

V.
"Evelyn, when are you going to meet a Nice Jewish Boy? Eh? You'll never get one the way you talk to your parents. You'll have to dress nice, be neat and presentable. Which boy wants to marry a girl who doesn't take care of herself? All you wear is jeans. What kind of example are you giving your sisters? I don't want them to be like you. You'll just be tall and good for nothing. Don't you realize you'll never get a boyfriend...."
  I quietly say, "Goodnight, mother," and hang up the telephone.

VI.
My world is Diana, grade twelve Latin teacher. I survive on adequate doses of the fifth declension and teaspoonfuls of varied verb forms.
  Amo, Amare — to love.

Diana is more than ancient history, she is present poetry. She lifts weights and wipes away tears. Her voice has definite intonations but it steadily commands. She expects academic excellence and shares hers with me.

Diana, my best friend. My world of primal aches and pains is hers for a moment. She helps me close the door gently. I bring her a birthday card, small and simple. My stomach squeals, shakes, screams loudly. The "runnies" race, pace, utterly disgrace me.

I leave the envelope at her desk and cry silently in the washroom.

The first dance
Irene Warner

Issue 55, August 1979

It wasn't that I didn't know who put what where in physical love between women. I had been involved with a woman for a year of decreasing passion; she had been my "lesbian" neighbour, a friend and lover over afternoons of wine and talk. But we had now become Joan Didion's wounded sparrows nuzzling against each other for warmth. No one in my "real" life knew about this relationship or its end, nor had I done any more than read about Toronto's lesbian community.

So, it was all there—but all in the closet—when I put on my Birkenstock boots, jeans, and leather jacket and went to an "All Women's Celebration" closing International Women's Day in Toronto.

With Sixties chants still in my head, I floated home from the march, collected my daughter at my neighbour Susan's. She said, "I would have marched too, but I thought there'd be only lesbians there."

"Oh, no," I replied.

The last time I had marched had been to integrate the Binghamton, New York, Howard Johnson's in 1963. I didn't know about lesbians then, though I was obsessed with Virginia Woolf.

I delivered my child to her father for the weekend and proceeded to celebrate women. And, incidentally, to confirm for myself whether I was really gay, straight or bisexual. Dressed in what I thought to be appropriate costume, I proceeded to the "celebration" being held in an Annex church where, five years before, I had taken yoga.

I arrived promptly at the advertised time of 8 pm. It was obviously not the right time to arrive. Undaunted, I paid my admission, refused to buy a liquor ticket (I was dieting) and, with some trepidation, entered a large room scattered with tables, candles, a sound system, and three women talking enthusiastically with each other. Not unlike my experience of such heterosexual things: it was not going to be a celebration, it was going to be a disaster.

I sat a a table near a long-haired girl reading Wilhelm Reich. A somewhat masochistic thing to do at a lesbian celebration I thought. My politics had advanced since my passion for Reich, I sneered quietly to myself. I had concluded that Reich was a victim of patriarchy, had unresolved homosexual feelings toward Freud, and had spent his declining years as an American imperialist and Cosmic warrior. This was hardly the stuff of radical feminism.

My first stereotype had been broken.

I looked to my left and saw a blue-denimed figure in shaded glasses and a cap. I imagined her in my bed. I imagined her in my kitchen. I bought a liquor ticket and returned to my table clutching a beer.

Women were entering wearing "Women's Self-Help Collective" T-shirts. I was envious. And absolutely no one looked my way.

And then, fantasy of fantasies, I heard a voice asking, "May I join you?" I turned and saw a version of myself. "Were you at the parade? It was great. This doesn't look like a celebration, it looks like a dance. This is a lesbian dance! I've never done this before. My boyfriend thinks I'm crazy to be a feminist, if he knew about this...."

The only straight woman at a lesbian dance had found me.

At this moment, the blue-denimed figure at the next table got up and joined us. "I don't like sitting alone," she said. "Were you at the parade?"

And we were off. I was a teacher. They were a student and a medical researcher. We all loved Emma Goldman, Anne Hébert and Marie-Claire Blais. We were all probably bisexual, though the blue-denimed person knew that she wanted to spend her life with a woman. The red-haired medical researcher questioned the difference between male / female and female / female relationships. In horror, I found myself explaining that the dynamic in my woman / woman relationship had been power and need.

We danced together, the three of us, to lesbian music, which sounded like ordinary music to me. We checked out the vegetarian buffet. We talked to a women's Self-Help T-shirted person. I resolved to give up therapy and help myself.

We talked.

I knew I wasn't going to meet any of the tall, thin, androgynous, political-looking women I lusted for. It didn't seem to work like that for women, or perhaps I hadn't learned this set of rules.

I wondered how these women become sexual with each other.

Sometimes I felt it was a grade seven dance before the boys came.

Sometimes I thought the boys had come.

We talked.

Marlene (for they had names) said she'd joined me because I looked non-threatening. I was pleased, though I'd thought I wanted to be desirable and sexual — powerful.

I said, "I don't feel uncomfortable here. I'm not sure if I belong here, but I don't feel threatened either."

I smoked dope in the men's washroom, as there were no men. I felt pangs of lust when I saw women necking in the dark, extinguished candles and plates

of ratatouille hastily pushed aside. Public heterosexual lust also affects me
this way after four beers, but not as keenly.

I asked an androgynous woman to dance. She accepted. We danced. She
returned to her table, I to mine.

I didn't feel threatened.

I talked.

I met two women I'll never see again.

I had fun.

I went home alone.

I did not feel diminished.

Heroes
Michael Riordon

Issue 44, June/July 1978

The initials below are invented only to protect heroes who would be uncomfortable as Heroes.

L and F, lesbians, live together in the kind of town that most lesbians and
gay men get out of as soon as they can. They were both born there, have never
lived anywhere else, have been together more than two decades now, and it
looks as if they will live there forever. A neighbour, in a place where your
neighbours usually know things, whether correct or not: "Sure we know
they're—like that. Everybody always knew." They build houses, that's their
trade. No one gives them any trouble. "They're big, you know, they're real big
women."

Restless, B went to his corner milkstore to pick up a copy of *Playgirl*. The
rack was empty. B asked the cashier if any other copies were available. The
cashier smiled (leered?): "For your wife?"

"No, it's for me. I like it."

The cashier, in whose life there are not that many events, watches B closely
now when he comes in for milk.

W, fifty-five or sixty years old, distinguished-looking, cruises the public
baths where I swim. He sits in the locker room for hours with or without a
towel around him, his legs crossed, a picture of decorum. Or he showers, at
length, getting rather pink. He smiles pleasantly at a variety of men, speaks to
them in an easy friendly way, often complimenting them. To a man on the
scales: "How does it look?"

"I guess I'm over, about fifteen pounds."

"Are you sure? You don't look that way to me."

Some ignore him, some return a smile but no words, some look ostentatiously offended. I've never stayed long enough to see what sort of return he

gets on his investment. The other day a friend of mine overheard an employee at the baths talking about "those perverts, they shouldn't be allowed in here with the kids." The woman speaking was, not surprisingly, reading the Toronto *Sun*. W continues to cruise gracefully.

C made her first protest phone call the other day. She did it in two parts. First, after seeing *The Killing of Sister George* on a local TV station, she called the programme director to say the movie was a "revolting mess" that insulted women and lesbians. She said she knew it because she was both and doubly enraged. C, who had never said to a stranger before that she was a lesbian, refused to give her name. About twenty minutes later she called back to tell them her name "so they wouldn't ignore the call."

R continues to resist the New Macho Look. You've seen it, you can't miss it: facial hair (on men), shorter haircuts, bigger muscles if it kills me, rigid joints (physiologically speaking), deeper voices (didn't Mario Lanza get throat cancer by forcing his voice down?), denim, leather, plaid shirts, boots, etc. R resists all this at considerable cost, because the more alike the rest of us look the more unlike he looks. He's a flutter of soft curls (his own), scarves, colours, bits of things that catch in the light, liquid movements the classical Greeks had the good sense and taste to admire in their men. On the street, at work or in a gay bar, many would say R is out of his tree. Better to say he's far, far out on his limb.

T truly doesn't like crowds. In her rural growing-up, after she knew she wasn't going to be a lady but before she knew she'd have to fight not to be one, she took long hikes alone in the bush, carrying tent, sleeping bag, food, hatchet and so on. This woman is afraid to read her poetry, some of it striking and moving, to more than one or two people she knows well. Unfortunately for her, this woman is also good with crowds, so she keeps ending up in front of them, either unruly predominantly heterosexual crowds with the usual percentage of bigots and intimidated potential allies, or unruly predominantly lesbian-and-gay crowds with the usual range of political wills. She's patient, angry, careful, provocative, funny, rude, supportive, scornful, determined. The performance costs her, among other things, a very urban ulcer whose bite varies with the size and mood of the crowd.

J is an enthusiastic and inventive photographer who wilfully breaks (or simply won't learn) most of the accepted rules. He belongs to a photographers' association, to which the members regularly submit samples of their work for other members' comments. The comments on the other photographers' work are all about composition, tone, light and colour. The comments that come back to J with enervating consistency refer to the number of male subjects in "odd positions." And the president of the association threatened to throw him out if he didn't clean up his *curriculum vitae*; that is, the gay liberation activities therein. He's fought the presidential bigot to a standstill on that one. Some hobby.

Week after week P's male therapist told her in an infinity of ways—he had to because she couldn't or wouldn't understand—that it wasn't actually *bad* to be a lesbian, it wasn't exactly sinful or particularly sick anymore, but since she was sure to be thoroughly unhappy wouldn't it be more *convenient* if she could just learn to relax with men. "We aren't so bad, you know."

There's a technique, it's called desensitization. It doesn't hurt a bit. P knew very few people, and all of them were heterosexual, or said they were. None of them knew she was in therapy, except her parents who paid the bills, gladly. One Thursday in the middle of her session P stood quite suddenly, said nothing, walked out and never came back. It says in her file "Therapy failed." She still knows very few people, feels lonely and afraid much of the time, but about a month ago she lifted a copy of *Rubyfruit Jungle* from the public library. She'll return it; she wasn't ready to use her card.

Getting off
Andrew Britton

Issue 56, September 1979

I had been in Toronto five days when it happened.

I'd come here for the second year running to teach a summer course in film studies. I was looking forward to meeting old friends and getting to know better a city I already liked.

On the evening of Wednesday, July 4, I went out to dinner with a close friend I'd known in England. We left the restaurant at about 1:15 am (his parting words were, I now remember, "Take it easy!") and, as it was a beautiful evening and I was feeling quite high after a fair amount to drink, I thought I'd go for a walk. We'd been eating at a restaurant on Church Street, and a five-minute stroll brought me to Allan Gardens.

Allan Gardens, I later learned, is one of Toronto's oldest parks. A patch of green the size of a large city block and dominated by a sprawling Victorian conservatory, it has long been a focus for the colourful street life of downtown Toronto. It once served as the city's modest version of Hyde Park Corner and, over the years, curious Sunday crowds might expect to be harangued by speakers as varied as determined suffragists and brown-shirted Nazis. Today, you may see drunks from nearby boardinghouses asleep in the sun, circles of men engrossed in picnic-table card games, prostitutes in spike heels strolling alone as dusk falls.

I'd never been in Allan Gardens before, but it was obvious at once that it was a popular cruising area. I walked round the park a couple of times, and then decided to investigate — the possibility of meeting someone suddenly seemed attractive. Eventually, I came upon a stretch of path running in front of a row of trees and bushes which backed onto a parking area behind the greenhouses. There were a number of men around, one sitting on a bench, and a few more standing at the edge of the bushes or on the grass between the bushes and the path. As I walked by, I passed another man—Alan McMurray, as I would soon learn—going in the opposite direction, and our eyes met. I found him attractive. When, on looking back over my shoulder, I saw that he had done the same, I walked over towards some bushes. He followed me, and we walked in as far as we could go, ending up next to a tall wire fence.

We'd hardly had a chance even to say anything to each other before we both became aware of a couple of men peering at us through the bushes. I was standing with my back to the fence, and one of them was almost directly in front of me at a distance of six or seven feet, walking slowly back and forth and craning forward to see what we were doing. I didn't notice the other one until Alan turned to one side and said, "Why don't you fuck off?" to a figure I then managed to make out crouching on the ground and trying to look up at us through the shrubbery.

Even at this stage it never occurred to me that they were policemen, though I had every reason to be aware of the lengths the cops will go to to get gays. I'm a member of the gay rights committee of the National Council for Civil Liberties in Britain, and for the past six months I've been working on a booklet called *Gays and the Law* and interviewing numerous people who've been caught in similar situations. Being a true academic, however, I never made the connection, and just assumed the men were voyeurs. As it happened, on this occasion there was nothing to see—we'd embraced once and kissed, but no more. In any case, it wasn't my intention to have sex there when it could be done in a far more leisurely and comfortable way in the apartment where I was staying.

But that isn't the point.

If I'd been married, or living with friends who didn't know I was gay, I wouldn't have had anywhere else to go—short of paying out ten dollars for the baths. Even if we *had* been doing what both policemen later claimed under oath, no one would have been around to find it indecent unless they had taken the trouble to crawl through the undergrowth to watch. The nearest light was a hundred and fifty yards away at least, and thick bushes hid us from the public footpath. The most upright Baptist family could have walked past without knowing that they were morally obliged to be disturbed. It was, in effect, a private place and, if we'd been a straight couple, it would almost certainly have been treated as such. As it is, straight couples can do what we were actually doing *anywhere* they like without being called indecent.

Both of us were disturbed by having these two men staring at us, and we were about to leave when they moved in. I felt a hand on my shoulder, and a whispered "Guess what?" in my ear. I expected to feel a knife go into my ribs, as my first thought was that they were bashers, and they didn't, then or later, either identify themselves as cops or officially arrest us for a particular crime. (One of them subsequently became aware of this omission and said to me at the station "You heard my pal say we were cops, didn't you?" He hadn't. Both, of course, testified in court that they had.)

They told us repeatedly not to make a fuss and to come quietly. They were afraid, presumably, that other gays nearby would have come to help us. I was so dazed and surprised that I *did* co-operate—and one of them was wearing a gun which he made very sure we could see. They walked us slowly across the grass to where their car was parked at the Jarvis-Carlton Street intersection. The one escorting me refused to take his hand off my belt even though I said I wouldn't make a break for it.

The rest of the evening was like a nightmare. I think it's probably impossible to convey to anyone who hasn't experienced it my sense of humiliation and powerlessness—the feeling of being in the hands of people whose authority gave them practically unlimited licence to say anything against me with impunity. We were taken to police headquarters on Jarvis Street and then up to the offices of the Morality Squad, where our pockets were turned out and personal details recorded. We weren't asked to make a statement at any point. Then we were taken downstairs, photographed and fingerprinted. I was struck by the matter-of-factness of the policemen. We weren't abused or pushed around, although one of them tried to unnerve me with the suggestion that I might not be able to get back into England with a criminal record.

We were simply two of the night's quota of faggots.

If we pleaded (or were found) guilty, it was just one more conviction. Even if we elected for trial and were acquitted, the police get extra pay for time spent in court to give evidence. Our lawyer told us that one officer had boasted to him that he'd got a holiday in Hawaii out of gross indecency cases. For all they knew, our whole lives might have been brought down in ruins by the public exposure of a trial. In this case, we both just happened to be out not only to our friends but also at work. They didn't know and they didn't care, and treated us with clinical indifference. One of them said he hoped the formalities wouldn't take long, as he wanted to get home to bed early.

We weren't told at any point what we were supposed to have done; we were simply charged with "gross indecency." The nearest we got to our legal right to know the nature of our offence was when one of the officers asked me, out of the blue as we were waiting to be fingerprinted, if I knew what a blow-job was. I said I didn't; the "innocent abroad" seemed one of my few available roles. He persisted: "D'you know what sucking a cock is?" I felt that I couldn't hold out anymore. "We call it a blow-job over here," he replied, with great seriousness.

It seemed farcical even then, but the humour was lost in the general atmosphere of unreality. If I protested or resisted the procedure, I'd end up in a cell with several other charges to my name—resistance of course, always indicating guilt. So I went along with it, and watched myself being reduced to data in a file.

The police have a wonderful ability to instill guilt; the following day, I felt ashamed to tell the friends I was staying with what had happened. Behind my concern not to worry and upset them lay a deeper sense that I *had* done something wrong, and had got my just deserts. The police rely on that as much as anything else — on a sense of shame, fear and humiliation only too easily aroused, even when you *know* that their having been there to arrest you at all should be cause for rage, not shame. The police expect guilty pleas, and each one (however understandable it may be, if you have everything to lose by publicity or simply have difficulty affording a lawyer) reinforces the likelihood that the methods the police use to get convictions will continue. If everyone picked up like us that week were to plead not guilty, the courts would be clogged for weeks.

Both Alan and I decided to plead not guilty.

The day after our arrest, I contacted a friend who put me in touch with lawyer Mitchell Chernovsky. We told him our story and he reinforced our decision with the opinion that we had a good chance. Our first appearance in court—on the Monday after our arrest—was simply a matter of fixing a trial date; we were in and out in about ten minutes. I'd been afraid there would be a long delay before the trial, which would mean staying on in Canada longer than I'd arranged for, and thus losing my charter flight home. Even if it came to that, I was determined to do it. Apart from the moral issue, a guilty plea would have meant a criminal record, and that would probably make it impossible for me to return to Canada. After a submission from Mitch, however, a date was fixed for three weeks later—Thursday, July 26.

The waiting was in some ways the toughest part of all. I fluctuated fairly regularly between optimism (of course we'd win), depression (we didn't have a hope) and anger that the thing could ever have happened. Alan and I were continuing to see each other. But simply because it was possible for policemen to spend their time and other people's money sitting in bushes waiting to spin fictions about us, a friendship that could have made a marvellous summer had been placed under needless and ridiculous pressure. Alan was worried for me because he had three previous convictions (the last in 1967) and I had none, and he assumed that this would completely destroy our credibility. The same thing worried me on his behalf; I saw myself being cast as the young tenderfoot being led wickedly astray by an incorrigible felon. We tried to reassure each other—more successfully at some times than others. And Alan became more and more militant as time went by. He told me that all his life he hadn't felt able to do more than sit back and take the kind of thing that was being handed out to us now. But he never would again.

We were confronted at once by two major problems:

1) Whatever happened, the case was going to turn on a conflict of evidence between us and the police. And the police, in Quentin Crisp's phrase, "never lie." As it was, the conflict wasn't limited only to the question of whether or not sex had taken place. Everything they said—about the brightness of the light at the time, about where they'd been standing in relation to us, about the length of time we'd been in the bushes—directly contradicted what we said. Our lawyer told us that even if the judge wasn't disposed to believe the police (and he usually would be), the pressures on him to accept their account were enormous. To do otherwise would be to imply that an officer had perjured himself, with possibly adverse consequences to his career. In addition, no judge could get away for long with finding against the representatives of pub-

lic order. Besides, as Crown Attorney Larry Feldman told me during my cross-examination, neither of the officers knew me and therefore no personal animus could be involved.

This argument assumes, of course, the majestic impartiality not only of the law but also if its executors. It was inconceivable, apparently, that the laws themselves were anti-gay, or that those officers (or any others) could have any other motive than personal dislike for lying about us. Indeed, the Crown attorney went out of his way at the beginning of cross-examination to assure me smoothly—and he was very smooth—that he had no anti-gay feeling at all, and that he hoped I believed him. I reflected silently that his liberal conscience didn't make much difference to me either way.

2) Our case would depend centrally on what kind of judge we had. Several of the judges on the provincial court circuit were demonstrably anti-gay. One of them had sentenced a gay man to fourteen days in jail on an indecent act charge. On the other hand, we might be lucky—we might get a new man who wasn't yet jaded and cynical after twenty years on the bench and who still, in our lawyer's phrase, "listens to people." If, on entering the courtroom, we discovered we had got the first kind of judge, we decided we would opt for trial by jury in a higher court, with all the extra delay and expense which that involved. In the event, we *were* lucky. But that such an issue should arise brought home both the arbitrariness of the outcome and the way in which the cards were stacked against closeted gays as well as lower-income groups. Whether or not we'd actually done anything would be the last factor involved in what happened.

We'd been asked to be in court at 10 am, but our case didn't come up until 12:15—we were the last on the list. In that two and a quarter hours, nine or ten cases were dealt with, and it became apparent from Judge Thomas Mercer's handling of them that he was the best we could have got. A shoplifting case—almost exactly analogous to one which the judge we'd encountered in the conveyor-belt atmosphere of the previous court had handled with monstrous severity—was dismissed on the ground of reasonable doubt.

The two police officers—Sergeant Peter King and Constable Gary Gordon—gave their evidence first, and were obviously unused to doing so. They'd been spoiled, clearly, by a long tradition of guilty pleas. Their manner was shifty, evasive and hesitant. For the first time we discovered what it was we had done: we had been masturbating each other for a minute or two, and then Alan had sucked my cock. Mitch Chernovsky, during cross-examination, wasn't able to produce any substantial disagreements in their testimony, though he did cause them both some embarrassment.

Why, he asked, did they stand watching us masturbate for so long? We were already committing an offence—why didn't they move in? Much hesitation and shuffling ensued, before both of them concluded that they had been too far away from each other to coordinate their plan of attack. One of them added, to give credence to the point, that "these people sometimes fight back when you try to arrest them," and it was dangerous to attempt to do so without reinforcements. On being asked by Mitch if he expected him to believe that, the officer replied, somewhat testily, that he didn't care whether he believed it or not.

Despite the less than convincing rectitude of the police performance, Mitch was depressed by our prospects when the court recessed for lunch. He asked Alan and me if there was any further information we could remember which would minimize the contradictions between our evidence and the police's. The greater the conflicts, he argued, the more difficult it would be for the judge to find for us. But the only option would be for us to lie, and this both of us refused categorically. On the simple, practical level, I couldn't see how such niceties could have much effect when the disagreement was so fundamental. More important, I gagged on the thought of accommodating myself to the system in that way. This was, perhaps, in one sense illogical. As Alan said, his impulse was to tell the court to fuck off, yet we'd both turned up in a suit, shirt, tie and all the signs of respectable middle-classness. In another sense, this seemed a perfectly acceptable way of playing the system. There would be no point in martyring ourselves for our own satisfaction, but for no productive purpose whatever. Lying was very different and, while I saw the reasons why someone might consider doing it, it wasn't a possibility. Even in the event that it could have made any difference at all, it would have put us on the level of our accusers.

After lunch, I gave evidence first, and had been on the stand twenty seconds when the court reporter's tape deck broke down. The fifteen-minute wait that followed was the worst point of the day. As I walked up and down outside the courtroom I felt faint, slightly nauseated and very, very tired — too tired, I thought, to be able to stand in the witness box. This feeling passed as soon as we resumed. Mitch's depression had communicated itself to me but, as soon as it came to the point, I felt inexplicably self-confident. I spoke clearly and distinctly, and addressed myself directly to the judge, who was sitting to my right. We had been warned previously that we should be prepared for catcalls and abuse from the spectators' gallery when the charges were read out. This prospect had been my main cause of alarm. but the court had cleared by now—only court officials and our two "character witnesses" were left.

I felt pleased with the way I behaved under cross-examination, and it was far less nerve-wracking to be actually *doing* something than sitting by while Alan went through the same procedure. Then came the summing-up by both counsel. "A very clear-cut case," concluded the prosecution.

Then it was Mitch's turn. My heart sank as he got underway; the second half of his submission seemed suddenly to concede the prosecution's case. He began talking about how "gross indecency" was defined, and brought forward three precedents which underlined the ambiguities of the available rulings. He'd already proposed this course as an alternative — we could either deny the charge or argue that it wasn't really grossly indecent. Both of us had rejected the second course; we wanted to win the case on the ground that we were innocent. As Mitch continued, I felt we no longer had a chance. Subtle theological debates about the definition of "privacy" and "indecency" wouldn't carry much weight, I thought, when everyone knew that cocksucking was disgusting anyway. I didn't understand until later that counsel must deal with all possibilities in one submission.

I felt unsteady on my feet as the judge asked us to rise to receive his decision, and his first words confirmed the sense of defeat that overwhelmed me already. "I have no doubt," he said, "that you were doing more than you've admitted." He went on to accept the police evidence that we'd been masturbating each other. Then he suddenly changed course. He said there was reasonable doubt, given the uncertain condition of the light in the gardens, as to whether oral sex had taken place. He would, consequently, acquit on all charges.

I was staggered. I didn't properly realize we'd won until the judge was halfway out of the courtroom. Alan seemed as dazed as I was, and we stood looking at each other stupidly for a moment before suddenly embracing.

But the verdict still made no sense to me: why should the judge believe one half of the police story and not the other? Mitch suggested one explanation. On the one hand, by saying he accepted some of the official story, the judge avoided implying that the police had perjured themselves. On the other hand, the use of reasonable doubt to acquit us probably didn't indicate faith in our testimony, but the belief that the police shouldn't be involved in park entrapment anyway. An ambiguous victory at best.

But it's all over at last. Walking in Allan Gardens one afternoon before leaving the city, it struck me that I had been lucky in every way. I had lost nothing by taking the case to full trial, I had the money to do so and I had some wonderful friends around to support and encourage me during the heavier moments.

Unfortunately, there will continue to be lots of gay men who will not be so lucky, men who will feel that heavy hand on the shoulder when they least expect it, men who will be subjected to the same demeaning, confusing—and useless—procedure. Unless we begin to challenge an arrangement that allows policemen to earn Hawaiian vacations by skulking in the shrubbery to arrest harmless victims.

A police cruiser, on one of its apparently routine daytime sweeps through the park, crept slowly toward me on the walkway. I had to step aside to let the bright yellow car and its uniformed occupants pass.

At least this time I could see them coming.

The mirror of violence
Michael Riordon

Issue 63, May 1980

In high school JB suffered from a lot of taunting: sissy, queer, fairy, the usual. One night he was walking home from a friend's house. He was not yet operatively gay. Three men approached on the same side of the street—J felt a familiar unease—they said nothing to him. He awoke the next day in hospital with a broken nose, a badly bruised face and deep lacerations from his own eyeglasses. The time lost remains a blank to him.

A chudo is a white-knuckled tight fist you make that describes an arc starting at your waist, coiling upward close to your chest, springing outward from you and ending in an efficient snap. You don't have to be very strong to do it well, but when a decently-executed chudo connects with the point where the nose abuts the face of an assailant, there's a reasonable chance the owner of the nose will be distracted, to say the least, for a short time. This interval can be very useful, especially if you're a good runner.

PD and a friend were cruising in David Balfour Park on a muggy summer night. Three men and two women, all in their late teens, appeared quite suddenly behind them. One of the men had a baseball bat; he waved it over their heads. The others laughed and joked about smashing the fruits. P and friend kept walking. "I could hardly breathe," he recalls. They reached a lighter part of the park, close to a subway station; the assailants withdrew, back into the dark. P: "We felt bad we didn't do anything, but what could we do? Call the police? Are you kidding? What for?" Later P heard that the same gang had attacked other gay men the same night in the park, and put one of them in hospital. The attackers were arrested eventually, sentenced and paroled before their victim was released from hospital six weeks later. They were of good families, the judge noted.

Surprisingly, given the sensation of receiving it, a well-delivered kick to the groin probably won't do permanent damage. To do the kick you raise a leg in front of you, making right angles at hip and knee. Your toes strain upwards. Your foot lashes out sideways, frontwards or backwards—depending where your attacker is—and the ball, heel or side of it slams into your assailant's groin, knee or shin. If you do happen to cause permanent harm, it's most likely covered by the attacker's medical insurance. And he (assuming it's a man) would simply have to accept it as a dramatic lesson in the changing politics of queer-bashing.

Attacks on gay men *seem* to be increasing in North America. We are becoming more visible and more demanding, both offences against a bigot's sensibilities. But it isn't exactly clear yet whether the actual incidence of attacks or only the frequency of reporting them is increasing. We're becoming less likely to swallow an attack as a natural phenomenon, a fact of "gay life." We're more likely to talk about it, more likely to listen, and more likely to do something about it.

For its first gay men's self-defence course last summer, Toronto's Gay Liberation Union auditioned — if that's the word — several instructor candidates, and chose from them a quiet, pleasant, courteous woman with a black belt in karate. She'd already taught women, disabled and blind people a potent mixture of karate, judo, aikido and jiujitsu that she calls, smiling, "dirty fighting." She would, she said, teach unskilled and, yes, even unathletic gay men to defend themselves against verbal and physical assaults. She would use a Zen-based approach that reflects back on the attacker the gist or the spirit of the attack. That, I found out, is easier said than done. Victims die hard.

The best victims aside from animals are undoubtedly children. From birth their lives in all respects hang on the good will, competence and sanity of people whose only qualification for the job of "parent" is that they got through puberty. The duties of the job, on the other hand, are heavy: to make of the raw material a productive member, or unit as it's often called, of society. School, church and other authorities will lend a heavy hand where they can. But when our economic system looks more like a post-iceberg Titanic every day, and governments hack away at social services—like daycare—that were already inadequate, parents remain pretty much on their own. Some of the more direct results we can read about in the newspapers.

Reported cases of child abuse—the degree that kills, maims and starves—have more than doubled in Ontario over the past five years. At least ten children have died at the hands of their parents in each of the same years. And since child abuse is still tolerated in many quarters, reports of it lag far behind actual incidence. In state-run homes, children aren't any safer; reports of torture under the guise of psychotherapy are surfacing. But when governments suggest even the mildest initiatives against the abuse of children, voices from the right underworld like Claire Hoy, Toronto *Sun* columnist, and Renaissance International shriek that the state is mangling the rights of parents. In their eyes the issue is not one of human rights; it's plainly one of property rights. The victims haven't much choice: to be owned by your parents or to be owned by the state.

All of us have been children at one time or another, some for longer than others. As such, most of us have experienced victimhood. We know where power resides — in parents, teachers, priests, policemen, generals and employers, maybe a little in certain politicians. Almost never does it occur to us that any of it might reside in us. That is, not unless we become parents, teachers, priests, policemen, generals or employers, or maybe politicians. It's either eat, they keep telling us, or be eaten.

Women have made quite satisfactory victims for much of world history. (The times when they haven't been tend to be called "prehistory," to suggest perhaps they never really happened at all.) Rape is one of several methods by which women have been, and still can be, reminded from time to time of their place. A woman's place is in the home, where it's safe. If she comes out, she must understand that men will be men. They may well rape her or beat her. (This may happen to her at home as well, if she's difficult.) Of course it isn't right, but then it isn't exactly wrong either. That is to say, it's human nature. After all, it *is* a man's world, is it not?

According to the quiet, pleasant, courteous woman with a black belt in karate who's taught all the initial self-defence courses, "Most bullies aren't looking for a fight, they're looking for a victim." And you're only a victim as long as you think you're a victim — or don't know you're a victim, which amounts to the same thing. *But*—here's the plum—you *can* learn, as others have done, to defend not only your body but your*self*, your being.

First, it seems, you have to locate it. Women from a rape crisis centre in Vancouver have started direct public confrontation with confirmed rapists as a self-defence tactic. Howls of indignation from all sides: they're taking the law into their own hands!! Not such a bad place for it to be, the women argue. The victim rises up and lo, as much to her surprise as to that of "the stronger sex," she whacks him right where it hurts. It's all a matter of Attitude.

Getting to the gay men's self-defence class by public transit is a fair test of one's attitudes. Here's this mob of heterosexuals — if gay people use public transit you'd certainly never know it from *this* bus—tired at the end of the day, many of them trapped in unsatisfactory lives and all of them, you suspect, restrained only by the sheerest filament of social convention from killing someone. And who would that someone be? If you're with a friend, you lower your voice on the word "gay"—if you use it at all. You check each other almost unconsciously for telltale signs, and you hold the Dominion bag containing your gym clothes to your chest, where the pink triangle is pinned. Then you think, goddammit who the hell do they think they are, etc. You lower the bag, look around defiantly, think rude thoughts about heteroburbia, and are hugely grateful that here's the stop for the school.

The men in the class—seventy or so have taken the four courses offered so far, and another twenty-five or so are taking the first advanced course—have no more in common, as far as I can see, than any other random group of gay men. Few of us have been attacked physically, or few will admit it. Most of us have been verbally abused, and most of us have learned to ignore it, at varying costs to ourselves. I presume that most of us are speculating about sexual prospects in the group. Some of us have never been in a group of gay men in smoke-free, brightly-lit surroundings, some never at all. Some of us are shyer than others, some in better shape. Our bare feet, winter-pink-and-white, look very vulnerable.

Why are we taking this course? Everyone answers in almost the same words — some variation of self-confidence. As I say it now, it doesn't seem clear enough. A feminist friend I told about the course snorted: "Why do *you* have to defend yourself, you're a man." I said I'm also gay, but that didn't seem clear enough either. The answer came later.

First we learn to make noise. Gay men tend to be rather soft-spoken in public, have you noticed? It's sometimes referred to as "masculine reticence."

The Screaming Queen, on the other hand, is an appalling person who makes so much noise that he attracts attention not only to himself but to anyone who's in the same room, on the same street, in the same province — to every soft-spoken masculinely reticent one of us, the beast.

Four bullies, a man in the class told us, descended on Fire Island and for one ghastly afternoon made havoc among the gorgeous hunks who were basking and cruising there. Not one ounce of all that splendid muscle flexed; we got quieter and quieter and scattered like sparrows in their path. No wonder we take so much valium. The bullies roared into a bar — shocked silence — and spied a Screaming Queen. After enduring their gross abuse for about thirty seconds he let fly with some breathtaking filth of his own. "He screamed his tits off," we're told. The bullies walked straight out of that bar and haven't been seen on *that* island since. Noise, we learned, is a primary mode of self-defence; bullies don't like it unless they're making it. We learned to roar from deep in our bellies — "don't squeak out of your throats, come on, let me hear it from way down here!" — out of a deep well of old anger and fear. We could have brought down Jericho.

We would not, we'd been told, each be turned into Bruce Lee, rippling exquisitely-tuned killer machines. For forty dollars we'd get eight three-hour classes, no guarantees of immunity or even safety but a decent range of choices to respond to violence. We'd learn to turn back aggression onto the aggressor, to mirror the violence.

We learned how to make weapons of our feet, knees, elbows and hands: chops, rams, punches, jabs and kicks. In case our opponents didn't collapse immediately under this onslaught, we learned to block their blows. How to stand and how to move so we'd look dangerous. How to throw an opponent, how to break a fall, how to do an Eagle Claw. (That's an unpleasant trick of stabbing your fingers into an opponent's eyes, twice, very quickly. The idea makes me shudder, but in a close-enough and bad-enough situation, who knows?) We learned to disarm an attacker wielding a knife. "You may get your arm slashed," the instructor said, "But you won't get stabbed where it counts." We practised with drinking straws.

We made lots of jokes in class, an older form of gay men's self-defence. "Jesus, if I kick that high I'll split my skirt." "Can I ask him to hold my shopping while I hit him?" "What do you do if someone gets you in a choke like this?" (An assistant demonstrates.) "Ask him home." "Why do we do the Eagle Claw twice?" "Once to take the eyes out, once to put them back." "What's the first line of self-defence?" (Correct answer: awareness.) "Spit." And we heard stories, gradually, as people came to trust each other more.

CD came out of a gay bar. A man on the sidewalk caught his eye, grumbled something at him — the man was drunk. C walked away. The man hit him from behind, knocking him half under a parked truck. C recovered and ran away down the street, a busy one. The man chased him with a piece of wood out of a garbage can, but C outran and lost him. He spotted a patrol car. Another gay man was speaking to a policeman through the half-opened window. This man's face was bleeding, his glasses smashed. After he'd left, C told his story. The policeman said he'd investigate, and drove off. By now C was deeply, grimly enraged. He went looking for his assailant, without knowing what he'd do if he found him. "I wished I'd had a gun, I felt like I could have shot the bastard." He saw the man sitting with a companion on the steps of another bar. Both of them were drunk or stoned. C called the police from a phone booth. A car arrived in minutes — no sign of the first one. They tried to persuade C to forget the whole thing: the guy would say C had come onto him, and it would be his word against C's. "As if 'coming on' to someone was legitimate grounds for assault!" C refused. They found the man, he was arrested, tried and convicted of assault. C joined a self-defence class.

DH met a man on Yonge Street. They walked awhile and talked. The man, about twenty, asked if he could come home with D. "From a sense of danger or lack of interest, I don't know which," D said no thanks. He noticed two other young men behind them, keeping pace. D walked faster, then ran. They followed. He jumped onto a bus, so did they. D asked the driver to alert the police (buses are equipped to do this). The man who'd asked if he could go home with D now shouted to the crowded bus, "This queer came on to my fourteen-year-old brother here!" The driver refused to help. With surprising presence of mind, or randomly somehow, D blurted, "Don't they have to pay?" Between them they had only a five-dollar bill and wouldn't tender it, so they had to get off. D didn't look at the other passengers.

LT emerged from a restaurant a little after midnight. He stretched, turned and was hit in the open mouth by a fist. His arms were grabbed from behind and he was dragged kicking down a lane. There he was punched — he never saw the face of his attackers — and kicked for what seemed a very long time. Then they left, tired or satisfied. "What's the point of self-defence?" he asks. "Who could have done anything there?" One of the most elusive factors we talked about in class is awareness, a sort of heightened sensitivity to your surroundings and where you are in them. It needn't make you paranoid — paranoids tend to be helpless — but it certainly makes you sober. One man in the class reported floating out of his apartment high on acid. "These two guys started following me. I heard one of them say 'It's a faggot!' It didn't sound like a compliment. In one second — less maybe — I was right down and completely clear." Nothing happened.

Attitudes kept coming up in the class, from deep unquestioned sources. "Maybe he *did* come on to the guy." "If you're going to swish down a public street with a beaded bag, jewellery and make-up you've got to expect that kind of treatment." "I'd like to think that no one knows I'm gay unless I want them to — why would *I* be attacked?" "You'd better not advertise that gays are taking self-defence." Why not? "They'll be ready for us." "Isn't there supposed to be something about people who get attacked that invites it?" "It's the ones who are obvious, who *look* gay that get it." Which of us here in the class would you say looks gay? "Oh, none of us here do."

Lesson Five tonight — our first "simulated attacks." The instructor and several assistants — gay men who've taken earlier courses and some of whom want to become instructors — wander among us in a half-dark room and pick on us individually, without warning and at random. We are to respond as well as we can.

One of them comes up to me. His eyes are cold. "Faggot," he says, nastily. I smile, this is silly. "What're you grinning at, faggot??" I smile and look down at his feet, at other people. They're engaged, they have their own problems. But I'm a quick-thinking, articulate person. He pushes my shoulder, once, twice, several times, a little harder each time. Nothing comes from me, no sound, no thought. I back away from him. "What's the matter, faggot, can't you speak?" Of course I can speak, you monstrous fool. He pushes again. Then he stops. "That's not very good, you know. You could be all over the pavement by now."

So here's my answer to the woman who asked why a man needed self-defence. I'm a man and then again I'm not—I'm not John Wayne, James Bond, Starsky or Hutch. I'm polite and gentle and I don't want to fight anyone. A little wrestle between friends in bed, sure, but not this. Please, I'm no thug. I was truly horrified by the gulf between what I thought I'd do and what I did.

The assistants told me of remarkable changes in people during the courses. One man, a lawyer, cringed visibly and shut his eyes when he was attacked, even just verbally. The threat of exposure seems to act as strongly on us as the threat of violence. But the same man "paralyzed" an assistant for an instant when, faced with verbal abuse, he suddenly let out a wild scream *"Fuck off!!"* whose volume and intensity you'd have to hear to believe. It gave the man just long enough, the assistant said, to get his breath and make his next move.

When another man was called a faggot in a simulated attack he felt a powerful urge to shout "No, no, not *me!*" Instead he turned back on the attacker the spirit of the attack—a punch to the solar plexus, to be specific. He make his point, you might say, *as* a faggot.

Lesson Six. This time I'd practised verbal defences all week in my head. I was full of assertive fantasies. Time for the simulated attacks. We deep-breathed, which is supposed to relax us. It didn't me. From the corner of my eye I could see him sidling toward me as people do when they're simulating attacks. My heart pounded. Remember to breathe; to do a proper takedown... there were two attackers, *three*... to do a proper takedown... "Here's one," they said. "Hey cocksucker, what do you think you're doing on our street? Eh?" "I'm gay and I'll take no shit from *you!*" That was *my* voice. "Oh you won't, eh?" A shove by one of them, another raises his arm. So I kicked one of them in the balls—well, it was the instructor, but it's the thought that counts —punched one of them in the throat and broke one or more knees of the third. "That was wonderful!" they all exclaimed.

I was smugly, blissfully astounded. Two days later I walked down Yonge Street with a friend at bar-closing time. *They* were pouring out of their bars, and unlike us they're noisy, pushy and belligerent. Normally I'd skirt such impediments, but not tonight—I didn't push or challenge anyone, but I was definitely conscious of not avoiding them either. I was as bristling with righteousness as any Reborn Christian. Just one of you goons give me or my friend any trouble and you'll never know what hit you.

Thank heaven none of them noticed me. I'd forgotten to breathe.

As many people in the classes have reported threats and sexual assaults by other gay men as attacks by bigots. Most of us learn to avoid bigots as much as possible. But most of us learn to be male before learning the possibilities of being gay: we learn very early to take what we want, to impale on our cocks the various fruits of the earth. Some of us think it's expected of us.

BR went home with a man from a bar. Usually he asks questions, tonight he didn't. Shortly after they arrived at the man's apartment B decided he'd made a mistake. He wanted to disconnect, go home. The man locked the door with a key and put the key in his pocket. For an hour or so B talked, made excuses, pleaded. Women are familiar with the reasoning that no means yes. The man became physical. A much bigger man, he shook B, pushed him onto the bed, pulled at his pants. B bounced around the room for most of another hour. The man was getting rougher. B: "I was so scared I suddenly started to cry." The man said, disgusted, "Go." B went. He joined a self-defence class. "Never again do I want to be that helpless. There's a kind of freedom in feeling you can take care of yourself in situations like that." So we learned bed defences. If you're one of those men who likes being rough with people who've indicated they don't want it, check first to see whether your intended has taken a self-defence course. You could lose something you value very highly.

The last night of the course we smashed boards—not terribly thick ones, softwood and we went with the grain—and got to take them home with us, a sort of diploma. Afterwards we had a party. HV said he was fed up with the closet. RD said we're never going to be loved—or at least we had better not hold our breath—but we're going to get stronger. How does he know? Simple. We will because we have to.

But the police, someone said, are buying themselves bulletproof vests with their own money. Someone else said his mail had been opened and an official number attached so he'd know it. Another told of an argument he'd had with a fashionable downtown faggot who laughed at the very idea of self-defence. "It's the Eighties, dear," our narrator replied. "War-fever, unemployment, food riots, scapegoats" (he made a fist and pounded the heads of imaginary scapegoats — thump, thump, thump) and "and we're one of them. Either we're down here" (he indicated where he was thumping) "or we get out from under." Does that mean we want to be on top? "Not me, just out from under."

I asked in one of our class discussions whether people felt they would use their shiny new attitudes and skills to defend *other* people, should the occasion arise. The responses were surprisingly candid, I thought, but not encouraging. Some, including me, said they hoped so but didn't know; others said it was unlikely. The politics of self-defence class are strongly individualistic. "Let's turn back," our instructor said gently, "to how to defend *ourselves*." When I asked, like a thorn in her side, about defending ourselves against the people who make climates where brutes can freely play—when goons are licenced and armed and elevated to govern over us, does it matter how awesome my lonely chudo is? — our instructor looked as close to cross as I ever saw her and said, "That's another course, I think." She told me privately that she didn't believe a teacher should impose her politics — in her case "fairly radical feminist"—on her students. The assistants from the Gay Liberation Union, then... but they too seemed very shy of placing our solitary self-defence in the wider context where it surely belongs.

A new course begins at the end of April, with instructors drawn from the ranks of the assistants. Lesbians in the Gay Liberation Union demanded that the courses no longer be restricted to men. The attacks aren't. CV and KR were assaulted violently by a man who was offended by two women holding hands in a more-than-European way.

LM, the mildest sort of person you could ever hope to meet, was strolling down the avenue with friends, women and men. They saw three bullies beating up a faggot—one of the obvious ones. The friends suggested crossing the street to pass by. (I know this story sounds suspiciously biblical, but L is to be trusted, and there were witnesses.) L: "I hate violence, I felt it wasn't right for them to be doing that." In a small voice he said to the attackers, "Leave him alone." Either they didn't hear him or they weren't impressed. (L's friends watched him from across the street. "It was my decision, I felt I had no right to involve them." He's more charitable than I would have been. But they hadn't, after all, taken a self-defence course.) He breathed deeply and ordered in a loud voice: "Stop! Leave him alone!" The three men looked at him in amazement. And retreated, with one of their victim's shoes—a trophy? L ordered them to bring it back. They did, and were gone. "I was so surprised. I've never done anything like that before. Always I'd think of good reasons to avoid these things, and then I'd feel bad. There — I felt wonderful. I was so surprised."

I know the feeling.

Exorcising ghosts of friendships past
Lorna Weir

Issue 65, August 1980

My past is returning to haunt me. It is arriving by letter, telephone, and in the flesh on my doorstep, bag in hand. I thought I had successfully severed connections with it, but it keeps insisting that I respond.

Sartre remarks somewhere that we are all faced with the choice of living from within or beyond our childhoods. Mine having been the usual disaster, the farther I get from it the happier I feel. Coming out as a lesbian reinforced the necessity of breaking with my childhood: I took the geographical course and moved to a different city, thus conveniently cutting off connection with my straight friends and previous sexual identity. I, or rather the shell of me, returned periodically to perform the social role of daughter. An altogether common way of coming out: flight is often a splendid solution to an existential predicament.

Of course, the predicament was just as much gay as existential in origin. As a tender young dyke, I didn't have the ability to bridge the gap between my former circle of straight friends and the gay male and lesbian networks and culture that I was busy trying to learn, a process which took several years. Until I felt strong in being a lesbian I simply wasn't in a position to face struggling with my straight friends' sexual politics (or lack thereof) and probable homophobia. Initially, too, I was ashamed of myself for being a "homosexual," although I would have vociferously denied feeling such shame had I been questioned on the subject.

Six years after discovering my attraction to other women, my suppressed past returned to demand my attention. Women and men came tumbling out of the archive of memory, with mixed effect.

Don arrived on my doorstep one evening from rural Quebec bearing his homemade muffins and jam. With the passage of time, Don had matured into a disco bunny—quite an out of the ordinary visitor for our lesbian-feminist collective house. Unacquainted with feminism, contemptuous of gay liberation (according to Don's reasoning, unnecessary in Quebec, where sexual orientation is included in the human rights code—choke!), his major concern in life was getting fucked at the baths every night, coming home to wake everyone in the house up at five or six in the morning. The women in the house did their best to give him a chance, and treated him with polite neutrality.

After two days it became clear that if I didn't ask him to leave, no one was going to like me anymore. Don, you see, assumed that he was completely fascinating to us, in the way men think it their right to be the focus of women's time and energy. How could we have had anything more important to do than to wait on his every wish? Conversations revolved around his life and interests; the women of the house, including myself, and their concerns could never be worthy of his consideration. He preyed on the time and energy of any woman who happened to be in the same room as himself. We were all infuriated.

The ways of sexism are devious; Don thought that a man who bakes muffins surely could not be sexist. He then proceeded to use highly sexist patterns of conversational style against us. Women are generous in lending an ear to subjects which are of importance to men; when talking with women, men feel no compunction in being completely self-centred. Small wonder our collective feminist rage at Don's predatory conversational habits, despite his beautiful blueberry muffins.

The last straw came when I went to my room, which was in a state of complete disarray, to find Don's porno collection by the side of my bed. Reaction: a "typical" feminist one of shocked violation—an immediate reaction which I'd cheerfully defend on the soundest of political grounds. Still, how could one avoid seeing the high comedy of the man who refused to leave his teddy bears behind, thus inconveniently doubling the weight of his luggage over a long journey? Don's visit concluded with an invitation to pack up and leave.

The next act was Matthew, my first lover, a relationship that lasted four years. "Just passing through Toronto, want to get together for lunch?"—seven years after we had last met. Despite the fact that Matthew had been picking up men in bars for years, it never occurred to him to mention this to me, although I did muster up the courage years ago to come out to him.

During our relationship I always had the intuition that there was something lacking: exactly what, I never could quite put my finger on. Last fall I found out what it was: feelings. Every time I would put myself in a vulnerable position by revealing my emotions, Matthew would look uncomfortable and change the subject. He was highly secretive about his own emotions, unable to grant mine a measure of reality, and completely incapable of being vulnerable. In short, I had spent years trying to teach an unwilling man emotional responsibility, trying to be intimate with someone incapable of intimacy, a skill which at bottom Matthew found contemptible. Yes, I did feel a bit lonely and crazy at times.

A few days after Matthew's departure, Ilene of the two young sons, happy marriage and liberal unease with lesbianism phoned to say that she loved me. Twenty years after our first meeting, this message came as a considerable surprise. She explained that she was trying to share her feelings with people more openly. By the end of the conversation I had decided that, despite her ambivalence and liberal blocks, there was something in this friendship for me.

Then Helen, her life bounded by her children and her husband's work. Fanciful Helen of the many-coloured inks and fat handwriting, cogent as ever. Both of us with a passion for carpentry. There will always be an element of difficulty for me in dealing with Ilene and Helen because they have no real idea of the depth of heterosexism. Their feminism, too, they unconsciously keep within severe limits, for fear of jeopardizing their marriages. Deny it as they might, I represent a threat to the choices they made unreflectively years ago.

And, lastly, Gérard, former film editor, now apprentice carpenter, a militant, and interested in sexual politics prior to me: straight, but not narrow. Of the men I formerly considered friends, he alone is capable of intimate discourse. Curious, that this bonding between past and present should occur through a straight rather than a gay man.

This is much more than a story of a treasure hunt in which much sand and several pearls were redeemed from the wastes of time. Don, Matthew, Ilene, Helen and Gérard are more than a number of individuals: they collectively represent my straight past, which I fled years ago. To talk with these people again is in a sense to go back to that unfinished past and those abruptly terminated friendships and finally come to terms with them. When I left I felt that my lesbianism was *my* problem, when I came back it was *theirs*.

Being at ease and proud of my lesbianism was achieved through years of struggle in the lesbian, gay, and feminist movements. Leaving town was a mark of self-rejection, and returning an act of self-acceptance: an insistence of my worth before my family and friends, knowing that my lesbianism does not constitute valid grounds for their alienating me. If anything, I now feel a bit arrogant for having had the good fortune to avoid the grotesque cliché of married life, which I now behold with the deepest revulsion. Lesbianism is a difficult choice, offering a woman neither the exciting inanities of the gay male ghetto nor the hazardous security of the heterosexual couple.

The return to my straight past didn't mean that I wanted to clasp it all to my bosom in utter rapture. Some of these people (all of the women and one of the men) I will keep in touch with; two I have cheerfully rejected. Through this filtering process I have gained a much better understanding of my own personal development, for one's reflection is found in one's friends, past and present.

As lesbians and gay men, we have an uneasy relationship with our personal histories. Our general level of acknowledgement consists of a few compulsory sneers and frozen silence. You'd think that gay people were born the day they came out. Other than the place a person *was* born, the details of our past experiences are hidden from each other, cloaked in mystery. We are especially uncomfortable with any mention of our heterosexual pasts. Our individual pasts are repressed and are a source of unconscious conflict: our concealment of the past from others and ourselves has the hallmarks of domination of the unconscious: anxiety, rigidity, compulsory silence, inability to accept or discuss differences and disagreements.

I am happy that my past friends have re-established contact with me, and I see this rediscovery of my past as part of a larger struggle to develop close personal and political links outside the gay and lesbian movements. Having spent several years learning lesbian social and political culture, I have no intention of making an about-face and rejecting my community. On the contrary, it is only because I feel established in this community that I have the confidence to develop ties outside it.

To refuse to talk about one's oppression is to perpetuate it: political work and personal friendships formed outside our communities must not be predicated on the denial of our lesbianism or gayness.

Over the last decade, our struggle has been to create gay and lesbian social and political institutions, and to forge a positive social identity for ourselves. To do this, we have been forced to isolate ourselves to a certain extent, both socially and politically.

It is true that the lesbian movement, operating within the women's movement, does not suffer the same degree of isolation as the gay movement. But we should not overestimate the extent of that integration. Certain sectors of the feminist movement, especially those concerned with trade unions, have no idea what a dyke looks like. Many lesbians in the women's movement do not politicize their lesbianism in any way, even where tactically possible. In those feminist groups that do raise lesbianism as a political issue, I have seen remarkably few friendships formed outside the organizations between heterosexual and lesbian feminists.

Making peace with our personal histories consolidates our lesbian identity in a process that mends the mind and establishes links with our pre-Enlightenment past. Sorting out friendships abandoned in the midst of coming out accomplishes an emotional synthesis that has many implications for our ability to form friendships and work politically with progressive heterosexuals.

Chapter two
Living our lives

"Stephen returned a forgotten textbook to a student on the school bus. As he turned to get off, someone said, 'There goes the fruit!' Another day he found GAY carefully large-lettered in ink on his desk, with an arrow pointing to his chair."

*

"In a bar one night, a fabulous specimen stared in my direction. Summoning up all my cool courage, I stared back. He intensified his gaze—I did the same. I took in the keys dangling from his belt loop. I counted the squares on his plaid shirt. He glanced away, then turned back to me..."

*

"Steve yakked away endlessly with the young woman working beside him, and when the male hets in the vicinity told him to shut up, he told them to get fucked. If they could talk about their lives, he could talk about his, he said. And the row was on."

*

Getting royally fucked
by a perfect sissy
Michael Riordon

Issue 67, October 1980

I hadn't done it, not really, for almost four years. You've seen those movies where people rush out onto the Kansas plains in overalls and aprons after months of killing drought to cry and laugh into the first rain splashing their faces? It was a little like that. And it had to be a perfect sissy, no one else could have managed it.

I'm no easy fuck, let me tell you. Anyone who wants to has to get over, around or through some very formidable barriers before he even reaches the palace gates, much less gets at the treasures within. Fewer than a handful of people have ever got a clear enough view of the treasures within to consider the challenge worth their while. Yet it's not for lack of wanting on my part.

Let me tell you a little of my history. It has three chapters: growing up, getting out and now.

Growing up was fairly grim. I learned that love was conditional on good behaviour; violence was the alternative. Sex was something obscure and distasteful that men did to women, and women put up with. Chapter One included a shocking number of friendships and possible loves sabotaged by me before they could become too — too anything, I never knew what.

Chapter Two included leaving home, getting into and out of electric shock therapy. The practitioner tried to teach me to hate men, their cocks and all the rest. Not to make me heterosexual, you understand, simply to kill the perverse desire for males. He called it adjusting to society.

Gay liberation threw a bit of a wrench into this calm destruction. Here we were suddenly taking on the whole world, ignoring its ugly, stupid commands about men being men and women being pretty, forging from moment to moment our own laws of loving and playing and growing. Suddenly I found myself fighting for freedoms I'd never tasted. At the same time that I was shouting from the rooftops what we do in bed, I was actually doing far less of it than the average outraged listener must have thought.

I suffer badly from being remote — oh no, several people will protest, you're not the least bit remote, on the contrary you're very easy to meet once we get past the answering service. Then let's say I'm impenetrable. That is, indiscriminately nice to almost everyone, open as a harbour to casual chat or a good argument but beyond that, in the murky realm of Real Feelings, absolutely, relentlessly terrified of being fucked.

There are two ways of fucking, of being fucked. (Surely there are more.) One is coyly described thus in an article in *Drummer*, "America's Mag for the Macho Male":

"With one quick forceful jerk I shoved my cock into the stud's shit chute. Buck bolted, his ass slid off the end of my cock. 'What the fuck you think you're doing, you dirty motherfucker!' I bellowed at him. I drove my fist into his back. Again and again I slapped the dude's milky white, hairy ass, till it glowed as red as the spotlight overhead. My cock plowed its full length into the stud's tight hole. Buck writhed in pain, trying to get off my cock. 'Oh shee-it,' he moaned, 'Fuck, you're killing me.' 'Shut the fuck up, boy—you're just making it harder on yourself.' Listening to this he-man stud grunting like a pig on the end of my dick made me even more determined to fuck Hell out of him. I pounded into him like a jackhammer."

And so on—I won't spoil the ending. Is it any wonder I'm terrified? Lest anyone think I'm pooh-poohing this kind of adventure, I confess to getting a ghost of a hard-on as I reread it; don't know in which role I see myself, probably both, would much prefer to see myself in neither, neither a stuck pig nor a jackhammer. There doesn't seem much of a future in either.

There's something uncomfortably close to Real Life in the above drooly fantasy. It's being done to us all the time by military and religious fanatics, by thugs, market analysts, parents and other official guardians; people with power of one sort or another can't resist using it to make openings in other people through which they get into us, have their way with us and wreak havoc in there. It doesn't seem right somehow that we should do the same to each other.

You may well argue that Sex is properly separate from Real Life, a good way of venting things, boys will be boys, etc. Perhaps so, but can you see the dilemma it causes someone who wants to be neither stuck pig nor jack-hammer?

Fucking *with* someone, as opposed to fucking someone or being fucked by someone, seems to me a true test of mutual consent. If the person entering is not also entered, then not enough has happened. Consenting people aren't just ones who agree to things, but ones who have real choices, and who know it. I've had sex with people when I didn't want to; I wasn't raped, but neither was I a consenting adult.

I'm not pleading for sex to be all glances, vapours and sighs. Though I still tend to apologize for sweating on people, I'm learning that tidal sex, now taut and muscular, now sweet and silly, works best for me. Brutish sex is tyrannical, and the last thing we need is more tyranny.

You're probably wondering when we get to the good stuff. All in good time. It took *me* long enough, it won't hurt you to wait a little, too.

Tired of my constant complaints, a dear friend finally decided to get me a dildo to practice with. Twenty-two dollars for a decent model, nothing more than a piece of molded rubber from Taiwan. (Are these things modelled after someone, and does he get royalties?) But neither of us had the financial resources for me to feel comfortable about sitting for very long on twenty-two dollars. Various vegetables were recommended, but that seems to me criminal when three quarters of the world don't even get to *eat* them. No progress.

Another friend suggested fingers, mine to begin with. I played one whole evening and it was lush, swoony fun; I rolled about demented on the floor until I banged my head against a rocking chair and got a little scar. Still, it was clearly progress.

Then I met C. This man is not a *Blueboy* fantasy. Though a number of people of impeccable taste claim to lust after him, he's no hunk. He was out in high school before that was fashionable — will it ever be? — and got called sissy a lot. He's never lifted a weight he didn't have to. (I'm keen on men who look as if they belong in their bodies, and as if their bodies belong to them. Near where I live a new store is opening: The Muscle Shop. I see it filled with racks and trays of pecs, with and without hair and a variety of nipples, washboard abdominals, tins of slightly damaged biceps and so on. Opening special: free tool kit with every purchase over twenty-two dollars....) C is graceful in his own way. His best (men) friends he calls Sis. Walking on the street one night, we collected almost a dozen insults. On a continent bulging with men all apparently trying to look like the Michelin Man, C is a wonderfully visible minority. And he's a yummy swampy kisser.

On our third encounter, C said he wanted to fuck me. Oh god, this is it then, I thought. Not my skinny fingers this time, but his actual cock, as large as life. (I'm sort of an inverse size-queen: the bigger it is, the less enthusiastic I'm likely to be. His is larger than average.) But "Yes" I breathed, lay under his hands, and hoped for the best.

Well. He certainly knew his way around. He could have been Imperial Oil the way he rummaged among the treasures therein. I was astonished: it didn't hurt after the initial bloop except for a few bumpings very deep. I didn't hear bells and see stars but I was well pleased, felt warm and moved, didn't want him to pull out. It's very difficult for me to see what I was doing as passive in any way. C said: "Some of the squeezes you gave me nearly made me pop. You have a very articulate asshole." Tee-hee, *this* old thing? Some of those cunning deep muscle exercises I do to soothe my writer's back are finally paying off.

Interesting, though, when he said the next morning that he'd like "to roll me over and poke me again," I balked, subtly and mysteriously. First, I didn't trust my newly articulate heavenly gate to have got its second wind, as it were. Second, it was twenty minutes before he had to go to work, and that seemed to me entirely too casual.

Most important, however: while I could celebrate being fucked once, what did it mean to be fucked twice in succession, what did it say about me? Wasn't it my turn at bat, so to speak? (I put it down to democracy, but who knows—in any democracy I've observed, the same people always get fucked.) He consented gracefully, and I promptly lost my erection by thinking about how much better at it he'd been than I was going to be!

Oh hell. Oh well, Rome wasn't built in a day.

Home and mother
Jane Rule

Issue 60, February 1980

I have met a few lesbian couples who have lived together for years without sexual connection, one maintaining near-celibacy, the other leading an active sexual life elsewhere. I have encountered this model of Victorian marriage more often between men. The older they are, the more this fact about their relationship is kept a guilty secret. Younger people are apt to talk about the convenience rather than the commitment of being "just friends." Though increasing numbers of people reject the ideal of one-flesh-faithful-unto-death, it still haunts us, making what we think of as more rational arrangements still dubious and guilt-ridden.

Is celibacy in a long-term relationship an attempt at a different sort of fidelity, removed from sexuality which, if combined with love, so often produces those monstrous children, possessiveness and jealousy? Remove sex from a relationship, and there may be freedom to enjoy commitments less likely to pall — work, hobbies, house and garden, friends and animals. That is often the explanation after the fact, but it is not usually on those terms such a relationship begins.

Romantic love offers no model for passionate peers. Most men fall in love with women, after all. Those who are attracted to other men, if they are to follow the romantic model, must assert their superiority or relinquish it. W H Auden and E M Forster, for example, both chose men much younger than themselves, less competent or inferior in social status, in need of protection and support. Auden's lover finally rejected the role of inferior by rejecting Auden sexually. As often, the rejection comes from the man who has perceived himself the superior. Once he recognizes his lover as a friend and peer, he can no longer see him as an object of passion. Sexual attraction depends on both partners accepting basic inequality.

Inequality in casual relationships, where love is not an issue, may seem more tolerable. So, just like the Victorian husband made to feel ashamed of his sexual needs, the homosexual spares his partner the humiliation of his appetite and takes it instead to the bars, parks and baths. Sex is sport, recreation, which has nothing to do with the centre of living, home.

But there has to be a centre, one who rarely strays, for the relationship to continue. Of those men who accept the role of tender of the hearth, it has been recently said, "They need women's liberation more than most women do." For, like women, they are expected to nurse and comfort those home from the game with bruised egos and hepatitis. Alas, without sex there can still be jealousy, and the contemptuous bitchery directed at young punks and tricks again sounds very much like the Victorian wife on the subject of prostitution.

The lesbian pattern of celibacy within relationship seems more often to come from guilt about all sexual experience which in one may result in rejection of the body, in the other a "sinning" and "being forgiven," virgin mother and child into old age.

It may be that the homosexual community is taking longer to emerge from Victorian attitudes towards sex, having suffered a great deal more from hostile disapproval of its appetites. As people with growing self-respect and deepening self-knowledge, we don't need to go on imitating heterosexual models which don't suit heterosexuals all that often and certainly have little relevance for us.

It may also be more difficult for men than for women, who have the support of the women's movement in radically changing their ways of living. I hear far more genuine questioning among women, far more fierce defending among men, whether of bars and parks or sex with children if I'm listening to homosexuals, of patriarchal privilege among my heterosexual male friends: "Well, maybe I just want to be an old fart; it's my house!"

Every choice in relationships has obvious limitations. We are not all alike in our needs and aspirations. A nun friend explains, "Celibacy is the only way I can manage loving so many people. Otherwise it would be far too complicated." "Give me the complications!" retorts one of my young, experimenting friends. "But sometimes I feel," says a recently divorced woman trying to figure out her new life, "as if I'm using everyone."

If we dared to use each other for real understanding of our experience, our sexual daring might be less compartmentalized, defensive, and guilty.

Fear of cruising
Jeff Richardson

Issue 71, March 1981

I'm not, I confess, very good at cruising. Through some reprehensible negligence, none of the schools I attended offered courses on the subject. Guidebooks abound listing the great cruising spots from Peterborough to Xanipateptl, but none of them seems to tell me just what to do once I'm inside José's Honcho Haven. The assumption, I guess, is that we're all born with an innate understanding of cruising technique. It's true that as a newborn lying in my hospital crib, I *did* make direct eye contact with the doctor. But you know what came of that? He circumcised me.

My subsequent cruising episodes have been equally distressing. Let me give you a typical example. One evening I went into my local grocery store to pick up some milk. As I was passing the soups, I stopped dead in my tracks at the sight of a gorgeous guy nearing me. He too stopped and began to peruse the pickles on the shelf in front of him. My heart was pounding so fast my keys were jangling. What do I say? What do I do? Even Erica Jong didn't tell *how* to get it. For moments that seemed like eras, I stood transfixed by the tins of soup. Somewhere in the "Chunky Manhandlers" there had to be a sign! Suddenly the guy glanced over at me and, with just the trace of a seductive smile, lifted a jar of Polski Ogorki from the shelf. My God, I gasped inwardly, look at the size of those things! It was too much for me. Trembling, I stumbled away from him toward the comfort of the produce section. "Spinach," I muttered, "I've got to eat more spinach."

For most of my sexual career, I have dealt with my inability to cruise in the same way I approach most other problems: irrationally. When in doubt, deny, distort or ignore. A thousand roles I could play, each designed to obscure the one basic truth: I wasn't getting it.

The scenario usually ran something like this. It's evening. Alone in my living room, I'm craving to go out. "No," I argue with myself, "remember your resolve!" I close my eyes and tap the heels of my ruby slippers together three times. "There's no place like home... there's no place like... like...." Doubt shuffles in. "I could cruise if I really wanted to," my mind bluffs defensively, "but I just don't want to, so there." (I stick out my tongue to add extra conviction.) I puff myself up, listing all the tremendously significant things I ought to do instead (take a nap, watch *Dallas*, buy a dog). Friends, I tell myself, are so much more meaningful to my life than anything cruising could bring — until I discover that all my friends are out cruising.

Needing to bolster my resolve, I reach for a book on my shelf: William Thackeray's *Pendennis*. If anything can keep me home, this great satire on the foibles of passion will. Quickly I turn to my favourite passage. There I read of a young man madly in love with a lady who, enamoured of another, barely knows this man exists. For weeks he roams about London, exhausting himself in the effort to get just one more glimpse of her. Finally, standing on an embankment in a park, he catches sight of her riding in the distance. "Ahhh," he swoons in triumphant glory. "But what," interjects the narrator sarcastically, "is the earthly good of looking at a girl in a pink bonnet across a ditch?" Exactly, WT, you said it. "And what," I deduce for myself, "is the earthly good of looking at a muscled number in skin-tight jeans across a dance floor?"

The analogy somehow fails, and within an hour I'm ogling pink bonnets across some ditch of a disco. Now that I'm out in the midst of the scene, my ineptness presses upon me. My knees begin to buckle; streams of sweat stain the name of Calvin Klein. There's only one escape, I decide: cynicism! Swiftly I scramble high atop my aristocratic nose to peer knowingly and mockingly down at this strange breed of Sassooned and Coppertoned lemmings. I sneer, I slander, I survive. Someone complains that the bars are too unfriendly and that Toronto gays are too uptight, but I don't even deign to express my agreement. To turn a cold eye on all the uptight, unfriendly coolness is not only acceptable, somehow it's *de rigueur*. Frigid is hotter than cool. And I — seeing through it all and scorning it all — wouldn't miss a night.

On my way home, alone, the cynicism subsides and I quiver for a moment in the throes of self-pity. I invoke the spirit of Sylvia Plath. "Death by fire or by drowning?" I debate. The storefronts, the lamplights, the freezing shadowed streets play *film noir* backdrop to my angst-ridden Outsider. Long as I might to cruise and be cruised, I will always be alone. Half an hour later, in bed, my snoring brings down the curtain on this existential melodrama.

It was the language of cruising I couldn't understand. I was nostalgic for what I supposed was the simplicity of words. "What's a nice guy like you doing in a place like this?" may at best be an uninspired line, but I could understand it and respond to it. But keys and scarves, poppers and pinky-rings—these were mysterious symbols I was unable and unwilling to decode. It was so much easier to play stranger in a foreign land than to interpret the language.

But finally a quotation from Balzac struck home with me. He had written of a princess that "She was learned and she knew that the amorous character has its signs in what are taken for trifles. A knowledgeable woman can read her future in a simple gesture." All right, I vowed, I would learn, I too would be knowledgeable. If no one would teach me, I would teach myself. (God knows, I'd been a "self-made" man for some time already.)

So the crash course was on. Assiduously I studied—on the streets, in the bars and restaurants, taking notes, compiling lists of gestures, postures, attire, strategies. Finally I felt I had it all together. I was ready for anything.

In a bar one night, a fabulous specimen stared in my direction. I glanced quickly about. No one stood near, so he had to be looking at me. Summoning up all my cool courage, I stared back. He intensified his gaze—I did the same. I took in the keys dangling from his belt loop, I noted the angle of his trucker's hat, I counted the squares on his plaid shirt: each a propitious omen. He glanced away, then turned back to me, raising his eyebrows far into his forehead. I—so suave, so sure—raised mine. He winked. I winked. With such heavy eye-contact, I could feel an epiphany approaching.

Then he put his hand in front of one eye. This, I thought, is a signal I've never seen before. It must be reserved for something very hot. Should I also raise my hand? As I pondered this expectantly, he suddenly lifted the other hand to his eye and blinked at me meaningfully several times.

Then, carefully, he extracted a contact lens.

Nice pickles, eh?

Faces of sisterhood
Mariana Valverde

Issue 66, September 1980

I arrived in London on a Monday, for a six-week period of library research. After the initial confusion was over and I was no longer stupidly waiting for buses on the wrong side of the street, I set out — on Friday — to meet some women.

So I bought *Time Out*, a wonderful what's-on-in-the-city publication which gives details on demonstrations and meetings as well as movies, and decided that a "Women Against Imperialism" benefit dance was my first choice for the evening. The dance was to be held at the Women's Arts Alliance, which turned out to be a combination bookstore/café/drop-in centre in a run-down building, oddly located just behind a series of stately white buildings with life-sized Greek statues guarding marble staircases. As I was staring at the monumental neo-classical complex (which faces the impeccable Regent's Park) and wondering what unknown lesbian feminists might be lurking behind the Rolls Royces, the unmistakable sound of Joan Armatrading told me I was not lost. I followed the sound down an alleyway and soon found myself surrounded by neat young dykes. Sigh of relief.

The women's punk/new-wave bands were great; the politics were unquestionably right on; the women looked lovely and lively. But—I hate to admit it —no one talked to me. At first I happily leaned against the wall and took in the scene, as they say, but as the evening wore on I naturally tried to talk with someone (when the music wasn't too loud) or dance with someone (when it was).

Alas. The new lesbian feminism prescribes that women shall dance in fives, threes, or ones, but seldom in twos—and I just wasn't suave enough to be able to ask four women at once to dance with me. Flirting was of course out of the question in this pure environment.

Anyway, I wandered back and forth between the dance floor and the library-cum-nursery, attempted to make conversation or even eye contact, and finally gave up and danced with everyone and no one. Needless to say, I left early.

Walking home, I had to pass an unashamedly apolitical women's disco, which I had been told was held on certain evenings in the upstairs of an otherwise ordinary pub. Although back home in Toronto I seldom go to discos, after the reception I had just got from my presumably like-minded sisters, the prospect of warm bodies and cold ale was too good to pass up. (To add insult to injury, the Women's Arts Alliance is not licenced, and I, stranger in a strange land, had neglected to bring my own.) So I threw caution to the wind and went in.

I had not even taken my jacket off when three friendly women came up to me, made small talk, got me a half pint, and proceeded to make me feel very much at home. They gave me info on where to go on what nights, who ran what, and other essentials, all sprinkled with jokes, pats on the back, and smiles. I cautiously asked one of the women to dance, and was relieved to discover that the critique of couple-ism had not yet made inroads among this crowd. A great time was had by all, especially me — and when closing time came around my "feminist emotional support detector" was registering a high concentration of sisterly waves.

Out on the sidewalk, as I stood for a minute trying to figure out the quickest and safest way home, a rather drunk woman in a tattered dress approached me. I was going to turn my back on her, but, remembering the evening's events, I did not avoid her pleading eyes. "Oh, I was going to ask you to dance, but I thought you were with someone... you're so good-looking.... Where are all the other women going?... Can we go for a coffee someplace?... You know, I've been a lesbian all my life."

I interrupted her stream of consciousness. "No thanks, I'm going home." She then gave me a look of desperation, the exact opposite of the self-confident independence of the lesbians I'm used to. Her despair was so profound, so childlike—I was torn between disgust and motherly concern. She was clearly discouraged by what she saw on my face, and said, "Good night, then," kissing me as if I were the last woman on earth. I put my hands on her shoulders and kindly but firmly put her literally at arm's length. I smiled: "Good night, then."

Making my way home down Tottenham Court Road, involuntarily looking at the sad gaudiness of sex-shop window displays, I wondered about sisterhood.

Forgotten fathers
Michael Lynch

Issue 42, April 1978

For forty hours a week Jack is a clerk in an automotive supply shop in Scarborough, Ontario. After each working day, he heads directly home where Jack Jr, eleven, and Sam, seven, are waiting. Since they got home from school they have been playing, watching TV, doing homework.

Jack prepares dinner, taking pride in serving a meat course, potatoes and green vegetables each evening. "Real food too," he says, "nothing precooked from the store." After cleanup and bedtime routines, he tucks them in and begins the evening work: a quick trip for groceries, mending school clothes or doing the laundry. Saturdays and Sundays he takes them on out-ings—to play hockey, to the park, downtown.

Jack's wife died five years ago, not long after Sam was born. For four years, Jack devoted himself entirely to "my boys." Then, about a year ago, "I real-ized that I was forty-five and had to start living a little for myself." He arranged for a sitter to come in every Friday, and now he goes out weekly to a Toronto piano bar where he enjoys relaxing among other men, gay men.

But only for these few hours a week. By 1 am, the sitter must be relieved, and then it is Saturday morning and Jack's a father once more. "There doesn't seem to be any way," he told me, "that I can be both a father and actively gay." When in the bar, Jack feels different from the men he meets there. They talk easily of new clothes, of winter vacations in the Caribbean, of theatre and rec-ords and the other props of extensive leisure and large disposable incomes. As a father, Jack has little of either.

Bob, on the other hand, seems to have both. He lives with his lover in the same Alberta city where his former wife and their four teenage children live. Although the law grants Bob only a few visiting hours a week, plus holidays, his children frequently visit his apartment as if it were their second home. All four of them know Bob is gay. So do their school chums, teachers, the princi-pal and Bob's employers.

Bob's daughters have no difficulty with his sexuality or his being out of the closet. One of them spoke with me at length, and very affectionately, about her father. One of the sons is equally at ease. But the other son barely copes; indeed, he often resents his father's gayness. His sister thinks that, uncertain about his own sexuality, he fears an inherited "contamination."

Jon, who is in his early twenties, separated from his wife several months ago. Unemployed, he lives with his lover in Montreal. After the separation, his wife quit her well-paying job and took their three-year-old to another province to deposit with her parents. Although she has no desire to rear the child and is now seeking a career in another city (the child remains at her par-ents' farm), she seems determined to deny Jon more than token visitation rights. She and her parents also plan a fight to keep the boy from ever visiting Jon in his own home.

Karl, after his separation, was allowed several hours each week with his young son, Robin. When last June he went before the Ontario Supreme Court to ask for more time, the judge lectured him on a text from Mrs Robert Green (she had just won her victory in Dade County, Florida), and refused to increase the visiting period. Indeed, he added two new conditions. During the short visits Karl now pays to Robin, two people must always be present: the man who lives with Karl's former wife (and who is periodically violent toward her, Karl says), and a psychiatric nurse who is to make regular reports to the court. Karl may never see his son except in the presence of these two people.

Four lives, forgotten lives. When was the last time you read about gay fath-ers in the press, straight or otherwise? If you are a gay male reading this, you may think them anachronistic (what faggot in his right mind would want children?) and certainly irrelevant to your own life. Of the several hundred gay men you probably know, it's likely that only a few are fathers and that even those few have little contact with their children. Gay fathers seem little more than a curiosity in the total picture of gay culture today and therefore are appropriately forgotten.

They are, however, more than a curiosity, and gay male culture's choosing to "forget" them might just signal something undesirable about gay male culture. The cause of lesbian mothers has been exalted; we certainly know that gay people can be parents. It's dangerous to forget that among those parents are fathers who are gay.

And not just a few, either. "I had no idea," says Brian Miller of Edmonton, "that so many gay men had children." Brian has been conducting a sociological study of gay fathers, interviewing in depth several dozen of them in the US and Canada. While there are no figures about the percentage of gay men who have children, there are informed guesses. George Hislop of Toronto, who has done as much telephone counselling over the years as any Canadian activist, believes that *most* gay men are still heterosexually married, and that of these a large majority have children.

Why, if they are so many, are they so invisible?

Preparing this article, I asked about twenty fathers if they could be pictured with their child or children. Almost all turned me down. They felt that being known as gay would entail a large risk of losing their children through the efforts of homophobic relatives, social workers or judges.

"The numbers of them weren't all that impressed me," Brian Miller recounts. "There was also an intensity of experience that I'd not expected." He described instance after instance where a father had broken into tears recalling the pain of having to decide between being honest about his gayness and getting to keep his children. "Every father I've talked with experiences a gap between his life as a father and his life as a gay man. As a parent he is part of his children and they of him; as a gay man he finds that the available social structures discourage the presence of children—or exclude them flatly. The invisibility is due not only to the homophobia of the non-gay world, but also to the failure of other gay men to make a place for children within their world as well."

Surely, one might think, a gay activist experiences this differently, does not feel such a gap. Surely the gay movement has made room for these men.

Not at all, says Maurice Flood.

"Jack," "Bob," "Jon" and "Karl" are pseudonyms. "Maurice Flood" is not. Maurice is a gay leader in Vancouver and is the father of Isabel, five, and Margaret, one-and-a-half. Maurice has chosen to live the life of what Don Mager, in a pioneering essay published in 1973, called the "faggot father": "A faggot father is not simply a faggot who at some point fathered a child, but more significantly he is a man whose sexual orientation is gay and whose daily life includes an active participation in the lives of his children."

Maurice and Cynthia Flood live in a large house with two gay men. All four adults have been active in feminist, leftist and/or gay politics. One might expect that such a context would make being a faggot father easier. But here's what Maurice has to say:

"The out-of-the-closet gay father is looked upon by heterosexuals and even by gays as a slightly ridiculous, bizarre creature. He doesn't fit any current conventional pattern of behaviour, and in that sense is considered weird and unacceptable. Many gays, particularly in the gay movement, regard parenthood as a retrograde step. The gay father who is out is seen as someone who has not quite rejected or escaped the family."

Maurice misses gay community support systems. "The gay father receives no positive social reinforcement whatsoever. Instead, people communicate in various ways the message, 'how could you?' or—which is more hurtful—'what right have you?' The most ordinary thing in the universe, having children, becomes freakish, a topic fit for gossip and jokes.

"The status of the gay father who is out is a lonely one, particularly in the gay community."

Maurice is also painfully aware of how little one hears about gay fathers, especially in comparison to lesbian mothers. Fatherhood has no priority in the gay male movement, while motherhood is often (though not always) supported in the lesbian movement. We need to ask why this is so, and perhaps be ready for some uncomfortable answers.

Men, of course, do not gestate and give birth to their children. There is always a mother to deal with: wife, lover, or ex-wife. At this point in our emerging gay culture, most gay fathers have been married, and coming out for almost all of them has coincided with marital deception, separation or divorce. The passage rites of coming out are complicated here by a special kind of pain related more often to grief than to simple anger. Many gay fathers still love their wives and want to continue a closeness with them, but the couple has to face their new world without models or guidance. Often the woman experiences her husband's coming out as a betrayal: she has not simply lost her breadwinner (and that can become an impulse toward feminism, when women break or are broken from their forced financial dependence on men); in addition, her husband is now understood to be no longer sexually attracted to her. Wives often suffer difficult times and express their anger, using the child as a weapon. If lesbians often find their divorced husbands enraged by their wives' rejection of male protectiveness, gay men often find their wives enraged by the loss of a protector.

Can gay men be married *and* be out? Many married gays, of course, keep their sexuality closeted. A few, on coming out, manage for a while to be both married and gay. But it's an uphill battle, and Don Mager has written that separation or divorce "is almost inevitable in being a faggot father."

Other problems arise when the man tries to integrate his fatherhood and his gay lifestyle. A lover, or a succession of lovers or gay roommates, are apt to dislike children. (A cynical John Kyper recently wrote, "I think gay men must dislike children more than they dislike women." But is he right in either case? I doubt it, but clearly many gay men are estranged from their own childhood and are unaccustomed to relating with children.) Children are virtually excluded from gay male social activities: bars, dances, dinner parties, demonstrations. The lesbian movement may or may not be more hospitable to children, I don't know; at least lesbians seem to offer childcare on a regular basis, which gay men usually fail to do.

Mike, a gay father active in the Canadian gay movement for five years, recently said that he'd gotten only two offers from the men he works with to help take care of his son—two offers in five years. "There are occasional small gestures," he said, "but more often a nearly complete indifference to or even flight from my child. Of course, people who dislike children should not be forced to care for them. But surely men and women without children, especially gay activists, should ask if they should not try to open themselves more to children—and thus to the children we all once were."

The problems of single parenthood are topped by the grinding labour of it, the unrelieved responsibility and chores. "I've discovered that care of young people is work, often gruelling and wasteful work if you are tired or slightly unwell," Maurice Flood says. "It took me some time to grasp that people viewed it as 'women's work,' and hence trivial." But it is important, and if much of it is trivial, much is also essential to the act of parenting.

Two quite specific problems concern the gay fathers I've spoken with. One is the anxiety about paternal influence on a child's sexuality. "You're a bad role model," a friend remarked to Don Mager. "Aren't you afraid your child will grow up gay?" is another refrain. The pressure is usually from others—fathers tend to know that a father-child relationship is too complex to yield before such comments—but it is recurrent and often much more intense than even the public debate over teachers as role models.

Their second problem is coming out to their children. (This, of course, is a homophobia-rooted concern; no one ever asks when *straight* parents should communicate to their children that they, as parents, are straight.) Court-inflicted psychiatrists, family counsellors, kindly relatives—many such people discourage coming out at all "until s/he is old enough to understand." They may insist on the father not keeping company with his gay friends when the children are present, or at least that he show no natural affection for his friends. "I realized," one father told me, "that what they meant was: don't come out to your daughter until she is taught to see your sexuality as odd or repugnant."

John Lee of Toronto has been out to his daughter and son since they were four and two, respectively. Now eighteen and sixteen, they have grown up comfortable in knowing of their father's sexuality. On occasion they have even been helpful, he reports, when he and a lover needed mediation or support. "The single most important factor in making a good parent," John says, "is being honest. My children have never had trouble with my living with men, though of course they have liked some more than others." He counsels gay fathers to come out as early as possible. "If you tell children more than they can understand, they'll let you know," he says. "So I prefer to exceed rather than underestimate their comprehension. Children are remarkable in their attention and understanding. At an early age they won't understand physical acts—heterosexual or homosexual—but they will understand affection, struggles, anger, tenderness. They can sense it, and resent it, when a parent is dishonest with them."

Above all, the problem facing the forgotten gay father is the spectre of isolation. Gay men may no longer be invisible, but gay fathers remain so. Like all subminorities, they suffer a more intense version of the general oppression experienced by the minority as a whole. Upon learning that I'd talked with other gay fathers, one almost shouted, "Where on earth did you find them?" The hunger to share experience is one that any gay person who has been isolated would understand. So would any parent who has been isolated from other parents. Parenthood, like sexuality, becomes a crucial component in one's sense of oneself.

"There's a lot I'd like to talk about with another gay father," one man told me, "but there's no place to do it. In the parent association at school we're not out to one another, if there even are any other gay parents there. And I feel completely apart from straight parents. In the bars there's an unwritten rule against talking about something like parenthood, except as an oddity."

"My loneliest hours," another said, "are those in the park while the boys are playing. I'd like to be with another gay adult then, to talk over the week's discoveries and decisions. I watch the heterosexuals who meet there to chat while their children play—but I'm alone."

Lesbian mothers may recognize this isolation, but I suspect they share it to a less intense degree. Gay fathers probably come closer in this respect to straight fathers: both suffer from an assumption, or ideology, that runs through our culture. It goes something like this: men are not suited for relating to children. They cannot be tender, compassionate, or nurturing with them. Only women are capable of nurturance. Men have another, nobler role: to teach the assumptions of the patriarchal succession—authority, emotional distance, toughness, competition.

The best book I know dealing with the way this cultural sexism bears on day-to-day fatherhood is a little one written by an apparently non-gay father. David Steinberg's *fatherjournal: five years of awakening to fatherhood* (Times Change Press, 1977) is an account through journal notes of David's struggle against the culturally imposed father-role, "the second, somewhat foreign parent." "I was going to be the perfect father," he writes not long after his son Dylan is born. "I was going to make up for all the men who leave the children to the women, who back away from intimacy with children, who are cold and distant. I was going to do it right.

"Tonight I see how scared I am. There is so much to do for this little creature who screams and wriggles and needs and doesn't know what he needs.... I am so small compared to what needs to be done."

Gay fathers may, in these respects, be more capable than straight ones. *May.* A Toronto father of two told me: "We don't begin with the assumption of the sexual division of labour and experience that many straight fathers have to begin by overcoming." Nonetheless, we have something of this sexism in us, and may empathize with David Steinberg's difficulties in trying to teach his son "to be a warm, loving, open man."

The opposition to nurturant fathers in general is, I suspect, reflected in the special opposition to loving sexual relationships between men and boys. (I avoid the use of the term "pedophilia" only because it considers the adult perspective alone, and I include here the boy's perspective.) Sexual relationships between boys and men in our culture are the object of far greater opposition than relationships between girls and men (we are amused, not rabid, when dealing with Lewis Carrolls and Humbert Humberts), women and boys, or women and girls (which are, even today, as invisible as lesbians were to Queen Victoria, despite all the gym teacher and camp counsellor jokes). Boy-man relationships do not dissolve easily into a melting pot with the other kinds of child-adult relationships, despite the repeated assertions that "pedophilia is primarily a heterosexual problem and not at all a lesbian problem."

The same cultural sexism that declares men incapable of tender or loving relationships with each other also dictates that fathers are incapable of nurturing their children. Men are not supposed to convey to children, particularly male children, more than token intimacy. To the sexist, the greatest traitor of all is the man who tries *not* to transmit the assumptions of patriarchy, who does not seek to cauterize his tender emotions, who seeks instead to undo his long-taught capacity for feelingless authority.

Gay fathers, then, have a special reason to think through this matter before dismissing the question of boy-man sexuality from their own politics. They should even be asking if the better fathers don't have something in common with the better pedophiles, and if the opposition to both of them doesn't come from the same source.

The core of opposition to gay fathers, then, is a sexist core, one that prohibits men from being loving, tender and nurturant with children, especially male children. This accounts for my own discomfort with a trend that seems to be surfacing among some gay groups: exalting, in nineteenth-century fashion, the saintly mother-role. Lesbian mothers, the message goes, are special people *because they alone can mother.* Fathers remain forgotten, implying that fathers, because they are men, cannot "mother," cannot nourish a growing child.

We need to recognize the sexism here, and rebuff it. Adrienne Rich has done just that in her book *Of Woman Born* (Norton, 1978), which deals with motherhood but has a lot to teach gay fathers along the way. "It can be dangerously simplistic to fix upon 'nurturance' as a special strength of women," she writes. "Whatever our organic or developed sense of nurture, it has often been turned into a boomerang." I would add that the boomerang is often thrown at men by unwittingly sexist gay male and lesbian groups—before it returns to harm the thrower.

A lesbian mother recently told me that a feminist lawyer advised her to fight her custody case by emphasizing the female protectiveness women show towards children, as opposed to the "exploitation" of children's sexuality shown by gay men. The lawyer, the mother, and the judge might continue to believe this lie unless gay fathers come out of their double closets.

We need aggressive battles for the rights of lesbian mothers. Their main liability, in general comparison to gay fathers, seems to me to be their economic disenfranchisement. Men already have a bigger piece of the (shrinking) pie and the muscle to hold on to that piece. But I will challenge any claim that men are better treated by the courts than lesbians are, and urge that our struggle for custody justice expand to include gay fathers. The techniques that have been developed to dramatize the plight of lesbian mothers—without overly risking their chances for custody—must be engaged for gay fathers as well.

Can all this lead to making gay fatherhood a more prominent issue in the gay male movement than it is now? Maurice Flood thinks not. "I don't visualize the issue of gay fathers becoming a pivotal point in the gay movement," he says, "except for child custody cases, which are a potential threat to every gay parent."

Perhaps he is right. John Lee argues that we should attend to the roles of gay men as surrogate fathers as a priority: the possibility for gays to work as Big Brothers, as teachers, as scoutmasters, to be childcare workers or adoptive parents.

But if we look to the future, when (presumably) fewer gay men will be marrying before they come out, we surely need to ask what those gay men who want children are to do. Lesbians have the option of what the straight press oppressively labels "test tube babies," some form of extramarital fertilization. Should we be seeking options for gay men to become biological fathers too? Not from motives of patriarchal succession, but because there are other, barely explored bonds between biological fathers and sons that can nurture both of them?

One matter, at least, is clear: right now gay fathers have a pivotal role to play in the gay movement. Gay fathers give the lie to two of our enemies' most pernicious untruths: that homosexual men cannot reproduce (thus they recruit, etc) and that they are dangerous to children (either as rapists or as bad role models). Gay fathers also have a unique chance to fight, as parents, against the sexism that heterosexuals in the schools want to recruit children into. Every gay father needs to aim towards coming out to his children, to their friends, to the school, to the public.

*

Last October, a father and his five-year-old son were visiting their neighbourhood library. After checking out four Babar books—which also propagandize for the nuclear family, despite their charm—the boy wondered why they weren't leaving.

Son: What are we waiting around for?
Father: I was hoping to meet that man over there.
Son: Is he gay?
Father: I hope so.
Son: Are you gay?
Father: I'm sure of that.
Son: You know, I don't really know what "gay" means.

Father: It means that if you're a man, you especially love and want to be close to other men. If you're a gay woman, a lesbian like Susan's mother, you want especially to be close to other women.

Son: Oh. (pause) Am I gay?

Father: I don't know. You'll find out someday, in time.

Son: How will I know?

Father: You'll have good friends who are both boys and girls, but you'll find you want to snuggle and be especially close to your boyfriends. You'll know.

Son: OK.

A week later, the boy was thumbing through a magazine and came across a cigarette ad with a smiling man and woman in it. He said, "Here are some gay people." "How do you know?" said the father. "Because they are kissing and they're happy together." "Close enough," said the father.

The father was, to come out of my closet, me. The son was Stefan, now age six. I originally wanted the analysis in this article to be based in our relationship, in our experience as father and son. I wanted to talk about the intimacy between us that has developed in the last two years. About watching him grow and, through him, seeking both my own childhood and something completely Other: him — the pleasure in his light spirits, of his unmitigated faith at times and his stubborn refusal to accept, at other times, my experience second-hand.

I wanted to articulate my growth into fathering. Learning about power. About how terms like "coercion" and "exploitation" and "manipulation" become difficult terms to use when I speak of children. Both because any adult-child relationship may be coercive, and because children, until authority drums it out of them, are native challengers of coercion, seldom passive recipients of attitudes or information from adults.

I wanted to talk about Stefan's sense of my sexuality and politics, and about my attempts to prepare him for the vicious homophobia he's sure to encounter in school before long.

I wanted to talk about privacy, since, next to the government, children are the greatest invaders of adult privacy. About the adult need to be away from children periodically. Likewise, about the ways adults invade the personal and peer group privacy of children.

I wanted to give the texture of moments in which these issues become clear, as they do in a close relationship with a child.

I've failed in this personal goal. Stefan's mother, reading this, pointed out that I haven't broken away from abstractions and loosely linked analyses. I haven't eased into the texture of the fathering experience, but had to rely on pointing towards Steinberg's book, which does just that.

Writing this final draft on March 22, I suddenly realize that it was eighteen years ago this morning my father died. What little I know of that father-son relationship has only been restored to me through my relationship with my son.

Two days ago eight gay fathers, and three of our children, gathered for the first time, and I found in that group a sense of commonality I'm not used to among gay men. "Being a parent," one of them said, "is a more engulfing experience than just being married or being gay—we are bound to have much more in common." All of us are battling sexism, both Out There and within ourselves. In each other's presence, we eight were no longer forgotten fathers.

Where do we go from here?

The words
Ian Young

Issue 4, May/June 1972

Six a.m. The party guests have all gone home.

I read his letter
(handed to me by our friend):
"drunken" he says (but too right to be),
honest, quiet, typed on school paper and
folded crooked:

"I'm very glad I met you"
and
"someone who likes you for YOU
    and not for your body" (OK I smile).

He likes only girls he says,
his tendencies are
in a "thigh-breast" direction.

Yet sitting behind the desk in my room
at six o'clock,
the letter in my hand,
I picture his quiet face,
slightly crooked, laughing,
beautiful I think.

Dawn, a milky light.
Books. Shadows.

Again I read the words;
again and again my eyes drop to the paper.

No sorrow, no pity: the gay disabled
Gerald Hannon

Issue 60, February 1980

Richard was a premature baby. Fifty years earlier he might have died at birth. But this was 1953, and little baby Richard was placed lovingly in an incubator of reputable American make. No one would know for many, many months, but some of the machines did not work very well, and babies across North America were quietly breathing an oxygen mixture so rich that their retinal tissue slowly burned away. "I was one of the lucky ones," Richard told me. "Some grew up with really horrible brain damage. I just grew up blind." Richard is officially a handicapped human being. He is one of an estimated two hundred thousand disabled persons in Toronto alone—though numbers are hard to come by because nobody's counting. The conventional wisdom is that the handicapped represent fourteen percent of the population—one in seven. But however many there are, the numbers, according to an article in *Physiotherapy Canada*, are growing. The "new paraplegics of Canadian society," it says, "are young people between the ages of fourteen and nineteen"—smashed up in car accidents, snowmobile disasters, even run-ins between ten-speed bicycles.

For Richard, an excess of oxygen slowly burned away his vision. For Scott McArthur, born in 1952, there were a few struggling minutes in the throes of birth when oxygen was cut off, and in those minutes brain cells died like lights going out in a panicked and desperate city. His intelligence was not affected, but Scott grew up with a condition known as cerebral palsy—CP. His days are spent in a wheelchair. His speech is distorted and laboured; anyone unused to it will find him very difficult to understand. His movements appear spastic and uncoordinated. If he is not careful, he will drool.

Like Richard, Scott McArthur is gay.

People like Richard and Scott have not been figures in our landscape. I know, I know that there are gay men and women everywhere—that they are single, that they are married, that they appear at every economic level and in every race and nationality, but.... Maybe it's our dogged insistence on our essential health as gay people, on our persistent view of ourselves in our own media as whole, active, healthy, bright and beautiful. Maybe that's it. But I feel that somehow, way at the back of our first closet we have built another one, and into it we have shoved our gay deaf and our gay blind and our gay wheelchair cases, and we've gone on with the already difficult enough problems of living as gay people.

If we've built that second closet, society has made it easy for us. We are not likely to meet the disabled in the workplace—of the employable blind, for example, eighty percent are unemployed. The general unemployment rate among the handicapped is usually given as fifty percent. And as for social-izing—next time you're at your favourite gay spot, count the stairs.

The lives of many disabled gay people are passed in institutions. Scott McArthur lives in one—he asked me not to name it because he has to continue living there. When it was built, it was widely seen as a progressive and innova-tive institution. But when Scott moved in five years ago, residents were for-bidden to shut their doors if they had a visitor of the opposite sex. That rule has changed, but even today there are no rooms that can accommodate couples, and it is generally expected that visitors will leave by midnight. No overnight guests are allowed.

Scott has known institutions most of his life, and this is not the worst of them. But in none of them has leading a sexual life been very easy.

"I can remember being interested in men since I was ten years old," he told me. "When I got into my teens, I began paying other boys in the hospital for sex. My parents gave me spending money, and I spent it paying the other kids to jerk me off. A few years later I was spending close to two hundred dollars a year for sex. But I didn't call myself gay—I didn't know what it meant. But I knew I wanted men."

Scott was caught, of course—one thing almost no one has in any institution is privacy. He was told it was bad to have other boys jerk him off. He tried to talk to the staff psychologist about his mysteriously developing sexuality, but it didn't work. He went back to paying the other boys. Shortly after that his parents received a letter saying that Scott was ready to be discharged.

As Scott said, "It was a nice way of kicking me out."

He stayed in his parents' home in Nova Scotia for five years. Not very much happened. Once, with the conniving of a sympathetic housekeeper, he man-aged to order some porn from the States. Shortly thereafter a letter from Can-ada Customs arrived—his mother was the first to read it—informing him that copies of *Hot Rod* and *Circumcision: A Study in Pictures* had been seized as "immoral and indecent." Scott was handed the letter, told it was obviously some business of his, and there the matter lay.

We who are able-bodied remember what coming out was like. It was not easy, it required privacy, a chance to surreptitiously look things up in books and magazines, a chance to get out alone for a while and maybe "accidental-ly" wander by that place you'd heard "those" people went to. Maybe, if you were lucky, you found somebody sympathetic to talk to. All of the people I talked to for this article have spent part or all of their lives in institutions where privacy is almost nonexistent, and where the administration, acutely aware of its dependence on "public money," has been quite frankly terrified of the topic of sexuality.

"Blind people don't fuck." That is Richard's summation of the attitudes of not only the School for the Blind in Brantford, but a lot of the gay people he runs into.

Richard went through grade twelve at the blind school. Every second Fri-day there was a very carefully chaperoned dance with the blind girls to which the blind boys dutifully went, and from which, before midnight, they were efficiently hustled back to their own residence. "I used to suck off one of my roommates," Richard said. "And I used to hear a lot of other people's doors opening and closing after everyone was supposed to be in bed. We had no privacy though—anybody could come in or out because we weren't allowed to lock anything. We used to call the place 'The Zoo'—there'd always be people coming on tours to see the 'poor blind kids.' "

Nothing was ever said about sexuality. Blind people don't fuck. For Richard, the rationalization that he was sucking off his roommate because women were unavailable was beginning to wear a little thin. "Anyway," he said, "from as far back as I can remember I loved being with men. I used to have this great crush on my old man. I loved climbing in bed with him when I was still a kid and we both just had our underwear on."

Again, the institution. The Canadian National Institute for the Blind—the CNIB, "snib," as Richard calls it—is one of the powerful ones. Richard is not very happy with snib. "Having your life run by the CNIB is like having your life run by a church group," he says. "They're arbitrary, they provide 'services,' they have a custodial attitude." BOOST (Blind Organization of Ontario with Self-help Tactics), of which Richard is a member, says that fewer than a third of the people on CNIB's board are blind, and that they've ensured, in fact, that the blind *can't* have control. Richard simply snorted when I asked him if the CNIB was a place for the blind to turn to for information on sexuality. I went to check.

I had to because the CNIB has basically cornered the market on information for the blind. Their braille and "talking book" library in Toronto is the blind person's national library. I spoke to the CNIB's Pat Trusty who, if she is nonplussed by my probing questions about the availability of adequate sex information for the gay blind, does not show it. She promises she will check their holdings. I ask about pornography; she promises she will check that too. In the meantime she lends me a great stack of catalogues giving a partial list of titles. Leafing through them, I discover they have *The Joy of Sex*—but not the gay male and lesbian versions.

Trusty, who is nothing if not cooperative, calls back in a week and says yes, the library does have one title. It is *The Gay Theology*. I do not tell her it is a dreadful book. There are, however, eight more titles in the US that would be available on interlibrary loan, if requested. There are some good titles — Peter Fisher's *The Gay Mystique*, for example, or Wainwright Churchill's *Homosexual Behaviour Among Males*. There is nothing specifically about lesbians, and nothing published in the last five years. There are no gay liberation periodicals. There are, however, volumes by those twin quacks of psychoanalysis, Irving Bieber and Edmund Bergler. There is also the temptingly titled *Homosexuality: Its Causes and Curses*. And no, there is no available pornography.

Trusty assures me, however, that a selection committee of the CNIB will consider any request for the conversion of printed material to braille or talking book. Fat chance. "Sighted" people may cruise a gay magazine for weeks before they dare pick it — even in the relative anonymity of a newsstand. It

"Four short, three long,
rotate hips and stick tongue in…
pull out to end,
slowly reinsert…
four short,
three long…."

"Rockets, bells,
erupting volcanoes…
I hear a symphony…
flights of birds,
waves, comets,
tornadoes…."

Gary Ostrom, Issue 38, November 1977

doesn't seem very likely to me that a gay blind person will put him- or herself on the line before an unknown quantity like a "selection committee"— no matter how badly the material may be wanted.

Richard, of course, had access to no information at all. Richard had to slowly stumble out of the closet. He called a gay counselling line a few times, but got nervous and hung up. And because he couldn't see, and because he had no access to any written material on gayness, he developed some very peculiar ideas about what gay people were like. All he had to go on was voice —and for him, gayness became the sterotyped lisping, mannered male voice. *He* wasn't like that, but somehow he knew that he and those "queenly" voices were after the same thing, and somehow it was all wrapped up in a man who would be taller than he, and have a deep, resonant voice and a furry, muscular arm—something he could get to check, by the by, since it happens to be perfectly okay for a blind man to take another man's arm when walking.

He went looking for that man at The Barn, a Toronto gay bar. And there he ran into some of the same paternalistic attitudes that enraged him at "snib." "One man came up and asked if I knew what kind of bar this was. I said sure, it's a gay bar. He said you mean you go home with people? And I said no, I simply stand around all night like a statue." Richard says he also got *very* tired of people saying "isn't that too bad." Or people yelling in his face because they feel he must be a little dim as well. Or people who want "to look after me." Now, he says, he gets a lot of the initial tension out of the way by introducing himself as "that weird blind person who may fall over you."

You get to say something like that, of course, only if you happen to have a pretty good self-image. That wasn't always the case for Richard, but it helped to discover he could pick up two or three people a week at The Barn during what he now terms his "whoring phase." A phase now over—he's involved in a relationship, has a job with BOOST, and plans to keep plugging away in the fight for disabled rights. "It means more to me than the gay struggle," he says. "I have more to gain for one thing—like a job somewhere other than BOOST, and independence."

Independence. Like most everyone else, the disabled want to control their own lives. And if they must live in institutions, they want to control those institutions and make them responsive to their real needs.

John Kellerman has been fighting that battle—until recently, a rather lonely one—for twelve years. When he tried to move back into a group home he'd left a year and a half earlier, he was told he couldn't because he "raised too much shit. And *I* thought I was doing everything I could to make it a better place by organizing the residents and so on."

Like Scott, John Kellerman has CP. It hits people in many different ways, though, and John can walk (although very awkwardly) while Scott can't. But John's speech seems to have been affected much more, and I find him more difficult to understand. He's patient enough to repeat everything five or six times if that's what it takes, and I'm persistent enough to keep asking, so we struggle through.

John defines himself as bisexual. He has fantasized about having sex with women, but remembers how he used to love to watch construction workers in the summer even when he was just a kid, how he was fascinated by their bodies. "I used to be afraid," he says, "of being condemned by gay people for wanting both. But it hasn't really happened—mostly it's having been brought up in a society that says we have to love one or the other."

John says that he was so desperate for information on sexuality that he helped organize one of the earliest conferences on the topic just so he'd finally learn something. "I went to Queen's Park in 1974 and got two thousand dollars and we actually got something going. I felt ecstatic—I'd been so hung up about organizing and about sex generally. But the conference was great."

That hadn't been his first effort, however. In the early Seventies he helped found a group called ALPHA, Advancement League for the Physically Handicapped, and that group successfully lobbied the city for the grading of sidewalks and the initiation of Wheel-Trans, the transit commission's project for the physically disabled. More recently, he has organized a citizens' committee to plan activities for 1981—the International Year of the Disabled. "One thing that sort of frightens me," he said, "is that we'll be inundated with do-gooders. That scares the hell out of me."

John Kellerman is an activist, but every activist has a private life. Or tries to. "I'm very lonely," he says. "I want to develop a relationship with someone, but nothing much has happened with either men or women. I've often wanted to go to the baths, but I'm afraid to because I'm afraid they wouldn't let me in. I went to two in Winnipeg, and they wouldn't let me past the door. I don't go to many bars because I have a real complex about going, though I haven't had any problems in the gay bars I've gone to here. It's been worse in straight bars and restaurants. Sometimes they ask me to leave. Sometimes they allow me to stay, but then I just sit there and nobody ever serves me. I was physically removed from the Hotel Toronto last September—nobody gave me any reason. I was just there in the lobby waiting for a friend."

The worst incident he remembers occurred when he left a friend at a street corner and hailed a cab. When he got in, the driver took a good look at him and refused to drive off. John refused to get out. The driver, in desperation, began offering money to passers-by if they would take John off his hands. He was offering two dollars. John says it was the most humiliating experience of his life.

I think John would call that taxi driver a "normal" person, and he does not have a very high opinion of normality. "Normal persons are very frightened persons," he wrote in a short essay. "They are frightened of themselves, and of people who are different, or who have different ideas, so why should we as disabled people try and degrade ourselves even more by becoming normal? Why not change the world...? Normal people need a purpose for living, and we need people to help us. They need people to look up to, we could be them?"

In those thoughts, John is beginning to reconceptualize the very categories into which our thoughts are straitjacketed. Already we have come some way from the times when a Sunday afternoon's entertainment was a trip to Bedlam to watch the mad cavort. And I suppose even that was an improvement over Justinian's Byzantium, where those born deaf were deprived of their civic rights. (Justinian was the emperor, though, who thought homosexuality caused earthquakes. Not a very scientific regime, that one.)

But we are still some way from seeing that to be handicapped means simply to be human in a slightly different way. UNESCO has published a paper which outlines the stages through which public attitudes develop with reference to the handicapped. There is the philanthropic stage, the public welfare stage, the stage of fundamental rights, the stage of the right to equal opportunity, and finally the stage of the right to integration. In that final stage, it is the very notion of norms and normality that is called into question. Suddenly one is faced with questioning whether there is very much difference between an individual with a baby carriage facing a staircase, and someone in a wheelchair facing a telephone booth. In both cases, the problem is not the "handicap." The problem is the telephone, or the stairs. "The difficulties of the disabled often reveal difficulties experienced by all," notes the UNESCO report, and cites the example of an American university where "the abolition of architectural obstacles for six handicapped students made life better for all the students."

Everyone of us begins life as a disabled person. We don't ordinarily think of infancy in quite that way, but it is a period during which we are entirely helpless and dependent. For many of us, old age has some of the same effects. And almost everyone, at some point in his or her life, will be briefly bedridden, or have a limb in a cast, or need psychiatric help. That is certainly not the same as spending your life blind or deaf or in a wheelchair, but it does indicate that we are talking about a spectrum here, not discrete and mutually exclusive groups. We are talking about ways of being fully human.

Sex is a fully human need. Sex that is masturbation, sex that's just a quickie with no names exchanged thank you very much, and sex that takes place as part of some broader relationship. Many disabled have known only masturbation. Not a few find even that impossible.

Scott McArthur works for the MCC as a referral person when that church gets calls from the gay disabled. "Someone called me last week," Scott told me. "He was desperate. He told me he couldn't even masturbate. Where could he go, he asked me, where could he go? I had to tell him there was nowhere he could go."

It's the big taboo. The disabled are supposed to have "more important" things to think about. A report from the Sex Information and Education Council of the United States notes that "in the name of benevolence and protection, many people still take the postion that sex information would 'hurt' the disabled. Why should Pandora's box be opened to a person who is unable to use what is there?... After all, disabled people are fragile and not expected to take care of themselves." As one straight woman said at a Sex and the Disabled conference a few years ago, "I had come out of the rehab centre and after twenty-two months of hospitalization we had never discussed the word sex, except amongst us, as paraplegics and quadriplegics. We were taught repression. We were taught that if we couldn't have something, don't rock the boat."

Blind people don't fuck, as Richard would say. But if the disabled do, or want to try, or — god forbid — if they're disabled enough to need assistance, then most of our institutions would really rather not hear about it. The public — not to mention Mom and Dad — might not be quite ready to hear that part of little Johnny's or Mary's physical therapy includes lessons on how to masturbate.

The topic, however, is finally beginning to surface among professionals at least. I spoke to Michael Barrett of the Sex Information and Education Council of Canada (SIECCAN). He has long been an advocate of sexual rights for the disabled — you're unlikely to find a seminar or conference on the topic which doesn't feature him either as an organizer, chair, or speaker. I ask about sex and the gay disabled, and he admits that he has run into almost nothing on the topic. He is a very gay-supportive individual though, and makes sure the topic is raised whenever he gives a workshop or seminar. He sends me a package of materials to look through, and it is depressing. I think homosexuality was mentioned twice — once in passing, and once thus: "When the patient's sexual activity is homosexual or otherwise variant, physician-patient communication is ordinarily further restricted." Indeed.

I did a bit of checking — again with institutions, because institutions are so frequently "home" for so many disabled. The general reaction might best be described as cautious. And where gay sexuality is concerned, a kind of benign neglect seems to be the rule.

Mrs Ann Pahl is the administrator of Participation House, a permanent residence in Markham for the multi-handicapped. There have been two marriages at Participation House. She says there is no problem with casual sexual encounters, but the individuals would probably have to ask the staff for assistance, at least out of their wheelchairs, and it would be given. There can be no overnight visitors, though—if residents want that sort of thing they're expected to book into a motel. She was quite frank when I asked whether a gay couple could set up house: "I certainly wouldn't be shocked, but to protect myself I'd have to present it to the Board for approval. I'm afraid we couldn't take it lightly; we're dependent on the community and the government for volunteers and funds. We're all very conscious of our community image, and we're closely watched by Queen's Park. People might be critical of anything that isn't pretty mainstream."

I was pleasantly surprised, though, that Pahl was equally frank about how the needs of those who can't masturbate are met. "Staff might help if requested," she said. "Some staff might be comfortable with this, others might not, and only those who can handle it get involved. We don't use mechanical sex aids yet, but that may come."

Ms Margaret Graeb, the administrator at Bellwoods, a residential centre for handicapped adults, is rather more cautious. She is "not sure" whether any of the residents would be completely unable to masturbate, and on the topic of staff participation says, "We're not ready for that yet. I'd be concerned about the kinds of relationships that might develop. I'd be worried about how other residents might feel. I guess I'm not prepared to see that happening yet."

Asked if homosexuality was part of general discussions of sexuality, she said she thought it was "touched on."

The situation isn't much better out there in the great wide world of the "gay ghetto." Everyone I talked to had a horror story to tell. Deaf men will have someone come into their room at the baths, begin to have sex with them, discover they're deaf—and get up and leave. Scott has been told to get out of the Parkside Tavern—or face the cops. Told he would not be allowed in Charly's, a local disco, without an escort. At gay dances he *can* get to, the music is usually so loud that anyone unused to his speech problem will find him impossible to understand. Richard has heard people say, loudly enough for him to hear, "Why does *he* have to come to a place like this?"

As disabled activist Pat Israel said at a workshop on sexuality, "Everyone's handicapped, only some people's wheelchairs are on the inside, not on the outside where you can see them."

Then there's the emphasis on youth and beauty — an obsession that pervades the entire culture, and one the gay world certainly shares. "It's one that *I* share," Scott told me. "I want an attractive man."

None of this is very easy for anybody. Disabled people used to make me unbearably uncomfortable. If I saw a wheelchair coming my way, I would make some excuse to cross the street. I spoke about this to Tom Warner, a gay activist who's been involved with handicapped groups in the Coalition for Life Together. "I have two disabled relatives as well," he told me, "so I should be used to it. But one night I got picked up by a man in a car, and it was only after I got in that I noticed the wheelchair in the back. I went home with him and we went to bed and it didn't really work out. I think he was quite depressed. But his legs were so cold. I flinched every time they touched me and of course he sensed it. But I couldn't help it."

None of this is going to be easy. But change is coming—partly because the disabled themselves are pushing against every constraint society has managed to put in their way, and not a few of the people doing the pushing are our gay brothers and sisters.

"Talk to us," Scott says. "If you see somebody in a wheelchair, talk. If you can't think of anything to say, go over and say 'I've never talked to anybody in a wheelchair before, and I don't know what to say.' Maybe it'll get something going."

"I want to see more cooperation between minorities," says John Kellerman. "We have to understand our commonalities and differences. We have to talk, we have to discuss problems and tactics."

"Solidarity," said André Malraux, "is the most intelligent form of egoism."

They do not want pity. They say listen, and understand. They do not want help. They say cooperate. To be handicapped is one way of being human. They say that they are all that men and women *can* be.

Neighbourly sentiments
Ken Popert

Issue 66, September 1980

Across the houseplants, woven baskets, pinwheels, clusters, stalks, heads and bunches which, overflowing onto the sidewalks, are sold under one roof in one of the Greek fruit-and-vegetable markets lining the Danforth, our eyes engaged.

A clone — well, clonish, at least — off duty and out of uniform; his dark limbs snuggled into white shirt and shorts. Our neighbourhood, somewhat gayified, shelters us in growing numbers.

I smiled, slightly. Enough, I calculated, to convey neighbourly sentiments, short of cruising. I smiled, but he didn't. Quickly he looked away, hesitantly back, quickly away again. He scowled, slightly. Enough to convey... what?

The scene is paradigmatic. I've played it now so many times that I've become as self-conscious as a poll-taker: "Let's see how this one reacts." Strangers dwindle down to specimens. Detachment dulls the disappointment.

Almost. A small anger warms by one degree each time this scene is re-enacted, as once again I consider the motives for his unneighbourly response.

It could be the rejection syndrome, more easily sampled in any bar or bath. Either he's not interested in me or he's afraid that, given a chance, I'll reject him. The injury to my self-esteem aside, it's discouraging to think that he evaluates me not as a neighbour, but solely as a sexual object.

Or maybe he frowns because I have unwittingly shattered a neat dichotomy in his life. Gay is something he *does*, at night, in baths, bars and bedrooms, not something he *is*, on Saturday morning, while shopping for groceries.

Or this: he's minding his own business, swaddled in his closet, securely anonymous, when suddenly I pull the door open, in a fruit-and-vegetable market, in broad daylight. He thinks he will stand revealed, for all to see, if he exchanges glances with this obvious faggot. Worse, is he himself so obvious that he can be picked out of a crowd, just like that?

This last speculation seems to me the most probable explanation for this behaviour, for I can remember a time when I used to play the scowling villain in this drama. Even now, that fear of being recognized in public by an unknown gay man, acknowledging him in return and being betrayed thereby to some third and hostile party, is not as alien as I would like.

It's almost funny now; I once naively believed that, if two gay men, strangers, could recognize each other, then most other people would recognize them too.

Since then, I've learned something about the relativity of observation. Walking down a busy street, I may see one or two transvestites, a few queens, dozens of clones (in and out of uniform) and uncounted pairs of searching eyes. Yet the straights around me will have noticed only the most egregious of the queens.

We can't, of course, spot every gay man. Many, probably the majority, are still deep in the closet and as invisible to us as they are to their families, friends and fellow workers. But those of us who belong to what is styled the gay community can see each other rather clearly.

I'm not sure how we accomplish this work of discernment. It has to do with the eyes, certainly, but not as much with fashion as some may think. Even in the shower rooms of the Central YMCA, the faces can be read. But that's another subject.

No, it was not the subtlety and safety of acknowledging other gay men on the street which convinced me to stop averting my eyes. It was the realization that, in turning away from unknown gay men, I was turning away from myself. I started smiling and nodding and even saying hello as tiny acts of rebellious self-love.

Each time I extend a casual greeting to an unknown gay man and receive the same in return, we both affirm that which joins us together and come away from the exchange newly knowing that it's good to be gay. We have added to the bond of gay community. And, in both of us, fear and shame, the wounds inflicted on us while we were too young to protect ourselves, heal a little more.

Three or four years ago, I got little positive response to my necessarily tentative gestures of solidarity. Now I find that gay men smile more readily. Maybe they've been able to relax a bit and smile more. Or maybe the smilers were always there, and it's me who has relaxed. Both, probably. Whether we've been active in it or not, the gay movement has touched us all.

The scowlers are still around. Like mastodons in blocks of ice, their cold looks and frozen faces are relics, I hope, of a bygone age.

They make me both less angry and more angry than they used to. Less angry, because, self-confident in my gayness now, I can afford some compassion for the anxieties sealed behind those unmoving masks. More angry, because those masks — fashioned at the time, perhaps, in reasoned prudence, but now maintained by raging paranoia — deny our common bond and deprecate our gayness, betraying both themselves and me.

One evening last summer, we were heading toward Church Street along Wellesley. Absorbed, we failed to see two towering and ostentatious queens until they had almost passed.

As they swept by, one of them glanced at us and smiled. But it was a complex smile, more a grin, in which I detected some malice, a grim conviction that the greeting would discomfit us.

We looked back; they were looking back. We smiled and waved. As we turned back to our path, I heard one of the men shriek: "They waved! They waved!"

That made me feel good. To be so flagrant, they must have suffered many indignities. I felt that, in turning and waving, we had given them something too often and too long withheld, something which would make up for the hostility and contempt which they must have long endured, not just from straights and queer-bashers, but also from their fearful brothers.

Confessions
of a lunchroom subversive
Chris Bearchell

Issue 40, February 1978

Riding home on the subway one afternoon last year, Pam, a friend and fellow worker, confided to me that she would never have guessed I was gay "except for the way you talk so openly about yourself at coffee and lunchbreaks." It wasn't intended as a barbed "compliment" the way that remark often is. It was an admission that lesbians weren't really part of her daily experience.

Pam and I and two other straight women, Marilyn and Mary Lynn, shared a table in the lunchroom at work for about a year. We also shared each other's writing, good conversation, humour and the occasional get-together after work. My experiences, opinions and perspective as a lesbian and an activist were a legitimate part of our exchanges. It was, and is, a good feeling.

Shortly after Anita Bryant's anti-gay message hit the media, Marilyn came bristling into the lunchroom and threw a copy of the Toronto *Sun* on the table. "What can we do about this woman?" She wanted to demonstrate. "I'll carry a sign for you." She and Pam and Mary Lynn were caught up by the anti-Bryant slogan: "A day without human rights is like a day without sunshine." Three straight women wanted to do something about gay rights.

Six months later Anita Bryant showed up in Toronto. It was a bitterly cold Sunday night, but we demonstrated in spite of it. Pam and Marilyn were there.

After the demonstration, Marilyn and I sat down at the lunch table to compare our impressions. Marilyn said she had come to the demonstration because she disagreed "with what Anita Bryant is doing. Really for two reasons. Because of Bryant's crusade against homosexuals and because of her beliefs concerning women — especially with regard to abortion."

She was impressed with the feminist emphasis of the demonstration. "It was a positive step to have the two groups (gays and feminists) together."

But demonstrating, she says, is something contrary to her upbringing. She was brought up to believe in established channels. She feels that demonstrating puts a person one step closer to violence, something she has always tried to avoid. But as she talked about her experiences that Sunday night it became clear to me where that feeling had come from. It wasn't that demonstrators were necessarily violent, but that their opponents certainly could be.

Despite the risks, Marilyn now feels it's important to demonstrate. "There are at least two sides to every issue. It is the responsibility of people who hold beliefs to stand up for them." In this case, she felt it was important to show Toronto that not all straights think like Anita Bryant.

Being able to show that depends partly on getting publicity. That was the source of a whole education, too. The media really downplayed and distorted what was happening that weekend. "Television didn't exactly give us equal time with Anita," Marilyn said, "and the newspapers would have had everyone believe there were only gay people in those demonstrations. There were lots of non-gay supporters besides Pam and me."

I asked Marilyn how she felt about being in a minority—meaning a straight person in a predominantly gay demonstration. But she took the question a different way. Her strongest reaction seemed to be to the hecklers at the demo, to those who stood and baited, trying to provoke the demonstrators. "It was my first real, concrete involvement doing anything for the gay movement. I was glad I did it, but I felt frightened by the reaction of some of the observers. I guess now I've felt the intimidation that gay people must face all the time." She felt not so much a minority among gay people, but, for a while, some of what it's like to be a part of the gay minority.

Like many of us that night, she was impressed that the demonstration was well marshalled. The provocateurs were probably disappointed. As she put it, "The demonstrators showed remarkable self-restraint."

Did she think that any of what the marchers said was offensive? "Not really. The chants were a bit boring — repetitive, and too much like high school cheerleading. Actually, I made one up myself: one, two, three, four, Renaissance is wrong once more; five, six, seven, eight, Renaissance discriminates. But nobody wanted to chant it."

Going home after the demonstration, thirty of us stragglers eventually took over a bus and then a subway car. We sang "offensive" songs, led by rowdy East York dykes from the Gay Offensive Collective, all the way from Sheppard Avenue to Bloor Street. Marilyn and Pam were among a group that walked to the subway — one and a quarter miles through the wilds of North York. Marilyn said the spirit was high and she felt a lot safer than she would have had they been alone. But she was still disturbed by the reactions of passers-by who knew or assumed they had been among the demonstrators.

"When people in our group were chanting on the subway, there was one creep that Pam pointed out to me who looked like he could have gotten violent. He was muttering under his breath about us being sick, that kind of shit. Most people just looked like they didn't believe it was all happening. When we got to Yonge and Bloor there were two punks I recognized from outside the church, hanging around the station. They had been really belligerent before and still seemed to be looking for trouble. I don't know, maybe I was just being super-sensitive; I'm not used to that kind of hostility."

When I asked Marilyn if she would do it again she said, "Yes, definitely," without hesitation.

Lesbians are not alien to these two women any longer. Our community and our rights are a part of their very real concerns now. And all because of what was once a very strange phenomenon on the other side of the lunch table.

Not the same old place: openly gay in the post office
Walter Bruno

Issue 10, November 1973

In the Vancouver post office, where straight workers have laboured for years beside "oddballs" (*ie*, gays, longhairs and Orientals), eyebrows were never more incredulously raised — and deftly plucked — than during last year's Christmas rush, when Stella was hired on *in full drag*.

Yet after a few days of thrill and uncertainty (Stella was *very* convincing) the men stopped taking bets on her gender, the women stopped circulating breathless tales of their Trips to the Bathroom, and Stella continued working in general tranquillity — having broadcast a threat to *scream* in the event of trouble.

Talk then turned to the alleged presence in our midst of a *second one*, who was *so* convincing....

*

"I see you're not married," intoned the interviewer, peering from behind his papers. "Why aren't you married?" He went on to demand to know when I was going to get married, was I living with a woman, and if not, "why not?"

Why indeed, I retorted. Why was he asking me personal questions which had nothing to do with my application for a promotion!

Both his questions and mine were largely rhetorical. I knew that he was trying to establish the fact that I was a self-avowed homosexual and a gay liberationist. That I had even "stirred up trouble" by making the lack of gay civil rights an issue in the job. And this was the stick he chose to hit me with. To my protests he simply said "We *have* to ask."

When I started working at the Vancouver Post Office three years ago, the last thing in my mind was raising gay liberation issues on the job. To be sure, I was a socialist and union militant, but for all my years of political militancy there were corresponding years of acting the role of "straight gay." Before I had come out, and before the re-emergence of gay liberation, you had to be a het to be a working class hero. Partly because the working class is soaked in heterosexual values, and partly because labour leaders from the Communist Party had peddled the Stalinist notion in the labour movement that "homosexuality is a manifestation of bourgeois decadence," the traditional tableau pictures socialism being born into this world on the brawny shoulders of the Family Man. Crap.

Crap, from beginning to end. For in the next few years I would discover that the best boss-fighters in the place, the ones least inclined to bow down to the authoritarian structures of capitalism, be bought off and intimidated were the young men and women who were proud to sleep in seven different beds a week, and not necessarily with members of the opposite sex.

I found that out slowly; it's never easy to come out. So for the first year I was content to take note of the sheer numbers of gay fellow-workers. And there were dozens in the place, playing every role—from House Faggot to Solid Citizen and from Stompin' Dyke to Lovely Lady. Yet we all got to know each other eventually. Sometimes it was a real trip-and-a-half, sitting together fifteen to a table in the cafeteria, cruising the new employees and screaming up a storm, to the general discomfort of other tables. I suppose that was one small stage on the road to liberation — just being together and "doing our thing" openly.

Most of my fellow gays accepted me as a gay liberationist, as long as it didn't become an issue in the shop. The attitude was, "Well, I suppose *someone* has to fight for our rights." Gradually I became notorious. I was less and less inclined to remain in the closet, and finally went out of my way to announce as subtly as possible to my fellow workers that I wasn't interested in the postcards of nude women they eyed and circulated endlessly.

Which produced the inevitable ostracism and enmity.

*

Old Jim was a case in point. A career soldier cast in true legionnaire mold, he was the worst gay-baiter in the place. He never missed an opportunity to tell you how much he hated homosexuals. So when he heard about my homosexuality (he had previously befriended me), he just walked up to me and said "Queer," and turned away. "Military mind," I thought, not much caring for his company anyway. Ditto for some of the workers, who snickered and looked on askance when I passed.

Within a few months, tension began to rise in the shop. The union had been trying to negotiate a contract for several months, without results. The workers wondered aloud what their leaders were doing for them. A right-wing movement arose, its object being the decertification of the union and its replacement by a company union. The local union leadership reacted in a hamhanded way, trying to stifle even legitimate opposition.

I decided to enter union politics, and with two other militants put out a call for solidarity and militancy in the face of the employer's intransigence. And there began a period in which my gayness became as much a political issue as the several points in the union programme we put forward.

Amongst the workers who suddenly fell into step with me was old Jim. Seems he hated the boss as much as he claimed to hate homosexuals, and he was a union militant to the marrow of his bones. He started talking to me as if our conversation had never been interrupted.

As tensions mounted and a strike appeared more and more likely, the boss and his friends in the right wing mounted a whispering campaign against me. Not only was I a commie, they said, but a faggot too. It was only mildly successful. One half of my fellow gays stuck with me throughout, the others heading for cover when I approached.

But the union local itself was now occupied to some extent with the question of homosexuality. This was a local with a strong tradition of fighting for minority rights: a very large proportion of its members are Asians or other third-world peoples. Many a supervisor had had his career cut short by an anti-Chinese slur uttered in public. The question in my mind: could the union understand gay rights as another minority struggle?

In a general meeting voting on union bylaws I proposed a clause barring discrimination in the union on the basis of "lifestyle." It was accepted unanimously, only to be suddenly overturned by an alerted right wing at a subsequent meeting which I couldn't attend. Rushed through with a scarcely-noticed vote, this reversal was motivated by the right-wingers as being necessary to avoid defending the rights of homosexuals! By this time rumours were circulating in the upper levels of the union brass alleging that I was the head of a "gay caucus" of two hundred people.

It was in this hilarious and hysterical setting that the most dramatic events were beginning to unfold. They involved Steve, one of the newer workers, and a gay's gay. He liked to talk about all the normal things: his lover, his sex life, his furniture, his plans for the future, the uptightness of heterosexuals.... He yakked away endlessly with the young woman working beside him, and when the male hets in the vicinity told him to shut up, he told them to get fucked. That's what they really needed, he said, and he was so right. If they could talk about their lives, he could talk about his, he said. I said Amen. And the row was on.

*

The shop was twitching with rumours and anxious glances. And then one of the shop stewards approached me and said, "Emergency shop stewards' meeting in the cafeteria at lunch." I was the last one to arrive. Jim was pounding his fist on the table: "I didn't fight a war for democracy for nothing! Either it's democracy for all or it's democracy for none." Another shop steward was explaining how Steve had been led by one of the right-wingers into the boss's office; how he'd been called on the carpet, and warned he'd be fired if he didn't stop "annoying the other workers." Yet another shop steward pulled me aside and whispered earnestly, "They've gone after Steve, but we know they're really aiming at you."

"An injury to one is an injury to all — that's our union motto," piped up another.

"My god," was all I could think, "it's happening. It's really happening."

*

Well, gay rights consciousness never again came up to the dizzying levels reached on that heady afternoon in the Post Office cafeteria. In the absence of legislated gay rights, such as the clause we sought for the local bylaws, and in the absence of sustained movement action, understanding tends to advance and recede, often rapidly.

But the Post Office is not the same old place anymore, new ideas having circulated through the dusty halls. Union officials urged me to file grievances against the zealous little interviewer's enquiry into my sexual status. That's a new attitude, albeit one whose impact will be felt only when the union bargains successfully for inclusion of "sexual orientation" in the clause prohibiting employer discrimination.

Not the same old place, though. Steve still fights with some of the hets, but the boss leaves him alone. Jim tells anyone who raises the subject that "homosexuals are as good as anybody else," and deserve equal rights.

In a short period of militancy, the labour movement embraced and understood the rights of gay workers. Surely that is the most hopeful sign for the entire gay liberation movement.

And for me, a closet-leftist who, until I quit the job recently, was wearing my commie-faggot label with some measure of pride.

A vulnerable man
Michael Riordon

Issue 47, October 1978

Stephen Whelan isn't his name. I'm not about to give anything away to his enemies, and when he's ready people will know who he is.

Stephen, forty-two, teaches history in a suburban high school. He's puzzled, sometimes alarmed, by the illiteracy in his students. And their cruelty. "They're more cruel than we ever were. We made fun of our teachers, you know, we had names for some of them, but nothing compared to what these kids do." Do they have less respect for authority? Isn't that a good thing? Does your perception change, perhaps, on the receiving end of cruelty? "Maybe, I don't know."

One afternoon Stephen found indelibly written into one of the blackboard erasers in his home room: GAY. "I was surprised because I've been very, very careful. I've lived for years in apprehension of being found out. I was aware of my sexuality as early as my own high school years, but my reaction to it was to deny it, to drown myself in work and to withdraw from people. The principal where I went to school had an affair with one of the students. The boy's parents found out. There was a big scandal and the principal had to leave. You remember things like that."

A few weeks later Stephen returned a forgotten textbook to a student on the school bus. As he turned to get off, someone said: "There goes the fruit!" Another day he found GAY carefully large-lettered in ink on his desk, with an arrow pointing to his chair. By now he had to be getting nervous. Only one boy in his class was accustomed to using an ink pen. Stephen watched him, but couldn't detect any change in his attitude or behaviour in class. If he was the poison pen, he was a closet one.

Stephen Whelan is a mild man. His voice is mild, his manner discreet, his clothes nearly invisible. His strongest opinions are usually put as questions. On bus duty in midwinter this man was supervising the loading of school buses to take the students home. Three boys were throwing chunks of ice at the bus windows. Stephen interfered. One of the boys, about seventeen and at least a head taller than Stephen, told him to go screw himself, or words to that effect. Stephen replied that if he was abusive he wouldn't be allowed on the bus, he'd have to wait an hour for another. The boy challenged: "Try and stop me!" Stephen stood in front of the door and asked the driver to close it. The student threatened to fight his way through Stephen and the door. Stephen spun him around and pinned his arms by his sides. The student began to scream: "You bloody faggot! He's attacking me!" Mortified, in the face of thirty very curious spectators Stephen let go. The boy ran into the school, to the principal's office, where he continued to accuse "that faggot" of "molesting" him.

After a hearing with Stephen, the boy and his mother, the principal suspended the boy for three days. A month later he was expelled for stealing a school master-key, making copies and distributing them to other students. Stephen, meanwhile, hung in a state of quiet terror that the world would fall about his ears. "The principal is a decent guy. He put his hand on my shoulder once or twice, I guess to reassure me. He's married, by the way, with a couple of kids." Written on the wall in the boys' washroom one day: MACKAY (the principal) IS GAY.

"By the end of the school year I felt pretty awful. I didn't think I'd be able to go back in September and face them. But if you transfer out of your particular board of education, you know, you lose all your seniority. I was planning a year-end trip, like I do every year, taking about twenty kids history-hunting in another province. I thought for sure everyone who'd registered for it, especially the boys, would drop out. But no one did. I feel a little stronger now. I'm going back. I don't know what will happen. What would you suggest I do?"

What can you say to another person's life? Join with other people, gather strength. We're always easier to pick off one by one. Fight for sexual orientation in human rights codes. But don't trust your legislators farther than you might want to throw them. Fight for job protection in your teachers' association contract negotiations. Fight for decent sex education: at Stephen's school, after a brief ramble through "Lifestyles" which didn't include ours, they're reverting gradually to "Humanities" which is turning out to mean comparative religion! You can guess which one comes out on top in the "comparison." Fight. That's all you can do.

It comes down to this, doesn't it: you, standing alone and vulnerable in front of twenty-five to forty energetic young people groping their way, if you'll pardon the expression, through puberty into the fearful and messy responsibilities of "adulthood" with almost no sensible help. You can be sure no one in their world is teaching them to value the splendid range of human potential, least of all the sexual and sensual riches to be found in it. Everyone they hear or see preaches conformity and blindness, orders or beguiles them to reject contemptuously and violently anything in themselves or in others that threatens "our way of life," an orderly backward march of obedient worker-consumer ants. The people who command the march have as much to lose as we have to gain from our freedom. They will fight as they have always fought, dirty. That's what you're up against, Stephen.

Fight for your life.

Chapter three
The making of the image
of the modern homosexual

" 'All prisoners with the pink triangles will remain standing at attention!' We stood on the desolate, broad square, and from somewhere a warm summer breeze carried the sweet fragrance of resin and wood from the regions of freedom; but we couldn't taste it, because our throats were hot and dry from fear."

*

"For millions of readers, the ultimate dreadfulness of *1984* has been brought home as the system where love was to be a crime, where lovers could not even be seen to touch, where the smallest sign of affection was a political gesture. And how many of them consider that all this was so for homosexual lovers in the *real* world of 1949, of 1959, of 1969, of 1979?"

*

"We have to stop mimicking their language, stop living on borrowed words, and refuse to become homosexual experts on homosexuality. We have to recognize that, in the war of words, there are no experts, only fighters. We, as women and gay people, have to take over the house of language, sit down in the best chairs, and decide whether we want to stay—or move out."

*

Homosexuals and the Third Reich
James Steakley

Issue 11, January/February 1974

In recent years the pink triangle has been widely adopted by individuals and gay organizations around the world as a symbol of gay visibility and gay resistance. Used by the Nazis to identify homosexual prisoners in German concentration camps, it is a powerful reminder of a grim episode in the history of gay oppression. The first account in English of the situation of homosexuals in Nazi Germany appeared originally in The Body Politic *as part of a series by James Steakley on the development of an early German homosexual emancipation movement. The discovery of the existence — and abrupt disappearance—of this first wave of homosexual organizing has had a lasting impact on the contemporary movement's sense of its place in history. Perhaps no other* TBP *article has so jolted the imagination and political consciousness of gay activists and other readers. It is reprinted in full below.*

"After roll call on the evening of June 20, 1942, an order was suddenly given: 'All prisoners with the pink triangles will remain standing at attention!' We stood on the desolate, broad square, and from somewhere a warm summer breeze carried the sweet fragrance of resin and wood from the regions of freedom; but we couldn't taste it, because our throats were hot and dry from fear. Then the guardhouse door of the command tower opened, and an SS officer and some of his lackeys strode toward us. Our detail commander barked: 'Three hundred criminal deviants, present as ordered!' We were registered, and then it was revealed to us that in accordance with an order from the Reichsführung SS, our category was to be isolated in an intensified-penalty company, and we would be transferred as a unit to the Klinker Brickworks the next morning. The Klinker factory! We shuddered, for the human death mill was more than feared."

Appallingly little information is available on the situation of homosexuals in Nazi Germany. Many historians have hinted darkly at the "unspeakable practices" of a Nazi elite supposedly overrun with "sexual perverts," but this charge is both unsubstantiated and insidious. Upon closer examination, it turns out to be no more than the standard use of anti-gay prejudice to defame any given individual or group — a practice, incidentally, of which the Nazis were the supreme masters. The Nazis were guilty of very real offences, but their unspeakable practices were crimes against mankind.

That homosexuals were major victims of these crimes is mentioned in only a few of the standard histories of the period. And those historians who do mention the facts seem reluctant to dwell on the subject and turn quickly to the fate of other minorities in Nazi Germany. Yet tens, perhaps hundreds of thousands of homosexuals were interned in Nazi concentration camps. They were consigned to the lowest position in the camp hierarchy, and subjected to abuse by both guards and fellow prisoners; most of them perished.

Obviously, gay people are going to have to write their own history. And there is enough authentic documentation on the Nazi period to undertake a first step in this direction. The words at the beginning of this article were written by one concentration camp survivor, L D Claassen von Neudegg, who published some of his recollections in a German homophile magazine in the Fifties. Here are a few more excerpts from his account of the treatment of homosexuals in the concentration camp at Sachsenhausen:

"Forced to drag along twenty corpses, the rest of us encrusted with blood, we entered the Klinker works.

"We had been here for almost two months, but it seemed like endless years to us. When we were 'transferred' here, we had numbered around three hundred men. Whips were used more frequently each morning, when we were forced down into the clay pits under the wailing of the camp sirens. 'Only fifty are still alive,' whispered the man next to me. 'Stay in the middle—then you won't get hit so much.'

....

"(The escapees) had been brought back. 'Homo' was scrawled scornfuly across their clothing for their last walk through the camp. To increase their thirst, they were forced to eat oversalted food, and then they were placed on the block and whipped. Afterwards, drums were hung around their necks, which they had to beat while shouting, 'Hurrah, we're back!' The three men were hanged.

....

"Summer, 1944. One morning there was an eruption of restlessness among the patients of the hospital barracks where I worked. Fear and uncertainty had arisen from rumours about new measures on the part of the SS hospital administration. At the administration's order, the courier of the political division had requisitioned certain medical records, and now he arrived at the camp for delivery. Fever charts shot up; the sick were seized with a gnawing fear. After a few days, the awful mystery of the records was solved. Experiments had been ordered involving living subjects and phosphorus: methods of treating phosphorus burns were to be developed and tested. I must be silent about the effects of this series of experiments, which proceeded with unspeakable pain, fear, blood and tears: for it is impossible to put the misery into words."

Dr Neudegg's recollections are confirmed in many details by the memoirs of Rudolf Höss, adjutant and commander of the concentration camps at Sachsenhausen and, later, Auschwitz. Neudegg's account is something of a rarity: the few homosexuals who managed to survive internment have tended to hide the fact, largely because homosexuality continued to be a crime in postwar West Germany. This is also the reason why homosexuals have been denied any compensation by the otherwise munificent West German government.

The number of homosexuals who died in Nazi concentration camps is unknown and likely to remain so. Although statistics are available on the number of men brought to trial on charges of "lewd and unnatural behaviour," many more were sent to camps without the benefit of a trial. Moreover, many homosexuals were summarily executed by firing squads; this was particularly the case with gays in the military — which encompassed nearly every able-bodied man during the final years of the war. Finally, many concentration camps systematically destroyed all their records when it became apparent that German defeat was imminent.

*

The beginning of the Nazi terror against homosexuals was marked by the murder of Ernst Röhm on June 30, 1934: "the Night of the Long Knives." Röhm was the man who, in 1919, first made Hitler aware of his own political potential, and the two were close friends for fifteen years. During that time, Röhm rose to SA Chief of Staff, transforming the Brownshirt militia from a handful of hardened goons and embittered ex-soldiers into an effective fighting force five hundred thousand strong—the instrument of Nazi terror. Hitler needed Röhm's military skill and could rely on his personal loyalty, but he was ultimately a pragmatist. As part of a compromise with the Reichswehr (regular army) leadership, whose support he needed to become Führer, Hitler allowed Göring and Himmler to murder Röhm along with dozens of Röhm's loyal officers.

For public relations purposes, and especially to quell the outrage felt throughout the ranks of the SA, Hitler justified his blatant power play by pointing to Röhm's homosexuality. Hitler, of course, had known of Röhm's homosexuality since 1919, and it became public knowledge in 1925, when Röhm appeared in court to charge a hustler with theft. All this while the Nazi Party had a virulently anti-gay policy, and many Nazis protested that Röhm was discrediting the entire Party and should be purged. Hitler, however, was quite willing to cover up for him for years—until he stood in the way of larger plans.

*

The Nazi Party came to power in 1933, and a year later Röhm was dead. While Röhm and his men were being rounded up for the massacre (offered a gun and the opportunity to shoot himself, Röhm retorted angrily: "Let Hitler do his own dirty work"), the new Chief of Staff received his first order from the Führer: "I expect all SA leaders to help preserve and strengthen the SA in its capacity as a pure and cleanly institution. In particular, I should like every mother to be able to allow her son to join the SA, Party, and Hitler Youth without fear that he may become morally corrupted in their ranks. I therefore request all SA commanders to take the utmost pains to ensure that offences under Paragraph 175 are met by immediate expulsion of the culprit from the SA and the Party."

Hitler had good reason to be concerned about the reputation of Nazi organizations, most of which were based on strict segregation of the sexes. Hitler Youth, for example, was disparagingly referred to as Homo Youth throughout the Third Reich, a characterization which the Nazi leadership vainly struggled to eliminate. Indeed, most of the handful of publications on homosexuality which appeared during the Fascist regime were devoted to new and rather bizarre methods of "detection" and "prevention."

Rudolf Diels, the founder of the Gestapo, recorded some of Hitler's personal thoughts on the subject: "He lectured me on the role of homosexuality in history and politics. It had destroyed ancient Greece, he said. Once rife, it extended its contagious effects like an ineluctable law of nature to the best and most manly of characters, eliminating from the reproductive process precisely those men on whose offspring a nation depended. The immediate result of the vice was, however, that unnatural passion swiftly became dominant in public affairs if it were allowed to spread unchecked."

*

The tone had been set by the Röhm putsch, and on its first anniversary—June 28, 1935—the campaign against homosexuality was escalated by the introduction of the "Law for the Protection of German Blood and German Honour." This law, the first revision of Paragraph 175 in its sixty-five-year history, brought a sweeping extension of legal criteria for "lewd and unnatural behaviour." Until 1935, the only punishable offence had been anal intercourse; under the new Paragraph 175a, ten possible "acts" were punishable, including a kiss, an embrace, even homosexual fantasies! One man, for instance, was successfully prosecuted on the grounds that he had observed a couple making love in a park and watched only the man.

Under the Nazi legal system, criminal acts were less important in determining guilt than criminal intent. The "phenomenological" theory of justice claimed to evaluate a person's character rather than his deeds. The "healthy sensibility of the people" (*gesundes Volksempfinden*) was elevated to the highest normative legal concept, and the Nazis were thus in a position to prosecute an individual solely on the grounds of his sexual orientation. (After World War II, incidentally, this law was immediately struck from the books in East Germany as a product of Fascist thinking, while it remained on the books in West Germany.)

Once Paragraph 175a was in effect, the annual number of convictions on charges of homosexuality leaped to about ten times the number in the pre-Nazi period. The law was so loosely formulated that it could be—and was—applied against heterosexuals whom the Nazis wanted to eliminate. The most notorious example of an individual convicted on trumped-up charges was General Werner von Fritsch, Army Chief of Staff; and the law was also used repeatedly against members of the Catholic clergy. But the law was undoubtedly used primarily against gay people, and the court system was aided in the witchhunt by the entire German populace, which was encouraged to scrutinize the behaviour of neighbours and to denounce suspects to the Gestapo. The number of men convicted of homosexuality during the Nazi period totalled around fifty thousand:

1933: 853	1939: 7,614
1934: 948	1940: 3,773
1935: 2,106	1941: 3,735
1936: 5,320	1942: 3,963
1937: 8,271	1943: 966 (first quarter)
1938: 8,562	1944-45: ?

The Gestapo was the agent of the next escalation of the campaign against homosexuality. Ex-chicken farmer Heinrich Himmler, Reichsführer SS and head of the Gestapo, richly deserves a reputation as the most fanatically homophobic member of the Nazi leadership. In 1936, he gave a speech on the subject of homosexuality and described the murder of Ernst Röhm (which he had engineered) in these terms: "Two years ago... when it became necessary, we did not scruple to strike this plague with death, even within our own ranks." Himmler closed with these words: "Just as we today have gone back to the ancient Germanic view on the question of marriage mixing different races, so too in our judgment of homosexuality—a symptom of degeneracy which could destroy our race—we must return to the guiding Nordic principle: extermination of degenerates."

*

A few months earlier, Himmler had prepared for action by reorganizing the entire state police into three divisions. The political executive, Division II, was directly responsible for the control of "illegal parties and organizations, leagues and economic groups, reactionaries and the Church, freemasonry, and homosexuality."

Himmler personally favoured the immediate "extermination of degenerates," but he was empowered to order the summary execution only of homosexuals discovered within his own bureaucratic domain. Civilian offenders were merely required to serve out their prison sentences (although second offenders were subject to castration).

In 1936, Himmler found a way around this obstacle. Following release from prison, all "enemies of the state"—including homosexuals—were to be taken into protective custody and detained indefinitely. "Protective custody" (*Schutzhaft*) was an euphemism for concentration camp internment. Himmler gave special orders that homosexuals be placed in Level Three camps—the human death mills described by Neudegg. These camps were reserved for Jews and homosexuals.

The offical SS newspaper, *Das Schwarze Korps*, announced in 1937 that there were two million German homosexuals and called for their death. The extent to which Himmler succeeded in this undertaking is unknown, but the number of homosexuals sent to camps was far in excess of the fifty thousand who served jail sentences. The Gestapo dispatched thousands to camps without a trial. Moreover, "protective custody" was enforced retroactively, so that any gay who had ever come to the attention of the police prior to the Third Reich was subject to immediate arrest. (The Berlin police alone had an index of more than twenty thousand homosexuals prior to the Nazi takeover.) And starting in 1939, gays from Nazi-occupied countries were also interned in German camps.

The chances for survival in a Level Three camp were low indeed. Homosexuals were distinguished from other prisoners by a pink triangle, worn on the left side of the jacket and on the right pant leg. There was no possibility of "passing" for straight, and the presence of "marked men" in the all-male camp population evoked the same reaction as in contemporary prisons: gays were brutally assaulted and sexually abused.

*

"During the first weeks of my imprisonment," wrote one survivor, "I often thought I was the only available target on whom everyone was free to vent his aggressions. Things improved when I was assigned to a labour detail that worked outside the camp at Metz, because everything took place in public view. I was made clerk of the labour detail, which meant that I worked all day and then looked after the records at the guardhouse between midnight and 2 am. Because of this 'overtime' I was allowed seconds at lunch—if any food was left over. This is the fact to which I probably owe my survival.... I saw quite a number of pink triangles. I don't know how they were eventually killed.... One day they were simply gone."

Concentration camp internment served a twofold purpose: the labour power of prisoners boosted the national economy significantly, and undesirables could be efficiently liquidated by the simple expedient of reducing their food rations to a level slightly below subsistence. One survivor tells of witnessing "Project Pink" in his camp: "The homosexuals were grouped into liquidation commandos and placed under triple camp discipline. That meant less food, more work, stricter supervision. If a prisoner with a pink triangle became sick, it spelled his doom. Admission to the clinic was forbidden."

This was the practice in the concentration camps at Sachsenhausen, Natzweiler, Fuhlsbüttel, Neusustrum, Sonnenburg, Dachau, Lichtenberg, Mauthausen, Ravensbrück, Neuengamme, Grossrosen, Buchenwald, Vught, Flossenbürg, Stutthof, Auschwitz and Struthof; as well, lesbians wore pink triangles in the concentration camps at Bützow and Ravensbrück. In the final months of the war, the men with pink triangles received brief military training. They were to be sent out as cannon fodder in the last-ditch defence of the fatherland.

But the death of other pink triangles came much more swiftly. A survivor gives this account: "He was a young and healthy man. The first evening roll call after he was added to our penal company was his last. When he arrived, he was seized and ridiculed, then beaten and kicked, and finally spat upon. He suffered alone and in silence. Then they put him under a cold shower. It was a frosty winter evening, and he stood outside the barracks all through that long, bitterly cold night. When morning came, his breathing had become an audible rattle. Bronchial pneumonia was later given as the cause of his death. But before things had come to that, he was again beaten and kicked. Then he was tied to a post and placed under an arc lamp until he began to sweat, again put under a cold shower, and so on. He died toward evening."

Another survivor: "One should not forget that these men were honourable citizens, very often highly intelligent, and some had once held high positions in civil and social life. During his seven-year imprisonment, this writer became acquainted with a Prussian prince, famous athletes, professors, teachers, engineers, artisans, trade workers and, of course, hustlers. Not all of them were what one might term 'respectable' people, to be sure, but the majority of them were helpless and completely lost in the world of the concentration camps. They lived in total isolation in whatever little bit of freedom they could find. I witnessed the tragedy of a highly cultured attaché of a foreign embassy, who simply couldn't grasp the reality of the tragedies taking place all around him. Finally, in a state of deep desperation and hopelessness, he simply fell over dead for no apparent reason. I saw a rather effeminate young man who was repeatedly forced to dance in front of SS men, who would then put him on the rack — chained hand and foot to a crossbeam in the guardhouse barracks—and beat him in the most awful way. Even today I find it impossible to think back on all my comrades, all the barbarities, all the tortures, without falling into the deepest depression. I hope you will understand."

The ruthlessness of the Nazis culminated in actions so perversely vindictive as to be almost incomprehensible. Six youths arrested for stealing coal at a railroad station were taken into protective custody and duly placed in a concentration camp. Shocked that such innocent boys were forced to sleep in a barracks also occupied by pink triangles, the SS guards chose what to them must have seemed the lesser of two evils: they took the youths aside and gave them fatal injections of morphine. Morality was saved.

The self-righteousness that prompted this type of action cuts through the entire ideology glorifying racial purity and extermination of degenerates to reveal stark fear of homosexuality. Something of this fear is echoed in the statement by Hitler cited above, which is quite different in tone from the propagandistic cant of Himmler's exhortations. Himmler saw homosexuals as congenital cowards and weaklings. Probably as a result of his friendship with Röhm, Hitler could at least imagine "the best and most manly of characters" being homosexual.

Hitler ordered all the gay bars in Berlin closed as soon as he came to power. But when the Olympics were held in that city in 1936, he temporarily rescinded the order and allowed several bars to reopen: foreign guests were not to receive the impression that Berlin was a "sad city."

Despite, and perhaps because of, their relentless emphasis upon strength, purity, cleanliness and masculinity, the all-male Nazi groups surely contained a strong element of deeply repressed homoeroticism. The degree of repression was evidenced by the Nazi reaction to those who were openly gay. In the Bible, the scapegoat was the sacrificial animal on whose head the inchoate guilt of the entire community was placed. Homosexuals served precisely this function in the Third Reich.

The ideological rationale for the mass murder of homosexuals during the Third Reich was quite another matter. According to the doctrine of Social Darwinism, only the fittest are meant to survive, and the law of the jungle is the final arbiter of human history. If the Germans were destined to become the master race by virtue of their inherent biological superiority, the breeding stock could only be improved by the removal of degenerates. Retarded, deformed and homosexual individuals could be eliminated with the dispassionate conscientiousness of a gardener pulling weeds. (Indeed, it is the very vehemence and passion with which homosexuals were persecuted that compels us to look beyond the pseudo-scientific rationale for a deeper, psychological dynamic.)

*

The institutionalized homophobia of the Third Reich must also be seen in terms of the sexual revolution that had taken place in Germany during the preceeding decades. The German gay movement had existed for thirty-six years before it (and all other progressive forces) was smashed. The Nazis carried out a "conservative revolution" which restored law and order together with nineteenth-century sexism. A system of ranking women according to the number of their offspring was devised by Minister of the Interior Wilhelm Frick, who demanded that homosexuals "be hunted down mercilessly, for their vice can only lead to the demise of the German people."

Ironically, the biologistic arguments against gay people could be supported by the theories advanced by the early gay movement itself. Magnus Hirschfeld and the members of the Scientific-Humanitarian Committee had made "the Third Sex" a household term in Germany; but the rigidly heterosexual society of the Third Reich had no patience with "intersexual variants" and turned a deaf ear to pleas for tolerance. The prominent Nazi jurist Dr Rudolf Klare wrote: "Since the Masonic notion of humanitarianism arose from the ecclesiastical/Christian feeling of charity, it is sharply opposed to our National Socialist worldview and is eliminated *a priori* as a justification for not penalizing homosexuality."

Towards 1984
Andrew Hodges

Issue 59, December 1979/January 1980

As the real 1984 approaches and becomes just another calendar year, one thing is certain: there will be no lack of voices claiming to draw political lessons from George Orwell's book. Indeed, the election posters for Mrs Thatcher's Conservative Party have already suggested that we should believe Labour policy to be leading Britain into an Orwellian nightmare. *1984* has sold millions of copies; it is a standard text for school examinations. But what does it hold for us?

A number of Orwell's suggestions have become reality; a number have not. That is not the point. The real value of the work is as a modern *Gulliver's*

Travels, as serious political satire, and in particular as a thesis on the politics of language. It was Orwell's idea that language was not simply a means of communicating thought, in the way that an open road affords space for every kind of traffic. Rather, language could be more like a railway system, with a laid-down schedule which could convey only ideas of a defined shape and size, fitted into the compartments which the managers provided. Only these right ideas could ever be used.

But Orwell's target was narrow and distinct: not the language of everyday conversation, but the official languages of his own class and time, the British educated middle class of the 1930s and 1940s. Wartime censorship, Communist Party theory, military euphemism, *Times* leaders and newsreel journalism —every case involved its own *trahison des clercs* in which state violence of revolting enormity could be justified or concealed by the manipulation of language. It was his thesis that language was not merely symptomatic of engineered thought; rather, that language *determined* what thoughts it was possible to have. "How *could* they believe it?", "How *could* they accept it?" Orwell asked of his contemporaries, and his answer was that once they had accepted a political language their thoughts could not be other than would fit inside its concepts.

It was a small step for him to suggest in *1984* that the State might consciously impose its official language upon its servants with that very objective in mind. This was a major theme of the book, summed up in its definition of "Newspeak," the officialese of the Anglo-American superstate. It was its purpose that:

"...the expression of unorthodox opinions, above a very low level, was well-nigh impossible. It was of course possible to utter heresies of a very crude kind, a species of blasphemy. It would have been possible, for example, to say 'Big Brother is ungood.' But this statement, which to an orthodox ear merely conveyed a self-evident absurdity, could not have been sustained by reasoned argument, because the necessary words were not available...."

The modern Newspeak of "extremist," "moderate," "security," has continued to keep Orwell's political critique as alive as ever. But our reaction to Orwell's ideas must necessarily be more critical. In *1984*, it was possible to escape from the official thought by means of ordinary language, the old English language, associated with good old ordinary decent things and feelings. Orwell seems to have thought the common language of his day to be a perfectly adequate vehicle for thought. But was it? Was it only the official, or state-imposed, language that constrained what it was possible to think? Clearly we can see that it was not: in Orwell's own description of Newspeak, he wrote:

"In somewhat the same way, the Party member knew what constituted right conduct, and in exceedingly vague, generalized terms he knew what kinds of departure from it were possible. His sexual life, for example, was entirely regulated by the two Newspeak words 'sexcrime' (sexual immorality) and 'goodsex' (chastity). Sexcrime covered all sexual misdeeds whatever. It covered fornication, adultery, homosexuality, and other perversions, and, in addition, normal intercourse practised for its own sake...."

Millions of readers must have swallowed unquestioningly Orwell's defini-tion of homosexuality as a "perversion," together with the connotations of "immorality" and "normal"—just as they would have gone along with the use of "he" in that paragraph to imply (as a "rule of grammar") a person of either sex. Why not? These were the available concepts, the "proper words" that English had to offer. Whether Orwell intended this classification con-sciously or not is beside the point; in either case this was simply the ordinary written English of 1949, in which sexual expression had to be packaged and valued by a tiny range of nasty words.

To be more precise, a writer who was explicitly sensitive to value-judgment might, by a sufficiently laborious discussion, avoid the unconscious com-munication of received ideas. Thus in 1948 the authors of Kinsey's *Sexual Be-havior in the Human Male* had been able to used the word "homosexual" in a very precise sense, carefully detached from the connotations of "abnormal." It was no easy task, as they themselves explained, and one which met with pro-found resistance from the "scientific" world as well as from popular opinion. But for those without access to the language of academic authority, words im-posed the bounds of possible thought, in which "queer is good" was almost as self-evident an absurdity as "Big Brother is ungood."

Another observation to be made on reading *1984* is that all those features of the State which Orwell presented in imagination as the most deeply appalling were none other than those which, in 1949, were being experienced in reality by homosexual people in Anglo-America. Not only the commonplaces of censorship, blacklisting, guilt by association; not only imprisonment on pol-ice say-so; but compulsory drug treatments, castrations, electric shocks, even brain surgery; the implication and betrayal of friends or lovers; the re-quired confessions of thoughtcrime in the dock. Worst of all, according to Orwell's book, defiance was robbed of all meaning when history would never know or care, when the past would not even be known to exist.

But Orwell would never have perceived the connection. And we too are so well trained to think of homosexual oppression as not counting, not matter-ing, not being "real" politics or history, that it seems fanciful to make the comparison, a slur on "real" political martyrs. But this training is itself per-formed by the available language, which has defined homosexual expression as a "non-political" form of dissidence, as a "social" or "psychological" or "medical" problem. Perhaps most poignant of all is the fact that Orwell chose as a symbol of escape from the official system the drama of a spontan-eous heterosexual affair. For the millions of readers, the ultimate dreadful-ness of *1984* has been brought home as the system where love was to be a crime, where lovers could not even be seen to touch, even to know each other for fear of the State; where the smallest sign of affection was a political gesture. And how many of them have considered that all of this was so for homosexual lovers in the *real* world of 1949, of 1959, of 1969, of 1979? Indeed, our position is in a sense worse than that of Orwell's rebels, who at least had the cultural re-sources of "ordinary language" in which to express their spontaneity. But for us, the ordinary language of sexuality is something that must be fought for:

childhood training and cultural values must be discarded and a second language learned in order that spontaneous feeling can be realized.

And yet, for that very reason, one cannot but be cheered by reading *1984*. The figure of Winston Smith was brought to say and believe that "Big Brother is good," just as so many of us have succumbed to "Queer is bad," yet so many of us have not given in. Not only have we continued to utter the "crude heresies" that the old available words allowed, but we have, since 1949, since 1969, found new words, new images, new language to express ourselves. So often we are immersed in conflicts over what seem mere words: our words (the straightforward use of "gay") are hated; the available "ordinary" words ("promiscuous," for instance) constrict a million different experiences into the straitjacket of one foolish epithet; the official words of psychology and of law degrade and imprison thought as well as people.

Yet we are gaining: with an ever-expanding vocabulary of word and picture, poetry and history, music, film and art. Orwell, against his own will, reminds us that the expansion of language is no ignoble cause, nor some unreal shadow of "real" politics, nor our own strange peripheral problem.

It pays to increase your word power
Michael Riordon

Issue 27, October 1976

The trouble is, no two people mean exactly the same thing by the same word. The resulting confusion leads directly to high art, adventure, war and chaos. Clearly a hopeless means of communication, but what are you going to do?

Let's get off to a good start with something we all disagree on. I've heard any number of arguments against the word "gay," most of them from usually unreliable sources, most along the lines of "Gay means cheerful and you people certainly aren't *that*." Yawn. The *Toronto Star* still bans the word, a staff writer told me, I suppose because of its political more than its cheerful implications. My own feeling is, as always, mixed: it's the only name we have that didn't get foisted on us by nasty, ignorant straights, and it's tacitly accepted by a majority of the people who are it and many who aren't. It would be a hell of a job to find or invent, distribute and sell another. I think what bothers me about it is that it's not exclusively ours and its meaning isn't entirely clear, even to us. A male homosexual trumpeted defiantly: "*I'm* not gay, I'm *queer*." Notable sentiment; trouble is, he *was* decidedly peculiar, therefore not a good example of the creative or rebellious usage. To some people it means simply homosexual (*is* there such a thing?), to others it can only mean *openly* homosexual (dare I say "aggressively"?), a word that's earned by paying a certain kind of dues. Another interesting objection, oddly enough from a straight woman, was that it doesn't *ring* as it should, the way "black" does—she said it's inadequate "because it's a *silly* word." I suppose we'll just have to *build* the ring into it over a period of time, by repetition and tone of voice. I'm glad it's one syllable....

Gorgeous word challenges are thrown out all the time by good writers, even in reasonable translation. Genet described one of his lovers as having "mobile buttocks." A ravishing term; I couldn't figure it out but began earnestly to look for examples. Gradually, with the help of some body-insights from a dance class I was taking, it made the prettiest sense: a wonderfully graceful flow of freedom through the back and the legs that makes some men's buttocks—it isn't common by any means—not sloppy, never sloppy, but *mobile*. There's no other way to describe it as well. (Someone accused me of "objectifying" in this little search, but I wasn't: I was "particularizing," which is quite different. What sly tricks you can play with words.)

Speaking of "gay," isn't "straight" a stupid word? You can wring some rude possibilities from it, but generally it implies "correct." As in Molson Diamond lager beer advertising itself as "straight lager"—if there weren't already ample good reasons for a boycott, surely *there's* one for us. An intriguing alternative to "straight" was offered in a newspaper headline over a milk-marketing story: "Skim subsidizes Homo." If we're the homos and they're the skims, would 2%'s be bisexual? And I guess cream would be on our side, wouldn't it?

Also speaking of "gay," there are a great many public washrooms in the world, and a great many people visit them fairly frequently for one reason or another. So why not more gay graffiti? Not of the "Frank likes hot heavy cocks, call such-and-such a number" variety (though it's probably a reasonable if risky form of communication—or public relations) but higher forms, funny or ringing. I did almost all the washrooms on the New York State Thruway (southbound, at least) last month, nothing classic, just "Gay Rights Now!" Maybe I should have shut up, will I ever get into the US again? Penknife is good if you have the time, spray paint if you have the pockets, either if you have the nerve, magic marker a practical alternative. I'll be looking for you.

Promiscuous/Effeminate/Deviant. What hateful things have been done with and in the name of those words. Stupid people always ask: "Is it true homosexual men are more Promiscuous than heterosexual men, or lesbians?" Possible answers: "Yes." "No." "Stupid question, no answer required." "We are more flexible in our relationships because, except for a giant umbrella NO, we haven't suffered under the petty restrictions applied to heterosexuals; once we come out from under the NO we can be pretty free in our comings and goings—heterosexuals, by the way, crave this kind of freedom and go to all sorts of bizarre lengths to simulate it. As for lesbians, it seems that if they throw off their doubly onerous NO burden, anything is possible." Then they ask: "What is the basis for the belief that homosexuals are effeminate?" That's a mischievous question, because they avoid saying whether *they* believe it. Possible answers: "None of the lesbians I know are the least effeminate." "My dear, the very idea is patently thilly." "The basis is: instead of sensibly recognizing and enjoying a full, lively range of human behaviour, the headless have swallowed whole the idea of arbitrary categories, and most of the minority ones have negative connotations. Thus, "effeminate" men, "masculine" women — *eg*, East German swimmers with broad shoulders — are considered in some circles to have lost any legitimate claim to womanhood." How brainless it all is.

Deviant/deviate is another matter; I rather like it. I give it my own proud inflection. Webster says: "an individual who differs considerably from the average." Having no respect for the average, I'm enchanted. And "characterized by or given to considerable departure from the norms of behavior in a given society." Finding the norms of the given society to be by and large a mess, I'm doubly pleased with myself. Of course, there's no denying the word is flung at us like mud, as are "promiscuous" and "effeminate."

Words say worlds about people, they spring out in bright relief if you watch for them. A man asked me if I would mind terribly if he "sodomized" me. Imagine. That's a very rich word, purple with implications of crime, sin and hellish perversion. I declined, it sounded to me a very dangerous undertaking. He slipped imperceptibly from "interesting" to "odd" in my ratings.

Why on earth is a "blow job" called a "blow job"?

Friends (not lovers)
Ken Popert

Issue 65, August 1980

A three-by-five card tacked to a bulletin board announced that "Two gay friends (not lovers) seek a third to share an apartment near Queen and University."

The phrase is arresting: "friends (not lovers)." Placing it almost first among the details of the situation, the writer must regard the distinction as crucial.

It might well be so for a third person. The word "lover," transplanted to the gay world from a sexual tradition which extends full approval only to the heterosexual, patriarchal, life-long monogamous coupling, carries an exclusionary flavour.

The gay man who joins two friends to found a household may fairly anticipate a union of equals. But a gay man who takes up residence with two who call themselves lovers is flirting with crowded loneliness.

The assumption that some precision is purchased by distinguishing between friends and lovers is worth considering. In a recent summer evening conversation, an acquaintance mentioned that he and his roommate had been lovers for several years, but now classify themselves as friends. I wondered out loud about the content of the distinction. Did he mean that they had ceased to have sex with each other? No. They still made love from time to time. But as friends, not lovers. The nature of this distinction, so casually drawn at first, eluded us for some minutes. It came down to this: as lovers, each took the other's plans into account in making his own; as friends, neither does.

Thinking about it later, it seemed to me that this conversational eddy exposed the essentially private character of the meaning of the word "lover." Many of us use it with an individual precision which is illusory, not being shared with others.

It now occurs to me that often in the course of those conversations with strangers which promise to lead to other things, I contrive to mention Brian, whom I allude to as my lover. This discourages those looking for more than an evening's diversion.

But I have always to couple that reference with the news that we're not monogamous, to preclude a further undesirable inference. The word "lover" is so empty of specificity that it serves as little more than a signal that significant information about my relations with other gay men is available.

Now the vocabulary of gay male relations does not suffer from a quantitative poverty. Many terms of gay male kinship can be found in the anglophone parts of the country: lover, special friend, companion, partner, attachment and even spouse-substitute (that's how Brian's employer, the Government of Canada, delicately refers to me).

But our vocabulary is impoverished in another way. Every one of these words refers to the same ill-defined area of gay male relations. We lack the means to render distinctions easily. Why don't we have a word for non-monogamous lovers? Or for friends who make love? Or for lovers who don't?

I think we don't have those words because we haven't yet developed the concepts which would lie behind them. We haven't reached a consensus which would bring meaningful order to the infinite welter which gay relationships offer to the observer.

The root of the difficulty is that our relationships fall outside of the reigning taxonomy of human relations, which is concerned exclusively with heterosexual couplings and the family. To find order and regularity in homosexual relations would be an undesired act of legitimization.

As gay life has flourished (relatively speaking) during the last decade, we have been able to meet needs long unmet and, in our necessity, we have been inventive. The gay male couple, for example, may appear to the liberal eye as a tolerably minor variation of marriage. But it is in fact profoundly novel, not least because a gay couple is a relation of social equals. Even if the established view of human relations is opened up to include us, it cannot do so without a thorough and transforming revision.

The absence of a constructive, ordering consensus about gay relations works very much against us. A kinship system is not primarily a description of what is; it is a prescription of what ought to be. It defines expectations and obligations, anticipates problems and poses solutions.

Without the aid of a map drawn up from our common experience, each gay man and woman must locate the pathways and dead ends on their own. We are exposed to individual and collective defeat.

Example: Brian and I have called ourselves lovers for six years. About eighteen months ago, we stopped having sex with each other. We didn't talk about it at first; we still haven't fully discussed it; but we have at least reached the point of joking about it.

Initially, I was disturbed and depressed by the apparent end of the sexual aspect of our life together. It seemed somehow to make us a failure. Worse, the nagging voice of authority from which the oppressed are never truly free was there in the back of my mind, denying the stability of gay relationships.

I knew these feelings were irrational. I knew this change didn't really seem to affect our relationship. I knew that the vaunted longevity of heterosexual interests is the product of a tyranny of restrictions from some of which we have escaped. What lifted the cloud was the discovery that some of my friends had had the same experience. To learn that our personal history was common was, for me, to restore it to full authenticity.

It is a truism that the politics of gay liberation touch not just our public stance, but also our private lives. The personal is political, the saying goes. It is a hard lesson to remember.

Now that we gay people are attempting to gain some control over our lives, we are searching for solutions. If we can discuss gay relations openly, giving them names and shapes, we can expect to become more confident in our way of life.

The material is all around us. The way we live now is the rough draft of our future.

Taking over the house of language
Mariana Valverde

Issue 50, February 1979

"Oppression" is a familiar word and, like so many familiar words, it can easily lose its meaning if used as a short-circuit to avoid thinking. To know what it really means is to know the concrete ways in which we—as gays, as women, as ethnic minorities, as youth—are oppressed. One of the least visible but most insidious forms of oppression is the way in which groups outside the mainstream are prevented from using language to say what we want to say, to name ourselves and name our world.

Words are not ours, but theirs. They, under the guise of scientific classification, define us as "perverts," as "witches," as "deviants"... you name it. Words are not neutral vehicles in which anyone can ride; they are weapons in a cold war in which the "in" groups, notably the white/straight/middle-class male group, use language to define everyone else as "outsiders" and to "keep us in our place," as they say.

Women (or rather "ladies," or maybe "girls") do not write operas or TV detective shows, advertising copy or newspaper editorials; ladies do not write scientific books, girls do not give famous speeches or make police reports. Even that which makes us female, our sexual organs, were christened by men, so that the names of our bodily functions sound vaguely foreign when (male) experts say them; even when we say them we have to assume the air of professional superiority male doctors are so fond of using. Try to say "radical mastectomy" without wincing, and you'll see what I mean.

Women always speak softly, and any word which does not lend itself to that "feminine" tone of voice (high-pitched, a question mark soaring above every statement) might as well not exist. Harsh words are banned and assertive phrases ("I can categorically state") are replaced by the meek "Don't you think that...." Words implying that the speaker has a special knowledge or skill are also unfeminine, and nothing more exotic than a wrench is allowed to enrich our vocabulary. After all, can you think of anything more butch than "foreclosure," "spectrometer," or "ontological"?

Like children confined to the playroom, we do not have the run of the house of language. We excel in kitchen words, baby talk, and *Reader's Digest* clichés, but if we attempt to phrase something in an original way, the nearest man will make us feel as though we've just blown our noses in the tablecloth.

What is "brilliant" in a man is "bitchy" in a woman. Even when men are not present we cannot use their languages, any more than a maid can comfortably use the parlour when the master is not at home. We are torn between outdoing men's professional seriousness (the career woman syndrome) and ridiculing it, between childishly exaggerating "correct" forms and breaking out in giggles.

So what words do we use? Well, we've always been good at keeping diaries, because, as Virginia Woolf noticed, that could be done in snatches on the kitchen table. We certainly couldn't write long books — the baby had to be changed, the soup was boiling over — so poetry was rather convenient; we were encouraged to be emotional, so sentimental poetry was just right. We were allowed to be perceptive, so we could describe our cute children, our home-sweet-home, and even our inner anguish, but we were excluded from knowledge.

While women were expected to be silent, gays were expected to be invisible. We existed only as *objects*, to be named, described, examined and laughed at. From the "decent homosexual" to the hated faggot or the despised dyke, we are all *defined* as outcasts and hence expected to act accordingly. Even the seemingly "value-free" terms used by the medical professions are weapons used to hurt us—the category of "homosexuality" is the scientific equivalent of the eggs thrown at drag queens on Halloween, being designed to confirm the otherwise dubious virility of the advocates of normality.

And when we choose words for ourselves ("gay") and for certain others ("homophobic"), the same people who want to save "our" children jump to the defence of "our" language. The letters column of the *Globe and Mail* has published a series of complaints by well-meaning citizens protesting the kidnapping of the nice, clean word "gay" by us horrid homosexuals. We are accused of abducting a young, tender, fun-loving word for use in our witches' cauldron. Do we have to rape and plunder the sacred mother tongue? ask English professors. Don't we have enough with "faggot," "dyke," "queer," and all those labels that have been lavished on us by "normal" speakers of Standard English?

This attack does not come only from the save-the-children bigots, however. Even well-wishers of the other sexual orientation wonder why we insist on being called "gays," not homosexuals. The answer is very simple: we are trying to break the ancient custom by which we are classified as defective goods because of our sexual preference, and we will no longer tolerate being shunted off into a corner of the psychiatrist's showcase of deviates, along with necrophiliacs, nymphomaniacs, and other victims of the medical profession's mania for classifying sexuality.

We have to destroy the scientific jargon of normality by showing that, far from being neutral and "value-free," it is distorted from the very start by the prejudices of the name-givers and classifiers. We have to stop mimicking their language, stop living on borrowed words, and refuse to become homosexual experts on homosexuality.

We have to recognize that, in the war of words, there are no experts, only fighters. We have to talk with those who, like ourselves, have been kicked out of the house of language—minorities whose cultures are being eroded, children who are told to be seen and not heard, mental patients whose lives are controlled by those who control the language.

We, as women and gay people, have to take over the house of language, sit down in the best chairs, and decide whether we want to stay—or move out.

Six of One:
a review of the Rita Mae Brown novel
Lorna Weir

Issue 49, December 1978/January 1979

Lesbian-feminist hero Rita Mae Brown has refurbished her image for the dustjacket of her latest novel, *Six of One*, cleverly disguising herself as the Medusa of the Chanel No 5 ad. Brown, the impoverished lesbian who made a sizable sum writing a book about a destitute lesbian, currently works as a scriptwriter in Hollywood, where she has purchased what her recent interview in *Publisher's Weekly* calls a "spacious mansion." *Rubyfruit Jungle*, justly billed as "the first lesbian comic novel," sold 70,000 copies in its Daughters' (a small feminist press) edition, and is now available at your corner grocery story as a Bantam book with 330,000 copies in print. Lionized by both feminists and Hollywood, Rita Mae Brown has met with a far different reception than Radclyffe Hall fifty years ago, and the very warmth of this reception creates its own problems.

The publicity for *Six of One* makes clear that lesbians don't hold the copyright to Rita Mae Brown. How could we be so selfish? She is a universal cultural treasure. Harper and Row hasten to assure us that "Rita Mae has broken through—this is not a lesbian novel or even a 'women's book,' it is a literary groundbreaker with immense universal appeal." How convenient for the company that she has broken through her previous lesbian-feminist identification and can now be sold to everyone. More alarming are Brown's own comments arguing that she is no more a lesbian writer than James Baldwin is a black writer, such categories being the stereotypes of oppression. Objecting to confinement in such categorical ghettos, she recently said, "Next time anyone calls me a lesbian writer I'm going to knock their teeth in. I'm a writer and I'm from the South and I'm alive, and that is that." (The bite is still there.)

The ideal of universal humanity is a moral balm which, assuaging the pain of specific oppression, causes forgetfulness to set in. The content of this universal humanity has been fixed by white, occidental, publicly heterosexual males. In order to be considered part of it, one must have "broken through" one's gayness, blackness, womanhood or other particular oppression because the universal is a stereotype which, paradoxically, excludes almost everyone. To say that someone is a "male writer" or "white writer" sounds redundant, while "woman writer" or "black writer" are not. The words "writer" and "universal" are much like the pronoun "he," which in a wonderful economy of expression, theoretically includes but practically excludes women.

To be a lesbian writer or a black writer is to write from a particular oppression which has been excluded from "universal," public acceptance. It is to insist that the words "universal" and "human" be rethought. The qualifier "lesbian" in lesbian writer will not vanish into the writer until the social oppression of lesbians has disappeared. To insist that these modifiers vanish immediately is to pre-empt the social struggle for their acceptance, and to side with those who hide their interests behind a smokescreen of universality. Those who belong to oppressed groups have no interest in disguising their struggle. There is a battle being fought over Rita Mae Brown's "universal appeal," and she is on dangerous ground if she resists being categorized as a lesbian writer.

With these reservations about the publicity, *Six of One* can be safely chortled and guffawed through by lesbians and gay men. It is an immensely enjoyable account of twentieth-century American history as it affected a handful of people in Runnymede, a town smack on the Mason-Dixon line. Unionbashing, class struggles, two World Wars, Prohibition, and a series of births, deaths and murders proceed apace in merry abandon through the decades. The central characters are two sisters who have a lifelong relationship of loving mutual insult, their mother, and a filthy rich, beautiful, cultured lesbian couple. It is a thoroughly woman-identified piece; Rita Mae Brown's male characters are superficially drawn, but described in a warm and understanding fashion.

It is unfortunate that the major lesbian character, Celeste, is so wealthy. The largesse of the lesbian couple can only perpetuate the stereotype that lesbianism is a vocation for rich literati, since only the rich can afford to protect themselves from social disapproval. Ironically, the woman who broke away from the myth of the aristocratic lesbian living off her inheritance, and gave us a model of a working-class lesbian in *Rubyfruit Jungle*, slides back into Vita Sackville-West gentility. The novel has an equally unfortunate tendency to divide the elite of Runnymede into the self-interested, money-grubbing bourgeoisie at the munitions factory and the natural, landed aristocracy, and to subtly idealize the latter: a repeat of American Civil War ideology without mention of slavery. We are not charmed by the fact that, in the best Stephen Gordon tradition, the representative of the southern landed gentry, the lesbian appropriately named Celeste, never needs to trouble about her income because the shoe factory is so far away and is tended by her brother.

Still, Rita Mae Brown has not broken faith with lesbians, gays and feminists, and *Six of One* remains a spirited and entertaining book.

Robin Tyler: comic in contradiction
Val Edwards

Issue 56, September 1979

The late August sun has disappeared behind a low ridge; the skies are just beginning to cloud over. Six thousand lesbians from across North America nestle in a nook between three hills that form a natural concert bowl. On stage Robin Tyler, dressed in a black tuxedo, is making her debut at the Michigan Women's Music Festival.

"Of course you may have noticed I'm wearing a tuxedo," says Tyler. "On Liza Minnelli it's called cute; on me it's called drag.

"I went to my first drag ball in New York City in 1960. There were five hundred men dressed up as women — crinolines, everything. The police raided that drag ball. I went up to one cop and said, 'Excuse me. Why are you arresting these gentlemen?' He said, 'You don't fool me, you're one of them!' So he throws me into handcuffs—which is how I got into bondage—throws me into the paddy wagon and takes me to jail for female impersonation. They allowed me one phone call. Did I call my mother? Are you kidding? Did I call my lawyer? No. I called the New York *Post*! And the next day the headline read 'Forty-four men and one woman arrested for female impersonation.'

"So of course I was trying to break into show business, and I decided if I could fool the police maybe I could fool the public. So I went down to Club 82 and did Judy Garland. For one year I was Stacey Morgan, one of the most famous female impersonators in the United States. And why shouldn't I be a female impersonator? Phyllis Schlaffley is.

"Phyllis Schlaffley is to women what the Hindenberg was to flying. But don't get me wrong—I happen to agree with the right-to-lifers. 'Cause if you don't agree with them, they'll kill you!"

We are on our feet, cheering. Encouraged, she launches into a humorous, yet impassioned, declaration of the rights of women and gays. Booming to be heard above our roars, she cries, "We are everywhere! We are everywhere!" Lightning flashes in the sky behind her—it will continue until dawn. A tornado touches down two miles away. Rain sweeps in and lifts our tents off their moorings. The local old-timers call it the worst storm in living memory: the gods are not amused. Robin Tyler's terrestrial audiences are generally heterosexual. They may be no less outraged by her act than their heavenly counterparts, but they *are* amused. Robin has been booked for two television shows and has released an album, *Always A Bridesmaid, Never A Groom*. She is one of only a handful of women stand-up comics making it in a medium where male comics still rely on tits-and-ass jokes for their biggest laughs.

Working out of the Comedy Store in Los Angeles, Tyler has now largely abandoned the "sexist nightclub circuit" in favour of college tours. Her performance at the Michigan Women's Music Festival, however, was something of a first. Performing before a lesbian audience both as a comic and as master of ceremonies put her in an unusual position; she admits that it is the substance of her humour, rather than her style, that distinguishes her from other comics. Stand-up comedy is, as Tyler puts it, "a precision art form" that depends almost entirely on the comic's ability to control an audience. "In Michigan, I was an MC and it was very hard. I had to maintain control of an audience that believed in collectivism and that was determined nobody on earth was ever going to control them again. And when there were six thousand women shouting at the moon, I wanted to run off stage. I was scared. I didn't want to stop them. But because I'm disciplined and I'm a performer, I have to listen to the producers. Art has to be disciplined. The more natural it looks, the more disciplined you are.

"When they sent me out to keep everyone quiet I had no idea what to do. So I asked people their signs. I knew if I asked who was Aries, eleven-twelfths of the audience would be quiet."

It is a testimonial to Tyler's skill as a comic that she receives standing ovations from lesbian audiences on their guard against an entertainer's manipulation. It is also a study in contradiction. Robin Tyler is a feminist who consciously uses her sex appeal on stage; a star in a lesbian movement that refuses to acknowledge stars; a revolutionary in an entertainment industry that mollifies the masses; a performer who, through commanding her audiences, urges us to toss off the command of others. The contradiction lies in the *exotic* dissonance of message and medium.

Stand-up comedy is not only a precision art form, it is a craft unto itself. Tyler is quick to point out the distinction between a comic and a comedian.

"Comedians are people who say things funny, who hide behind the characters they create—women like Lucille Ball, Carol Burnett and Lily Tomlin. Comics say funny things. I am my own instrument, and consequently I rely on my own energy."

On stage, stand-up comics are naked. No other performer is so at the mercy of the audience. If a comic's act bombs, it's because he (or, rarely, she) is a bomb; bad comics are despised as *persons*. Because the stakes are so high, the comic's relationship to an audience is an extraordinary power struggle. The conflict is usually subtle—the great comics manipulate us without our knowing it. At times, however, the battle is overt: some comics' best lines are devastating put-downs of hecklers. Regardless of how the campaign is waged, final victory comes when the comic has wrested, or the audience has relinquished, control.

"Then," says Tyler, "we can lead an audience in and out of where we want them to go. Laughter becomes involuntary. If I want to, I can get the most radical people to laugh at a racist joke because they'll be off their guard."

Robin Tyler is a superb stand-up comic. She skillfully combines timing, aggressiveness, and vulnerability to get an audience laughing with her. All good comics rely on some combination of the above. Bob Hope, whom Tyler admires for his discipline on stage, consistently allows a four-second gap before delivering his punch line. Johnny Carson on the other hand "is not great on timing. What makes him acceptable to middle America is that he's vulnerable. You must appear vulnerable on stage."

All comics are self-deprecating to greater or lesser degrees, setting themselves up as the objects of their humour. In making herself appear vulnerable, Tyler generally bypasses self-deprecation. Robin's humour is rooted in her own experiences — she is more akin to Lenny Bruce than to Bob Hope or George Burns. Lenny Bruce was the first comic who dared to get up there and be emotional, to tell his truth and his pain. He didn't do mother-in-law jokes.

"Humour comes from pain. It takes maybe ten years to be a strong, seasoned comic. I've been out as a lesbian for twenty years, but at first I didn't know how to make my past funny, I didn't know how to make my anger funny. Then I started to perform solo in a small club in Los Angeles. I just got on and started talking about my past and coming out and found that, years later, I was able to deal with the pain of it through humour—like when I talk about falling in love, or having my mother send me a letter 'To whom it may concern.' It took years to make that pain funny."

Tyler's appearance and personality do not lend themselves to self-abasement. She possesses an omnipotent stage presence and is altogether irresistible — a remarkable alloy of belligerence and sensuousness tempered by a humour wrought in pain. She also has an uncanny ability to read the mood of her audience. "A singer stops when the song stops and the audience applauds. I've got to know when to end. I have to know when the mood is dropping and the moment is over." Misreading an audience is a costly mistake; it destroys the dynamic so carefully constructed and forces the comic to scramble to re-establish it.

Robin Tyler has not always been a comic. She started her career twenty years ago as a singer and dancer in New York City, like many other comics who had to survive somehow before they could make it in comedy. For women, breaking into comedy was hard enough; for a feminist, the difficulties were compounded by the expectations of nightclub audiences.

"I worked in Miami Beach and formed a comedy team with Pat Harrison. And we were Harrison and Tyler. But we called ourselves Rachel and Robin Tyler because we had to be a sister act."

Sexist jokes were the mainstay of the profession, and women comics were expected to make themselves, as women, the brunt of their own jokes—witness Phyllis Diller. "But we wouldn't be self-deprecating," says Robin, "and at first we weren't funny. Then all of a sudden feminism came along. In essence what we did then is now called the new women's humour, a humour which finally gave women the opportunity to make not themselves the brunt of the jokes, but rather the society that was oppressing them."

Tyler hates to be compared to women who indulge in the old-style humour —comics like Joan Rivers. "She didn't have our support system. We can't blame those women." Robin acknowledges the debt she owes to the women's and gay liberation movements. "You must remember that comedy reflects the political state of the times. In the 1940s the focus was on anti-Semitism and a lot of Jewish comics came up. In the 1960s we had the third world problems, and we began to get other minority comics like Richard Pryor and Freddy Prinze.

"The greatest humour has sometimes come out of oppression. The most oppressed groups have had to use humour as a pressure valve. Laughter illuminates the trouble." But to Robin Tyler, comedy is more than a means of relieving political tensions. "It's a powerful political tool. We have to take the weapons they traditionally used against us, turn them around, and aim back.

"I am aggressive. We always talk about our right to be assertive. Assertion is taking your own power, aggression is taking your power over others. I'm going to take power from the people who took power from me. A comic must be aggressive with an audience. It's not assertive, it's not sharing. Social satirists and people who deal with political analysis have to be very strong. They're not just getting up there and doing self-depreciating jokes.

"I know that people who have not been exposed to my kind of humour and my kind of presence might feel uncomfortable. I think we mustn't be afraid of our own power. If my aggression is threatening to some women—only some —then I feel I don't have to deal with my aggression, they have to deal with their lack of it."

Recently Robin Tyler has taken her comedy out of the nightclubs and into the streets. She made regular appearances at gay rallies in California when the Briggs amendment reared its ugly head, becoming the first gay entertainer to actively rabble-rouse for gay rights. "In Hollywood, you can be gay but you can't be political. They can know you're gay, and make references to it, but you can't go out and say it to the people. I'm the first one to come out and do it. But I'm still getting booked. I don't know why it's happening."

Robin views her role in the movement as that of a spokesperson rather than a leader. "You can't lead people. You can only show people, and hope they'll be inspired to take back, to kick ass back. Kicking ass, as Flo Kennedy says, is the highest thing. They're using machine-guns against us, so we can't use pop guns."

No one entirely escapes Tyler's barrage, although she takes particular delight in spearing male chauvinists. She has a few deliciously vicious cock-and-balls jokes. "And why not? We've been listening to the tit-and-ass jokes for fifty years! Now let's see who doesn't have a sense of humour!" She also does an outrageous takeoff on sexist television commercials, and of course Anita Bryant and Phyllis Schlaffley get their comeuppance.

But some of Tyler's lines hit closer to home: "I always believed monogamy was a kind of dark wood you polish. I don't know if coupleness is for me. Why does having sex with someone give them the automatic right to persecute you?" She kicks off her album with a hilarious cut entitled "Politically Correct Introduction." Tyler has little use for ideological rigidity, a phenomenon she attributes to a lack of political sophistication. "I remember when we all first came out everybody had to wear workshirts and bluejeans and nobody could shave under their arms or they weren't a radical lesbian feminist. People who are rigid have no right to define themselves as revolutionary. Because what we are really fighting for is freedom of choice."

She isn't afraid to be blunt. She has this to say, for instance, about *The Body Politic*'s controversial article "Men loving boys loving men": "Inopportune, tacky, poorly researched and written, too graphic. Pedophilia is not our issue. Children are in a one-down socio-economic position. Seducing them is simply not right." Tyler tells it as she sees it. "If I've offended any of you," she says at the end of her album, "you needed it."

Her directness isn't surprising in a lesbian who was bold enough to come out more than twenty years ago in Winnipeg, where she grew up. "I remember standing on the corner of Portage and Main when I was about sixteen with a sign saying 'Gay is Good,' and people thought I meant happy and gave me money. We were actually out on the streets, but there were only a couple of us, and we were ostracized by other homosexuals who thought we were making it hard for them to stay in the closet. One of my most valuable lines is 'When a heterosexual shows us a picture of his family, it's called sharing. When we show them a picture of our lover, it's called flaunting. Isn't it time we shared?'

"I don't tell people they have to come out, but the least they can do is work for the community. They can lick stamps or send letters. I was speaking to the Community Guild of Los Angeles, to gay millionaires. I said 'We're tired of carrying you on our back. You're millionaires. If you won't come out, you're gonna start writing cheques in the closet. We'll give you flashlights and pens and just write the cheques.' They have to give something — time, money, something — to our movement."

Robin has a keen sense of her own roots in the movement, roots that date back to the bars of the Fifties and Sixties. "The older dykes of years ago had to take roles. They were our forerunners, women who had to survive in a world of such pain. There was no movement. Today lesbian feminists can afford to come out with a support system. Then there were only the bars. They are our elders, and they're being disrespected."

"I call myself a born-again butch. Which means I still have the choreography, but I don't do the dance. That's why I wear tuxedo and leather jackets on stage. These women are coming to see me, and through my humour I hope to make it okay to be a butch."

Her tuxedos do more than make butch women feel welcome. They help Robin establish a visual image in keeping with her aggressive delivery, though she usually dresses "collegiate" for straight audiences. She makes no other efforts to adapt her act to the audience ("an audience knows when you're talking down or kissing up"), but does admit to "flirting a little more" with a lesbian crowd. "Since Michigan, I've gotten more comfortable with projecting my sexuality on stage. Before that I went through a stage in my feminism where I tried to appear asexual. But I am sexual; it's a part of me, it's valid. I don't think it contradicts my feminism."

Like many activists, Robin Tyler is striving to integrate her career, her feminism and her gay politics. This is no small task for a stand-up comic; even in her satire, contradictions will invariably show through the performance, giving us a glimpse of Tyler unmasked. Are the contradictions irreconcilable? Probably. A good lesbian-feminist does not manipulate people; a good comic must. Does it matter? Only to a purist.

Robin Tyler is making an important contribution to the feminist and gay rights movements, and in the process is giving us a much-needed break from our own endeavours, from work that can get too heavy.

It's good to laugh. Let the purists be damned.

La cage aux folles: a review of the film
Gerald Hannon

Issue 56, September 1979

Somewhere in the middle of this frequently hilarious, sometimes heart-breaking film, a baroquely effeminate character called Albin throws up his hands in exasperation at his inability to appear even modestly conventional, and cries, "I am a monster! A monster!"

He isn't. As played by Michel Serrault, Albin is a wonderfully camp confection, so warmly played as never to be entirely ludicrous, and so certain of his comic powers that even his eyebrows can put an entire scene on hold.

There *is* a monster in this movie, however, though he will not be recognized as such. The normative centre of this frantically paced French farce, Laurent, is a blandly sweet young man, the product of a short-lived heterosexual indiscretion on the part of Albin's longtime lover and partner, Renato (played by Italian star Ugo Tognazzi). Together, Albin and Renato run La cage aux folles, a St Tropez nightclub featuring transvestite performers. The plot is set in motion when Renato's son announces to his distraught father that not only is he going to marry, he's engaged to marry a *woman*. Matters are further complicated by the fact that the girl's mother and father are moral rearmament types, and that they are planning a pre-nuptial visit to the boy's "parents." When you realize that Renato and Albin live in a rather feverishly frou-frou apartment serviced by a young black man who favours frilly aprons, panty hose and little else, you can see the potential for farce.

Farce is a delicate thing. It cannot engage real feelings. It can offer people you love to love, and people you love to hate, but a more direct claim on the emotions can only clog its headlong pace. Evelyn Waugh understood this. When he dispatches Mary Mouse in *Vile Bodies*, all for the sake of a one-liner, the reader is thrilled as much by its heartlessness as by its humour.

Writer Jean Poiret may have intended Renato and Albin to be uncomplicated stereotypes of the aging, effeminate homosexual, but the characters are so warmly realized by Tognazzi and Serrault, so lovingly crafted, so delicately built detail by detail from the inside, that one finally cares rather deeply about these two men and the life they have built together over a twenty-year relationship.

Because one cares, actions that would otherwise simply impel the plot along its antic way seem curiously harsh and wounding, and the son, an otherwise bland, stock character, becomes the monster I mentioned. All he asks is that Renato send Albin away for the period of the potential in-laws' visit, and that he redecorate the apartment somewhat more astringently, but the effect is devastating. The action summarizes the whole history of homosexuality in a heterosexual world—there is the smug, bland superiority of the son, certain that his way is the way of the world and rightly so, the amused tolerance with which he regards the two men, the ease with which he dismantles the apartment (and the relationship), the contempt as he slowly smears along the wall makeup he has rubbed from his father's face. Renato and Albin protest, there are scenes, there is weeping, Renato says something brave about knowing what he is and accepting it—but at every point they surrender. In those brief and almost unbearably painful moments, one understands much of our social history—a history of small accommodations, concessions, sacrifices made by us so that their world might have its way.

I do not much like violence in movies, but I would have watched happily if the son had been slowly disembowelled.

To be fair, I must record that few people have had so marked a reaction to those scenes, and that by the end of the film I had half forgotten them myself in the exhilaration of watching Albin and Renato finally take devastating control of the plot, and set the action's hilarious dénouement on *their* terms. There is a particularly brilliant grace note near the end when one realizes that even the priest performing the marriage ceremony is swoopingly one of us.

That delighted the largely straight audience as much as it did me, but there were all too many occasions when one had to endure an audience convulsed by some minor effeminacies. The people I've talked to about the movie have been unanimous in wishing they could have seen it with an all-gay audience. One grew bored at spotting the suburbs in the audience by locating the patches of inappropriate hilarity. Straight people still seem to find role reversal so threatening (or so tantalizing) that they'll laugh themselves silly if a man so much as sashays across the stage.

I have said there is a monster in this movie. At some level, of course, we need our monsters. Children know that—private terrors need a public substance, a habitation and a name. How else would one know where to go to kill them? But, buoyed as I was by the final moments of *La cage aux folles*, I left the cinema with the disquieting feeling that my monsters are living in other people's homes—and that they are welcome there.

Not even a brilliant farce can make me feel very good about that.

Hosanna:
a review of Michel Tremblay's play
David Mole

Issue 31, March 1977

Hosanna—"the fourteen thousand, two hundred and twelfth episode of our great love story, 'Cuirette and Cleopatra,' conceived, imagined, produced and lived by Claude Lemieux and Raymond Bolduc,"— has just finished playing at Toronto Workshop Productions (TWP) theatre.

Claude and Raymond, Hosanna and Cuirette, face a crisis. The bits and pieces of role-playing and fantasy, dressing up and theatre, that they have carefully made into lives and into a relationship, no longer cohere.

"When I'm dressed like a man I'm ridiculous," says Hosanna the motorcycle queen, Hosanna the transvestite. "When I'm dressed like a woman I'm ridiculous. But when I'm stuck between the two... with my woman's face... and my own body...."

For Cuirette, Hosanna's question hangs, "Is it my dresses that turn you on, or is it me? Is it Hosanna the drag queen, or Claude the farmer?" Cuirette is unemployed and lives off Hosanna. He does the chores around the apartment, "a cleaning lady who rides a motorcycle." If Hosanna is ridiculous, what is he?

The fragile accommodation that these two men have toiled to produce, between their own sexuality and the sexual roles of society at large, is coming apart. The times are changing and they are growing older. "All right, all right,

I know what I used to be," says Cuirette. "I'm fat... I was good-looking once... and now I'm not any more." It takes her humiliation, when she appears as Cleopatra at the Halloween party, to convince Hosanna that her day as the motorcyclist's girlfriend is over. After that, Hosanna is afraid to take off her make-up, afraid of what's underneath.

By the end of the play Cleopatra is dead for Hosanna. She has destroyed her *papier mâché* set because her *papier mâché* life is over. Cuirette's nemesis is a visit to Parc Lafontaine, where he made a dark and secret début. It is ablaze with lights. "The bastards have changed everything," he complains. "I don't want things to change."

But brought to this point, where their fantasy is destroyed, they can at last exist for themselves and one another. They can shed their clothes, their drag, their make-up. Dressed only in their genitals, they embrace simply as men who need and, perhaps, love one another. The embrace is charming and lovely and the play finally touching.

As a love story, *Hosanna* works. It has pace, solid characters and some good writing, especially Hosanna's monologue, which is superbly acted by Richard Monette. Both Monette and Richard Donat as Cuirette act throughout with skill and enthusiasm. They bring Hosanna and Cuirette to life and still pull off the happy ending, without more falseness and sentimentality than is inevitable.

Is *Hosanna* more than a love story? A play about a transvestite is bound to explore the paradoxes of sexual roles. As we laugh, or fail to laugh, as Hosanna fights the hooks on her dreadful dress or drowns in cheap scent, we laugh, or fail to laugh, at a stereotype Hosanna only mimics.

Is this, then, a play about straight sexuality? Does it hold up a mirror to its largely straight audience? If this is the point, it shoots wide of its mark. For this audience, the imitation of Elizabeth Taylor is not the leading edge of sexism. If it shows that sexual roles exist and are destructive, then it isn't saying anything that a liberal, intellectual audience doesn't already know. The play, after all, has no women in it and has little to say about women or to women.

Does it talk then to gay men? It explores two versions of gay sexuality—an extraordinary version, a piece of theatre played between Hosanna and Cuirette in which few will recognize themselves, even in parody, and, in the final scene, another version: the love of two men unencumbered with the false and artificial. But most of us, gay or straight, live lives between drag and nakedness. We do not dispense with the psychic and social baggage of our sexuality —we cannot. It is our condition. Nor do we allow our condition to become a prison of leather or perfume. Tremblay indicates the extremes of the problem. It is between these bookends that we must find a way. It is a start, but this far down the road of our liberation, it makes better theatre than politics. As politics it dates, its message becomes too general, its critique less keen. As theatre it remains a warm and sometimes powerful play.

As far as I can see, this play has nothing whatever to do with the struggle of the people of Quebec for their national rights.

Trading on secrets:
the making of a TV documentary
Chris Bearchell

Issue 71, March 1981

New Gays; Old Wounds? *Not Afraid Anymore*? They finally settled on *Sharing the Secret: Selected Gay Stories.*

"The film you are about to see contains powerful subject matter, including rare and rarely glimpsed aspects of homosexual life. It is *not* about the obvious homosexual stereotypes, such as drag queens or boys in heavy leather. Nor is it, to any great extent, about vocal gay militants. This film takes us into a still largely closeted world, to meet a few of the other gays, people who have come forward, at whatever risk, to share some of their secrets and their feelings with us. No single film could hope to encompass the entire gay world or the complex of people and attitudes within it. Instead, six individual subjects have been chosen. Their stories are their own, and what they say is not necessarily representative of other gay people. The film contains scenes which some viewers may find disturbing. Parents with children present are urged to exercise discretion."

Sharing the Secret, a television documentary, was made by the renowned mother-and-son team of Rose and John Kastner. As a young journalist for the *Toronto Telegram*, John Kastner used to cover all the social movements of the late Sixties. He says he got the idea for *Sharing the Secret* when, looking back over those days, he came to the conclusion that the only one of those movements that wasn't dead was gay liberation. It was more alive than ever. He wanted to know why, and what its impact had been on gay people.

The Kastner team has two Emmy awards to its credit, for *Four Women*, a documentary about breast cancer, and *Fighting Back*, about childhood leukemia. It was on the basis of this reputation that mother and son were able to secure the cooperation of the six gay men and three of their parents who participated in this latest venture. John and Rose spoke to some five hundred people before choosing the six men who would be featured. They discovered that the gay community was so complicated as to include two genders, and that the two genders were too complicated to be encompassed in a single documentary. John Kastner says they've already filmed about one third of a follow-up on lesbians.

Sharing the Secret: Selected Gay Stories was telecast across Canada by the CBC on Sunday, January 11, 1981, in prime time, from 9 to 10:30 pm. Before, during and after that ninety minutes, the film was the focus of attention and controversy in the media, in all those Canadian homes, in many workplaces and, above all, in the Toronto gay community where the film was made.

Television viewers were introduced to the cultured son of a wealthy businessman who tried to subdue his homosexuality with physical abuse; two lovers—one of whom's parents went through incredible anguish in the struggle to accept their son; a man who is obsessed with his appearance, wardrobe and the fear of growing old; and a brilliant musician, the son of a former Anglican priest, who cruises bars, baths and parks in search of sex for the thrill of it.

"Accept that no gay life is every gay life, and *Sharing the Secret: Selected Gay Stories* can be considered a useful and a creditable documentary, the best probe yet of a world many fear," began a review by *Ottawa Citizen* television critic Richard Labonté, who is also a contributor to *The Body Politic*. Labonté told me that his editor was responsible for the direct praise in that statement, although he approved the change. "I would not have been so uncritical if I'd been doing it for TBP and not a straight audience. It wasn't as negative as CBS's *Gay Power, Gay Politics*. Sure there were twits in it, but they could have chosen worse."

A lesbian acquaintance said to me, "It seemed okay to me. That's what life's like for gay men, isn't it?"

"I thought we left the pardon-me-for-living mentality behind years ago," said one friend. "Although the bar, bath and park stuff was handled well enough to look appealing, mostly it was boring." Said another, "If this had been the tenth good film on homosexuality to come out of Canada, then maybe it would have been okay to do an 'Everything you've always wanted to know about cruising (but were afraid to ask).' But that's hardly the case."

But the most enlightening comments of all came from the men who shared their secrets with the Kastners. I was able to talk to five of them.

*

"André Fortin," said the voice of narrator Margaret Pacsu, who also delivered the introduction quoted above, "patrician and ambitious, who regarded his homosexuality as an obstacle to his success to be stamped out at any cost."

André Fortin is actually Pierre Robitaille. The Kastners suggested the name change because it would contribute to the drama and because there were other Peters involved in the film. Pierre called me as soon as he heard I was interested in writing about *Sharing the Secret*.

On camera, Pierre had slowly and calmly related what he'd experienced growing up gay—before he'd come to terms with his homosexuality. He described his fear of hurting his parents with the revelation, the agony of keeping up a straight facade, and an impulse to mutilate himself while masturbating.

"My mother started getting sympathy calls the next morning," he told me. Unlike some of the other participants, Pierre was not disguised physically. To make matters a little more confusing for his mother's friends, he has a brother whose name *is* André.

Pierre Robitaille says *Sharing the Secret* "took what I said about myself, about the way I was ten years ago, and made it look like I'm still that way today. The segment in which I reflected on my adolescence was sincere in content. But the film did not in any way reflect the process I've gone through, and how what I went through was a result of my *status* as a homosexual, not something intrinsic to me as a gay person. I'm a much happier, wittier, laid back person since I've come out. I've evolved, matured. The joy, the uplifting, the struggle of working out my gayness with my family and friends—that was all on tape too, but it was shelved away."

*

Rocco Fermi—"who even as he cruises the bars for men dreams of another life with a wife and children," said the Kastners' script—comes from a large, Italian Catholic family. A small-town boy with small-town values, Rocco (not his real name) describes how he is caught up in the bar scene—on a perpetual quest for "Mr Wonderful." He is shown, at twenty-seven, dreading the day he reaches thirty, and perusing a huge wardrobe which, he estimates, along with cosmetics and jewellery, consumes almost fifty percent of his income.

"I did the film," Rocco told me, "because I thought the gay issue was important. I thought it was worth it if I could help somebody." When I asked if he thought the film or its producers treated him fairly, he paused and finally said he got across what he wanted to. "When I first saw the film I was very critical of myself in it, but when I saw it again later I felt good about it. I'm gay; I accept it. Some people have said they feel sorry for me. That wasn't what I intended."

I asked why what he had to say seemed limited to a very narrow range of concerns. "They were trying to get different perspectives from different people—we couldn't all say the same thing. I was taped for two and a half hours and I said a lot more than what you saw, but I put it in John's hands. I trusted John."

Tracy Angles (the Kastners dubbed him Lee Murdoch), remembers "so distinctly sitting on the couch while someone was putting a wig on me, and asking them whether they were going to do stuff on the baths and the parks. And they said no. I remember it really well."

Tracy's parents, "the Murdochs," were described as "the straitlaced parents who discovered that the homosexual lifestyle they find so repugnant has been taken up by the son they cherish." Tracy and his parents, who live in a small town in Ontario (not in Vancouver as the film suggested) have argued vigorously about the film. "I guess it's important that people think it was good; mind you I can't imagine *why* they would think that," he sighed.

Steven Tattle, Tracy's lover, says the Kastners didn't ask him about anything besides his relationship with Tracy. "They seemed to think my involvement with the community was too political. A lot of older straight people I've talked to really liked the film. I think that's because their stereotypes were upheld. There were no challenges to what they've always thought about us."

June Tattle, Steven's mother, was also among those who were not happy with the way they were treated by the Kastners. June is the founder of the Toronto Parents of Gays group; in the film she was the mother who didn't get to say much. They taped a lot of her (saying very positive things, she says) but told her they were having technical difficulties and most of the footage wasn't usable.

She spent a year helping the Kastners pull together some aspects of the show. "Over the last year I was on the phone to Rose Kastner two or three times a week," she told me. "If you only knew how many people I talked to for them. People who trusted me. And trusted *them*—because of their reputation. They said they wanted to do something positive. I must have heard that word a million times."

June feels the assurances came to nothing. "The film was so depressing. Things were thrown in for shock value. The scenes in the bar, for instance. We all know bars exist. Straight bars exist. So what? What do they have to do with a positive image?"

June was also very upset that, despite her efforts to do so, she was not able to see a preview of the film. Tracy and Steven didn't get to see *Sharing the Secret* in advance, either. Steven says he "felt really bitter every time I read in the press that all of the people in it had been given the opportunity to see it."

The Kastners have said contradictory things about the kind of power the participants had over how they were portrayed. They have claimed that everyone in their films has veto power over what is said and shown about them. It was the first question I asked when, at the beginning of their project, Rose Kastner approached *The Body Politic* for assistance. She boasted that it was standard practice for them.

John Kastner later told the *Toronto Star* that *The Body Politic* threw up a major roadblock in their way by telling people to make sure they had that veto power before cooperating with the film-makers. "You just can't work with those kinds of restrictions," Kastner told the *Star*. The paper went on to say, parenthetically, that "In the end the Kastners did screen the program for the six principals. None of them, or their families, objected to the treatment they received."

That information presumably came directly from John Kastner. Later, Kastner told me that *most* of the gay people in the film had seen it. When I told him that I'd been talking to some of them, he clarified: "At least two thirds of them. We tried to set something up for the remaining ones—those kids who were so upset they didn't see it, Steven and Lee (Tracy Angles). We thought they should see it with the parents, as a bunch. That couldn't be arranged, but we tried. Just ask the parents." Tracy told me they approached his parents, who have a very inflexible schedule, once — the night before they wanted them to come to a screening.

In a later conversation, Kastner finally told me that he and Rose "did this film differently from the others. We didn't give the subjects veto power. We had them sign contracts for small honorariums which were, in effect, releases. We only agreed to show it to people in advance as a courtesy."

*

Peter Shaffter is described by the Romper Room voice of CBC narrator Pacsu as "a proud gay who embarked on an odyssey of erotic pleasure through the secret world of gay male sex." Shaffter, whose name was changed only slightly to Shaver at the Kastners' suggestion, *did* get to see the film, twice in fact. He made a number of suggestions—some of which made it into the final version. "But the one specific request I made was ignored. I never, in the film, call myself a 'sexual revolutionary.' While I may hope my actions are revolutionary, I don't like labels of any kind. I found the repetition of 'sexual revolutionary' and 'sexual extremist' embarrassing and silly, so I asked them to take those references out. They didn't."

Peter Shaffter is the director of Toronto's Gay Community Choir. He and I mused over coffee about the Kastners' insistence that they were not focusing on vocal militants, and the apparent contradiction in the fact that even though they didn't listen to him, he seemed to have more control than the other participants. "John Kastner doesn't know what a gay militant is," Peter laughed. "And he probably thought that, since I was doing what I wanted with my part in the film, he wasn't in danger of losing me by showing it to me."

Peter took the Kastner film crew on a tour of the three-storey Richmond Street Health Emporium—one of the Toronto steam baths that was raided a couple of weeks after the show went on the air. It turned out to be the most controversial part of *Sharing the Secret* for straights and gays alike — including some of the film's other participants.

"I have a strong personal belief that gay people are almost never portrayed accurately because we talk about trying to liberate ourselves without addressing why. We say that we're oppressed because we're different, but we don't address what it is that makes us different — our sexuality.

"I knew that the Kastners would be using extreme examples to delineate the things they wanted to show. I ran that risk in cooperating with them. I convinced them I could play one of the roles in their documentary with the intention of using the role to transform, or at least inform, the film. I wasn't going to be a tortured, suffering homosexual for them. I did something which I saw as factual rather than personal. I thought I could use them to give a dispassionate, factual account aimed at demystifying some of the more misunderstood aspects of gay male sexuality.

"I treated some things with more levity than I should have. Hustling, for instance. What I said was an honest description of what it was like for me. It wasn't particularly painful, but it was more complicated than I wanted to get into with the Kastners. So I treated it lightly, without thinking about what it is like for other people, without realizing I was trivializing it."

Lesbian comic Robin Tyler called *TBP* from Los Angeles after she'd heard that the show had been broadcast. She hadn't seen it, but she was angry.

"I let those guys film my act, but I said I wouldn't sign a release until I could see how it was going to be used. On June 6, I received a 'performer contract' from the CBC, dated March 1980, for four hundred dollars. They were trying to buy me off. I contacted them and said 'There's nothing in here about my right to see the thing.' They said, 'There never is.' I said, 'Well then, you can't use anything from my act.' They said, 'You can't stop us; this is Canada.' "

The only other shot of lesbians in *Sharing the Secret* showed the Salukis, a women's softball team. The sequence was filmed at the time when the programme was still supposed to include women. A couple of members of the team were to be featured; the others were told they would only be in the background. One of the women who was supposed to be a subject of the film didn't appear in the shots at all. Many others did. As the coach explained to me, "There are women on the team who are in the closet, and there are straight women as well. For those of us who happened to be watching the film that night, our appearance in it came as a complete shock."

Sharing the Secret also contains scenes of a Metropolitan Community Church service which had been taken for another CBC programme a couple of years before. MCC's pastor, Brent Hawkes, contacted *Man Alive* only to be told that the Church's permission had not been sought because the people at *Man Alive* were unaware, until receipt of MCC's letter, that their segment had been used.

Brent Hawkes has a particular reason for being upset at the use of MCC in the film. "I talked to Rose Kastner early on in the production of the film. I put her in touch with people who I thought would be helpful. Then I began hearing rumours that there were bad feelings among some of the people who had talked to her. It became so pervasive that I called John Kastner. I told him I would feel a lot better about trying to put people at ease about the film if I could see it myself. He was reluctant at first, but he called me back and said he could make arrangements if I promised not to tell anyone what I saw. So I pledged confidentiality.

"I took three full pages of notes of things that I saw that upset me. I was so angry I almost walked out a couple of times. When Kastner came back in at the end I told him how angry I was and he was amazed at my reaction. He said that everyone who had seen it—gay or straight—had really liked it and that my reaction was way off base. I gave him my notes saying, 'Take this temptation out of my hands,' and left.

"Confidentiality is very important to me. I wrestled with it for a long time. Finally I called Nancy Wilson, my elder in Los Angeles. She agreed that confidentiality was important, but said that if I thought a trust with the gay community had been broken, I should do something about it. I called Kastner and told him why I didn't feel obliged to keep the pledge.

"In trying to talk me out of it he kept contradicting himself. Then he said, 'Brent, we have things on film about you that could prove very embarrassing. If you continue to protest, I can't guarantee that those things won't get into the film.' I told him I wouldn't be pressured that way. He said, 'We also have things on gay business that could prove really scandalous.'

"Finally I said, 'If you're correct and my reactions really are off base, I want to know that. I'll select a small committee, made up of men and women, political people and non-political people, to see the film and I won't prejudice them in advance. If enough of them say it's all right, I'll shut up about it.' He agreed. He told me that the documentary wouldn't be broadcast until late spring and that he'd get back to me by early January to set up another preview. The next thing I heard was that the film was going on the air on January 11."

I can understand how the subjects of *Sharing the Secret* went along with Rose and John Kastner. Early in her work on the film, Rose Kastner called me, gave me a brief description of what she and John wanted to do and asked if we could meet. We went for lunch.

I handed her a long letter in which I'd outlined some of my initial concerns based on that first brief telephone conversation. She had, for example, promised to avoid "all the stereotypes, the obvious ones."

To which the letter said, "There is no doubt that your average man is uptight about the mincing queens he thinks all gay men are. The way to deal with that is not to overlook anyone who might give some credence to the image (and thus contribute to their oppression — to the perception of them as invalid, an embarrassment, as less than human) in favour of those who are more a reflection of yourselves, your world, your values. The real challenge is to show the person who is obviously and often proudly gay as a survivor in a hostile world."

I was full of that kind of advice for Rose and John. I told them how it felt to be reduced to the status of a case history or to be subjected to the roving eye of the voyeur, how insulting it was for lesbians to be relegated to invisibility. And I know I am not the only one to have shared ideas, information, and names and numbers from my phone book with these people only to be disappointed.

Sharing the Secret was shown to the press in advance—all the press, that is, except the gay press. I asked John Kastner if the exclusion of *The Body Politic* was an oversight. "It was a conscious decision. We thought you were already prejudiced against the film because you told people not to cooperate with us. We didn't want you stirring things up in advance."

John Kastner has been patiently sending *The Body Politic* clippings of favourable reviews with cute little covering notes. They say things like:

• "Richard Labonté, a *Body Politic* contributor, has praised the film in the *Ottawa Citizen* as the best film ever made about gays (see enclosed clipping)."
• "Linda Difalco of the *Ottawa Citizen* called me about a follow-up piece she is writing, and said that Ottawa-area lesbians are demanding to know when we're going to do a similar type of show on lesbians. This positive reaction is the sort of thing we have been hearing from many gays, especially from those outside of Toronto, whose reaction, I fear may be influenced by some highly political activities from within the gay community."
• "Any film which (Toronto *Sun* columnist) Claire Hoy sneers at as a ninety-minute commercial for homosexuals can't be all bad!"
• "There has been a deliberate campaign on the part of some people in the gay community, for reasons of their own, to discredit the film, including what was supposed to be a highly secret, well-orchestrated phone campaign to the CBC. I am also aware why these individuals are doing this—that it is extremely important to their personal interests to do so."

People did phone in their protests to the CBC. The idea was suggested at a public meeting where a group of community activists watched the broadcast of *Sharing the Secret*. It was one of the few ways people had to make their feelings known, it was hardly a secret campaign, and it was probably no better orchestrated than such things usually are.

In a letter to Tracy Angles and Steve Tattle, Kastner claimed, "We have just learned that there is a petition supporting the film, with two thousand signatures, from within the gay community on its way to us. Furthermore, at a gay community event this summer we are to be presented with a trophy for service to the gay community."

Said Tracy, "I haven't heard anything about a petition and I can't imagine anyone in the gay community giving them a trophy for anything." Neither can I. As far as I can determine, no such petition has materialized.

The Kastners traded people off against each other in the film (Tracy and Steven *vs* "the Murdochs") and pitted people against each other during its production as well—Peter against June and Steven because he didn't like the way they laundered the gay experience of its sexuality; June and Steven against Peter because they didn't like the way he left gay sexuality open to sensationalism. They also succeeded in using the people in the film against the rest of us by exempting themselves from responsibility for the content of *Sharing the Secret*. The six men in it, they warned us, were "telling their own stories." Anyone who got upset at what that content seemed to be saying about gay people, all meaningless disclaimers aside, was left resenting those six gay individuals (the creeps, the freaks, the mentally ill) rather than the Kastners.

Much of this exploitation of division is designed to deflect criticism. John Kastner calls his critics, in a letter to Peter Shaffter, "the sour grapes set," meaning that they are jealous because they weren't selected to be immortalized in *Sharing the Secret*. Criticism from gay activists is made to seem especially untrustworthy. The vocal militants, as Kastner calls them, are disqualified from talking about gay people because, to hear him tell it, "they are the most untypical gays. An open, out-front gay person, who lives in a ghetto surrounded by gay people, gets relatively few bruisings by the straight world. We wanted to look at the other eighty or ninety percent who are still in the closet and are therefore suffering gays. The majority of gays lead secretive, troubled, fearful lives—that's the gay mainstream, the gay silent majority. If we had produced a portrait of gay people as well-adjusted, problem-free people it would have been a phoney-baloney portrait. But not only would it have been false, it would have been useless. You're not going to win any friends among straight people by saying you're proud and happy to be who you are."

The fact that five hundred people came forward as potential participants in a documentary for national television goes some way to answering John Kastner's question about the impact of gay liberation on the lives of gay people. I don't think Kastner was forced to reject most of those people because they were afraid to come out of the closet. I suspect many of them were simply familiar enough with the ways of big media to recognize a disaster heading their way. The Kastners seem to have gone through five hundred people by eliminating anyone who was (a) an activist, (b) a queen, or (c) some other "obvious type,"—and by alienating a good number of (d) all of the above.

Rose Kastner brags that she "has an unusual ability to relate to people. I know that as a researcher for a subject I can get anyone."

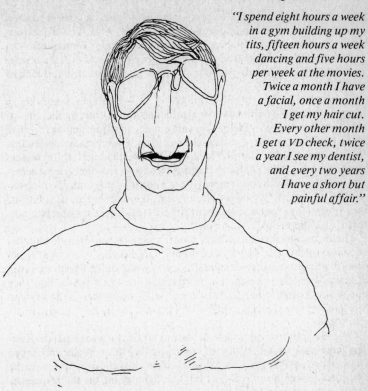

*"I spend eight hours a week
in a gym building up my
tits, fifteen hours a week
dancing and five hours
per week at the movies.
Twice a month I have
a facial, once a month
I get my hair cut.
Every other month
I get a VD check, twice
a year I see my dentist,
and every two years
I have a short but
painful affair."*

Gary Ostrom, Issue 48, November 1978

Rose's sensitivity to gay people has been well-documented by the straight press in what promise to become some of the most quotable quotes of the decade. "Whatever the subject is, I want the viewer to think, 'There but for the grace of God go I,' whether it's a film on cancer or on gay people." Rose began her research by screening *Boys in the Band*, and said about gay people afterwards, "It's the first time I could ever relate to them." Her research has apparently proven to her that lesbians, unlike their male counterparts, tend to like older partners. Indeed, during the preparation of the documentary, she told the *Edmonton Journal*, "girls young enough to be my daughters came on to me. I'd roll my eyes to the ceiling and say, 'God, what am I doing for the CBC!'" Best of all: "I've probably got everything that's been written about homosexuals in the last ten years. It really sounds presumptuous, I know, but I really think I know more about gays now than any gay."

John, who's truly his mother's son, says that as a media person he has always counted gay people among his friends. Odd, then, that he should also say of himself when he began to research *Sharing the Secret*, "I was afraid I was going to be molested or jumped on or something. I was also amazed at how few gay men are mincing, lisping, limp-wristed people." And: "We're not interested in subjects like cannibalism or pedophilia." And: "We wanted to get people who would be honest about the pain, people who could tell the average person about the inevitable agonies you must go through with this kind of thing."

The Kastners' refusal to talk to "militants" or "stereotypes"—and the gay community's well-developed survival mechanism of distrust for the untrustable—were not the only factors screening out people from among their five hundred prospects. There was also the fact that they were really auditioning. Rocco Fermi said there were different perspectives that each subject was expected to cover. Peter Shaffter's description of roles is probably most accurate. Roles like: wealthy but maimed (André Fortin); lonely and youth-obsessed (Rocco Fermi); the odd couple nurturing their cats instead of kids while their parents long for grandchildren (Steven and Lee); the sex-obsessed, tortured artist (Peter Shaver).

The distortions inherent in this approach are more than just little white lies or convenient twists of fact for the sake of emphasis. They are a part of something that calls itself a documentary. The very word sounds like it's engraved in stone. People hear it and think lofty things like Truth and Reality. They don't stop to consider the changed names, the disguised faces, the liberty with fact and the myriad preconceptions of a straight filmmaker on a visit to the gay world.

Given such an approach, it should be no surprise to anyone that the Kastners have come up with a view of homosexuality substantially unchanged from the period which they say piqued their curiosity about gay people in the first place. Except for the slightly brighter lighting and the slightly greater candour about things sexual, this film could easily have been made ten years ago.

All the distortions are, in turn, combined with dubious dramatization to achieve the final effect. André Fortin escapes from his world of adolescent self-hatred into his beautiful universe of three thousand classical records; sitting in shadow, headphones on, music building in a shivering crescendo. Alice Murdoch weeps her way through a prolonged and embarrassing reconstruction of her reaction to her son's coming out, complete with bizarre and unflattering camera angles. Tragic music wafts in periodically, just in time to remind us to be sad. Peter Shaver takes us on a walking tour of David Balfour Park, where the most innocent of shadows take on all the qualities of a nightmare. The hidden depths of a gay steambath are probed by a camera that sees no faces, only dim, empty hallways, a camera that peers suspiciously into darkened rooms and then zips away at a crazy angle as if embarrassed at having caught some dirty business. Accompanied not by the baths' usual disco-muzak but by the eerie sound of footsteps, these shots subvert Peter's attempt to demystify gay sex, snatching his experience from him and redefining it as something creepy, cold, frightening. For those occasions when Peter, or alter-ego Rocco, take us into the bars, the camera is ever ready to slip into slow motion and the sound track into weird electronic noise, just so no one will miss the point that it's time to be grossed out.

The Kastners' camera does not just passively record and reflect; it selects, frames and shapes. They are formula filmmakers specializing in "sensitive" issues, complete with close-up invasions of private pain. When they don't find exactly what they want or expect, they're not above using a little creativity to achieve the desired effect.

There's a fine line between a historical record of anguish and a sensational exploitation of it. The Kastners' documentaries derive their appeal from treading that line. And crossing it fairly often. They cross it every time they censor a little bit of reality that is inconsistent with their long-sought saga of misery. When they wrench individuals out of their context and isolate them on the tube—when they extract the gay person from the gay community, for instance. When they take someone's story, like Pierre's, to the point of coming out—but not beyond to the joy of self-knowledge at last, to the strength of struggling and surviving, to the affirmation of community: of our friends and lovers, ourselves and each other.

There is something inherently dangerous in these apparently safe and liberal dramas or docudramas masquerading as documentary fact. Certainly they present people with the opportunity to experience something painful or problematic or controversial. But always from a distance. From over there in the corner of a room, in that safe little box, nicely and neatly packaged for them so they don't have to do their own thinking.

*

The day after I'd finished the second draft of this article, John Kastner called me to ask if I'd filed the story yet. I hadn't quite. He said he had one or two thoughts he wanted to add.

"I'll have to say this carefully because I am, in a certain sense, representing the CBC," he began. He went on to reassure me that he and his mother had the best interests of gay people at heart, but then said that "when you spend as much time in the gay community as we did, all kinds of things come your way. The temptation was there. We could have done some really shitty things."

He was proud of having resisted that temptation. This from a man who had told a reporter from the *Globe and Mail*'s *Broadcast Week* magazine, "The gay community is such an armoured one. You come in saying you're going to do a film on homosexuality, and understandably people are afraid you're going to do another *Cruising*."

John Kastner did, however, say one thing that *was* reassuring. He and Rose hadn't anticipated the negative reaction they got from so many gay people— not, he hastened to explain, that it was a majority reaction, but that it had been so intense.

"You know that film on lesbians that we're working on? Well, there's no question. If we get the same kind of enormous hassling, we'll drop it right away."

I suspect he thought he was threatening me.

Bad Exposure:
a review of *The Gay Picturebook*
Gordon Montador

Issue 49, December 1978/January 1979

What importance has the photograph in the development and expression of gay culture? It's certainly crucial to heterosexual life, tying the nuclear family together on Christmas cards, documenting the growth of children, and furnishing the real proof of matrimony. For most of its history, for most homosexuals, the camera has been feared even in not explicitly homosexual situations. Exposure wasn't sure to stop with the shutter. Pictures were evidence that could only be used against you.

Photographers took from painting the genre of "the nude," and developed an industry around it. From the classic studies of Thomas Eakins, Edward Muybridge and Baron von Gloeden to the heavy pectorals in contemporary magazines like *Blueboy*, photographs of naked men have supplied male homosexuals, in largely anti-gay and anti-sexual societies, with the stuff of their erotic imaginations. These pictures not only help masturbation, they act as talismans: promises, however insincere, of attainable youth and beauty.

Historically, "gay" photographs seem to come from two sources: from straight photographers' forays into the city of night, and from the lives of famous homosexuals. The latter crop up increasingly in biographies of writers and artists, and while usually no more than group shots of people on lawns, or studio portraits of loving couples careful to regard the camera rather than each other, much is suggested to those who understand the importance of appearance in our culture.

Most photographic treatments of modern urban society have included pictures of the bits of gay culture available to the camera. Some of these images, retrieved from their dismal company of "decadent" night-life studies, have extraordinary power. The famous Brassai photograph of two lesbians dancing in a Paris nightclub, their calm round faces confronting the camera, their stance utterly assured, has become an indispensable part of our history. Portraits like these are evidence not merely of homosexual desire, but of the cultural complexity such desires can create. But for the most part, pictures of transvestites and the denizens of dark bars were true only to the heterosexual imagination. What the camera seems to record is in fact an interpretation.

In her constantly illuminating collection of essays *On Photography*, Susan Sontag notes the attraction of photography to the Surrealists, who found in the camera many new ways to document "unofficial reality." Sontag claims that the photograph is necessarily surreal, "in its irrefutable pathos as a message from time past, and the concreteness of its intimations about social class." One of the great subjects of American photography has always been How The Other Half Lives (the title of an 1890 collection of Jacob Riis' photos of the New York slums), alternate realities laid bare for the shock and titillation of the bourgeoisie. Of course, "the other half" isn't restricted to the poor, it includes the sexually disaffected as well. People unable to cope with societal demands for conformist behaviour, who "choose" to make the sex act their livelihood, who manage to live their fantasies, have been the subjects of almost as many photographs as the deserving poor.

Until recently, gays who were the camera's subjects tended also to be its victims. For many, this situation has radically changed, and a strong aggressive image (not to be confused with masculinist swagger) has been developed that confronts the aggression of the camera head-on. The culture becomes more complex as more of the threads of gay sensibility emerge from the blanket assumptions of heterosexuality.

Arthur Bell has wondered whether we wouldn't be better off if our skins were lavender, but in black and white photos lavender would probably just look beige. The real test of a "gay picturebook" would not lie in its ability to document once again the superficial surrealities of "gay life." Times have changed, and many more gay lives are available to the camera now.

The Gay Picturebook, edited and largely photographed by Michael Emory, designed by Carl Barile, with an introduction by Dennis Sanders, contains twenty pictures of lesbians; fifteen pictures of drag queens; thirteen pictures containing political statements (all taken at gay pride marches); nineteen pictures relating to sado-masochism (not including three two-page spreads of models trying on various leather "gear"); thirty-six pictures of sex-film stars, theatres, and Colt models; thirty pictures on Fire Island; nine pictures of "Entertainers Popular With Gay Audiences" (the only people identified in the whole book); one picture of a man giving himself an enema, one of someone dressed in a space-age rubber suit (for water sports?); one of a penis very tightly bound in thin leather straps, and two huge blow-ups (each fills a page) of crab lice. Most of the rest of the photographs are of anonymous gay men. In five pictures only, out of at least a few hundred, are two men shown in any sort of embrace.

The best feature of the book is its design, which calls to mind Sontag's warning that artful collections often create historical lies. Barile has given a kind of "new-wave" graphic style to the book, through his use of photo-endpapers of graffiti that boldly claims PUNK QUEER LIVE, in his concentrated, asymmetrical and angled layouts (most pages have from two to five photographs), and by leaving the furry black lines at the edges of many of the prints uncropped. The slick surface of the page and the right angles of the book give these rough edges a very contemporary sophistication, and make the photographs themselves very accessible.

But the quality of most of the photographs, especially those taken by the editor, is incredibly low. Badly focused and poorly exposed, shot for the most part without imagination or flair, they've been arranged in little groups according to content, with no apparent regard for the way one image might gain strength or truth from the images around it. Several of the photographs are at least five years old, recognizable from old movement publications.

As Sontag remarks, a photograph can be either art or evidence, and not many are both. The photographs in *The Gay Picturebook* approach no subtleties of texture, lighting, composition or movement; they are static, posed, unnatural, dull. They are evidence only.

Evidence of what? According to the introduction by Dennis Sanders, the photographs are evidence of "a lot of very different people being different together." Not only is the statement meaningless, it's a lie. Most of the people in this book are exactly the same. Sanders' introduction consists of one incredible simplification after another ("gay life is very *in*, very *chic*, very Seventies —what blacks were to the Sixties, Jews to the Fifties, GIs to the Forties"). The only thing to learn from this shallow and stupid essay is that for the purposes of this book, "gay" is an adjective that relates *solely* to style, and that this style finds its apotheosis in the phenomenon of the "gay bar." Of course, the result is a book no more adventurous, no more perceptive, than the pictures of drag queens taken by the heterosexual mobs behind Toronto's St Charles Tavern on Halloween.

Finding pictures that would document homosexual oppression wouldn't be all that easy. Queer-bashers don't hang around for photographers, a lesbian mother trapped in a heterosexual marriage looks to the camera like any other housewife, John Damien leaving the racetrack would just look like a man leaving the racetrack. Pictures alone don't tell stories very well. And Sontag points out that photography and the rest of the contemporary arts have "lowered the threshold of what is terrible" to contemporary eyes. Photographs intended as social comment are easily neutralized by the distance between the picture and its jaded audience. This complaint concerning the paradox of the *effect* of photography reverberates throughout *On Photography*: that while "there is no way to suppress the tendency inherent in all photographs to accord value to their subjects," a parallel tendency can frame and isolate the subject of a photograph, limiting the force of the image to the size of the print. Undue attention to subjects of little importance can in certain contexts utterly distort the truth, and this is the greatest effect of *The Gay Picturebook*.

But photographs documenting the fight against oppression would be easy to find, easy to take; in fact many of the pictures of unidentified gay men in *The Gay Picturebook* are of movement activists, from New York, Toronto, Miami, and likely half-a-dozen other centres where the faces are less familiar. Emory and Sanders dismiss the political struggle while taking advantage of the freedoms achieved by it. "Gay" doesn't simply apply to disco and the Marlboro Man. The word was popularized by the gay liberation movement, it applies to every field of human endeavour in which homosexuals have played a part, and it involves a special understanding of every social circumstance.

If not all of this is readily accessible to the camera, then perhaps some hard thinking about what photographs could reveal is in order. There's no evidence of thought in *The Gay Picturebook*, no captions either, to give the images some weight. It's a lazy production, a marketing trick, a waste of paper. For Sontag, photography is suspect because it keeps us from making necessary judgments, from drawing "distinctions between the beautiful and the ugly, the true and the false, the useful and the useless, good taste and bad." Photographed, everything becomes "interesting." And faced with the literally infinite number of photographs and their reproductions, the lines between what is real and what is an image become blurred.

Sontag's "conservationist remedy," limiting the role and extent of photography to gain a better perspective on both image and reality, is wishful thinking. Gay people like Emory and Sanders will continue to exploit their superficial understanding of gay society and culture as long as there's money in it, and images acceptable to profiteering publishers will continue to cloud our knowledge of what is real.

Letters
Jane Rule

Issue 56, September 1979

I save the letters written to me about my work. From the time my first novel, *Desert of the Heart*, came out in 1964, there have been many more than I expected, thanking, asking for help, challenging, telling their own stories.

A writer for some people is like the stranger on a plane, someone to confide in, with a real, if only half-consciously recognized difference: the stranger is chosen as someone unlikely to betray secrets; the writer, on the other hand, is a teller of tales. Though some of my correspondents have offered their life stories as material of books I ought to write, I have never used material from any of the letters. Yet I feel my heart far better informed for them, the range of my understanding greater. And they, as much if not more than reviews, describe the climate in which my books have been written.

Archivists have argued that the letters, for their sociological and psychological value, should be among the papers preserved for the future. When that suggestion was first made, I protested that people who write to me don't imagine that their sometimes very personal revelations will end up in the public archives. Though I didn't write books for the purpose of soliciting people's confidences, once I received them I felt I had a trust, protecting the real people who wrote those letters from exposure and abuse. To that objection, a fifty-year seal was suggested. In, let us say, the year 2030, there would be no one left with any personal stake in letters, and their social value could be fairly assessed. Though legally the dead can't be libelled, I feel no freer to abuse their memory. Yet, I wondered, isn't one of the motives in writing to become part of the testimony of what it has been like to be alive? To destroy the letters might be a greater offence than to save them.

I talked with a number of people who argued on both sides. For some, privacy is absolute. To expose it no matter how far into the future is a betrayal. I have friends whose letters, at their request, I routinely destroy once I've answered them. Others, however, feel just as strongly that our personal lives belong to history, and to destroy evidence is to participate in the lie that reduces the truth to a guilty secret.

One afternoon when an archivist was visiting and helping me to sort out various other problems about preserving papers, I told her that I hadn't been able yet to make a decision about the letters. She was still arguing strongly for their inclusion in the archives.

"Would you mind if I looked at some of them?" she asked.

Though for some clear-eyed moralists this request in itself would be a violation of privacy, I felt no hesitation, respecting as I do this woman's discretion. I thought if she could see the range of the material, she might understand better both my hesitation and my concern. I handed her the file of letters written after *Lesbian Images* came out, then offered her a cup of tea or a drink, which she refused. I went off upstairs to get myself something and also to start dinner. By the time I got back down to my study, she was sitting with the file in her lap, staring at the fire.

"Could I change my mind about that drink?"

"Of course," I said and went to get her one.

When I got back, she asked for a cigarette as well. She doesn't ordinarily smoke.

After some moments of silence, she said, "These should be burned, all of them, right now."

"You begin to see the problems they pose for me?"

"One of them," she said, "is from a good friend of mine."

I stood, watching her trying to recover from the shock of it, having so inadvertently exposed her friend. Hadn't the writers of those letters been real people to her before that, rather than cranks and kooks about whom I was being over-fastidious?

At that moment, I made my own decision. Though I don't intend to dispose of my papers for some time, having uses for them myself, when the time comes those letters will be among my archives. For only when people can read the power and diversity of response to persecution will they begin to learn that the people in pain are, in fact, their good friends. The solution is not to throw their testimony into the fire but to face it.

To read those letters is not only to recognize suffering but to encounter remarkable courage. No hate mail I've ever received has been signed. Apparently self-righteousness needs anonymity. But from those who had real reason to protect themselves, the letters have invariably been signed. They have been a support for me without which it would sometimes have been nearly impossible to go on writing.

Preserving pain and courage and love betrays nothing but the world's hypocrisy. Our only real defence has always been the truth.

Dreams deferred: the early American homophile movement
John D'Emilio

Issue 48, November 1978; Issue 50, February 1979

"Dreams deferred do explode"— Langston Hughes

On a Saturday afternoon early in November 1950, five men met at the home of Harry Hay in the Silver Lake district of Los Angeles, California. They were discussing for the first time a proposal Hay had written which had as its focus "the heroic objective of liberating one of our largest minorities and guaranteeing them self-respecting citizenship." After several hours of animated and exhilarating conversation, the others left Hay with the promise to meet again in a few days. All of them were pledged to secrecy.

The need for secrecy flowed from two very different sources. All of the men were homosexuals, and they were discussing the liberation of the gay minority in the United States. In mid-twentieth century America, homosexuals were well advised to keep their sexual preferences secret. Discovery virtually guaranteed that a man or woman would be ostracized by family and friends, denied most means of earning a living, and consigned to a marginal existence.

But the five men who met that November afternoon had another, just as pressing, reason for exercising caution. Two of them were members of the Communist Party, a third had been an active party member in the Midwest after World War II, and the other two might well have been described as fellow-travellers. It was difficult enough to be gay in postwar America; to be a communist or communist sympathizer compounded the danger.

Despite the odds against it, however, a homosexual emancipation movement did take root in the America of the Fifties. Several months after their first meeting, the five leftist homosexuals founded the Mattachine Society. The name "Mattachine" was chosen after Hay told the others of the mysterious wandering figures by that name who during the Middle Ages performed at festivals wearing masks, and who Hay suspected might have been homosexuals. The founding of the Mattachine Society in Los Angeles in 1951 marked the radical beginning of a continuous history of gay political organization in the United States.

In a three-part series first published in The Body Politic, John D'Emilio examined the little-known early days of the Mattachine Society. In the following excerpt from "Part one: radical beginnings" (Issue 48, November 1978), D'Emilio takes a look at the movement's founders who—fueled by their radical political beliefs and Marxist worldview—ignored the risks of McCarthy's America to make their vision a reality. The excerpt concludes with the Postscript from "Part three: reaction, red-baiting and respectability" (Issue 50,

February 1979), in which D'Emilio analyzed how the Society's radical begin-
nings were betrayed by later events and why the history of this recent past has
been so thoroughly suppressed.

Henry Hay was the man most responsible for the founding of the Society.
Born of American parents in England in 1912, he spent his early childhood in
Chile, where his father was a mining engineer for Anaconda Copper. The
family returned to the United States in 1917, and Hay spent the rest of his
childhood and adolescence in southern California. After graduating from
Los Angeles High School in 1929, he entered Stanford University in the fall of
1930. At Stanford, Hay developed an interest in drama, and returned to Los
Angeles without completing his studies in order to pursue an acting career. In
the depression-ridden years of the early 1930s, Hay found it difficult to secure
steady work as an actor, and when a friend asked him to join a group of agitprop (agitation/propaganda) players, he accepted the invitation.

Hay's participation in the agitprop company awakened in him a political
consciousness. The street performances at the sites of strikes and other demonstrations were "dangerous stuff," he said. "The Red Squad was always
busting things up." He remembered the players narrowly escaping arrest on
several occasions. Soon after joining the agitprop company, Hay was taken
to a Communist Party study group by some of his actor friends. Though he
understood little of the theory being discussed, he admired the seriousness of
the party members whom he met and enjoyed the theatre which he discovered
the party was sponsoring. Early in 1934, Hay joined the Communist Party.

Hay might well have been one of the many party recruits who joined hastily
and as quickly fell away, except for his experiences during the summer of
1934. A strike by West Coast longshoremen in May had escalated in San Francisco into a stoppage of all the maritime workers, and the Communist Party
sent Hay and many other Los Angeles members to aid in the strike effort.
Early in July violence erupted as employers tried to open the port with scab
labour. When the Governor called out the National Guard, labour leaders
appealed for a general strike. In the heady days which ensued, Hay's commitment to the party was born.

"The strike was just something tremendous!" Hay remembers with excite-
ment. "That did it! It was pure emotion, a gut thing. You couldn't have been a
part of that and not have your life completely changed."

For the next fifteen years, Hay's life revolved around the Communist
Party. Initially assigned to the artists and writers branch of the party, he continued to do agitprop theatre as well as to participate in many of the party's
mass organizations. Active in the Los Angeles chapter of People's Songs Inc
(PSI), a leftist organization of songwriters and musicians, Hay represented
PSI at the People's Educational Center, a worker education project whose directors ranged from American Federation of Labor (AFL) representatives to
Communist Party members. Early in 1948, Hay began teaching a class at the
centre on the history of popular music.

Hay's commitment to the party also profoundly affected the shape of his personal life. When he joined in 1934, Hay was an active homosexual. Becoming aware of his sexual attraction to men during his adolescence, he had gradually discovered the male homosexual subculture of Los Angeles and San Francisco and slowly begun the process of accepting his sexuality. Joining the party led Hay to question his choice. The Communists shared society's general condemnation of "sexual deviance" and, in the total world of the party, Hay found it difficult to incorporate his sexual identity. Deciding to suppress his homosexuality, Hay in 1938 married a party member with whom he had worked closely for a long time.

"I determined that I would simply close a book and never look back. For fourteen years I lived in an exile world."

Unable, however, to make a complete break with his homosexual inclinations, Hay occasionally had sexual encounters with men. But he deliberately isolated himself from gay social circles and ostensibly conformed to society's — and the party's — sexual mores.

An unexpected occurrence during the summer of 1948 upset this precarious equilibrium. The Communist Party was concentrating much of its effort that summer on the Henry Wallace presidential bid — a third party effort organized by some liberal Democrats and leftists who opposed the Cold War policies of the Truman administration. Hay was working on the campaign while continuing to do research for his history of music class at the People's Educational Center.

Early in August, Hay attended a party where he was expecting to meet another musicologist. When he arrived he found, to his surprise, that all of the guests were gay. Hay began talking about the Wallace campaign, and before long he and several others were jokingly spinning out the design of an organization to mobilize gay men behind Wallace's Progressive Party. Calling it "Bachelors for Wallace," they imagined the group gathering support among male homosexuals in return for a sexual privacy plank in the Wallace platform.

Although Bachelors for Wallace never moved beyond the stage of idle talk, this chance discussion set in motion in Hay a re-evaluation of his personal life. He now began to perceive that homosexuality might contain the potential for political organizing and, in the months that followed, he mulled over the idea of a gay organization. Hay began to realize that "somehow or another, my life as a heterosexual, a pseudo-heterosexual, was coming to an end. Suddenly I was forced to admit that the relentless difference between me and the world of my choice had grown imperceptibly into an unscaleable barrier."

But the imminent break with his past had its exhilarating side, too. Hay saw that he would be bringing "to my own people, magnificent experience and training in organization and in struggle which I had learned on the other side." He would be using the organizing skills he had acquired in the Communist Party to launch a homosexual emancipation movement.

Sometime during the spring of 1950, Hay elicited his first signs of interest when he spoke to Bob Hull and Chuck Rowland about his idea. Hull was a student in Hay's music class; Rowland was Hull's roommate and closest friend. The three men met one evening at a concert and Hay, who suspected that the pair were gay, decided to broach the subject of a homosexual rights organization. As it turned out, the three men had more in common than their homosexuality, since Rowland and Hull had also been members of the Communist Party.

Rowland was born and raised in a small town in South Dakota. He too grew up feeling isolated by homosexual urges which he could discuss with no one. Going away to college at the University of Minnesota in Minneapolis provided the opportunity for him to come out, to meet other men like himself and begin the process of self-acceptance. Rowland also found himself participating in the campus disturbances of those years, including demonstrations in support of the Loyalists in the Spanish Civil War and against compulsory military training for students.

Hull attended the university in the same years as Rowland, although the two men did not know each other as students. Hull had a graduate degree in chemistry, but had passed by a career in science in favour of pursuing his interest in music. When he met Rowland in 1940, he was just beginning to break into Twin Cities music circles as a pianist. The two men became lovers and, when that relationship ended, moved easily into a close relationship that would last for twenty years.

Rowland served in the army during World War II, and toward the end of the war, while still in the service, he became a charter member of the American Veterans Committee (AVC). The AVC tended to attract New Deal liberals and progressives who were determined, as Rowland described it, "to build a world in our own, idealistic image."

Rowland decided to join the Communist Party, recruiting his friend Hull in the process, and, when he was finally forced out of the veterans' organization for his politics, he returned to Minneapolis to work as executive secretary of the branch office of American Youth for Democracy (AYD), a communist-dominated organization. Late in 1948 Rowland migrated to Los Angeles, at the same time abandoning his active involvement in the party.

Hull followed Rowland to Los Angeles toward the end of 1948. Maintaining his party affiliation, he joined one of its cultural units and participated in the activities of the People's Educational Center where Hay was teaching.

Hull and Rowland were both excited by Hay's suggestions for a homosexual organization, and a few more conversations about it ensued. Their informal discussions ended, however, as abruptly as they had begun. After the conclusion of Hay's music class, the men lost contact with one another and Hay was once again left alone with his plan.

The disappearance of Rowland and Hull, in fact, was due to more than the conclusion of Hay's class, although Hay did not know it at the time. According to Rowland, he, Hull and another Communist Party member left the country in late spring, 1950, and "departed for Mexico where we had decided to spend the rest of our lives." In describing their motives, Rowland said,

"That was not just a wild, romantic spree; we were fleeing the witch hunts along with *thousands* of other Americans from all parts of the country. On several occasions since then I've met previously unknown people who spoke of that crazy summer of 1950 when *everyone* became a refugee in Mexico."

Although Rowland most likely exaggerated the numbers, the incident points to the depth of the fear and panic felt by many communists and their sympathizers at the height of the postwar anti-communist hysteria. By the end of the summer, however, Rowland and Hull had returned to Los Angeles, chastened after several aimless months in Mexico and having decided that their flight was "ridiculous."

Early in July 1950, Hay met R at a rehearsal fo the Lester Horton Dance Theatre. A costume designer and dancer with Horton's company, R had fled with his mother from Austria in 1938 to escape the Nazis' genocidal persecution of Jews. Settling in Los Angeles, he joined Lester Horton's dance group in 1942. He found the company an intensely political milieu, as Horton's dance pieces frequently had social injustice as their theme, and troupe members who did not share these concerns quickly left. At the time of his initial meeting with Hay, R was performing in *The Park*, a dramatization of police brutality toward Mexican-American youths, and *Brown County*, the story of a fugitive slave.

Hay spoke to R about his idea for a political organization to defend the rights of homosexuals. When he expressed interest, Hay resolved to commit his scheme to paper and wrote a lengthy prospectus for the proposed organization. Upon reading it a few days later, R enthusiastically committed himself to the venture. After almost two years of cautious effort, Hay at last had found his first recruit.

Hull, meanwhile, had enrolled in another of Hay's music classes and Hay, who had been somewhat puzzled by the sudden termination of their earlier discussions, decided to show Hull the prospectus he had written in July. Hull and Rowland passed it on to another gay friend, Dale Jennings, a writer active in campaigns to defend the civil rights of Japanese-Americans. Hull arranged a meeting for them with Hay, and on a Saturday afternoon in November 1950, the five men — Hay, R, Hull, Rowland, and Jennings — gathered at Hay's home to discuss the formation of a homosexual rights organization.

Frequent meetings over the next several months led to the formation of the Mattachine Society. As the first organization in what would become a nationwide movement, the early Mattachine Society had several features that reflected the leftist orientation of its founders and that would distinguish it from most of its successor organizations: it had a secret, cell-like, and hierarchical structure; it developed an analysis of homosexuals as an oppressed cultural minority; and, as a corollary of that analysis, the Mattachine Society pursued a strategy for social change that rested on mass action by homosexuals.

The founders' perception of a need for secrecy grew out of the specific political climate in which they lived. By 1950, American communists and their sympathizers were an embattled, increasingly isolated political minority, subject to severe repression. In the five years since World War II, the popular front of the 1930s, in which communists, New Deal liberals, and other radicals frequently worked together, had fragmented. The Truman administration's hard-line foreign policy toward the Soviet Union had spawned a rabid anti-communist crusade in the United States. Although its most extreme expression was found among right-wing Republicans and conservative Democrats, liberals also actively promoted domestic anti-communism.

In 1949, Communist Party leaders were indicted under the Smith Act for supposedly conspiring to overthrow the government by violent means, and in September 1950, Congress passed a tough new Internal Security Act requiring party members and front organizations to register with the Justice Department, and providing for the internment of communists during periods of national emergency. With the Korean war raging in Asia, the threat of internment loomed large. Following the lead of the federal government, many states enacted laws aimed at suppressing the Communist Party.

To the founders of the Mattachine Society, the attacks on radicals were not an abstraction: Rowland had experienced the effects of anti-communism in his work with the American Veterans Committee; Jennings' involvement with Japanese-Americans in California made him appreciate the threat of internment; R had fled his native country to escape a fascist regime bent on exterminating not only leftists but an entire people as well.

Above all, Hay was acutely conscious of the growing climate of repression. With much of his party work centred around cultural activities, he was aware of the targeting of leftists in Hollywood by the House Un-American Activities Committee (HUAC). California, moreover, had its own anti-communist investigating committee whose head, Jack Tenney, came from Los Angeles, and which held highly publicized hearings throughout the postwar years. The two organizations in which Hay was most active, People's Songs and the People's Educational Center, had already come under official scrutiny.

Hay and the others also felt themselves under attack as homosexuals. By 1950, the anti-communist crusade included "moral perverts" among its targets. In February 1950, Under-Secretary of State John Peurifoy testified before a Senate committee that the State Department had uncovered homosexuals among its employees. Over the next several months, the Senate pursued this revelation and ultimately issued a report that recommended the dismissal of homosexuals as security risks from government and defence-related employment. One result of the investigation was that the number of homosexuals dismissed from government service increased tenfold in 1950 over the preceding three years.

The prospectus that Hay had written in July 1950 for a homosexual rights organization, and which served as the starting point for the founders' early discussions, revolved around his awareness of government repression. Taking off from the Communist Party's thinking of the time, which saw the country moving rapidly towards fascism, Hay gave its analysis quite a different twist by placing the plight of the homosexual at the centre of contemporary American politics. After drawing an analogy with Nazi rule in Germany, where homosexuals were "ruthlessly exterminated," he went on to warn against an "encroaching American fascism" which "seeks to bend unorganized and unpopular minorities into isolated fragments." The full significance, he wrote, "of government indictments against Androgynous Civil Servants lies in the legal establishment of a type of *guilt by association*" which the accused cannot disprove. If the government succeeds in isolating and attacking the homosexual minority, it will have a weapon, Hay argued, which "can be employed as a threat against any and every man and woman in our country to ensure thought control and political regimentation." While this danger made it imperative for homosexuals to organize, it also pointed to a need for caution. Hay's prospectus suggested that membership be by careful recommendation only, that all members be sworn to protective secrecy, and that they remain anonymous to the community at large and to each other.

The structure that the five men ultimately devised for the Mattachine Society reflected their own intense fear of repression as well as their recognition of the need to provide security for their homosexual constituents. As its model it drew heavily upon the experience of Hay — and to some extent of Rowland and Hull — in the Communist Party where secrecy, hierarchical structures, and centralized leadership predominated.

They created a pyramid of five "orders" of membership, with increasing levels of responsibility as one ascended the structure, and with each order having one or two representatives from higher orders of the organization.

The founders also brought to their planning meetings a concern for ideology that grew out of their leftist politics. Although communist ideology in the mid-twentieth century largely ignored questions of human sexuality, and certainly did not describe the persecution of homosexuals as something to be fought, the worldview of its adherents rested on an analysis of society that saw injustice as rooted in the social structure. Exploitation and oppression came not from simple prejudice or misinformation, but from deeply embedded structural relationships.

Hay himself was well read in Marxist literature, and the other four, according to Rowland, had at least "some coloration of Marxism" in their thinking. This led them to reject a narrowly pragmatic approach to the problems of the homosexual, one that focused only on a set of reform goals, and instead pushed them to seek a theoretical explanation of the sources of the homosexual's inferior status. The concern with theory as a guide to action—a standard feature of Marxist thought — set them apart from the leaders of the movement who emerged later in the 1950s, and who had no contact either with the Communist Party or with Marxism. These later spokespersons tended to reiterate a single theme: they had neither an analysis of the sources of the oppression of gay women and men, nor any sense of strategy. They expected to change society's treatment of lesbians and homosexuals simply by plugging away at prejudice.

The founders' lack of an already developed analysis of the oppression of homosexuals forced them to generate one by scrutinizing the main source of information available to them — their own lives. Throughout the winter of

1950, the five men met frequently to share their personal histories. They exchanged stories of coming out, of discovering cruising places and bars, of the years of loneliness.

Out of these discussions an analysis gradually emerged of the sources of the oppression of homosexuals. Pointing to the heterosexual nuclear family as the "established vehicle for the outlet of social impulses," the founders of the Mattachine Society argued that it constituted a "socially predetermined pattern" for human relationships. Homosexuals "did not fit the patterns of heterosexual love, marriage and children upon which the dominant culture rests." Excluded from the basic unit of society, the family, they found themselves "an enclave within society... an undesirable and despicable group worthy only of ridicule and rebuke." With no socially approved models for their lifestyle, homosexuals "mechanically superimposed the heterosexual ethic on their own situation in empty imitation of dominant patterns." The result was a daily existence predicated upon "self-deceit, hypocrisy, and charlatanism and a sense of value distorted, inadequate, and undesirable."

Victimized by a "language and culture that does not admit the existence of the Homosexual Minority," and that viewed their sexual behaviour as an individual aberration or personal moral failing, homosexuals remained largely unaware that their efforts to adjust to society constituted "a culture in itself" and that they were in fact "a social minority imprisoned within a dominant culture."

Their definition of homosexuals as a minority group suggested to the founders an initial course of action. Committed to a Marxist worldview that saw progressive social change occurring through the mobilization of masses of people with common interests, they were at first stymied by traditional thinking about homosexuality: if "sexual deviance" was merely a personal problem, on what basis did one organize a mass movement of homosexuals? But if the ideology itself was a primary agent of oppression, then the first task of a homosexual emancipation movement was to challenge the internalization of that ideology by homosexuals, to develop among the gay population a consciousness of itself as an oppressed minority. Out of that consciousness homosexuals could then evolve a "highly ethical homosexual culture and lead well-adjusted, wholesome, and socially productive lives." And, from the cohesiveness that such a process would stimulate, the founders expected to forge, in time, a unified movement of homosexuals ready to fight against their oppression.

*

The hallmark of the Mattachine Society during its first year was the discussion group. In these informal meetings, gay women and men broke down their isolation and slowly developed a sense of common identification growing from their perception of themselves as members of an oppressed minority. Through this process, they came to recognize the need for collective, militant mass action as the means by which they would challenge their inferior status.

In "Part two: public actions, private fears" (Issue 49, December 1978/January 1979), D'Emilio described the group's first opportunity for such action. Early in 1952 one of Mattachine's founders, Dale Jennings, became a victim of police entrapment. The group resolved to fight the charges. Mattachine members rallied support by distributing flyers throughout the Los Angeles area. When Jennings came to trial the jury voted eleven to one for acquittal. The charges were later dropped.

The successful defence led to a period of phenomenal growth for the Mattachine Society. By the spring of 1953, more than a hundred discussion groups had been formed. Members of one Los Angeles group took on the project of publishing a gay magazine and in January 1953 the first issue of ONE was distributed. The Mattachine Foundation was established as an educational organization to reach out to the public at large. One of its first actions was to send candidates for local office a questionnaire about police harassment of homosexuals and the availability of nonprejudicial information on homosexuality in the school system.

A March 1953 column in a local Los Angeles newspaper marked the first step in a long retreat from the radical hopes of the Mattachine's founders. The columnist raised sinister questions about the potential power of organized homosexuals. "A well-trained subversive could move in and forge that power into a dangerous political weapon," he wrote. It was all the evidence that was necessary in the paranoid atmosphere of the McCarthy period to "damn the organization." The Mattachine was soon torn by suspicions, demands for loyalty oaths and calls for an end to the secrecy which its founders had seen as necessary for the protection of Society members.

In "Part three: reaction, red-baiting and respectability" (Issue 50, February 1979), D'Emilio documented a series of organization-wide conventions which took place throughout 1953. The gatherings gave a hitherto-isolated conservative segment of the Mattachine Society membership an opportunity to make contact with each other. This opposition, upset by the accusations of communist subversion and fearful of public political action, quickly gained in power and influence within the organization. By May the founding members had relinquished control and the Society was completely reorganized into a single membership organization.

The new leadership rejected the notion of a homosexual minority and were convinced that the pervasive sanctions against homosexuality in society were the result of misinformation and false ideas. They felt that their best strategy was to rely on professionals and experts to change society rather than to pursue collective action themselves.

In November 1953, a convention of the Mattachine Society adopted a statement which not only dropped reference to a homosexual culture but also avoided all mention of homosexuals. Although the membership rejected the leadership's call for loyalty oaths, the bitter infighting and accusations at these conventions had cost the Society dearly. Over the next year and a half the Mattachine Society declined dramatically in size until only a few dozen *members remained. Along with the drop in membership went a programme which opted for interminable waiting for public enlightenment.*

Under its new officers, the Mattachine Society sought respectability and abandoned the quest for self-respect.

*

In its pursuit of a respectable image for itself and for the homosexual, the new Mattachine offered little to attract its gay constituency. In place of consciousness-raising, challenges to police practices, political action and efforts to achieve penal code reform, the organization sponsored activities — blood drives, the collection of clothes, books and magazines for hospitals, and the like — to demonstrate that homosexuals were solid citizens. The leadership expended its energy denouncing indecent public behaviour and disassociating itself from those who contributed to the "delinquency" of minors. The Society witnessed the sorry spectacle of members investigating and exposing each other's private lives under the guise of preserving the Mattachine's good reputation, as if any homosexual in the 1950s had a reputation to protect.

The outcome of the Mattachine Society's internal struggle was almost inevitable, and cannot be understood in isolation from larger currents in postwar American society and politics. By 1953, the Cold War anti-communist crusade had succeeded in driving leftists from hard-won positions of influence in the labour movement, blacklisting them from the motion picture industry, silencing them in the schools and crippling most of the organizations in which communists played an important role. As a result, not only had communists become an insignificant force in the United States, but for a time the country as a whole appeared to have reached a consensus which left little room for militant movements for social change. Under these conditions, one could hardly expect that a small band of leftists would retain leadership in a movement that by its nature was offensive to most Americans of whatever political persuasion.

The predictability of the outcome, however, should not obscure its disastrous impact upon the Mattachine Society and upon the movement which the Mattachine initiated.

In abandoning the perspectives of Hay, Rowland and the other founders, the organization's new leadership discarded several elements that would prove crucial for a successful gay movement: the recognition that the oppression of homosexuals had structural roots that ran deeper than simple prejudice; the bold rejection of the complex of theories and attitudes that labeled homosexual behaviour as sin, sickness or crime; the espousal of a self-affirming pride in one's gay identity; the determined assertion that gay life could be ethical and dignified, and that a gay culture had something of value to contribute to society as a whole, and the conviction that only mass collective action by homosexuals themselves could initiate significant changes in the status of the gay population.

By contrast, the conservative, essentially accommodationist course pursued by the founders' successors left the Mattachine without a dynamic strategy for achieving its goal of equality for gays, and with little appeal among its natural constituency.

*

Our ignorance of the radical roots of the early gay movement in the United States is a compelling example of our oppression. The failure of those efforts meant, in effect, that twenty years later the system of gay oppression survived intact. The silence and invisibility which until recently surrounded our lives extended to our history, including its most precious parts — the organized attempts not only to survive but to fight back and to use our gayness, as Chuck Rowland once said, "in the interests of humanity."

But it is also important for us to realize that the history of the early Mattachine Society has remained hidden not solely because of external forces. The individuals who took hold of the Mattachine in 1953 systematically buried every trace of its left-wing origins. Accounts of the early history that were printed in the *Mattachine Review* and passed on to newer members later in the 1950s told merely of a semi-secret organization that had grown so rapidly that it outlived its initial structure. The changes of 1953 are painted as the triumph of the democratic strivings of the membership and as a sign of the maturing of the movement.

One cannot help but draw an analogy with the American labour movement of the 1930s, whose enormous achievements owed much to the commitment, daring and sustained efforts of thousands of Communist Party members. Not only were they, too, ruthlessly purged during the Cold War era, but their contributions have also been ignored and denied.

*

When I began my research three years ago into the early history of the gay movement, I had little idea of what I would uncover. I also had little idea of what "gay history" could mean to me personally, a gay socialist of the 1970s.

These explorations into our past have been an intensely emotional journey. Of Harry Hay, whom I visited for several days at his home in rural New Mexico, and of Chuck Rowland, with whom I have had an extensive correspondence, I could say that I fell in love, though that phrase barely touches the depth and variety of feeling that I have for them. I was three years old when they wrote the Mattachine initiation ceremony: "No boy or girl, approaching the maelstrom of deviation, need make that crossing alone, afraid, and in the dark ever again." They were talking about me.

We have a special need for history. Raised as we were in heterosexual families, we grew up and discovered our gayness deprived of gay ancestors, without a sense of our roots. We need to create and carry with us a living awareness of gay generations, to incorporate in our consciousness not only the organized struggle of our predecessors, but the everyday struggle to survive that our ancestors engaged in. We need to affirm and appreciate our past, not in some abstract way, but as it is embodied in living human beings.

Just as a knowledge of our history can strengthen us today, the way we carry on that tradition validates those who came before us.

Maybe Chuck Rowland, in a letter he wrote to me during my research, should have the final word:

"You say, John, that you are grateful and filled with love for me. You won't feel the need to apologize for these feelings when I say: What the hell, man, *you're my son*, blood of my blood, flesh of my flesh, in a deeper, truer sense than any literal blood or flesh could possibly be! You represent our future and our fulfillment. You are the greatest and finest progeny we could ever have aspired to conceive when we met in our little, fear-struck rooms filled with brave words and great dreams back in 1950."

Dangers of the minority game
Ken Popert

Issue 63, May 1980

From the perspective of our society, gay people are new and strange. Our attempts to conceptualize ourselves and our relation to our society have turned on several different analogies: the Third Sex (analogy with women), the Minority Community (analogy with racial and ethnic groups) and the Lifestyle (analogy with a pattern of commodity consumption).

The notion of gay people as a Minority Community is pre-eminent at the moment. The reasons for its popularity, among liberals and gay activists alike, are not obscure.

First, superficial observation lends plausibility. Gays, whenever we become numerous enough in any one place, tend to ghetto behaviour, like Toronto's Chinese or Greeks or Italians. We develop our own small-business structure, along with typical community institutions: rights groups, churches, newspapers, charitable organizations.

Second, since civil and human rights are mainly an interest of minority communities, such a vision of gay men and women fits together nicely with our struggle for those rights.

Third, the minority community picture of gays directs attention away from those aspects of gay life which straights find so offensive and alien: things like washroom sex, steambaths, one-night stands.

Because it is an analogy, this minority community view of ourselves is only partial. And it is partial in a rather damaging way, for, in failing to accommodate those features of gay life which constitute its historical meaning, it pushes them to the margins of our consciousness.

The vision of gays as a minority community rests, in part, on the Kinsey finding of an exclusively homosexual population amounting to a few percentage points out of the total. It is this percentage which anchors the social category of gays. But just as significant was Kinsey's discovery that half of the supposed heterosexual majority is tinged with degrees of homoeroticism.

Under the social fiction of a homosexual minority and heterosexual majority lies a more complex reality. If we view ourselves simply as a minority group, we run the risk of dead-ending ourselves into a political strategy which neglects the large number of so-called heterosexuals who have a personal stake in gay liberation.

An ethnic minority group relies on reproduction to perpetuate itself: as long as its members continue to have children by each other, it will continue to be part of society. If they do not, it may disappear. That can and does happen.

In the Germanies, there are now few Jews, but almost as many gays as ever, although Third Reich policy was to exterminate both groups.

Gays do not reproduce or replace themselves; we rely on heterosexuals to do that for us. This is possible precisely because we are not like an ethnic group, detached from the rest of society and perpetuating ourselves alongside it. On the contrary, we are an integral and organic part of our society. Cut us out, as Hitler did, and we grow right back.

Gays exist because straights exist. In the act of isolating and exalting heterosexuality — thereby dividing human sexuality — our society also isolates homosexuality and ushers gay people into existence.

Ethnic minorities are accidents of history; gay people are part of the working out of history.

Although we do not reproduce, we do undergo a kind of birth as gays: we say that we come out. Coming out, in its several different senses, is the essential gay experience. But how many Ukrainians are born at the age of eighteen or twenty? As we increasingly look at ourselves as a minority group, coming out loses its centrality. The gays-as-minority approach, when combined with fears raised by the "recruitment" theme of our opponents, can smack of a cop-out. It becomes easy to divorce ourselves from those — mostly young people—struggling to come out, to take the personally safe but socially irresponsible position that they must fend for themselves.

Finally, the minority community is essentially a family affair. In the work world, people must be identical, interchangeable parts. Ethnicity can be indulged only in private, in the theatre of the family, the core of ethnic life.

Gay life cannot be construed in this way; there are no gay families. To the extent that we have a community, it rests, not on families, but on our desire for each other. It is our inclusionary love-making ("promiscuity") which is the glue of our collectivity.

Looking at ourselves as a minority community has definite survival value. But it is a precarious shelter which can be demolished at any time, for it is easy to show that gays are not just another tile in the multicultural mosaic.

And the analogy can blind us to our own realities. But it cannot cancel them out.

The historical forces which find their expression in us cannot be denied. However much we struggle to fit into the world as it is, we must fail, for we do not fit. But in our struggle we will reshape the world, so that *it* will fit *us*.

The day the homos disappeared:
a cautionary tale
Robin Hardy

Issue 68, November 1980

The day the homos disappeared, Nora Lindquist had planned a dinner party. First, the bakery didn't have any spinach quiche. Nor could she get any of that delicious key lime pie she'd hoped to impress everyone with, and the cheese soufflé she attempted fell in like a punctured basketball the moment she took it from the oven. In desperation, she phoned out for Chinese food—at least it was from one of the best restaurants in town.

Her guests arrived late, and two didn't show at all. Nora wasn't surprised that her husband Bill Lindquist absented himself. In fact, she was quite happy; they didn't like each other very much, really. If it wasn't for the corporation's disapproval of divorce, he would have walked out long ago, taking Nora's lifestyle with him.

But no Wayne Simon! That made Nora furious. It was important to have one gay man at her dinner parties. It was as important as the right arrangement of flowers in the centrepiece. It was, well, fashionable. She never asked lesbians though. They made her uncomfortable. And lovers made being gay seem too serious somehow — more than one gay person and they started flaunting it. Wayne Simon had been perfect. He was single, he was a famous fashion designer — but he wasn't here! The homos must have been planning this for weeks; why couldn't they have waited for some other day, or at least warned her in advance? It was quite rude, Nora bristled, putting every homo who had ever lived firmly in place once and for all.

And now Emily Tilchrist, who sat across from Nora at the Roche-Bobois dining table, wouldn't shut up about it.

"It was just dreadful today, dear," Emily crooned, tucking a forkful of Ming-yung-poo tastefully into her mouth. "Mmm, this is delicious. Did you get it from the corner take-out on Parliament Street?" Emily raised her eyes coquettishly and continued before Nora could answer. "It was simply dreadful. First, I couldn't get my hair done. Alain had disappeared. Vanished into thin air. In fact, his entire salon was closed. Then I met Adrienne for lunch at Crispin's and we had to wait an hour to be served—they only had one waiter left. When we finally did get the food—they cook artichokes so nicely there, you know, so much better than at L'Ombrellino — it was lukewarm. And *soggy*."

Nora thrust aside visions of grinding raw artichokes into Emily's facelift. "Yes, well, I was talking to John today about the homos disappearing. John *Sewell*." She dropped the last name less than casually. The mayor was someone worth knowing, and she always invited Someone Worth Knowing to her dinner parties. John had declined this time around, though. At her last party he had joked about joining the Tory party and found it reported the next day on the front page of the *Toronto Star*, thanks to that frozen tuna fish in the baggy grey flannel who had sat too attentively beside him all night. It would take Nora months of careful manipulation to get the mayor back to her table.

"John is just frantic. He told me—quite confidentially, of course—that no one seems to know where they've gone or why they took all those other people with them."

"All the other people?" exclaimed Emily, her curiosity overcoming her jealousy.

"Why yes," said Nora, victoriously sipping Chateau Yquem from her Boda wineglass. "It's not just the homos, you know. Ten percent of the population has disappeared."

"Darling," said Emily, her voice venomously chilled for the kill, "they're all homos. Ten percent of the population. The closeted ones are gone, too. "By the way," she added with a smile, "Where's Bill tonight?"

*

John Sewell gazed through the plate glass wall of his city hall office, out across the square to the serene plumes of water gushing in the fountain. The hanging plants, he noted, blocked too much of the view. He hated plants. Occasionally he had visions of the Swedish ivy spreading before his eyes, doubling in size, doubling again, shutting off the entire window and then reaching out across the floor, closing off the door, circling the legs of his chair, curling around his knees....

The pastel jungle print fabric on the wingback chairs across from his desk encouraged the nightmare. He hated those chairs, too. He wanted his office redesigned, but at the moment it looked unlikely. There were no more interior designers. Maybe he'd find someone with taste during his next term in office —if he had a next term in office. The homos, *his* homos, his *voting* homos had disappeared during an election year. His headache accelerated three throbs per minute.

Downtown had been particularly badly hit. Most of the good restaurants never opened, and the ones that did were running pretty sloppy service. Hundreds of boutiques were closed, and theatres by the dozens were cancelling performances. Traffic was jammed up because ten percent of the buses and streetcars had been abandoned in the middle of the streets. Hospitals lost hundreds of nurses; schools missed thousands of teachers. The switchboard at city hall was overloaded—telephone operators had vanished in droves— and even when people did get through to the departments they wanted, chances were the person they wanted to talk to wasn't there. And all the ones left were so grumpy. All the happy people had disappeared, or so it seemed to John Sewell.

But that wasn't the reason for the mayor's headache. The throb was coming from Queen's Park.

The provincial cabinet had called Sewell because Sewell was a friend of the homos. It shouldn't have upset Queen's Park that the homos had disappeared, but it upset a lot of Queen's Park's friends. Bell Canada was crippled. Hydro was at half power. Banks had lost loan officers and accountants, the stock market had lost brokers, and insurance companies were missing actuaries. The courts were being adjourned because court reporters and clerks had disappeared. Interprovincial trucking was at a standstill, with empty semi-trailers blocking the King's Highways. In the north, a third of the miners failed to show up for morning shift. Queen's Park's friends were pissed off. Queen's Park needed the homos back, and they had come to John Sewell for help.

"Look, John," the premier's administrative assistant had said on the phone, "we want you to make some kind of statement, you know, to calm the atmosphere—the way you did at that big gay rally a few years ago. Just say that we're in the process of contacting the, uh, gay leaders and that progress is being made on, ahh… certain justifiable grievances of the homosexual population. That's all. Nothing too specific.

"How about it, John? After all, how does John Damien expect to win his case if we can't get the courts open again? Ha ha ha."

Very funny, thought Sewell morosely. They hadn't thanked him in '79, but now they were dumping the whole mess in his lap. They were desperate. They needed the homos back.

His secretary buzzed. Nora Lindquist was waiting in his outer office to see him. The city was in chaos and Nora Lindquist was miffed because he'd begged off her last dinner party. Or so he figured. "Tell her to come in," he buzzed back, and his headache floored the throb throttle.

Nora strode into the room with an expression of Great Concern on her face and started talking even before she hit the floral print wing chair. "John, I just can't understand why Bill would do a thing like this. I mean, I'm sure it can't just be the homos who've disappeared. Bill's gone! They must have taken people with them."

The throbbing in Sewell's head left very little room for thought, but he knew Nora wasn't alone in her panic. Police Chief Ackroyd was demanding that the homos be found and punished for spiriting away twenty percent of his force. And it wouldn't be very many hours before Renaissance International discovered the absence of tens of thousands of schoolchildren.

Nora gave a well-practiced stifle to her sob, but before Sewell could sympathize, even before he could indulge his vision of the floral print wing chair swallowing Nora in one satisfied gulp, the intercom buzzed. The man from Queen's Park was on the phone again.

"John, I have some good news," the premier's assistant said cheerfully. "We've just got word on the whereabouts of a homo. Wayne Simon, the fashion designer, is still around and apparently he's announced a major show. There's an ad in the *Star.*" The *Star* was down to about ten pages, but at least it was still publishing. This morning its single editorial had called on the homos to stop this silly petulance and get back to work.

"We thought maybe you could go see Simon," the premier's assistant continued. "Maybe he could tell you where everybody's gone. It's not just the homos, you know. They seem to have taken about a tenth of the population."

Sewell buzzed his secretary. "Call me a cab."

"I'm sorry, Your Worship, but I'm told their lines have been tied up for hours."

"Oh, right. Never mind, we'll walk. Call Wayne Simon and tell him I'm coming to see him within the hour.

"Come on Nora, we're going to get to the bottom of this."...

Chapter four
Advice on consent
and other unfinished business

"Why we feel more concerned over children's sexual dependence than over their physical, emotional and intellectual dependence says more about us as sexual incompetents than as responsible adults.

Children are sexual, and it is up to us to take responsibility for their real education. They have been exploited and betrayed long enough by our silence."

*

"We need our own banner. If we're going to demand equality as women, let us not forget the fact that we are *gay* women, and that as such we must make the dyke issue a prominent one, retrieving it from the closets of feminism."

*

"Respectable middle-class gays can't have it both ways. They want the movies to reflect the private reality that they have always been unwilling to share publicly. They want most of all to be able to stay in the closets and not affiliate themselves openly as gay but at the same time they want nice middle-class motion pictures about two gay men who are account execs and are buying a co-op."

*

Advice on consent

Some debates have greater consequences than others. This one began, rather routinely, with the publication of "Men loving boys loving men," the third in a series of articles on consent and youth sexuality. It ended up triggering the transformation of *The Body Politic* and its relationship to the world around it. The magazine has been transformed from a small tabloid, operating virtually unnoticed in the marginal world of a dying counter-culture, into a minor institution and the major political voice of a visible and acknowledged gay community. In a sense, *The Body Politic* came of age January 5, 1978. On that date, after a police raid on its offices, criminal charges were laid against Pink Triangle Press and its officers under Section 164 of the Criminal Code— use of the mails to distribute immoral, indecent and scurrilous materials. Suddenly, the magazine found itself fighting for its very survival.

The hoped-for rational discussion of adult-child relationships and of power and consent within such relationships became completely submerged by more pressing concerns. In a political atmosphere charged with Anita Bryant-inspired hysteria, gay people grappled with the implications of a perceived state attack on one of the community's few visible organizations. The urgent issue became one of freedom of the press, the right of a magazine like *The Body Politic* to discuss topics of importance to its community in a manner most relevant to its readers.

Initially, in the wake of the criminal charges, many people in the gay community reacted with hostility. They blamed *TBP* for provoking—perhaps intentionally—the intervention of the attorney general's pornography squad. They accused *TBP* of bad timing in publishing the article at such a critical juncture. For others—and here there was support from many non-gay observers—the police seizure of large quantities of documents, including the magazine's subscription list, was cause for greater alarm. An unprecedented number of letters to the editor reflected readers' ambivalence—anger, fear, defiance, pride—towards the article and the police raid.

By the time the magazine came to trial a year later (January 1979), much of the hostility had been completely turned around. The trial helped to expand the ranks of *TBP* supporters. It put *The Body Politic* in the public's mind as a recognizable—if somewhat notorious—name. It also pushed the gay community into the kind of intense media spotlight it had not experienced before that date. The trial, sensational enough by itself, was given a further boost of publicity by the appearance of the then newly-elected mayor of Toronto, John Sewell, at a rally in support of *TBP*. In language so unequivocal that it set Christian fundamentalists raging, he defended the legitimacy of the gay community and *The Body Politic*'s role within it.

The discussion of adult-child relationships in the pages of *TBP* stopped dead until the magazine's acquittal in February 1979. The editorial collective immediately reprinted the "Men loving boys loving men" article, accompanied by a long analysis of the major criticisms that had been levelled against it. Discussion died again. Not until late 1981 did another article on the topic finally appear. The nagging weight of a prolonged court case had had its effect: it put a chill on the collective's desire to encourage further exploration of the issue. Only with the passage of time has it been possible to chip away at this self-censoring caution.

Although *TBP* was acquitted in a legal decision noteworthy for its sanity and common sense, victory was to be short-lived. The Crown appealed the decision and a County Court judge ordered a new trial. Subsequent legal appeals by *TBP* failed to overturn the retrial order. Four and a half years (and sixty-seven thousand dollars in legal and related costs) later, *TBP* found itself back at square one: a new trial and a second acquittal in June 1982. The debate around the merits of the original article and the important sexual political issues that it raised continue to be as relevant today as they were in 1977. Highlights from that debate follow.

Men loving boys loving men
Gerald Hannon

Issue 39, December 1977/January 1978

1977 has been the Year of the Children.

The year of the children Anita Bryant wanted to "save," of the children lesbian mothers lost. The year of the one child who died in a bodyrub parlour on Yonge Street.

We have been sensitized.

There is some irony in this. In the lives of most gay people, children are conspicuous only by their absence. But they are not unimportant to us. We have begun to realize, for one thing, that many gay men and lesbians are parents themselves. Their battles for custody of their children have given them new visibility.

These custody cases, though, are only one part of a much broader assault. Dark warning is being given: children are to be the last frontier of heterosexist bias. Hints have been dropped that our right to be free from discrimination—when and if that right is recognized—just might not include the freedom to be a teacher, a counsellor or a childcare worker. We have been told that our magazines can't fall before *their* eyes and that our television programmes, if they are shown at all, can't be aired until *they* have gone to bed. Regardless of the nature of our real everyday contacts—or lack of them—with children, all of us have been branded as every child's potential "molester."

Which brings us to the article below, "Men loving boys loving men," the latest in a series on youth sexuality by Gerald Hannon.

The people you will meet in it are "child molesters," "chicken hawks," "dirty old men." They are these things just as all of us are "pansies," "lezzies" and "queers." The names are only the most visible part of an elaborate and vicious mythology. (In Toronto this summer we found that the myth includes us all as "child-killers" too.) We know how much these myths and these words have to do with our real lives.

We know about some of them, that is.

The real lives of men who love boys and boys who love men are mysterious even for most other gay people. We are not immune from the general paranoia about children and sexuality, and many of us are willing to accept that part of the straight world's homosexual mythology even when we know the rest of it for the lie that it is.

A small part of the reality is presented below.

"Men loving boys loving men" is not printed here without awareness of the potential consequences. The decision to run the article was not taken lightly nor without debate within the editorial collective. We have had it on hand, typeset and laid out, for nearly six months, but we have hesitated, sensitive to the feeling that "the climate was not right" after the anti-gay media barrage which followed Emanuel Jaques's death in August.

We know now that the "climate" will never be "right." The Jaques trial is yet to come, and when that is over there will undoubtedly be something else we could point to if we wanted an excuse to move with the tide. The tide must be resisted, the discussion must be opened up.

We know that people who are more concerned with "respectability" than with rights will groan at our "irresponsibility."

We also know that the media are likely to react as though they had just found a delectably rotten plum in a Christmas cake from a bakery they've never much liked. The issue might well be splashed sensationally across the tabloids (especially on days when there isn't much real news), lines may be quoted out of context and juicy bits read over the air to satisfy prurient interest. Columnists like the Toronto *Sun*'s Claire Hoy will be delirious. We know about these things because they have happened to us—to all of us—before.

We also know this because we are aware of how desperate the enemies of gay liberation are. They are willing to hurl the bodies and minds of the very children they are trying to "save" into the fray.

The Body Politic, for instance, recently received a curious series of telephone calls. The voice at the other end of the line was that of a young boy, perhaps nine or ten years old. He asked on one occasion to speak to the author of this article (who, as we noted, has written on youth and sexuality before), asked where he might buy *TBP*, asked finally where he could go to have sex. At least once the prompting voice of an adult male was audible in the background. The sound of a tape recorder was not, but could be assumed: it is illegal even to advise people under the age of eighteen (and gay people under twenty-one) to have sex.

We can only speculate about the character of someone who would rather manipulate a child into an act of fraud than have him know anything real about the lives of men who love men and women who love women. But the characters of three people whom this man with the tape recorder must fear so much, three "child molesters," three men who love boys, are here to be examined.

We leave it to you. — *The editorial collective*

There's a painting in the foyer of my YMCA. It's a dedication portrait, the kind you still expect to see in banks over an "Our Founder" plaque, except that banks have pretty much surrendered to the framed fabric school of interior design. Not so trendy, the YMCA. The ones I know still rely heavily on dark wood veneer and respectable oil paintings like this one of C J Atkinson, "Leader in Boys' Work." Or so the dedication reads. It continues: "...here he realized a dream of his young manhood in the building of a community in which boys learned to do by doing."

He worked with boys, did Mr Atkinson. He cared about them, worried about their welfare, worried more about the ones society didn't seem to have much of a place for, and finally arranged for the construction of this building, a sanctuary—at least until recently—for boys, for young men, "a dream of his young manhood."

I think I know something about C J Atkinson. I think he was a pedophile.

I don't know for sure, of course. If I did — if anyone else had — there wouldn't be an oil painting of the man gracing the foyer of a building belonging to the Young Men's Christian Association.

But I *do* know what he did. I know, at least, why he was celebrated. He loved boys. He had dreams for them. He made them his life's work. If you are what you do, C J Atkinson, benefactor and "leader in boys' work," was very much a pedophile.

It's not a good word. The Greek origin, "lover of boys," is nice enough, but it's a clinician's word; it's like "homosexual," only worse. "People use it as a label for a disease," says Simon, one of the men we shall meet in this article, one of the men who says, "I'm gay, but I like to be called boy-lover. I like the word 'boy.' It's strange... whenever I even see the word boy...."

We'll meet Simon and others like him because what they *do* is important. Like C J Atkinson, if they are remembered at all, they will be remembered for what they do. Not for what they *are*, not because they are "nice people." Niceness is not enough. No, Simon and Barry and Peter and thousands of others like them will earn the esteem of their community for the work they do with boys; they will earn the affection of their associates and friends because they have lived honest and loving lives, have formed meaningful and responsible relationships.

If they don't get caught.

What *do* they do, then? What is it like—a loving, sexual relationship between a man and a boy? If you read the papers, this is one picture: a psychopath draws a circle of hapless boys to him and after months of wild, degrading sex he murders them—the Houston story. Another: a pathetic man incapable of forming meaningful relationships with adults finally turns to children for his social/sexual outlet—basically harmless, but pathetic and obviously in need of help. Another: a group of well-placed and usually wealthy citizens make clandestine use of a well-organized "boy bordello," one that recruits runaways and waifs and makes big money by selling their sexual favours to the well-to-do.

Those things happen. But they happen less often than wife-beating, or the battering of babies. Psychiatrists see far, far fewer young people from man/boy relationships than they see boys and girls unable to cope with the strains of their happy homes.

The media equate boy-love and child molestation. And they use that equation as a weapon against all gay people. Children are molested when they are physically or psychologically coerced into a sexual act, and that sort of thing is almost exclusively a heterosexual preoccupation. "Homosexual offenders against children almost never used force, but... heterosexual offenders against children often did"—the admirably clear and succinct conclusion of one American study. The same study noted: "Abuse is the major killer of children under two, and (intentional) neglect occurs ten times as often as abuse." And Barbara Chisholm, project director of the Canadian Council on Children and Youth, has said that as many as fifty percent of girls now in training school may have been subjected to initial rape by their own fathers.

Boy-love is not child molestation. Boy-love is C J Atkinson. Boy-love is Simon.

Simon is thirty-three. He is, I suppose, exactly the person that families worry about. He is a primary school teacher, and an active member of several social service agencies that deal with children, including Big Brothers. He has taught for ten years in four different schools and has formed sexual, loving relationships with boys in each of those four schools and in each of the service organizations of which he is a member, including Big Brothers. He has never been caught.

Simon is tall, genial, getting a little soft around the middle; a generous, rather private man with few close adult friends and a much wider acquaintance among the young. His lover, David, is twelve and in Simon's class at school. David writes poetry to Simon:

You are a friend that I love forever.
I will care for you,
And if we must to part
It would break my heart.
So let's stay together,
And be friends forever and ever.
With love, from David.

Kids are not usually romantics, according to Simon, and that is one of the reasons he finds the relationship with David so deeply moving. I asked him how it began. "He liked me, used to come by and visit. We used to lie on the couch together, I at one end and he at the other, with our legs together. But some of the things he did at first were quite touching and quite unusual and I have to tell you about them. We used to sit there and he would do things like just lean over and lick the bottom of my throat... I was dumbfounded and I said, 'What are you doing... stop!' But I didn't want him to stop. And all on his own he would take my fingers into his mouth and roll his tongue around them... it would just drive me up the wall. Then I would do it to *his* fingers and on one occasion I did it to his toes... that got him aroused. But this was before we'd been naked in front of each other, and all of this was without his being told what to do or asked to do it. *Any* gay person would have been overwhelmed by him."

The relationship seems on an even keel now. "I think it will last like this for quite a while," says Simon. "We satisfy each other. He satisfies my needs, not my desires." But like many relationships, it had its moments of strain. "At one point it cooled off a bit for a period of weeks, and I was very hurt and depressed. I had a talk with him and told him he was really hurting me quite a bit, and though I didn't expect things to be always the same, I didn't see any reason for his being so cold and distant. There were a couple of occasions during the conversation when I couldn't speak anymore and I had to get up and leave and when I came back he said, 'I didn't think it meant all that much to you.' And I said, 'It's not the sex, it's what you think of me. It's the affection you used to show me that I miss.' Since then, he's just completely warmed up, and though he's still cool at school, when we get out on our own he's completely relaxed."

I asked Simon why he thought the coolness had developed.

"I think he was genuinely a bit troubled about some of the things he'd done. He'd gone down on me. And perhaps I was a little aggressive and tried to kiss him on the lips, which is something he didn't want. But it seems to be settled. I suppose now we have more fun than sex... we both undress, and bring the mattress out here in front of the TV, and we eat and wrestle and giggle and blow into each other's bellies and generally laugh and have lots of fun. And that's really more pleasurable to me than having sex... because there's so much affection."

I wondered about teaching. Is it wise to have your lover in your class? Could one possibly avoid just a little favouritism? Simon thinks so. "If the boy I'm having an affair with does something wrong, I tell him off just like anybody else and he gets marked just like everybody else. If anything, I'm probably a bit harder on him because I want him to do better. And *he* makes sure that I don't treat him any better than any of the other kids. He'll act a bit cool sometimes... but I accept that. It makes him feel more secure with his peers. I mean, there's a lot of pressure not to be teacher's pet... and listen: I'm a popular teacher. I'm usually one of the most popular teachers in the school. I understand the kids, sympathize with them. My principals have always remarked on my special relationships with my kids in their reports on me. A few have even suggested that I have a little chat with some of the teachers that didn't seem to be doing so well. If they only knew my method!"

But then Simon's *classroom* methods aren't that traditional either. He's fed up with what he calls "a glorified baby-sitting service... that seems to exist to keep the kids out of the parents' hair. The schools aren't doing what they should be doing. They aren't teaching kids to live, they're not teaching them to think, and they're not teaching them to consciously relate to each other. You can't learn anything in the classroom anyway — except how to regurgitate information. They should be out in the factories, they should be seeing how other people work, seeing what it means to earn a living, seeing how institutions work, how the courts work… how businesses work…. You know how incompetent kids are when they first get out on their own. I was the perfect example—as soon as I started earning a living I went straight into debt. Been there ever since!"

For Simon, of course, teaching goes beyond the classroom, and he's willing to admit that his affairs with these boys form a kind of sex education. In many cases, it's the first time many of them have a chance to talk openly about something which is changing their bodies and minds in ways they're not sure how to deal with. "I remember talking to one boy years after we had our affair. He remarked that it was good for him, that it gave him a lot of confidence with girls. In fact, he thanked me for it. Before me, he was afraid and reluctant and didn't know much about sex, but through our relationship he learned quite a bit about his own body and what he could do. It also liberated him from the idea that sex was a no-no — which is what he'd been taught. I tried to relieve him, as I still do with my kids, of feelings of guilt that I went through. I try to get them to realize that this is a bodily function to be enjoyed, and nothing to feel guilty about.

"As well, I've never gone to bed with any kid that I haven't formed a friendship with. I just can't go out and seduce a kid. There has to be affection. I can honestly say I've never gone to bed with anybody that I haven't felt a great deal of affection for. Sex has always been part of friendship, of romance, of a love affair. I'm just not capable of going out and picking up a kid and sucking him and screwing him and paying him. If I did something like that, I would feel guilty, I would feel emotionally upset."

I wondered if any kid had ever made the first move.

"Yes, one fourteen-year-old I had in a grade eight class. We went camping one summer and I tried a few things but nothing obvious and he didn't seem interested, so I just dropped it. A few months later he turned up at my door one night and said, 'Do you remember the things we did last summer? Well, let's do them again.' And I said, 'I don't believe it.' He said, 'I mean it,' and I said, 'You'll have to prove it.' So he stripped. And that was that for the winter!

"The whole thing made a real difference to him. He began to talk easily about masturbation—he'd say, 'Boy, I had a good one this morning,' and he seemed to have no guilt feelings. Although he did before. He was from a very strict family."

I envy Simon that easy rapport. Kids are an uncomfortable challenge to me. When I'm with them I feel either condescending or oddly negligent; I suspect they find me either pompous or uncomfortably strained. We do not meet easily. For Simon, they are the most casual of meetings. They are neighbouring tribes, he and his boys, and their rambunctious energies still draw echoes from him.

"I can have as much fun with a kid running around in a field as I did when I was fifteen or sixteen. We go camping, we go downtown, we go to the Arcade, to movies, for rides on our bikes, we buy records and come home and listen, we bowl, we watch TV, we fuck. Actually, I've only really bum-fucked two kids. One of them asked me to, and the other indicated that he wanted it. They didn't like it all that much, but it seemed an experiment that they wanted to try.

"A lot of my relationships with boys have not been all that *sexually* satisfying to me. Especially with the pre-pubertal kids—there's never been anything really sexual. Mostly just affection, care. Anyway, I don't find pre-pubertal kids all that exciting—it's a physical pleasure of the hugging, cuddling kind. And it's an emotional pleasure too. I never felt any guilt about the fact that these were kids — I worried about being caught, that's all. And I've never wanted to be different than I am. I'm content. I just want to liberate my kids a little bit and help them find their own sexual direction. Help them realize their sexuality is nothing to be ashamed of."

If the word for Simon is romantic, the word for Peter is cool. He's rich for one thing, and that's always cool. Not rich in the way of smart young things winging their way noisily from "in" resort to way-out film festival and back, His is new money, and it resides quietly on the fringes of Rosedale, which is about as cool as new money in Toronto gets. Peter is forty-eight, trim and attractive. He has a swimmer's body and he's a meticulous and casual dresser. He runs his company with the same generous aplomb that characterizes Peter the host, very much at home in what is always an inhumanly meticulous townhouse. Thanks, in this case, to the "help," which has its own apartment below stairs, and which it is also very cool to have.

I suppose we ought to be enemies, Peter and I. Young money meets young radical. But we aren't. I like him, even when he answers my question about how we can change the way society and the law view boy-love with "I don't see that I'm willing to make much of a contribution in that direction. I suspect there's no cohesive group that shares any thoughts or experiences…. I see myself very selfishly satisfying my own needs by zipping off to Morocco twice a year and filling in the time here with whatever little delights I can scrape up."

I remember that there isn't a pedophile movement in Canada, and Peter is saying very much what I would probably have said had I been out of the closet back in the mid-Sixties before the gay movement gave me the chance to change my way of thinking. I think I would have had an "I'm all right Jack" attitude because anything else would have been too frightening to contemplate—anything else would have had to have been done alone. A pedophile movement would be more difficult to organize, would have more perils and pitfalls, than almost anything else I can think of. Neither Simon nor Peter expect to try.

I wondered how Peter met his boys. He did not have the kind of job which would put him in daily contact with them.

"With boys you have to impress them at first, you have to call attention to yourself. I do it with a big car, or a deep tan, or an ability. I used to be quite skilled at diving and I would have all eyes on me all summer. It's not the only way, of course. I've picked up boys in theatres. You sit down beside them and start making comments about the movie, and then you might say 'here's a quarter'— now it would have to be a dollar —'why don't you get us both a coke.' Then there's a long, long period of courtship, talking, driving around town, having a hamburger. And it might never happen. There were lots of boys that I would have loved to make advances to and never did. Or it might take several months. Relationships that were budding in the summer would mature in the depths of winter in a car parked in a secluded spot in the snow."

For Peter, as for Simon, it is the relationship that matters. So much so, that he is still in contact with many of the boys he began having sex with ten years ago and more. Many are married now and have children of their own, but they have no regrets about what happened with Peter, and see nothing odd about looking him up whenever they're in town.

"I remember a couple of kids, they were brothers, probably ten and twelve, and I especially liked the ten-year-old. And when he got a little older, I made an advance, but he made it clear he didn't want that—he said he didn't want me to touch him there because it wasn't right. And I said, 'Allen, it's not a question of right or wrong, but if you'd prefer not, that's fine....' Then he began to talk about his religious ideals and ethics, so I just retreated and didn't bother pursuing it. His brother, on the other hand, turned out to be quite a swinger, and we had marvellous sex over a period of years until he got married. Even then, the night before his wedding, he wanted to see me. We stayed in the apartment they were going to live in, and I fucked him in his marital bed. By that time he was really older than I was interested in: he was probably twenty-one.

"I still see Buddy. He's married, two kids. And he loves sucking me off. I don't think he has sex with other men."

Peter has a special interest in the detritus of heterosexual relationships, the unwanted or unloved boys, the boys from homes where the father is dead or has deserted. "It seems the more disadvantaged the child, the more he needs some stable, mature human being. And they're looking for love as well. Typically, they are not very articulate and not very well educated, and I think I am often a positive influence. I don't think John would ever have gone to university without my influence. We discussed that, and he agrees. He would never have placed the same value on his own personality if it hadn't been for our relationship. I valued him far more than his parents did. I taught him self-respect. I used to encourage him in school, we had a regular correspondence and he used to try and copy my style. He's a professor now, married, two kids, divorced. I began having sex with him when he was twelve.

"And then, I think my relationships give *all* the kids a real appreciation for a perfectly valid form of sexual activity. It takes the threat away from it and gives them some kind of balance, more sense of objectivity than they would have otherwise."

But can they choose, I asked Peter. Can a child actually choose to have sex with you when you have all the power and privilege that comes from simply being an adult?

"You can't treat sex as a mode of behaviour totally different from any other mode of behaviour. One doesn't worry about an adult buying an ice-cream cone for a child and thereby potentially turning him into an obese creature.... It's another form of experience, like going to the movies or playing football or hiking. I've never felt that sex should be seen alone and separate as some 'great experience.' And I can honestly say I've never been tempted to use even the tiniest bit of influence I might have to get some kid to come through. If there's the slightest bit of resistance, I'm not interested at all—I'm just wasting my time and that person's time, and it's silly to continue."

What does sex between a man and a boy consist of? For Peter—as for Simon—not much, it seems. Not much, at least, in an age when raunchy experiment gets all the publicity: "My sexual needs are very simple. I don't very often fuck somebody, though I like it once in a while. Most of the time it would be mutual masturbation, with some sucking. I prefer to be sucked: sucking doesn't interest me that much, though I do it if I think it gives someone else pleasure. But mutual masturbation would constitute the largest single practice."

And though the twelve to fourteen age bracket defines Peter's prime area of interest, he is, like most of us, willing to experiment: "The youngest? Seven, I think. He wasn't a very bright little fellow, but he just loved sucking. He used to come up to the apartment, and as soon as he got in he'd say 'I want some wine.' That meant he wanted to suck me off. And he learned *that* reference from a policeman. I'd asked him if he did this for anyone else and he said yes, there was a policeman in the neighbourhood, and the policeman told him that this was wine. We'd kiss, I'd suck him a little bit but he wasn't very interested. He just wanted to suck me. He'd suck me to orgasm and swallow it. He had very sharp teeth I recall.... I decided to put a stop to that one, and years ago I had sex with quite an old man on the beach. It just seemed sort of exciting. And of course, the fellow I'm having quite a regular relationship with is in his late twenties."

A simple question: had there ever been a time when he's wished he hadn't been a boy-lover?

A simple answer: "No, I'm crazy about lobster and there was never a time when I wished I didn't like lobster. Why would one wish not to like something one likes?"

Don is a friend of Peter's. He's forty, looks thirty, could look younger if he lost ten or fifteen pounds. He's married, and has a nineteen-year-old son. He's unashamedly and unrepentantly heterosexual. A species I rarely meet socially these days, but Don is scarcely a typical example, and we get along easily.

Don met Peter when he was eleven and Peter was nineteen and in his first year as a very popular lifeguard at the local pool. They became friends and it wasn't long before it became a sexual friendship and Don had his first orgasm in the change room at the pool. "It was very gradual—Peter just slowly got more physical with me until that day when he jerked me off. I felt a bit ashamed at first—my mother had always told me not to play with myself—but I really enjoyed it. In fact, I think I had a hangup about sex that Peter probably snapped. In any case, I was certainly masturbating myself within the month.

"I began looking up in books, though, about homosexuality and wondering to myself if I was one, but I guess I never really felt I was. Peter and I used to talk about it a lot, and I would try to understand it all. He's the only male I've ever had sex with—I never played around with kids my own age. And I guess we kept having sex on an infrequent basis until I was fifteen or so. Then I wanted to stop. I still wanted to be his friend, but I didn't want the sex anymore, so I guess I avoided him for a while."

They're good friends now, though, and they see each other about once a month for dinner or whatever and, by the by, Don meets, on a casual basis, the only gay men he ever meets. He's happy to admit it's been an education for him.

"If if hadn't been for Peter, I wouldn't be at all surprised if I'd grown up to be an Anita Bryant supporter. But I just don't have any of those crazy ideas about the typical homosexual waiting in a dark alley with candy to tempt some kid into the dark to fuck him. I know what happens. You know, I think it could have been good if the same thing happened to my son.... I think it might bring us closer together."

He can't take the final step though.

"No, I don't think I'd want my son to be gay. But I can't defend that. I guess it must be things in my upbringing... but if he came to me and said he was, and was sure of it—yes, I'd accept him."

Less of an endorsement than I might have wanted, I suppose. But I think I can understand it. If I had a son, and he were growing up straight, I think I would be disappointed, a little grieved, even a bit resentful—but I think I could handle it. It is a mark of love to want for those close to you those things in life that have been splendid—and, yes, what there is of splendour in my life happens along with being gay. I'm sure Don feels that about being straight. And I sometimes think we're doomed to feel about each other what one feels in a foreign country when everyone is, well, simply adorable but they all do everything *wrong*. Trying, but you can handle it.

Barry got in touch with me. He'd heard what I was doing, wanted to talk about himself, wanted to let me see how his relationship worked, and since I am not only an ordinarily curious individual but something of a voyeur, I said yes.

It was to be a weekend tenting in the woods. Billy didn't live in Toronto—he was a farm boy, lived in one of those houses in the middle of a flat area with cows in it somewhere north of the city, and since Barry wasn't known to Mom and Dad and crusty old grandpa he simply camped in the woods across the way. Billy, the boy he loved, the boy who loved him, came to him there out of one of those lazily large families where, thank heaven, not all of the kids are underfoot at the same time, and you don't question too closely a twelve-year-old boy who has the good sense to be out of the house all afternoon and half the night. Not if the chores are done anyway.

Barry is a chatterer. Five foot five and rather impish, he has the chatterer's ability to string together absolutely unrelated topics in a curiously coherent way—so though you feel you've been *talked* to, you don't feel exhausted. And I didn't as we barrelled down the dirt country road to be met, coincidentally, by Billy and two older brothers barrelling down the same country road in the opposite direction. There were great screams of "Barry!", screeching to a halt and then they were shy because I was there saying things like "How do you do" instead of "Hi." But they agreed to come and help us set up the tent.

They had fun. There was no doubt they were as thrilled to see Barry as he was to see them—that first great braying of his name out of their car window made that clear to me. The brothers were fifteen and sixteen, I think; they knew the score—Barry had had sex with both of them some years before, but with Billy it was something special and I could see that he got most of the attention. Nothing "romantic"—that would have been hooted, but when a wrestling match started it was clear who would be paired with whom.

I felt out of it. I mean sometimes I think farts are funny but I don't think a *lot* of farts are funny. And it's been a long time since I listened to people telling dirty stories. Or quarrelled over who could beat up whom. And I think it was probably then that I realized you practically *had* to be a pedophile to love kids —kids at their most outragously banal, kids when they're not being "nice" the way schools package them for mom and dad—and me, for that matter. Not that it was all unremittingly horrible—it was easy sometimes just to be carried away by the sheer energetic nonsense of it all, particularly after we'd knocked off a bottle of wine.

I was glad to see midnight. The two older boys crept off home and we got ready to slip into our sleeping bags—in our underwear, though I could tell by the giggling that Barry and Billy had taken theirs off as soon as the flashlight went off. Odd man out, I lay there listening to the murmuring, the giggling, the occasional explosive snort. But it didn't last long. And we were all asleep when the two older boys came back and moonhooted us outside the tent until they roused us and told us that Billy had to go home because his mom had discovered that he wasn't just sleeping out in the back of the truck the way they'd told her. He was dressed and gone in a minute.

The next day we talked. I mean Billy and I did after breakfast in a roadside restaurant. Barry went off to the can for longer than was really necessary and that had been arranged.

What did I discover? No startling truths, no insight into the human condition, not even any insights into this particualar relationship — though I think it became clear to me that it *was* a relationship, and a significant one. Billy didn't talk like that. He said Barry was his best friend. He said he wished Barry lived in the country so he could see him more often. He said he like "fooling around," which was their way of talking about sex, but he was shy about that and we didn't get into it. And that was that.

So. I had trekked off to the country and found—a relationship. Seen what I'd been hearing about from Simon and Peter, seen two people drawing delight from each other's company, seen two criminals at work. Let's not forget that.

Let's not forget that C J Atkinson and associates are criminals—the way we were before 1969, the way we still are if we try anything other than the things you can do with one (and only one) other individual over twenty-one and very much in private.

Anita Bryant won't let us—or anyone else—forget it.

"Save Our Children, Inc" is the name of the game, although the organizers seem to be cynically aware of just what that means: "The molestation tactic was the thing that particularly got the headlines. We now know how effectively it can be used," said Robert Brake, one of the top officials of that organization. Who *wouldn't* want to save our children, after all, save them from things like the Houston mass murder horrors, save them from being pawed by nasty old men? That's what molestation means to most people, it's what the media encourages them to believe, it's a belief "Save Our Children" does nothing to discourage.

They've added a refinement. Recruitment. Because homosexuals can't reproduce, they must recruit.

Anita should know. Because recruitment is what she is all about.

She wants our children. And, yes, they're *our* children too.

She's going to get some of them, and some of those are going to grow up gay, and some are going to grow up straight. If they're gay, they'll grow up miserable, hating themselves, their desires and their community; becoming mean, or robot-like, or blustering hypocrites because that's what happens to love that's taught to hate itself. And if they grow up straight, they'll grow up proud to be Americans, secretly proud to be white, a majority that's "quiet" because its soul is empty, in marriages that last and last because nothing is quite so binding as mutual distaste and suspicion.

Anita's recruits. They've been with us for a long time. They tried to save our children from witches, and turned the middle ages into a charnel house of burning and innocent flesh. They tried to save our children from Jews, and almost succeeded through twelve years of methodical and monstrous savagery. They tried to save our children from communists, and sat with Senator McCarthy in judgment upon heroic lives trying to salvage some dignity, some integrity from that degrading exercise. Now they want to save our children from homosexuals. They want to save our children from us.

Yes, we have *our* recruits, though they are not, as Bryant would have us believe, legions of hapless children diverted from the straight and narrow by the corrosive touch of some predatory homosexual.

Don is one of our recruits. He's *not* gay, but "when I'm with straight people and they say something derogatory or stupid about gays, I always try to turn it around, make them see they're stupid. I can't go as far as I'd like sometimes.... I'd be suspect myself and that would be hard to take. But I try."

Simon's students are recruits. If they grow up gay, they grow up remembering a loved role model, they grow up knowing sexual acts are not disgusting, they grow up with the possibility of coming out long before the early-to-mid twenties, the age when so many of us finally caved in, or came out.

If they grow up straight, they may not, like Don, do their best to defend gay people in the small ways he's chosen, but somewhere in the back of all that bliss they fall heir to, they are going to know the Anita Bryants of this world are out-and-out fruitcakes. And maybe, just maybe, if they're presented someday with a ballot which asks them to say a simple yes or no to civil rights for homosexuals, and they're alone in a polling booth and no one can see what they mark, then, maybe they'll remember what happened to them twenty years ago and vote the way they remember.

I have seen a photograph of Anita and family praying together before they go to bed—in pyjamas yet. Besides marvelling that anyone would consciously do anything quite so kitsch, I feel a real sense of sadness for those kids, down on their knees and huddled between momma and poppa Bryant. One or more of them could very easily be gay. And he or she would be the truly molested child.

Every homosexual has suffered that molestation. Every homosexual's sexuality has been interfered with—impeded, strangled, diverted, denounced, "cured," pitied, punished. That is molestation. And it has nothing to do with what Simon, Barry and Peter are doing.

They are the heirs of Mr Atkinson, "Leader in Boys' Work," community workers who deserve our praise, our admiration and our support.

Paying the price:
some letters to the editor

Issue 40, February 1978; Issue 41, March 1978;
Issue 51, March/April 1979

Why should a gay publication, aimed at helping out ten or fifteen percent of the population, speak out for pedophiles, whose numbers overlap only slightly our own?

To paraphrase *The Body Politic*'s masthead slogan: "The liberation of pedophiles can only be the work of pedophiles themselves." Why should gays stick out their necks for them? What have they done, or are they doing, or are they going to do, for us?

The legitimization of same-sex love among adults is a far more important and accessible aim than the legitimization of adult-child eroticism. If the two are linked, the latter can only hinder the former. Let's not spread our efforts too thinly.
Michael Johnson
Vancouver

It is so important to raise consciousness about the status of the more "exotic" sexualities and genders. Besides the injustice of the stigmatization of groups like pederasts, sado-masochists and transsexuals, such groups are most vulnerable to attack. I have been watching with growing horror the pattern of arrests in the last year: adults charged with statutory molestation, prostitutes, men having sex in public restrooms. We are all being attacked by such arrests. And the worst part of it is the ambivalence of the gay and women's movements towards such people.

Articles like "Men loving boys loving men" are important ways to get the rest of us to understand our biases, so that we may better defend each other. The publication of the essay was another example of the courage and political acuity of *The Body Politic*.

Gayle Rubin
Ann Arbor, Michigan

Your recent article made me proud to be what I am. Yes, I am a pedophile (odious term): I love boys. I love men, too, and have been known to love women. Having had entirely satisfactory, loving, sexual relationships with women, men *and* boys, I find that I prefer boys — boys generally twelve to fourteen years of age, some younger, some older.

I have never had sex with a boy who demonstrated any kind of reluctance or resistance. That would be tantamount to forcing an unwilling child to attend a symphony concert: neither of us would enjoy it.

There is nothing intrinsically undesirable in a youngster discovering the pleasurable aspects of sex with a mature, loving adult, male or female — so long as he is interested and is not coerced. Sexual pleasure should not be the sole preserve of "adults." Why should a child not be permitted to enjoy whatever physical pleasure his maturing body can afford him?

Proselytizing is a non-issue. A child cannot be "converted" to homosexuality any more than he can be converted to becoming a concert pianist — or, for that matter, a masochist. Homosexual experience will either please him and result in repetition, short-term or long-term; or it will leave him indifferent or repelled, in which case he will avoid further involvement. I find it curious that critics of pedophilia fear that an act which they consider so repulsive and so damaging to the child should in any way constitute a snare which could trap him into a life of "depravity." Why should it? Indeed, there is no evidence that it does.

It is regrettable that society is yet unable to strip pedophilia of its mystery. Pedophiles are not witches to be hunted down and burned at the stake. They do very ordinary things with very ordinary boys who typically welcome not only the physical exploration but also the entire relationship, of which sex is only a part. What, after all, is so sordid about a kiss — or an orgasm?

Anonymous
Canada

Your magazine can expect small sympathy and less support from anyone at your obscenity trial. Your reckless self-indulgence has done irreparable harm to the gay community throughout a North America already nauseated by the Gacy horror in Chicago and similar mass murders of boys and young men in California and Texas.

Extolling pedophilia, at best, could only harm and alienate otherwise tolerant heterosexuals, while at worst it plays straight into the hands of the Anita Bryants and official rednecks who are only too eager to grasp at any excuse for harassment.

You know, and ought to have known, that the vast majority of the gay community have no interest whatever in children. In the heterosexual community, even criminals in prison regard child molesters with such hatred that they will kill them, given opportunity.

It is against such a background that those who have worked so long and patiently after the Jaques shoeshine boy murder, to explain that most child molesters are heterosexual, were struggling. They need struggle no longer after the full glare of media coverage your trial will attract. It will be hopeless trying to convince a public that has been told that the "official" voice of the gay community has endorsed child molesting, even if that voice is in fact only self-proclaimed. The public will make no such fine distinctions.

What an enormous price for innocent people to pay for a stupid article in an obscure magazine that speaks only for itself! But since you lacked the judgment, decency and self-restraint to refuse to publish that article, you cannot now anticipate everyone else stepping forward to bear the formal penalty. They will be too busy trying to maintain their own reputations and integrity— if that is still possible.

Marlowe Amber
Toronto

I appreciate a great deal your finally publishing the article "Men loving boys loving men." The debate within the editorial collective mirrors the debate within the gay movement itself on the approach toward youth sexuality. I'm glad you chose to inform us and challenge our views on young people and sex.

The challenge is to inform, and the key may be to remind others of how they felt when young. What is also required is the right and expectation that young people become actively involved in the control of their lives and the decisions affecting them. The forms of oppression and its abolition are best determined by those who experience it.

We can't drop the issue of childhood sexuality, it is too important a component of our sexist society. And we can't soft peddle it for "pragmatic" reasons. To do so is to become part of the negation and hindrance of an important aspect of the personalities of our younger brothers and sisters.

Keith Sherwood Stuart
Vancouver

Perhaps you are not aware that freedom of the press assumes that the press upholds its responsibilities like any law-abiding citizen. By publishing the article, you have demonstrated an immaturity and irresponsibility that is shocking to me. You have a responsibility to your readers to print articles within the confines of the law. Now, by your action, you have caused exposure of your readership to the authorities. Was this your intention all the while? Don't ask me for donations to your cause—you deserve everything that you will get. Don't get me wrong—I think the authorities in their actions were just as wrong as you. Only *you* were the instigators of this action. You egged them on.

Gay people don't seem to understand that there are other ways of getting laws changed than breaking the law.

G Small
Ontario

I was shocked and dumbfounded at the news (of the raid on *The Body Politic* offices) and am truly saddened by the implications of the police's actions.

Though subscribing to *TBP* was a small step (and a tentative one, at that) along the road to coming out, I am pleased to discover that I am not at all intimidated by the fact that my name and address are included in the material seized. Indeed, I'm more ready than ever to fight for freedom.

Our freedom.

My freedom.

Michael Petty
Winnipeg

Teaching sexuality
Jane Rule

Issue 53, June 1979

The furor created by *The Body Politic*'s "Men loving boys loving men" posed hard political questions for me. On the one hand, I deplore repressive police action designed not only to stifle any discussion of the subject of sexual activity across generations, but also to intimidate anyone even so involved with the paper as to be a subscriber. On the other hand, I understand the rage against sexual exploitation by men not only of children of both sexes but of women and other men, the pleasures of which *The Body Politic* can sometimes be accused of advertising. I am convinced that censoring serious discussion of unconventional sexual relationships does nothing to protect those who might be exploited. To test, to contest, is the only way to reach forward into understanding areas of human experience vulgarized by either taboo or glorification.

As a society we are so fearful of sexual initiation we pretend that by ignoring it, it will not take place. What we really want is not to know when or how it does. We no longer frighten our children with threats of insanity and death as results of masturbation. It is, instead, clumped with picking one's nose, belching, farting—something not to be done in public, by implication not to be done by nice people at all—but we give our children enough privacy so that the guilty pleasure can be discovered and practiced not only alone but in the company of other unsupervised children. Children caught may be shamed, the more sexually aggressive children ostracized, but it is not, as it used to be, a cause for brutal retribution.

Our embarrassed liberality on this matter does not extend to encounters between children and adults. Though anyone who spends any time with very young children knows that they are aggressively curious about bodies — everyone's bodies—apt to stick a finger not only in another's eye or nose but to reach for a nipple or penis, we pretend that these assaults have nothing to do with sex, are only part of the random and *innocent* activity which can be ignored or distracted. The adult who actively participates in sexual instruction of children — whether the nurse who teaches a child masturbation as a sedative or the adult male who complies with a four-year-old's demand, "Show me your penis"—is simply criminal.

Sexual education in this culture, when undertaken at all, is presented impersonally in abstract diagrams, unlike any other teaching of bodily function or domestic habit. Once the breast is unavailable for nourishment and the lap outgrown, sexual pleasure is presented as a far off and nearly mystical reward for years of asexual (or at least secret) behaviour. If defecating and eating were left to the same secrecy and chance we might face the same problems with basic sanitation and nutrition that we do with sex. When the relatively simple task of teaching table manners takes so many years, why do we assume that sexual manners need not be taught at all?

Formal sexual initiations in other cultures may serve as bad examples of what we might teach if given permission: the mutilation of female genitals and the equating of sexual gratification with the kill in males. Both these puberty rituals express attitudes toward sexuality in our own culture, and it is no wonder that we can therefore be alarmed at exposing children to adult sexuality. If we viewed sex as a basic appetite normally satisfied and gradually cultivated, we would not need to keep our children isolated and in ignorance for so long, building in them what we have ourselves experienced: intense fear and desire which, so long uninstructed, produce dangerous stupidity. Of course we don't want dangerously stupid adults initiating our children. Fear of that leaves the children to themselves, not out of our conviction that children are, in this matter, the best teachers, but by default. We have so little trust in what we have to teach that we not only abdicate our responsibility but label criminal any adult who might attempt instruction.

There are adults who do sexually exploit, damage and kill children. It makes no more sense to deal with the question by taking them as the norm than it would to take rapists as the norm for heterosexual relationships between adults. To say that any sexual activity between adults and children is exploitative because of the superior size and power of the adult is really to acknowledge that, overall, relationships between adults and children are unequal. Why we feel more concerned over children's sexual dependence than over their physical, emotional, and intellectual dependence says more about us as sexual incompetents than as responsible adults.

Children are at our mercy. They are at each other's mercy as well. It makes about as much sense to leave children's sexual nourishment to their peers as it would to assume that the mud pies they make for each other are an adequate lunch. I use the term "sexual" rather than "sensual" because it seems to me that both our embarrassment about and focus on genitals make us the inept sexual creatures most of us are. A child's need for physical contact is as sexual as our own. It takes as little imagination to know that a child's sexual appetite is different from an adult's as it does to figure out that a newborn baby can't eat an apple or a steak. We don't therefore refuse to feed an infant.

If children's sexual independence were as thoughtfully taught as their ability to feed themselves, masturbation would become the satisfying accomplishment that it should be. Being able to gratify oneself provides an autonomy that is basic to self-respect and therefore respect for others. Sexual play based on the understanding of pleasure can have associated with it as many small courtesies as eating with other people, as much ritual wonder as the most sacred of games. Just as children gradually learn greater autonomy and responsibility in all other aspects of living, so their development in sexuality should be gradual until they come to the choices of commitment in relationships, in parenting, not as sex-starved barbarians willing to barter anything for the experience so long forbidden, not as infantile, gluttonous, guilty and dangerously stupid, but as warm, sexually intelligent human beings.

Until we have a responsible view of our own sexuality, we will go on shirking our responsibilty to our children. We live in so homophobic a society that most adults are terrified of expressing any affection with children of their own sex, and even discourage those friendships often most meaningful among children. Mothers can be jealous of, rather than delighted in, their daughters' sexuality, so ambivalent about themselves as women that they don't know what sort of victimization to recommend. Fathers compete with sons, warning them off the lotus land of sexual pleasure which will only deter them from the conquest of whatever world has been chosen for them, be it military service or medical school. For every child traumatized by overt and brutal sexual treatment, there are many, many more suffering the damage of ignorance and repression which makes masochistic women and sadistic men the norms of our society.

The choice is not really between child-rape and chastity into late adolescence, nor is it between perversion and orthodox heterosexuality. We do have the further option of accepting our own sexuality and therefore that of our children as a complex blessing which we and they must learn neither to exploit nor deny but to enjoy with sensitivity and intelligence.

Such a change in attitude doesn't come quickly or easily. It will not come at all unless we are willing to address the question seriously and openly. Police who use violence and intimidation to silence such discussion, who see in every adult interested in the sexuality of children a molester and murderer, are themselves victims as well as perpetuators of our sexual sickness. If we discover through reading "Men loving boys loving men" that we question the motives of the men involved, we must as certainly question our own in allowing our children to choose such experiments while pretending not to. We must also examine the motives of all interaction between adults and children—how much has ever been done "for their own good," how much we simply reinforce our own values—before we are too purely suspicious of anything but disinterested altruism in adults who relate to children.

More important than judging the quality of other people's experience and relationships is the exercise of our own memories. Certainly my own initiation came long before I was legally adult. Though a number of males around my age offered to participate, a woman ten years my senior was "responsible," at my invitation and encouragement. The only fault I find with that part of my sexual education was the limit her guilt and fear put on our pleasure, the heterosexual pressure even she felt required to put on me. What she did "for my own good" caused both of us pain. If I were to improve on that experience now, it would not be to protect children from adult seduction but to make adults easier to seduce, less burdened with fear or guilt, less defended by hypocrisy.

If we accepted sexual behaviour between children and adults, we would be far more able to protect our children from abuse and exploitation than we are now. They would be free to tell us, as they can about all kinds of other experiences, what is happening to them and to have our sympathy and support instead of our mute and mistrustful terror. There are a thousand specific questions, all hard to answer, but we can't begin dealing with them until our basic attitude changes.

Children are sexual, and it is up to us to take responsibility for their real education. They have been exploited and betrayed long enough by our silence.

Another look
Chris Bearchell, Rick Bébout
and Alexander Wilson

Issue 51, March/April 1979

As the editorial collective's original introduction noted, "Men loving boys loving men" first appeared at an especially significant—and sensitive—time for gay people.

The defeat of the gay rights ordinance in Miami was still a fresh memory, and the impact of the strategy Anita Bryant and her allies used there was lost on no one: "children" had become a very hot property.

The fundamentalist forces were driven to the polls by the fears tapped whenever children and sex are mentioned in the same breath. There they demanded a halt to the "moral corruption" being advanced by the women's, youth, and gay liberation movements. Miami, they said, was just the beginning. Future crusades would be fueled by the same fears and, as in Miami, they would be focussed on the most terrifying monster of them all: the "child molester."

The fact that this creature was largely mythical stopped almost no one. Myth and reality were hopelessly blurred, a situation which the fundamentalists found both comfortably familiar and strategically convenient. Where the monster was not known, it could be invented: it was a man, first of all; he preyed on little girls sometimes, but his violation of boys was somehow more important. He was a man who wanted boys. He was a homosexual. He was all homosexuals.

The "molestation tactic" was tailor-made for the compressed and unsubtle world of the mass media. It was direct, unencumbered by sophisticated analysis, and could make a dramatic impact in less than ten seconds. Sometimes the air time or page space had to be bought, but the fact that "Save Our Children" could, with devastating effect, fill their ads with news reports and clippings of "boy sex rackets," "kiddie porn" and "homosexual use" of children showed that the media often provided them with their best copy for free. In August 1977, the Toronto gay community was given a frightening lesson in this editorial generosity to their opponents, when the murder of a twelve-year-old boy by four men became the "homosexual orgy slaying" for which all gay people might, in some way, be blamed.

It was these times which the December 1977/January 1978 issue of *The Body Politic* confronted. The issue, intended as a review of 1977, included feature articles on three of the major themes of the year. Each was preceded by an introduction written by the collective. One was an analysis of the defeat in Dade County, and another dealt with the use of television *by*, rather than *on*, gay people.

The third feature was "Men loving boys loving men." The collective was aware that reactions to the article could be unpleasant; much of what later transpired (with the now glaring exception of the raid and criminal charges) was predicted in the introduction. But the molester myth was not going to be defeated until we refused our opponents their exclusive claim on the subject. Many agreed, but certainly not everyone. Collective members were regularly asked why we chose to run the article when we did, with Toronto about to face the trial of Emanuel Jaques' accused killers, Anita Bryant on her way and, it was thought, with the sexual orientation amendment of the Ontario Human Rights Code about to be discussed in the legislature.

These impending events, so apparent late in December, had not been known to the collective when the decision to publish was made early in November. That fact could have seemed an excuse, and in making it clear we may, at times, have leaned on it as such. But it said only that we failed to pick a time that was as "right" as we might have originally thought, and that was not the point. A truly safe time to publish an article like "Men loving boys loving men," we knew, would never come. Gay people had not achieved what gains they had by waiting to come out until the time was right. They had come out in bad times and had worked to make them better. Seeking change means taking risks.

However, neither the objections to publication of "Men loving boys loving men" nor the outpourings of support for *The Body Politic*'s right to publish it, which characterized the period following the police raid, really dealt with the questions the article itself raised. But discussion was beginning.

Reacting to an anonymous writer who, after criticizing *TBP* for publishing the article, had gone on to say that "I find boys pleasant, and there is poetry about their love that moves me," Ronnie Allen of Somerville, Massachusetts wrote: "Does he mean that boys are pleasant like a cup of tea? The 'poetry' business suggests some 1950s mentality, a chauvinism, that I find unpleasant and dangerous. It sounds more like a Milky Way bar having just been consumed by some burnt-out diabetic."

Body Politic Free the Press Fund member Lorna Weir, picking up on Gerald Hannon's admission that his attempts to deal directly with the boys in the relationships he examined were not very successful, noted that this left him dependent on the point of view of the men. "It would have been hard for the men *not* to define the boys in terms of the adult needs they fulfilled. Of course, this really isn't so different from the way men define women for men's needs, as floozies or nursemaids or saints, depending on the needs of the moment. But if men involved with boys see them as the embodiment of lost innocence, or as sensual creatures completely unencumbered by adult guilt, then they're failing to deal with them as whole, complex human beings with needs of their own."

Much valuable criticism of "Men loving boys loving men" came from feminists who reacted not against the subject matter per se, but against a treatment of it which they felt left too many important areas unexplored.

In a letter sent in support of *TBP*'s legal struggle, the Atlantic Provinces

Political Lesbians for Example (APPLE) made clear the deficiencies they saw: "It is not, nor do we think it was meant to be a definitive article on the subject. It was written from the point of view of the men's, more so than the children's sexuality. The inequality inherent in most child-adult relationships is not adequately dealt with."

This last concern — that the article did not reflect sufficient awareness of the element of power in sexual relationships — was shared by most feminists.

Their criticisms were based on experiences common to women but, for the most part, unknown to men. Many lesbians and feminists speak with authority about child-adult relationships from having participated in such relationships themselves — as children. Their recollections conform to the pattern established in the statistics on sexual encounters between adults and children: they were more often psychologically than physically coercive; they involved members of, or persons known to, the family; they were, in the overwhelming majority of cases, heterosexual. They were not usually pleasant experiences. Knowing this, many women doubt that the situation is really so different for boys.

In the lives of both girls and boys, men are generally cast as authority figures and disciplinarians. Our culture reinforces this role and doesn't encourage men to develop warm, tender or physically affectionate contacts with children, not even their own offspring. Some of the discomfort expressed by criticism of "Men loving boys loving men" seems implicitly to accept, rather than question, this conditioning and the sharp division of sex roles it encourages. In writing about gay fathers in *TBP*, Michael Lynch quoted Adrienne Rich: "It can be dangerously simplistic to fix upon 'nurturance' as a special strength of women. Whatever our developed or organic sense of nurture, it has often been turned into a boomerang." Men may be more nurturant, more capable of dealing warmly and positively with children, than either their critics think they are or society encourages them to be.

The full implications of "mothering" fathers, however, have yet to be explored. Most children are still presented with a cool, threatening image of men. Boys and girls react in different ways to this image — and thus to men — because of the ways they have been taught to see themselves and their own sexuality.

Girls are given little reason to feel positive about sex. They are taught that they do not really have sexual feelings of their own. Their lot in life is to please others in all things, and when they grow up that will include pleasing a husband sexually.

Girls learn that they may pay enormous and often terrible penalties for "indulging" in sex. They are raised in the shadow of the spectre of rape, and surrounded by the demeaning myth that it doesn't happen to "good girls." Rape victims, society insinuates, invite and deserve their fate. Even if a girl is pleased at the prospect of a (hetero)sexual encounter, it is she and not her partner who faces the possibility of pregnancy. She risks not a brief fling, but the fate of her body and her life for months — or years — to come.

Unless sex conforms to very specific conditions, girls are expected to see it as devaluing. Women who act on or even acknowledge their sexual needs are "loose," divorced women are "cheap," victims of rape have been "used." Nonetheless, by a cruel twist of logic, most straight men have traditionally viewed women's resistance to sexual advances as a deceit camouflaging their real desire to submit — if "seduced."

At the heart of all these experiences lies the assumption of sex-as-heterosexuality. The prospect of relationships with other women would probably not give rise to the same anxieties, but then, girls are not generally raised to be lesbians. They, and all children, are taught to view the world in heterosexual terms.

It is no surprise, then, that women do not usually see sex as a casual and recreational activity; they have long experienced it as a serious and potentially dangerous matter. Women might understandably be sceptical of the notion that sexual relations between men and boys could be mutually satisfying and beneficial. Their own experiences with men were anything but.

It's dangerous, though, to apply heterosexual judgments to homosexual acts. Feminism and gay liberation both make clear that girls are not raised like boys, nor boys like girls.

Boys are expected to be more active and aggressive than girls. They are taught to take risks, to set their sights on the things they want and to go after them. They are "toughened up" to deal with failure, taught to be resilient, to bounce back from reverses and expect success.

These expectations naturally affect the way boys are encouraged to deal with their own sexuality. While they may not be actively urged into sexual encounters, it's assumed that by the time boys reach their teens they will have begun to seek them out for themselves. Specific instances may cause a bit of trouble, but beneath the scolding a boy may get if he's "caught at it" there lies tacit parental—and especially paternal—approval of his acts. Little Johnny is growing up, "sowing his wild oats," learning, thank God, to be a heterosexual man.

Sex is less a threat to boys than it is a tool, a thing that is theirs to apply in casual play or in their battle for social prestige and authority. As with girls, the end result of their training is intended to be heterosexuality, but even boys growing up gay carry with them the notion that sex is not something that will be imposed on them, but rather something they control, something that can be serious or fun, as they see it.

Both boys and girls would bring the results of their different sexual socialization to any relationship with an adult. Boys, more confident of getting what they want, could bring more genuine willingness to a sexual encounter with a man than most girls would — more willingness, in fact, than many women might believe possible.

It seems clear that judgments based on heterosexual experience cannot fairly be lifted, unmodified, and applied to encounters between adults and young people of the same sex. But feminist concern about power and the possible abuses of power in these relationships remains a valuable touchstone for analysis.

Power is an element in *all* relationships, but the obvious social inequality of children and adults makes power a more visible element in any relationship between them. In two areas especially—those of physical strength and economic clout—adults have glaring advantages.

People over twenty-one can take for granted their right to earn money, to live on their own, to go about unaccompanied and to enter into relationships without having to get anyone else's permission. Children and teenagers can't count on any of these freedoms, regardless of how capable they may be of exercising them.

But, as Boston gay activist and boy-lover Tom Reeves points out, boys are not completely without power in relationships with men. "Seduction of men *by* boys is at least as frequent as seduction *of* boys by men," says Reeves. Boys are aware of their sexual allure and of the ways they can use it to manipulate the men they're involved with. Despite their own superior physical and economic strength, these men say, it's the boys who hold the final card: they can always talk. Exposure of the relationship is a constant threat to the man.

This logic, however, ignores the fact that exposing the relationship could have disastrous consequences for the boys as well. The contention that the boys' power lies in their seductiveness and in the threat that they might "blow the whistle" also has a familiar — and suspicious — ring for many women. "Arguments that boys seduce men sound frighteningly like what men have always told us about rape," wrote Amy Hoffman in a recent issue of Boston's *Gay Community News.* "The power attributed to the boys sounds like the devious passive/aggressive modes of gaining some control which are the only ones powerless people have available to them."

The basic inequalities inherent in an encounter between a man and a boy—those of physical strength and freedom of economic and social mobility—are not unique. They are the same, in kind if not degree, as the inequalities affecting relationships between men and women. Straight relationships provide a model of power unbalanced and open to abuse. If there is hope for heterosexuality (and not everyone thinks there is), it must rest on the assumption that abuses can be controlled and imbalances rectified.

Forces more subtle and sophisticated than physical strength and socially-sanctioned power also come into play in any human relationship. Psychological power may be less concrete than money and muscle and it may finally be secondary to them as well, but it is nonetheless real and must be considered in any calculation of equality or inequality.

To shift the discussion of child-adult relationships away from the notion of age, and suggest instead that the most useful criterion for judging the validity of any human relationships be the distribution of power, does make one thing clear: most relationships are based on inequality. Despite this, many interactions between people of unequal power are seen to be of mutual benefit—to a point.

Teachers are usually assumed to have more power than students, even if they are of the same age. Yet students benefit from their relationship, at least ideally. Many high school students and even those younger, however, may question just how great the benefit is when weighed against the control teachers and schools impose on their lives.

Parents are clearly more powerful than their children. In infancy and early childhood that imbalance more often than not serves the child's interests: among the powers she or he doesn't have is the ability to provide the necessities of food and shelter. Parents do. But even at this early age, children often suffer at the hands of those who take care of their physical needs. The imposition of parental will may be necessary in the socialization of children, but the means used have been known to cause harm that never heals. Children who are beaten do not usually have the power to hit back.

The very language used to describe children indicates that the function of the family goes well beyond merely providing for the material needs of the child. Mothers and fathers talk about "having" children who, once they are born, are "theirs." This arrangement is convenient for society: able to count on parents to feed and clothe "their" young, our social system escapes the need to treat children as citizens by saying that, in return for their efforts, parents get to control the lives of their offspring.

Nowhere is this control more apparent than in the increasingly insistent claim that parents and parents alone have the "right" to determine the sexuality of their children. Any interference from outside the family — sex education programmes, birth control information provided by public clinics, even a friendship with another boy or girl whom parents find a "bad influence"—is seen as a threat to parental prerogatives.

Clearly, the ultimate threat is another adult willing to interact directly with a child's or teenager's own sexuality. In defiance of the fact that most sexual abuse of children takes place within the family, the mythical "molester" is cast as an ominous, tempting stranger. He embodies not the fear of injury to the child, but the fear of a threat to the "rights" of the parents.

Susan Brownmiller, in her classic work on rape, *Against Our Will*, notes that a stranger who has sex with a person under the legal age of consent "may draw a life sentence in many jurisdictions, yet a conviction for incest rarely carries more than a ten-year sentence." In her analysis of the history of rape legislation, Brownmiller shows that it was less often intended to protect women from assault than it was to avenge men for damage done to their property—wives and daughters—by other men. Rape, marriage and divorce laws codified the terms of the social deal by which women gained material support and "protection" from men; in return they gave up control of their sexuality.

Age of consent laws strike the same sort of deal: parents provide for and protect children, and children must, in turn, submit to parental control of their sexual lives. Age of consent legislation is as much an expression of property rights as the laws which "protect" women from rape, and both are equally ineffective in defending anyone from assault. Rape victims find themselves interrogated in public cross examination about their past sexual experience in order that the "value" of the property damage can be assessed. Children assaulted in the home rarely get their cases heard in court; those genuinely abused by strangers may end up there as witnesses, to be grilled by the defence. And those under the age of consent who willingly gave consent anyway may find themselves categorized as juvenile offenders, "incorrigibles" or if they have already escaped parental authority, "wards" of the state.

Despite this, Brownmiller still sees value in age of consent legislation. Feminists who have studied the problem, she says, conclude that anyone under the age of twelve deserves "unqualified" legal protection, "since that age is reasonably linked with the onset of puberty and awareness of sex, its biologic functions and repercussions." As perceived here, sex is not warm or sensual. It is a serious, possibly reproductive and probably coercive experience, something from which children should be protected. It is the heterosexual invasion which women (especially a woman dealing with the subject of rape) would understandably see as a threat.

The concepts of coercion and consent are critical to an understanding of how power operates in sexual relationships. Discussion has hardly begun on what these words really mean; up to now, they have been used not as terms on whose definitions there is common agreement, but as brickbats.

"We are taking the bait and accepting straight society's definition of the constraints of the problem," Ian Johnson, a social service worker who deals with young gay men, wrote recently in *Gay Community News*. "The real issue is not one of *age* of consent... but the more elusive concept of consent itself. Central to this concept are: an informed awareness of alternatives, the ability to discern and accept responsibility for the consequences, and free choice from a position of self-power." Consent might be defined as saying yes in a situation where one has the power to say no and be taken seriously. It might be defined as the power not only to enter relationships but also to leave them without suffering drastic consequences.

Until recently, coercion has almost always been defined in law as a matter of physical force. Rape was a "forcible" act, and signs of violence were helpful as evidence that the victim had not given consent. Few would now say that pressure has to be that extreme in order to be called coercive; how subtle or unintentional it has to be before it no longer qualifies for the term is less clear.

However we decide to apply these concepts to judgments of sexual relationships between adults and younger people, it's clear to us that the ways they are now enshrined in law not only fail to prevent abuse, but actually *contribute* to it. "Laws are responsible for the bulk of abuse and violence among men and boys engaged in sex," says Tom Reeves. "Laws lead men to panic, to paranoia, to hit-and-run relationships. The laws lead boys to blackmail, to secrecy and lying, and to link sex with crimes. Sex between men and boys does not lead in this direction, the law does."

Sexual abuse of children and teenagers *does* really happen, and sometimes it *is* committed by strangers who have no concern for the well-being of the unwilling victims. Young people do deserve legal protection from this kind of assault, just as everyone else does, and we need laws to provide it. But laws that can be used to lock up a twenty-two-year-old man for fourteen years because of a single, consensual sexual act with a sixteen-year-old "boy," laws that can land the same sixteen-year-old in a juvenile detention centre for his part in the "crime," are not the kind of laws we need. Laws that define an act as criminal because of its sexual nature, rather than for its violence or injuriousness, are not the kind we need, either.

Laws designed to reinforce the control of one group of people over another, cheered through legislatures under the guise of "protecting children" or "stemming the tide of filth" are the kind of laws we should be eager to expose for the repressive measures they really are. Further repression is not the answer to abuse of power between people.

*

Like "Men loving boys loving men" itself, these remarks are clearly not intended as the last word on the subject of child-adult sexuality. Discussion has gone on despite legal efforts to limit it; we have tried to reflect that discussion and to show how it has influenced our own thinking since Gerald Hannon first presented his article to the rest of the collective in the middle of 1977.

It should be apparent by now that this topic is too complex to be dealt with as a debate "for" or "against" sexual relationships between adults and people under the age of twenty-one. We should be beyond that point. We should be trying to find out more about those relationships themselves, trying to discover the ways in which power operates within them, and for whose benefit.

We should also be applying the same kinds of questions to other relationships. No one group of people alone should be called to answer for shortcomings in their dealings with each other if the "flaws" in their interactions are common to most human relations.

In December 1978 more than one hundred and twenty-five people directly involved in man-boy relationships met in Boston. It was the first such conference ever to take place in North America, and was an incredibly emotional and cathartic experience for those who participated. Getting their personal stories of rage, frustration and grief out in a collective forum and coming to a realization of their common oppression, they took the first small steps toward working together to confront society with the reality of their lives.

Almost all of these people were boy-lovers, not boys. It's unrealistic to expect, at this point, that it could have been otherwise. But it's also unrealistic to slip into the old, comfortable pattern of letting those with the power to speak define the truth for those who are stuck in silence. Boy-lovers do suffer a special and vicious oppression in a society that has fabricated its own rigid notion of what they are like, a notion truer to the paranoid purposes it serves than to any reality. But the boys these men love are at least as much oppressed, and nobody will have the whole story until the boys tell their half of it in their own voices.

Many at the conference were aware of this, realizing that their own predicament is a result of the controls society has imposed on the sexuality of its younger members. Common ground with the youth liberation movement is being discovered; the next meeting planned by the people who met in Boston will occur in New York in March, and members of that city's gay youth group will be there.

Terminology is still a problem. We have very consciously avoided the one term most commonly used to name what we're dealing with: pedophilia. It is inaccurate technically in that it refers to an attraction to pre-pubescent children (the "correct" term for male adult-adolescent love is "ephebephilia"), but it is even more objectionable for naming the emotion of only one of the parties involved. "Boy-love" clearly serves no better as the name of a relationship, "boy-lover" says as little about the loved one as "cat-lover" or "art-lover" does, and "transgenerational love" brings to mind bizarre images of an airline that flies back to 1967 and lands only at San Francisco. Even the catch phrase we have favoured, "child-adult relationships," says too much and too little at once, categorizing eighteen-year-olds as children and evading the clear statement that sex is part of what we're talking about.

There's a danger in naming things too neatly, anyway. The urge to slice up sexuality into distinct categories may simply cover a defensive desire to put its more unacceptable manifestations into a box clearly different from the one we've decided to take for ourselves. We are not all the same, to be sure, and the realization of our difference is necessary for the development of minority self-identity. But rigorously marginalizing and disassociating ourselves from "transvestites," "pedophiles," "coprophiles," "fetishists" — in short, "freaks"—verges on the nervous assertion that we can't begin to comprehend these variations on sexuality, that we're just nice normal gay people—almost as normal as straights.

Applying an analysis of power to human relationships means looking beyond these pigeonholes. People who are young or female or gay, and who have tried to examine the implications of being these things in a world that is run primarily for the benefit of those who are adult and male and straight, have a perspective on power because they know powerlessness. Those used to power rarely perceive it, rarely see how it works. But we have seen it from the bottom up; we have watched it in operation and have kept careful notes.

What we know about power's intersection with sexuality, about coercion and exploitation and violence, as well as consent and sensuality and affection, can contribute to an understanding of all sexuality, not just that between adults and the young, or between men and men or women and women.

Our job is to keep watching, to keep taking notes, and to keep open a discussion of what we find.

Working together

Can lesbians and gay men work together? Should they? Can they at least find political unity on issues where their interests coincide?

Since the beginning of the gay liberation movement, the history of attempts to establish workable political relationships has been a troubled one. Linked always to the central issues of lesbian visibility and autonomy, it is a history riddled with accusation, counteraccusation and guilt-tripping.

Lesbians, unlike activist gay men, have always been put in the position of making a choice between directing their political energies toward fighting their oppression as women or struggling for their liberation as gay people. "What's a woman to do?" asked one writer who described her dilemma in an early issue of *The Body Politic*.

A full debate about lesbian political priorities never found its way into the pages of *The Body Politic*. Editorial policy has always been more than cautious; the volatile nature of the issue and the fragility of existing alliances apparently inhibited free-wheeling discussion, at least in print. A survey of *TBP* issues spanning the Seventies reveals only fragmentary attempts at dealing with the perceived causes of the problems or at proposing solutions to them. Some of these articles are already historical documents: they capture critical moments in deliberations about the issues, both among lesbians and between lesbians and gay men.

Early in the Seventies, lesbians found that they were outnumbered and their concerns often ignored in mixed gay organizations. Most withdrew, some into lesbian separatist organizations, some into the work of building an autonomous lesbian movement, others into feminist activities and projects. With the passage of time, both men and women began to analyze the limitations of the "cosmetic" ideal of gay unity. For a period during the latter half of the Seventies, lesbians almost disappeared from the gay movement; between gay women and men only sporadic interaction, an uneasy coexistence, seemed possible.

Differing social and sexual needs push lesbians and gay men away from common ground much of the time. Opinions differ as to whether or not that divergence is necessarily an obstacle to *political* unity in areas where our experiences overlap. Feminism and gay liberation are not just any two social movements vying for the loyalties of a common constituency. Historically, gay liberation has relied heavily on feminism for theoretical foundation, although feminism hasn't felt so direct an affinity. Thus gay liberationists—male and female—have been reluctant to voice public criticism of the directions taken by parts of the feminist movement, while feminist and separatist lesbians have felt freer to express their displeasure with developments in the politics of gay liberation. Guilt, whether or not directly manipulated by feminists, has often served to silence criticism in the other direction.

This second phase of lesbian-gay male relationships is currently undergoing another change. The first signs of this change could be glimpsed in 1977-78 in the successful, if short-lived, coalitions of gay men, lesbians and feminists which formed to combat the Anita Bryant crusades. As political circumstances throw feminists and gay liberationists together again, a dialogue is developing which includes a gay liberationist critique of lesbian participation in separatist and in feminist activities. Lesbian separatism, by definition isolated and opposed to alliances with either gay men or straight feminists, is increasingly viewed as political suicide, however *personally* appealing it might continue to be. The right-wing trends in the larger political scene have caused many pragmatic lesbian feminists, as well as lesbians recently coming out, to seriously rethink the separatist solution. Also coming under scrutiny is the wide-spread tendency among lesbians in the feminist movement to maintain a low profile in order not to jeopardize feminism's potential for popular appeal — or funding.

Visibility *is* a gay liberation issue and, viewed from this perspective, the refusal to be publicly lesbian is more than simply an insidious form of closetry on the part of politicized women who should know better. It is also the collective shirking of political responsibility to meet the needs of non-feminist lesbians who are abandoned to an even more isolated closet. Consequently, lesbian adherence to the more "official" or orthodox strains of feminism has led to the odd situation whereby lesbian sexuality becomes a political embarrassment. The current debates around pornography, censorship, public sex and S/M, initiated by feminists over differences with gay liberation, have also begun to reveal differences among lesbians, who until recently have often disappeared from *visible* participation in the discussions.

Although *The Body Politic* has been produced largely by gay men, there consistently has been lesbian input as well. The nature and extent of lesbian contributions have been dependent to some degree upon the state of lesbian politics at the time. *TBP*'s editorial policy, equivocal or silent in the past, is slowly becoming more explicit on this issue. It could be summarized this way: candid but respectful exchanges between lesbians and gay men can only be mutually beneficial; coalitions around selected issues make political sense; gay liberation does address some of the concerns of lesbians; lesbians have as important a role as men to play in the movement. The second decade of gay liberation may well witness the full flowering of these new initiatives.

The following selections represent published fragments of a decade-long debate, carried on for the most part by other voices, in other rooms. Incomplete in many cases, dated in others, they are offered as essential background reading for a rather large item of unfinished business.

We need our own banner
Marie Robertson

Issue 24, May/June 1976

After four years of asking myself, "Where are all those women?" I've decided to change my focus and question what, if anything, the gay movement has to offer us dykes. Contrary to the belief of many lesbians who are inexperienced in working with gay men, but who nevertheless are amazingly outspoken in their criticism of gay liberation, I have done much more than make coffee and answer telephones. However, of late, I've been looking at the large amount of energy that I expend fighting for equal power in a male-dominated struggle, educating my gay brothers about their sexism and feminism in general, and trying to recruit more women.

Who gains in the amalgamation? It seems to me that men are getting quite a bit for our time. Besides the work we do, having a significant number of active women in an individual group has become a basis for credibility and status in the contest for "Most Together Gay Liberation Group of the Year." But what are lesbians gaining? A growing sense of alienation from our sisters; fatigue as we struggle as a minority to let the public know that the term "gay" also means *female* homosexual. This is not to underplay all the good feelings I've experienced in past years. Spending one's formative years with faggots has definite advantages (I'm a great dancer). Nonetheless, it has begun to strike me as ludicrous when in seminars I expound the virtues of loving women and then upon reflection realize that I've been spending most of my time with gay men.

The problem is obviously much deeper than the superficial male chauvinism in the movement: the meatballs who insist on saying "*man*kind," "him," "he" when referring to both sexes. I perceive a clear conflict of interest. Gay liberation, when we get right down to it, is the struggle for gay men to achieve approval for the only thing that separates them from the "Man"—their sexual preference. All right, all you self-proclaimed "male feminists" who are at this point desiring to bend, spindle and mutilate my poor Polish neck. The point is that if you were not gay you would be part of the powerful prestigious male ruling class that oppresses women, whether you choose to face that reality or not. Your birth as males defines that; you don't. My female birthright places me on the bottom rung, regardless of my sexual orientation and that is where I must fight from. Thanks for letting me take a step up to your rung on the ladder, but no thanks.

Should we dykes then fight alongside our straight feminist sisters? Enter lesbian pride to complicate matters even more. Some lesbians put a lot of energy into the feminist movement, committing themselves to working for the benefit and eventual liberation of *all* women. No one can deny the importance of this since dykes are oppressed first and foremost as women. But it has been my experience, (and I know I'm not alone) that the mere mention of including gay issues in the feminist struggle arouses a complete gamut of negative responses from outright refusal to the more pseudo-liberal (but harder to detect) queasiness of inner parts, characterized by a sudden tightening of the vocal chords and nausea. I refuse to kow-tow to the closetry strongly encouraged by uptight straight women concerned with the "image" of the feminist movement and also, sadly, by those paranoid gay sisters who rationalize their own closetry by viewing their lesbianism as a private personal matter, of little consequence to the liberation of women.

I want a separate dyke movement through which we can fight the women's fight openly and proudly as upfront lesbians. I want gay women finally to get credit for all the work we've been doing and presently are doing under the banners of the gay and women's movements.

We need our own banner. We have nothing to lose by separating; we are already losing in movements that do not meet our needs. As feminists we're compromising ourselves in the gay movement, as lesbians we're "hushed up" in the women's movement. If we're going to educate, let us educate our lesbian sisters, not our gay brothers. If we're going to demand equality as women, let us not forget the fact that we are *gay* women, and that as such we must make the dyke issue a prominent one, retrieving it from the closets of feminism.

Divided we stand
Andrew Hodges

Issue 30, February 1977

A new dialogue has to begin on the subject of the relationship between lesbians and gay men. Major events, like the Canadian Fourth Annual Gay Conference (September 1976) and the Gay Academic Union conference in New York, end in set-piece battles resolved by the same vacuous demands, resolutions and promises that I have heard and seen fail many times before.

I have come to question the assumption that underlies these conflicts, the assumption that there is one coherent group that can be described as "gay people" or as "lesbians and gay men." The latter contrived phrase, which is the one now most favoured, makes particularly plain the difficulty of finding even a *word* for this group, for as everyone knows the words "homosexual" and "gay" are male-identified.

This difficulty is not some mere accident of vocabulary. It occurs because society is male-identified and sexist. And these problems with words are reflected at every level of social and political organization. I have come to the conclusion that the conception of "lesbians and gay men" as a single entity is an artifice that no one can really believe in and still less act upon.

Others are pointing to the same conflicts, but in a way that verges on suggesting that sexism is not a real issue or that women's oppression pales before the persecution of gay men. In contrast, I feel that sexism, by which I mean the institutionalized inequality between the statuses of men and women, is of overwhelming importance.

In the conventional view, there are supposed to be "people" who identify themselves as gay. Some just happen to be women, others men, just as some are black and others white. All alike are oppressed as "gays" in this picture; all oppose the imposition of heterosexual values, all suffer discrimination or the threat of it, all are denied openness and spontaneity, all are alienated from the family system. In this model of the movement, all "gay people" would put aside their differences (gender, race, class, and so on) to fight back.

But this model failed as soon as it was invented. Lesbians realised immediately that "putting aside their differences" would mean adopting male definitions of what were issues and what were solutions. Hence the women's groups, the women's caucuses, and lesbian separatism — all much to the annoyance of gay men.

Differences due to gender are just too great to be "put aside." Lesbians and gay men are oppressed in different ways, these differences being dictated by the heterosexist society. Lesbians need economic and social equality as women for their own material survival, for one thing, which gay men do not. Lesbians also have difficulty in being taken seriously as regards their preferences, choices and ideas, simply because they are women. Gay men do not. Lesbians have to overcome the notion that a woman partner is less than satisfying sexually, being "only" a woman (ie, "lacking" a cock). Gay men have no such problem — dullness is one of the few things that male sex has not been accused of! But they suffer from sexism in other ways. Expected to support the myth of masculinity, they attract a special anger for letting the side down, an anger which in the hands of Christians, Nazis and psychotherapists has taken more intensive forms than has usually been thought appropriate for controlling "mere" women.

Of the many divergences here, sexual expression itself is a focal point and is currently drawing particular attention. But attitudes to sex do not stand in isolation; they make sense only in the context of heterosexism.

All women, lesbian or not, suffer from being objectified sexually in a way that men rarely if ever experience. At work, or on the streets, women are attacked impersonally, arrogantly, by heterosexual male expectations. It is logical that women should want to remove sexuality from where it is irrelevant (employment, for example), to desexualize woman's public image, and to restrict sex to the private domain where a woman has at least some chance of being treated as a person.

Now in a very diluted way gay men do experience and share in women's situation. I remember moving when I was eighteen from a rather gentle co-ed high school to an all-male college. I was really shocked, and socially incapacitated, by the male chauvinism of the other students. Anything I thought or said in protest sounded like a confession of what I dreaded being discovered: that I had had no heterosexual experience. The other males might suspect from my "soft" attitude to women that I was (what I then deeply feared) a homosexual. They might deny me the respect and privilege I had in their eyes by virtue of being a male, might in fact treat me like a woman! I felt like a spy in their midst under false colours.

When gay liberation came along, I found that many other gay men had also experienced knowing male chauvinism from inside the enemy camp, and felt themselves similarly threatened by it.

And this is why it could be claimed that lesbians and gay men had a single struggle, that indeed gay liberation and women's liberation were identical. No analysis of gay men's oppression can do without this central connection. And yet it does not seem to me to be the whole story. Gay men cannot live by negatives alone, by not being sexist; they must have some positive way of expressing their sexual and social identity.

What gay men suggest they can do is to subvert heterosexism by their sexual expression. Gay male sexuality denies the assumptions of heterosexuality— that the words "woman" and "sex" are all but synonymous, for instance. That women and not men are sensuous, receptive; that there is something intrinsically female about making one's body attractive; that male bodies are naturally gross and ugly.

Gay men subtly or not so subtly undermine the image of the male as economic provider and political arbiter by extolling erotic attributes of men, attributes irrelevant to social status. They also, by a comparatively open admission of their need for attention, affection and passivity, subvert the concept of the purposefully striding, aggressive, impassive male.

Such attitudes do indeed run counter to sexist gender-roles—but they are also pretty well diametrically opposed to the feminist programme. Gay males encourage male-female equality, in the sense that they want men as overtly attractive, as open to erotic attention, as women are supposed to be. This is quite different from the feminist programme of removing sex from public life. Gay men are liable to see their sexuality as a redeeming, levelling force, their gift to the world. Women have had quite enough of men who think their sexuality is a gift to the world. Indeed, while feminism for the sake of equality wants *no one* to be a sexual object, gay men often speak and act as though they wanted *everyone* to be a sexual object.

These conceptions of equality are so very different that it is not surprising that contradictions occur. In particular, it is not possible for gay men honestly to do what they are often expected to do, namely, to give unreserved support to the women's movement. Though appreciating the strong connection between their own low status and women's low status, they cannot go along with the programme of desexualizing all public and social life.

On the street of Syracuse, New York, where I have been living, there are large posters which show a woman kicking a man in the balls, with the words: *Men! Next time you whistle at, hassle, ogle, rape, approach… may be your last!* How can gay men honestly accept the idea that making eyes is as bad as rape and deserves castration or death? They spend most of their waking hours looking and being looked at; they have to do a great deal of fending off of unwanted attention themselves, and find it hard to imagine that women are such delicate creatures that they cannot do the same. Of course, their more sanguine attitude is due to the fact that they are not objectified as *inferiors* by those who look at them. The fact remains that it is hard for gay men to consider non-violent sexual approaches as intrinsically evil and dangerous. For gay men, as Rita Mae Brown comments, "the easiness of rejection is incredible... sex isn't a weapon... it's a release."

Feminists are aware of gay men's sexual freedom, and sometimes attack gay men for objectifying each other. A nearby lesbian-feminist group attacks a Syracuse gay newsletter for defending those arrested for washroom sex. They say that the arrests are no worse than "the mutually exploitative and sexist nature of tearoom trysts," and that anyone who makes sexual contact in a toilet is being "oppressed by someone who doesn't view him in a fully human manner. Sexist tradition carries on." A similar attack is made by a person from the state human rights commission on all gay male casual sex, on the grounds that if uncommitted heterosexual sex is a sexist exploitation of women by men, then uncommitted gay sex must be an exploitation of men by men. But from a gay male point of view, the argument is the other way round. Gay sex can be mutual and unexploitative; if it were not for sexism then so could heterosexuality. Heterosexuality, in which women are allowed only the roles of victim or prostitute, should not be allowed to give all sex a bad name. (I think gay men should also be allowed to feel some sympathy for non-gay *men*, whose need for sexual release is just as great, and who do not have the same opportunity for achieving it in a decent way). Essentially gay males, by being males, have had the privilege of an environment in which a sex-positive attitude can work out well. They would like to see this extended to all — women and men, heterosexual and homosexual. Women have not had this privilege, and justifiably are apt to regard sexual liberation as simply an extension of male privileges.

To return to my main point, I feel that an honest appraisal of these conflicts is impossible if one is committed to the idea that "gay people" must have a unified view of sexual liberation. Lesbians and gay men necessarily have quite different standpoints.

It would be quite incorrect to try to draft lesbians into a gay men's programme for sexual expansiveness. For it must be remembered that in heterosexist society, a woman who says she wants sex takes on an incredibly low status. Lesbians have to resist being defined as particularly sex-hungry or sex-identified women. They have to do something much more radical: to redefine sexuality in such a way that it is no longer regarded as *something men do with cocks*. They have to get away from the idea of a "sexual act," and to develop verbal and poetic imagery in place of the intensely visual imagery imposed by males. These programmes are sex-positive, but in a quite different way from gay men's positiveness, and the result has been something utterly fresh and new — a lesbian feminist culture.

Gay men do not have this fresh and vigorous culture within the movement. One reason for this can be traced to the notion that in a movement of "lesbians and gay men," any accent on the male is anti-female and sexist. Thus male imagery is "glorifying men," and must be excluded. The result of this policy has been that the male body has been left to be trashed and packaged by gay capitalism. Exploitation of the sensations of the gay male as passive, desirable, masochistic, sensuous, with few exceptions has been abandoned to the crude and repetitive glossiness of profit-making publications, which model their imagery on "successful" heterosexist formulae. Comment on the enormous spectrum of male sexual possibilities has been restricted within the movement, sometimes explicitly for fear of offending lesbian sensibilities. Sado-masochism, pedophilia, baths and cruising, are often attacked by lesbian feminism for the objectification they all involve.

Accordingly, I cannot see that when we look at the positive aspects of gay men's and lesbians' identity (rather than at the purely negative facts of oppression), we discover any unifying feature that justifies the insistence on the unity of "lesbians and gay men." When in a particular group "unity" is achieved, I suspect it is at the cost of sweeping under the carpet all the difficult issues of sexism and sexuality. It is "unity" at the cost of the women's consciousness or at the cost of the men keeping a low profile as regards sexual expression.

Why are we all so hung up on unity anyway? Some of the standard reasons (strength, numbers, etc) look pretty thin in reality. A more subtle reason was admitted by gay men at a recent annual conference: they feared that an autonomous lesbian movement would threaten them by suggesting to the public that gay men couldn't get along with women. Using lesbians to make gay males more acceptable, however, is not exactly a strong ground for unity!

It is true that heterosexuals can diminish their terror of homosexuality if they can feel that there are women and men involved with each other at least somewhere in it. They won't be so afraid if they can be allowed to feel that, like other minorities, gay men have "their" womenfolk around. Nominal unity is used to *legitimize* gay men, who will applaud calls for lesbian autonomy as long as they know there will always be a few token lesbians attached to the "gay" (*ie*, gay men's) movement as well.

Unity and equality are so hard to achieve in practice! If "gay" and the "gay movement" are defined to refer to both women and men, then certainly every conference, panel, talk show, movie, dance, centre, etc, etc, must be organized with both in mind. But for anything which depends on voluntary, self-sacrificial effort, this is an all but impossible demand. Especially as, in practice, those who insist on equality of representation also support the right of lesbians to have separate, women-only events. The result, as everyone engaged in organizing knows but rarely admits, is that events done in the name of "lesbians and gay men" are done almost entirely by gay men who invite lesbians to make up numbers in a fashion redolent of Victorian chivalry. Males are thus perpetuated in the role of initiator and inviter, females as the quarry to be seduced, flattered, and never, *never* criticized in public.

The problem could be solved by abandoning the concept of "gay people" and speaking only of "gay men," where appropriate, and "lesbians" where appropriate. Why is there such resistance to this?

It would mean a confession of failure. And it would upset non-gay people. But probably the main difficulty is the implication of having something called a "gay men's movement," which even if not technically excluding lesbians, would in practice be organized by and for men only. It smells of male chauvinism. And in the words of Karla Jay, "women excluding men is different from men excluding women… because men excluding women reinforces our oppression. We don't oppress gay males as they do us, so we should be able to exclude them, but they should not exclude us." The model for this, the usual view, is eminently respectable. We approve of black-only movements for racial equality; we condemn white-only groups as racist. I suppose I have come to feel that the gay situation is different from what these analogies suggest. We need a reappraisal based on what really works.

Certainly, there *are* gay men who are male chauvinists, who do not want anything to do with women, who self-oppressively rationalize their sexual choice as choosing the "superior" sex. But the real male chauvinism is deeper and more subtle than this, and the current situation is nourishing it.

The editorial collective of *Gay Left* (London, England), used to describe their publication as "a socialist journal produced by gay men," which indeed it was. They were attacked for the use of the word "men," which was said to be used "with pride." They then retracted and now call themselves "gay people." By so doing they have in my view perpetuated the chauvinistic notion that *men* are allowed to call themselves *people*, while *women* are only *women*. I don't think they called themselves "men" with pride; I think it was an attempt to be honest. Conversely, I do not feel that current male gay organizations would like being cut down to size by having to admit the fact that they are *only* men.

Use of "gay people" or equivalents is presumably meant to combat lesbian invisibility, by reminding everyone that there are just as many lesbians as gay men. But the usage doesn't succeed. The *Advocate*'s recent article "Black and Gay" totally ignored black lesbians' existence. In response to complaints, we read that they "overlooked" what they hypocritically called "this important element of the gay community." Why can't they be honest? The *Advocate* is written for gay men. It wanted to run an article on black gay men. Why pretend that it was covering gay men and lesbians equally, but "overlooked" lesbians? I have come to feel that "gay people," "gay community" and so on do in fact serve to *perpetuate* lesbian invisibility rather than to combat it. It would be better to insist on always using the words "gay men" where appropriate, thus constantly provoking the question "so what about gay women?"

So often gay men form an organization, call it a "gay" organization, create male-oriented activities and then complain that "women won't come to our meetings." Steeped in paternalism, gay men are encouraged to believe that lesbians are in some sense "their" women, their rightful responsibility. This will do nothing for lesbians.

Dishonesty and pretense are greater enemies of progress than open dis-

agreement. The age-of-consent policy, for example, was supposedly affirm-
ed this year by a conference of "lesbians and gay men." In reality, it was formulated by gay men only. Many lesbians have since criticized it. How can we
deal honestly with important issues like this, issues which go to the heart of
what we mean by liberation, without acknowledging the deep differences
that arise between lesbians and gay men? Progress will only be impeded by the
sexist notion that gay men can organize and speak for "gay people." Polite
silence will achieve nothing. A new dialogue must begin.

Gay men and lesbians
can work together
Chris Bearchell

Issue 32, April 1977

In 1968, in a gesture of liberalism, the federal government broadened the
grounds for divorce in the Divorce Act to include homosexuality. In 1972, in
Prince Edward Island, a judge spent twelve pages clarifying that lesbianism
constituted homosexuality. Since that time there have been numerous cases,
recorded and otherwise, in which the use, or the threatened use of these
grounds has separated lesbian mothers from their children. In the eyes of our
oppressors, lesbians and homosexuals represent the same perversion — the
same threat. "Lesbians and gay men" have many differences and points of
disagreement, but we are oppressed by the same legal system, sometimes the
same laws, and, more important, we are all oppressed in a hundred and one
ways by the same ideology that has given rise to that system and those laws.
    Andrew Hodges in "Divided we stand" expresses scepticism about the
claim that we in fact have these things in common. I always look twice at
sweeping generalizations. Especially generalizations that say "men are or
want etc, etc; women are or want etc, etc." Especially when the generalization
is made by a man, albeit a gay man.
    Hodges tells us that the programme of men in the gay movement is "for sex-
ual expansiveness." On the other hand, it seems to me that the Canadian
movement, with which I am most familiar, represents the beginnings of a
cohesive bi-national movement with a growing lesbian caucus. And it is fortunately based on a strategy of public action and a programme of civil rights.
A programme which was developed because it is the most comprehensible to
the majority of gay women and men. One which most, if not all of us, could
agree on. One which would be able to include and mobilize the largest number
of people. One which would allow the handful of us who are gay liberationists
to contact, talk to, and — it is hoped — convince many more gay people that
civil rights are just a first step toward liberation.

What is missing from Hodges's article is basic gay liberation politics—in fact, politics period. Politics are dismissed and replaced with an unrealistic yearning after a common view of the sexual ideal.

Andrew Hodges has missed the point that it is not just lesbian feminists who think the male bars and baths are objectifying. I have spoken to gay men who think they are too, and who don't like it. I am a lesbian feminist who knows that women's bars can be just as objectifying. Rita Mae Brown, on the other hand, looks forward to the day when there will be "baths" for women with an inspired vision of what they'd be like. I was attacked for walking hand-in-hand with my lover—and yet Hodges says that, as a lesbian, I necessarily stand against "public sexuality." The point is this: not all gay people have reached a consensus about whether or not sexual expression should have a high or low profile. Neither have all gay men. Neither have all lesbians. And a movement that seeks to eventually include all gay people cannot afford to try to reach such a consensus, or to decide how many angels can dance on the head of a pin, either.

I will be the first to admit that, while I see a basis and a need for unity between gay women and men, I don't see the unity. It does not yet exist. Of course, the movement as I hope to see it does not yet exist either; that doesn't mean I'm packing it in and heading back to the hills (though sometimes I'd like to).

Unity will only be forged when those few dykes who are in the gay movement can convince the movement as a whole to give priority to lesbian demands and struggles. Yes, lesbians have been burned by sexism in this movement. No, saying you're sorry won't make it better. Doing something on the other hand just might. Throwing full support behind a child custody fight, for instance, just might. We can't say for sure, because we haven't had the chance to try, yet.

It is also true that lesbians need our own movement—while unity and the needs we share with gay men are political, not all lesbians' needs are. Caucuses, or our own organizations, which do not dilute the impact of our common protest, are the only ways to ensure that past mistakes are not repeated. Whether we are in the same organizations or not, we can be united. Political unity in action is far more important than formal unity in name. And meantime, autonomous lesbian organizations can work toward mobilizing the lesbian community in a way that the gay movement has never been able to—and can fulfill other, less explicitly political needs. That does not mean that we have to forget the fact that, when the weight of the straight world comes down on queers, they don't care whether we're faggots or dykes.

Sexism is not simply, as Hodges would have us believe, "the institutionalized inequality between the statuses of men and women." It is also, and perhaps more importantly, conceiving of individuals in terms of narrow, stultifying roles determined by gender. Hodges takes many of the ingredients of the traditional stereotype of woman and recombines them to portray lesbians and lesbian sexuality. As if dykes haven't had enough of that very shit. Who is Hodges to tell me what, if anything, I have to overcome to accept the validity of my sexual identity? Who is he to concern himself with lesbian invisibility? We'll do what we can to take care of that ourselves, thank you. What makes him think he can attribute a monopoly on striving for a "sex-positive attitude" to men? We live in a sex-negative society. The psyches of the sexually exploited and the sexually exploiting are equally damaged. Individuals suffering from either *can* do much to overcome them. But no one can do so completely. And, I'd wager that this is one lesbian whose "sensibilities" are probably no more easily offended than Hodges's own.

Hodges's article begins with a reference to words, words, words. Will we ever arrive at universally accepted definitions of all the labels we have ever worn? No. Will we ever cease haggling over them? No. Is it important? Yes, but not enough to lose sleep over. By all means, let's discuss it, but let's not pretend we've concluded the discussion. Yes, "gay" and "homosexual" are male-identified to some gay women and men. The dynamic lesbian culture that Hodges describes includes a whole spectrum of artists who describe themselves variously as: dykes, women who love women, gay and proud, homosexual women, and just plain lesbians. I use gay when I'm tactful and dyke when I'm angry. I think lesbian is a beautiful and overwhelmingly sexual word. My lover, on the other hand, shies away from it as a word that, for her, has always been derogatory. There are probably as many opinions on this subject as there are gay people. But such differences can't be attributed to, nor can they explain, whatever incompatibility exists between lesbians and gay men.

The expressed intention of "Divided we stand" is to provoke a dialogue. Such a dialogue is necessary. But if it is to be a productive one, it must begin by recognizing that we are dealing with a political context. It is doubtful how productive it is for lesbians committed to the gay movement to be both angered and undermined by a supposed attempt at dialogue.

Confessions
of a lesbian gay liberationist
Beatrice Baker

Issue 57, October 1979

"God is coming. And is *she* pissed...."

So says the button a friend brought back from the Michigan Womyn's Music Festival. She takes it to mean that God will swoop down in vengeance and set this sexist world aright. Or at least zap a few male chauvinist pigs.

Myself, I secretly think that she's coming, like the Old Testament Jehovah punishing the wayward Jews, to kick ass because we've blown it. We've blown it by expending more energy hassling each other than trying to effect real change.

Sixteen years ago as a student in the United States I read Betty Friedan —
with curiosity, consternation and anger. As a student I embraced the student
rights movement. Out of horror at the carnage of the Viet Nam war, I committed myself to the anti-war movement. And because these movements in particular and the left in general were so incredibly sexist, I, along with many
other politically active women, broke with these groups. We began in earnest
to raise our consciousness, sharpen our skills and put all our time and energy
into the women's liberation movement. We worked not to end someone else's
oppression but our own.

It was a fearful and joyful time. We raged and celebrated, explored and
grew. And through the liberating influence of the women's liberation movement I discovered my lesbianism. I came out. Now I combat the oppression
that strikes at the essence of my being. Because I am a lesbian I channel most
of my energy into the gay liberation movement.

About ten years ago, when straight women were the majority of movement
activists, a dyke in the movement worked secretly and carefully because lesbians weren't always welcome. Straight women feared that society, the
media, men would dismiss the movement as "just a bunch of dykes."

But now, ironically, the majority of movement activists seem to be gay. In
fact, in most women's gatherings the unspoken assumption that everyone is
lesbian is so strong that I'm surprised straight women haven't sprouted "How
dare you presume I'm gay!" buttons. And yet at some feminist gatherings,
comprised largely of lesbians, I feel as welcome as an atheist at a Baptist convention.

Discussions with women who have, or are, working in the gay liberation
movement reveal common feelings of alienation. We have been called "*just*
lesbians," referred to as "not feminists," and even been accused of being
"anti-feminist" by lesbians active in other movements.

Perhaps because it is easier, we get sucked in by the seductiveness of the
single solution: as if that which will liberate mothers, will liberate native
women, will liberate working class women, will liberate older women, will
liberate gay women.

"When the revolution comes...." "When we all get wages for house-
work...." "When we live in a socialist state...." "When we've established
LesbiaNation...." "When you do things my way..." ...sexism will cease to
exist, homophobia will fade away, nuclear war will be no danger, the ecology
will be salvaged, there'll be no unemployment, etc, etc, etc.

Maybe there is a single solution to all of our problems. Maybe there is a God
(of whichever sex). But four years of Jesuit education simply taught me that I
could not prove the existence of God. And a year of studying communist
states, reading Marx, Engels, Lenin, Trotsky and Mao, simply taught me that
acceptance of a single systemic solution to all the world's problems is likewise
an act of faith. I'm quite willing to admit that I'm wrong. But I've yet to meet
anyone who has seriously tried to teach, persuade, convince or demonstrate
to me the validity of her particular "single solution" position.

Instead, my political philosophy is condemned without dialogue and without explanation as conservative. And my political activities labelled politically incorrect, or at least a waste of time, without suggestions as to what I could be doing on a day-to-day basis. Polite discussion wins more converts than condemnation. So, until the revolution arrives, I'll continue to do the best I know how.

James Baldwin and Franz Fanon, among others, have documented how much more psychologically damaging "invisibility" can be than actual physical discrimination. Straight folks say "homosexual" and see in their minds a gay male. I don't want to be invisible, and a homosexual organization, mixed or lesbian, is visible in the community *as* a gay group; a feminist organization is not.

I don't advocate every lesbian devoting herself to the gay liberation movement and I can't criticize lesbians simply because they don't work with us; their priorities could include doing things of benefit to me. In turn I expect the same courtesy and respect.

Don't rain on my parade, sister; I'm marching for you too.

Gay men's feminist mistake
Brian Mossop

Issue 67, October 1980

In debates of recent years about relations between lesbians and gay men, the special relevance of feminism to gay men has often been assumed. In Canada and elsewhere, some gay male activists have been vigorously promoting feminism as a basis for organizing gay men—often in language filled with charges of sexism and appeals to guilt, uttered in a particularly self-righteous, more-feminist-than-thou tone of voice.

The *substance* behind this has not been very clear, but here (I think) is the basic idea:

The gay male movement has gone off track. There was a time in the late Sixties and early Seventies when we were close to the "feminist roots of gay liberation." But now gay men have lost touch with these roots. The macho image is dominant and it is the centre of a commercial culture that is taking us away from the path of liberation. To return to this path, links must be made with lesbians and straight women, and the banner of feminism taken up.

This outlook is in my opinion thoroughly misguided. Feminism has arisen out of the situation of *women* in our society. That situation includes a system of gender roles, and a family institution based upon them, which I (like the gay male feminists) believe to be the reason both women and gays are oppressed. However, *nothing follows from this about how to organize gay men*. The source of oppression may be the same, but the form it takes is different.

Gay men are treated like women only in superficial ways, as in queer jokes. We do not earn sixty percent of the wages of straight men, we do not enter into contracts where economic support is exchanged for personal service to a man (indeed, we are legally prevented from marrying each other). Queer-bashing and hustling do not work like rape and prostitution.

We suffer in distinct ways as men-who-are-not-heterosexual. We are dragged though the courts for having sex with each other. We are treated as the monsters of society: corrupters of children, destroyers of the family and of civilization itself.

That is why here in Toronto you will find very few men at International Women's Day marches (this I know from personal experience)—but lots of them taking part in self-defence classes, in the defence of *The Body Politic*'s right to publish discussions of issues like pedophilia, and in the campaign against raids on the baths.

Feminism simply does not address these immediate concerns of gay men.

Which is not to say that the betterment of the position of women will not help gay men. I think it will, and we should devote *some* effort to supporting *certain* feminist demands. But before we can support, we must organize ourselves—around our own needs. I say *certain* demands because it is against our interests to support feminists who demand stronger pornography laws or ignorantly denounce gay S/M and pedophilia as manifestations of what they call male violence and power. Anti-lesbian trends in feminism are of course against our interests too; indeed, the fact that lesbians are still in an uphill fight against heterosexism in the women's movement underscores the impossibility of making feminism as it now exists a rallying point for gay men.

The advocates of feminism-for-gay-men might agree that it has little to say about raids on baths, but I have often heard claims that a feminist analysis *can* help us deal with such matters as gay male sexual and emotional interaction, creating better social environments for gay men, and defining a new sense of what it means to be a man.

*

Sex. Nothing I have read by feminists about straight men's or lesbians' sexuality has been particularly applicable to gay men. This seems inevitable, since women have no experience in the matter.

Gay male relations cannot be understood in terms of heterosexual relations, since neither partner has been raised as a woman. This frustrates attempts to ape straights, however hard some may try. Related to this is the absence in gay sex of the built-in *power* relationship of straight sex (unless it is present for some other reason such as difference in class, race or age). This is true of lesbians too, but since our different sexual upbringing has apparently resulted in somewhat different sexual fantasies and practices, we cannot take lesbians as models.

*

Social environments. Gay men regularly complain about the "bar and bath scene." Can we use the experience of the women's movement to make these and other environments better? I don't see how.

Women have had to find ways of coming together in the face of a lack of money and isolation from each other in marriage (hence the idea of "sisterhood"). But this is not the situation of gay men. We are much better off financially, and what we are trying to create is not environments supplementary to family life, but substitutes for it.

The environments that exist have their problems, some arising from the predominance of commercial motives, some from the difficulties of male sexual emotional interaction. But these are not the problems that feminists—straight or lesbian—have had to cope with.

*

Being a man. Men need to become less aggressive and competitive, and the mainstream feminist view—that both sexes should learn to be either passive or aggressive as the situation demands—does provide us with a goal. However, since as men we are coming from the "aggressive" end of the scale, we must find our own way to that goal.

In searching for a way, we will not be helped by trends within feminism that idealize traditional "female" characteristics and make men responsible for violence and war — and Evil generally. While a degree of antipathy toward men is perhaps necessary on the part of women, such an attitude has no place among gay men.

Yet I have actually heard gay men say that they don't really like men (except in the bedroom), that they want "to refuse to be men." It's hard to imagine a movement of gay men getting anywhere without the fundamental bond of "men loving men" *just as they are*, with all the contradictions of people raised in a sexist society. To hate ourselves as men is as harmful as to feel guilty about being gay.

The hope that feminism could help us redefine maleness arises, I think, from a belief that the current "masculine" gay male image is a step *backward* from the older image of the queen — and a step toward identification with straight men and "patriarchy." Actually it is more a step *forward*, because it is closer to the reality of our lives — that we *are* men, but not *straight* men.

The moustache-and-check-shirt look and its variants are in fact ambiguous. They *can* be closety and straight-oriented, but they can also express a refusal to let "man" and "straight man" mean the same thing. They can mock the straight male image, challenging it on its own ground. There are times in certain Toronto bars when you can find "masculine"-looking men cuddling and generally relating to each other in ways that straight men do not.

The "masculine" image is the latest attempt by gay men to define who we are in the face of the dominant idea that we are not really men (though, as already noted, our economic and legal situation *is* that of men.) Earlier attempts at self-definition involved various sorts of effeminacy. Drag queens, for instance, by adopting exaggerated traditional female dress and gesture, have shown how ridiculous society's identification of gay men with women really is.

However, neither drag nor other forms of effeminacy can challenge the male image on its own ground. The furthest they go is to define us as a mech-

"It's no fun being a lesbian separatist trapped in a faggot's body."

Gary Ostrom, Issue 38, November 1977, (thanks to Tommy Pace)

anical mixture of woman and man. Whereas if we look at the "masculine" gay men whom we know (rather than consider the macho image in the abstract), we can see that they have often subtly incorporated the effeminate tradition into the current image/identity.

Feminism is attractive because, if gay men could adopt some version of it, we would have an ideological basis for unity with lesbians and straight women. But such an alliance, however important, cannot be based on ideas that do not speak directly to gay men's concerns.

Feminism is also attractive because it is a relatively well worked out body of ideas, and gay men lack such a theory as a guide to action. But no theory can guide us successfully unless it comes out of the actual lives of gay men. It is no use trying to see our lives in terms of the lives of women or any other oppressed group.

We must find our own way.

Everyfaggot's dyke, everydyke's faggot
Chris Bearchell

Issue 44, June/July 1978

Stereotype One. A faggot is a person (male) who is weak in body and mind; who, at one and the same time, emulates and hates/fears women. He is bitchy, fastidious, swishy, neurotic and an all-round failure as a man. By the way, he also tends to be attracted to his own kind.

Stereotype Two. A dyke is someone (female) who is aggressive, overbearing and violent. She is a man-hater who acts like a man because she couldn't catch one if her life depended on it. She is a mean, ugly bull who is neurotic and an all-round failure as a woman. Oh yes, she prefers other women as sexual partners.

That is the world — ours — according to *them.*

The most oppressive thing about gay stereotypes is that they sometimes induce *us* to believe them. There are fortunately fewer of us now who think that accepting lesbian or gay sexuality means accepting straights' lies about us or parodying their twisted roles. But we are still tempted to believe the myths about each other. There are gay men who reacted joyfully when lesbians were excluded from "gay" bars because they were glad to be rid at last of the spectre of the brawling dyke. There are lesbians who have implied, or even stated, that gay men are in fact child molesters who've cost all gay people legal protection in the human rights code.

The most insidious thing about gay stereotypes is that we sometimes create our own. Have you met the faggot or dyke who is thrilled to the marrow when someone pays him or her the ultimate compliment: "I never would have guessed!"? The "new gay machismo" seems designed to provoke just such a response. New, subtle versions of our old, blatant stereotypes for each other have taken hold within (of all places) our movements.

There are male gay activists who tremble at the approach of "tough" lesbian feminists and shudder at their political "irrationality." This stereotype, shall we call it *Stereotype Three,* draws in part upon general male concepts of women. Its most dangerous tendency is to discourage discussion because lesbians and feminists are presumed to be inscrutable women — emotional rather than analytical and, above all, "sensitive" and apt to cry "sexist" at the least provocation (not that provocation is being invited).

Equally unjust assumptions about gay male activists are held by many lesbian feminists. One of the more common is that gay men believe that it is possible to change the definition of masculinity just enough to allow gay men to fit comfortably into a male-dominated society (thus leaving women, including lesbians, holding the short end of the stick). This assumption rests on several premises, some of which are true, others not. It is true that our society is male-dominated. It is also true that legal change does not equal social change.

It is not true that legal change alone could alter entrenched societal definitions of what, for example, it means to be male. Conceptions of masculine behaviour hinge on conceptions of feminine behaviour, and the other way around. It will not be possible to change the one without changing the other. It is also untrue that gay liberationists don't, by and large, realize this.

So, *Stereotype Four* might be the gay man who earns enough money to afford to be publicly gay in order to fight for the rights that will eventually enable him to earn *more*. With impunity, and at the expense of women and other oppressed groups.

Disagreement about who could and should be public has a lot to do with the hard feelings within our community between women and men. Openly gay men are far more numerous than public lesbians. Men are sometimes resentful that it is they who stick out their necks by being public and are then criticized for male-dominated press conferences, demonstrations, publications and so on. Lesbians are often resentful that the man standing next to them, doing the same job, is presumed to be a primary "bread-winner," whether he is gay or straight, and is paid accordingly, while lesbians are "worth" less simply because they are women. Lesbians have a justifiably greater concern for job security. For them, breaking out of the female role means taking a career and self-sufficiency very seriously. It is often a matter of survival in a world that systematically discriminates against women.

Reality One is a lesbian and feminist who, because she has a relentless respect for organization, waited until January 1 to come out, even though she decided to do so in November. She went to a drop-in one evening and found herself carrying a picket sign against Anita Bryant the next. Within three months, she was on the co-ordinating committee of one of Canada's fastest-growing lesbian organizations and now faithfully edits its newsletter. This woman loves to engage in debate and discussion and sees as one of her goals developing political unity between lesbians and gay men. When asked to appear on television, she overcame what she considered to be a "symbolic" obstacle easily and was only really concerned that she "say all the right things."

Men are not only not discriminated against, but for them a challenge to the traditional male role means a very different thing. *Reality Two* is a male gay friend who is breaking out of the male role in part by refusing to be competitive and career-oriented, at least in any traditional sense of that expression. Having made peace with his sexuality, he is determined to live according to his own lights. He walks down Toronto's Yonge Street holding his lover's hand (Yonge Street isn't bad, but watch out for College.) While he may recommend avoiding certain streets, he hasn't let violence, verbal or physical, stop him from being himself. He is a non-professional hospital worker who may earn more than women doing similar jobs. But he knows *they* will never let him climb the ladder. While he may worry about his future, success in their terms doesn't mean that much to him.

Two realities. They are individuals, exceptions, one-in-a-million kind of people—but they exist. And they have far more to offer us, to teach us, than stereotypes—our own or anyone else's.

Why I write for *The Body Politic*
Jane Rule

Issue 80, January/February 1982

Gay friends of mine, both men and women, who, like me, have established themselves in various professions like teaching, writing, the law, often question my involvement with *The Body Politic*, a paper they read only intermittently, about which they are nervously ambivalent.

They are quick to criticize, to focus on issues they themselves would not support, like sexual relationships between adults and children, sexual activity in bars and baths. They consider such behaviour exactly what makes it difficult for people like themselves to be accepted, for, as long as they are identified with those extremes of sexual behaviour, they feel unable to argue their right to be in positions of responsibility for children, for sick people, for people in difficulty with the law. Many of them are at odds with their churches and neighbourhoods and political parties only in the fact of their sexual preference, and are at pains to prove they are in all ways as responsible as other citizens for the moral health of their communities. If they do belong to groups advocating social change, they tend to choose humanitarian ventures like Save the Children and Oxfam, or causes like Amnesty International which to date excludes their own. They argue that their sexuality should be a private matter: to make it a public issue would be to distort its importance to themselves as well as the world they live in.

But then they do agree that they feel guilty, too, at not doing something, or something more, to change the climate for homosexuals. But they really don't see how I can appear in a paper whose policy is to advertise and support sexual behaviour which can only damage the homosexual image in the eyes of the majority and increase prejudice against us. Since my personal life seems so much like theirs, they really would like to know why, and I try to tell them.

Neither sexual liberation between men and women and boys nor the baths are priorities of my own, obviously. Though I am perfectly willing to listen to Gerald Hannon extolling the pleasures of sexual toys like whips and nipple clips, I will continue to have reservations about the celebration of master/slave games, not because they are kinky but because they are all too normal, not to say reactionary. The political value of his argument for me remains. Until our right to consenting sexual acts is established, limited only by the rights of others, no homosexual behaviour will be protected, because anything any of us does is offensive to the majority. Policing ourselves to be less offensive to the majority is to be part of our own oppression. Tokenism has never been anything else.

By writing for *The Body Politic*, I refuse to be a token, one of those who doesn't really seem like a lesbian at all. If the newspaper is found to be obscene, I am a part of that obscenity. And proud to be, for, though my priorities

and the paper's aren't always the same, I have been better and more thoughtfully informed about what it is to be homosexual in this culture by *The Body
Politic* than by any other paper, offered information the straight press refuses
to publish, whether about John Damien's case, or the legal niceties of crossing
the border or the prospect of being included in human rights codes across
Canada. I am kept informed about our scholars, artists, politicians, as well as
our victims and fighters. Most of the people I know who don't read *The Body
Politic* regularly are dangerously ignorant about what is actually going on
either here or abroad.

While too many homosexuals nervously debated the bad taste and / or bad
timing of the article "Men loving boys loving men," a number of heterosexuals acknowledged both the value of *The Body Politic* and the importance of
the issues when they took out an ad in the *Globe and Mail*, asking that obscenity charges be dropped. That statement was important, and it did impress
some homosexuals that people like Margaret Atwood and June Callwood
thought *The Body Politic* worth defending.

Whether we like it or not, our sexuality isn't a private matter, and the altruism of some good citizens hasn't changed the government's mind. What will
change the social climate is our own persistence, through government-
sponsored court cases and police raids, or silence and bigotry in the straight
press, to gain our rights.

The Body Politic has a proud history and future in that battle.

Agree to differ
Eve Zaremba

Letter, Issue 81, March 1982

The crux of my disagreement with Jane Rule lies in what I take to be the implications of her column: that for us the only alternative to being politically passive is to work for and through gay liberation. This may be true for gay men,
but it most assuredly is not for lesbians. We have the feminist movement.

Feminists view gay liberation as quintessentially male; almost all the issues
and priorities it espouses are male. Rule acknowledges this fact in her column. Rule's point is that by supporting gay liberation, in spite of its male character and orientation, we can best protect our rights and future as lesbians.
Many politically active and astute lesbians disagree with such a position
which explicitly does not differentiate between male and female sexuality—
thus between women and men—or take into account the divergences in our
respective political, social and economic positions in society. Indeed, the
straight majority does lump lesbians, when it remembers us, with gay men as
"homosexuals." That is rather like the use of "man" to mean the human race.
Subsuming the interests of women under those of men is standard practice.

It's what male chauvinism is about and is precisely what should be resisted.

Numbers of women choose to work with men in gay liberation, but many more prefer to look for opportunities to work altogether outside male control, no matter how benign. These opportunities they find in women's liberation: some aspect or current of feminism. That is where they put their energies as both women and lesbians.

Gay liberation is a male movement. There is nothing wrong in admitting it; it is an exercise in futility, if not hypocrisy, to deny it. It does not help our struggles, either mutual or separate, to ignore differences and their political implications. Better to agree to differ where we obviously differ and agree to work together where our interests coincide. Then there is a better chance of building real solidarity and cooperation.

Cruising and censorship

Occasionally a movie comes along which seems to crystallize all of the objections gay people have felt about the depiction of their lives on the screen. For a time the film becomes a touchstone by which all other Hollywood productions are to be judged. It becomes a measure of progress in the struggle to force the image makers to represent gay life accurately and in all of its diversity. *The Boys in the Band*, directed by William Friedkin in 1969, was one such film. It was a rallying cry to an entire generation of newly-politicized gay people who had long endured Hollywood's stereotypes and distortions. A decade later, *Cruising* was another. Released in 1980 and directed once again by William Friedkin, *Cruising* became a focus of protest for thousands of gay men in communities across North America.

Cruising, filmed on location in New York's West Village, taking over gay bars and employing willing gay men as extras, raised many urgent questions about self-oppression, censorship and control of the corporate media. Questions such as: were the protests that disrupted on-location shooting a form of censorship or a strategy of protection? Were the protesters opposed to Hollywood's distortion of their lives or were they opposed to the depiction of S/M sex, a particular sexual lifestyle that more conventional gays found distasteful or embarrassing? Does a film director have a "right" to make a film which exploits the resources of a community and then ignores all input from that community? Is corporate Hollywood *capable* of capturing the realities of the lives of gay people? When we talk about freedom of the press, of freedom of the media, whose definitions are we using? These issues — and more — were raised in the gay press throughout North America during and after the production of *Cruising*. *The Body Politic* dealt with many of them in a series of articles, columns and letters, some of which appear in the following pages.

Sex, death and free speech:
the fight to stop Friedkin's *Cruising*
Scott Tucker

Issue 58, November 1979

The Ramble, a bucolic thicket on the west side of Central Park, has been a cruising spot for as long as anyone can remember. Cole Porter celebrated it in song in 1935 ("Picture Central Park without a sailor..."), and it is still one of New York's most popular *rendezvous*, sun-dappled and casual by day, more intense at night.

And more dangerous. One night last summer a gang of toughs roamed through with baseball bats ("We went out to get the queers," one of them said later in his court testimony) and beat six men. Five were taken to hospital, seriously injured.

This morning, though, the place seems idyllic: gay men in cut-offs and swimsuits lie sunning, talking, now and then rising to go off into the woods. For a while I wander the twisted paths, picking my way through the dense growth, and finally sit down on a bench to read my book of essays by Rosa Luxemburg and eat fruit from my knapsack. Police barricades are still up nearby: the night before, William Friedkin had been shooting a castration-killing scene here for his film, *Cruising*.

I am in New York for the protests against the film. On August 20, 1979, eight hundred of us had marched from a rally in Sheridan Square to a film site on West Street. We had shrilled our disco whistles like a swarm of angry locusts and had whooped Indian warcries—"The streets belong to the people!" On West Street the cops surrounded us. Somebody handed me an egg and I figured eggs can't beat clubs—I was saving it for Friedkin when a cop took it. "But that's for my breakfast," I said, and then added, "Sit on it."

Mounted police charged into a large group that had broken away to get closer to the filming. Nightsticks cracked on skulls and some of the protesters began to throw bottles. One man tried setting fire to a camera cable with a book of matches and was quickly circled by kicking, clubbing cops. A dozen of us broke through, grabbed the cable and began a tug of war with the police until they pummelled us back. For the first time in my life I called cops "pigs."

Interviewed in the *New York Times*, Friedkin called the protesters "a gang of unruly fanatics." *Soho Weekly News* columnist Allan Wolper warned that "The Constitution isn't stamped 'For Gays Only'.... The people leading the sit-downs and whistle-blowing against the film will lose their war for equality if they manage to win their battle for censorship."

What constitutes censorship? What constitutes self-defence? The subtleties and ambiguities had been considered. The protesters themselves were acutely aware of them. Tugging on that cable—knowing I wanted to destroy that camera, stop the filming—I suddenly saw how it had crystallized for me. I knew exactly what I was doing.

This morning in the Ramble, though, certain questions remain. Should we have been trying to stop *Cruising*? Was that possible or realistic — or desirable? Should we have simply said, not in *our* neighbourhood, not on *our* streets? Should we have waited until the film is shown at theatres and planned protests then?

Because *Cruising* burst like a bomb in the gay community, there wasn't always time for these and other questions to become clear. Key issues were hedged or obscured or not recognized by gay spokespeople, by the film-makers and by the "free press" defending "free speech" without ever making connections with "free" enterprise.

Some questions can only be left open, but to others the protesters, the film-makers and the film itself can provide answers.

*

In 1969, William Friedkin directed the film version of Mart Crowley's play, *The Boys in the Band*. Earlier that year gays in Greenwich Village had fought back a police attack at the Stonewall Inn, and a new generation of activists—not just "politicos" but people from throughout the gay community—protested the film's depiction of gays as doomed queens.

Friedkin defended his film then by saying that *"The Boys in the Band* is not about gay life. It's about human problems. I hope there are happy homosexuals. They just don't happen to be in my films." "You show me a happy homosexual," says one character in the movie, "and I'll show you a gay corpse."

Cruising offers gay corpses in spades, and Friedkin is equally disingenuous in defending it. "This isn't a film about gay life," he told journalist Vito Russo. "It's a murder mystery with an aspect of the gay world as background."

Jerry Weintraub, the film's producer, told the *New York Daily News*, "The gay leaders keep asking me why I don't make a nice film about homosexuals. I don't know what that means."

Neither does the American public. The truth is that happy homosexuals "just don't happen to be" in *any* Hollywood films—unless they go straight. The more substantially a story deals with homosexuals, the more substantially sad or sinister the film. *The Boys in the Band* was a sad gay melodrama with campy comic relief. *Cruising* is an utterly unrelieved gay horror film.

The script of *Cruising*, written by Friedkin, is based on a 1970 novel by Gerald Walker, an editor at the *New York Times*. At the time the novel appeared, gay activists asked Walker what he thought the book's social effects would be. "Ah, it's not my business," he replied. A police lieutenant in the book says of gays, "They think the straight world is the enemy, but it's themselves." All but spoken, this remains the key message in William Friedkin's film.

*

A previous film by Friedkin, *The Exorcist*, portrays the gradual, gruesome possession of an amiable teenage girl by Satan. After great struggle Satan is finally exorcised, but dark powers still lurk and loom in the world.

The script of *Cruising*, which the filmmakers kept so secret that *Village Voice* columnist Arthur Bell described it as "more difficult to come by than knowledge of Skylab's crash sites," shows that possession and exorcism are still dominant themes for Friedkin.

In the first scene, a tugboat captain discovers "a severed gangrenous Human Arm" floating in the polluted Hudson. Later, in the city morgue, "the camera stays hypnotically on the lifeless limb" while a detective asks questions and a medical examiner deciphers on the arm a tattoo reading "Pleasure."

Friedkin claims *Cruising* is a murder mystery, but his script contains no puzzle as to "whodunit"—"it" in this case is a series of dismemberings of gay men—only as to *why*.

A straight cop, played by Al Pacino, is sent out as an undercover "gay" decoy to find the killer. "How far do I have to go?" Pacino's character asks his captain. "If we send out an undercover narc, he grows a beard and long hair but he doesn't have to become an addict." But during his immersion in the leather and S/M bars he becomes possessed. He breaks up with his girlfriend and becomes interested in an unsuccessful gay playwright, with whose jealous lover he has a violent quarrel.

The killer is portrayed as a failed artist, but a heterosexual, a narcissist fond of musicals. Whenever moving in for the kill, he speaks in "The Voice of Jack." The killer has a humiliating encounter with his father, and we learn that the Voice of Jack is, in fact, his father's voice. This encounter turns out to be imaginary: dad is long dead, though son continues to write him letters begging for approval. Killing exorcises the punitive father and the killer's own suspected homosexuality—briefly.

The cop and the killer finally cruise each other one night in Central Park. The killer muses nihilistically on the cosmos and "black holes," and both then enter a dark tunnel (shades of Freud). They drop their pants. ("How big are you?" "Party size." "What are you into?" "I'll go anywhere." "Do me first." "Hips or lips?" "Go for it.") Both reach for their knives, but the cop "garrotes" the killer first. As he dies he stares, unbelieving, at the cop "in whom he sees — his father — himself." The next script note adds that the cop is now "released. He's done his job, he's made a choice, and he's a civilized member of society." Granting that Friedkin intended irony here, it is the first sign of it in the script, and it occurs in a parenthetical note that the director may appreciate, but the public will not see.

The cop's own exorcism appears successful, but demons lurk again when a fresh gay corpse is found—the failed writer to whom the cop had been attached. The film ends with the cop's promotion to detective and his return to his girlfriend.

Friedkin adds one touch to this story that may seem gratuitous but which in fact perfects the emasculation of a predator driven to castrate his prey. In a morgue scene a medical examiner informs the police lieutenant that one victim's anus was "dilated at the time of death" and that he found some semen. "Aspermia," he said. "No sperm. Your killer is shooting blanks." Friedkin does *not* have the killer dress up in the clothes of a long-dead mother; he may have refrained only because Hitchcock's *Psycho* beat his psycho to it.

In what may have been a concession to protests against *Cruising*, producer Jerry Weintraub once mentioned the possible inclusion of "a good, healthy, gay relationship" in the film. In the context of the other characters in the script, this couple would look like vegetarians in a tribe of cannibals. The few gays with any character have but two roles: killer and victim, and not even all the victims are painted in more than two dimensions. *Cruising* doesn't explore the lives of gay people. It murders them in sequence and exploits their deaths.

*

When gay activists first learned of plans to shoot *Cruising* in the Village, many pleaded with the filmmakers simply to *consult* with the gay community. In an open letter to Friedkin, journalist Doug Ireland wrote, "You didn't want to talk to anybody. Instead you went to the Mineshaft... and hired its people as consultants. Now we know that the Mineshaft is owned by two heterosexual ex-cops.... Well, since you wouldn't talk to us, we decided to talk to you — in the streets."

By early June, the film was in the second of eight weeks of on-location shooting. In his regular column in the *Village Voice*, Arthur Bell reported that the film promised to be "the most oppressive, ugly, bigoted look at homosexuality ever presented on the screen," and urged readers "to give Friedkin and his production crew a terrible time if you spot them in your neighbourhood."

On July 23 more than six hundred gay people packed Washington Square Methodist Church for an emergency Town Meeting, responding both to Bell's warning and to the meeting flyer which read, in part: "*Cruising* is a film which will encourage more violence against homosexuals. In the current climate of backlash against the gay rights movement, this movie is a genocidal act." Doug Ireland, who helped organize the meeting, later reported in the *Soho Weekly News* that the audience was asked how many of them had been targets of anti-gay violence within the last year, or had friends who had been. More than half raised their hands. Outside, meanwhile, a group of young toughs sharing anti-fag jokes with the cops harassed the hundred or so gays who couldn't cram into the church. The gang later got into their car and tried running people down on Christopher Street; one woman was injured in the hip.

Ireland was asked at the meeting whether protests against the film might violate free speech rights. "We're not attacking Billy Friedkin's right to make this film," he responded. "We're just telling him we don't want it made off our backs. That's not censorship, that's self-defence."

The day after the July 23 Town Meeting, gay activist Ethan Geto led a group to meet with Mayor Ed Koch and ask him to withdraw Friedkin's film permit. Koch refused. "To do otherwise," he said, "would involve censorship. It is the business of this city's administration to encourage the return of film-making to New York City to whatever extent feasible with filmmakers." When Nancy Littlefield, the city's liaison with film companies, was asked by phone if she thought *Cruising* would be good for the city and its citizens, she replied, "Anything that brings this city seven million dollars is good," and hung up.

Koch was right: withdrawing the film permit *would* have been censorship. But Littlefield's point was lost on no one — the "principled" stand on free speech was also a very profitable one.

*

In an interview with Pete Hamill of New York's *Daily News*, Friedkin said, "I went to the Anvil and the Mineshaft (two Village leather bars) for three months. The guys in it seem to enjoy it; it's unique, unusual, and that's why I'm looking at it. I'm trying to capture the energy of it and the quality of ritual. I have no idea what it means to them, but it's a commitment."

Speaking of the undercover cop in *Cruising*, Friedkin says, "He's initially repulsed, as many people might be. If you dropped a citizen of Grand Rapids into the Mineshaft, he'd probably collapse."

Friedkin knows, of course, that good citizens will pay good money to collapse. There is a profit to be made from incomprehension and intolerance.

He takes pains to express his *own* tolerance: "There is no comment in this film that it is degrading or that it's wonderful — just here it is," he told Vito Russo in an interview. "These scenes could be run as documentary footage. I don't find what goes on in these bars particularly shocking. I find myself in opposition to the gay community people who find sex bars offensive and condemn them. There's no doubt in my mind that this film won't provoke violence against gays, but I think it might very well provoke more men into this kind of life."

A neutrality, a liberality, then, appropriate to a film on Eskimo domesticity or a flick on household plumbing — so Friedkin would have us believe. But what is "this kind of life" he portrays? Is it a kind of life we would care to see anyone provoked into? As one actor in the film, Paul Sorvino, put it: "It's dangerous to be gay." *Cruising* presents this danger as though it were the Nature of Things rather than examining *why* it is dangerous to be gay in this society at this time.

If Friedkin thinks he's directed a documentary, Jerry Weintraub thinks he's produced a morality play. "What if the film serves as a warning to a young guy who comes to New York looking for a thrill? What if it says to him, don't do this stuff — go and find a good relationship."

That young guy might like to take Uncle Jerry's advice, but *Cruising* gives no clue where to find such a relationship. It also makes S/M mythologically dangerous and evil, the medium for the message that homosexuality and homicide go together like Peggy Lee's "Love and Marriage."

"I don't pretend to understand places like the Mineshaft," says Friedkin. "But they exist. They are part of the world. And yes, they're violent. While I was doing my research, there were two murders at the Anvil." What he fails to mention is that those two murders were in no way sexual. One involved a pickpocket, the other a rowdy drunk.

Since *Cruising* is really a horror film like *The Exorcist*, and since the Incomprehensible is crucial to Horror, Friedkin has no profitable motive for understanding the context and meaning of gay S/M. Gay people themselves have every reason to be more comprehending.

*

When gay extras were being selected for *Cruising*, they were asked what kind of sex acts they'd perform and in what degree of nudity. They were also asked to provide their own leather gear, and so almost all who were hired were, in fact, regular patrons of leather and S/M bars.

"I have friends in there who are extras, and I need the money just as much as they do," said one protester at a film location. "But it's a political act to be in this film, and those people are dead wrong." I was among those who called these extras traitors.

Did we feel betrayed by these gay men being in leather in the film—or by them being in leather at all? That is, did we feel that gay S/M shouldn't be exposed, or that it shouldn't exist? Motives, like crowds, are always mixed. The extras who worked for Friedkin were indeed betraying the gay community, but the ambiguous impulses of those who called them traitors must be acknowledged.

In his book *Art and Pornography*, Morse Peckham writes, "it does not seem to me theoretically possible to cut more deeply into the very heart of human behaviour than does sado-masochism, for it reveals nakedly and with full intensity the adapting animal." After expressing some scepticism that loving-kindness is "naturally" human, Peckham notes, "To impose one's needs on some segment of the environment in the form of demands is aggression; submission is to permit some segment of the environment to impose its needs on oneself.... To call submission an act of will is correct, for the segment of the environment one manipulates is one's own body and one's own personality for the sake of what one judges to be one's own advantage. Actually, then, submission is really aggression...."

In contrast to Peckham's elegance and erudition, John Rechy is passionate and polemical in his book, *The Sexual Outlaw*. "Explore the dynamics of gay S/M: playing 'straight,' the 'S' humiliates and even tortures the 'M' for being 'queer'...." He adds, "I believe in the necessity of exploring the real, not the rationalized world of S/M. I believe the energy produced by this hatred turned inward dissipates the revolutionary energy. Redirected, refunneled, that inward anger would be converted into creative rage against the real enemies from without. The conclusion is inescapable. The motivation of the 'M'—*as well as of the 'S'*—is self-hatred. There is no 'S' in such gay relationships. The whimpering 'masochist' and the 'tough' posturing 'sadist' are, in reality, only two masochists groveling in self-hatred. Gay S/M is the straight world's most despicable legacy."

Rechy and Peckham represent only two points on a spectrum of polemic and speculation about S/M, but both strive to comprehend their subject. *Cruising* exploits S/M crudely to mythologize our lives, to make them fit material for Horror. Friedkin not only reveals, but *strives for*, incomprehension.

*

In his *New York Times* interview, Friedkin discussed his fascination with the leather bars. "Obsession—there was true obsession in those places. All the films I've made deal in one way or another with characters who are obsessed, driven, perhaps sexually confused, given over to a macho image, which is generally bluff, and living on the edge of danger."

During filming, Friedkin told Vito Russo that the killer in *Cruising* "is not gay" and the cop "doesn't kill anybody in the film." A crew member confided to Russo, however, that the cop *had* become a killer, and *is* gay.

But suppose the killer isn't gay, just "sexually confused." If queer-bashers and killers are false straights or latent queers, then true and tolerant straights are released from any complicity in crimes which *queers commit on queers*.

In reality, genuinely straight queer-bashers and killers do exist, and what they express is not only aberrant "homosexual panic." They express, in its most intolerant form, the average sado-machismo of the average straight man.

Sado-machismo is as pervasive as God and Kleenex, can be as invisible and seem as innocuous. *It* is as much the subject of *Cruising* as gay S/M is—if we can decipher it through the distortions produced by Friedkin's lens.

Sex itself is only one of the things that panic straight men about homosexuality. Beyond that panic is a deeper fear about the intimacy, the tenderness and the non-hierarchical relations such sexuality can engender between men. These are potentially subversive of the whole social hierarchy: sado-machismo cements each one of us into our "proper" place in the pyramid. It operates when dads jeer at sons for sissiness, when husbands beat and rape wives, when straight punks bash queers, when fundamentalists attack feminists — *and when we submit*.

Patriarchy would not be such an abstraction if we talked more about how sado-machismo is actually passed from father to son. A straight young Baptist recently asked me, "Don't all gays hate their fathers? Our pastor says that's why all gays hate God the Father." Underlying such mythology is the fact that fathers do serve as the punitive arm of the patriarchy, having themselves been punished into loyalty. The dominant ideology about gay men is that we were punished into deviance: the penalties worked too well, producing anomalies contradictory to the rule of the fathers.

What makes the killer in *Cruising* tick? His father. Sons like the killer serve as a warning to all fathers: to punish sons *out* of deviance, *punish with care*. The terms of this warning are fictional and personal: the effect is personal and political.

Gays can be a threat to patriarchy if we are not crushed or co-opted by it, but a positive effect can't be explained by a negative cause. Homosexuality has its own positive social dynamic for persevering against penalties. In gay S/M interactions, the 'S' may signify either Sadist or Slave, the 'M' either Masochist or Master. A reduction of S/M to the give-and-take of pain—or to murder, as in *Cruising*—ignores the permutations of power which it may involve. Masochists may be masterful and sadists slavish. Often S/M involves rituals and fetishisms where there is no pain or even contact.

Cruising, however, simplifies and falsifies: gay S/M means dying and killing. The film "documents" at a glance realities which require contemplation. Gay S/M roles may be "acted out" quite seriously, but they are not immutable. Friedkin was not serious in his claim that he wished "to capture the quality of ritual" in gay S/M: he confuses its consensual and reversible roles with the coerced and inflexible roles sado-machismo imposes on us in the world at large. The masks of gay S/M may sometimes mould the face, the postures may sometimes mould the person, but only rarely does the act become fact: only rarely are the roles chosen in gay S/M truly injurious or fatal. The roles sado-machismo imposes on us are often so. In Philadelphia, where I live, a cop was recently acquitted after he blew the brains out of a black teenager who was handcuffed. Many of the extras in *Cruising* also had handcuffs hanging from their hips, but while gay S/M may toy with that terror and may inevitably reflect the dominant context of sado-machismo, it is by no means equivalent to it.

*

During the protests, many gay men realized for the first time just what kind of struggle women are waging against media misogyny and abuse. Feminists at a recent conference on pornography watched a slide-show of media assaults, epitomized by a *Hustler* cover showing a woman being fed into a meat grinder. That kind of imagery is big business, and with its images of gay men dying with their cocks hacked off and stuffed in their mouths, so is *Cruising*.

When it came right down to the police barricades, *Cruising* had on its side Mayor Koch, mounted police and riot squads armed with guns and clubs, the film crew goons, the power of the "free press" (the *New York Times*, which barely noted the protests, saw fit to print a half-page of Friedkin defending the film), and, most crucially, the full power of "free enterprise." The film's budget was seventeen million dollars.

What did gay militance have on its side? A handful of gay journalists, a few informers from the crew, twenty extras who quit the production in disgust, fifteen hundred people at one protest, only five at another, weapons consisting of slogans, leaflets, whistles, and later eggs and bottles.

And next to no bucks. When gay bar owners exercised *their* free enterprise rights by covering their signs and refusing to become part of the film's backdrop, producer Jerry Weintraub likened them to members of the Ku Klux Klan. If cops barricaded Harlem streets so that the real Klan could film a racist movie there (using either Uncle Toms or whites in black-face as extras), would it be Klannish of blacks to boycott business that collaborated with the filmmakers? Nonsense: this would be seen as community self-defence, the kind of defence gays use against a clan of straight bigots and profiteers invading *their* turf.

"Mass rallies and marches and sit-ins — that kind of civil disobedience is welcome, it's important," said Friedkin in the *New York Times*. "If that had been directed against *Cruising*, I might very well have—no, I *would* have been persuaded to stop filming." Having made aliens of some of us, Friedkin tried to divide us further by pitting his idea of "welcome" protests against the "unruly fanatics" who *did* rally and march and sit in to stop his film. The great majority were moderate and became more militant only as the situation itself grew more provocative.

Who finally initiated the violence? I don't know, and I doubt that anyone does for sure. Some might say our puny power should never have been pitted against their great power, that doing that was in itself a delusion induced by sado-machismo, that such a confrontation could only lead to bad press, injured people and defeat. I can't dismiss that argument: I don't accept it, either.

I was made sick by the heads bloodied on the night of August 20, and I wasn't thrilled to be clubbed myself. But our puny power was sufficient for Stonewall. Defeat followed that occasion in the sense that business-as-usual was restored. But, in fact, oppressive Law and Order were from then on increasingly challenged. Without such a "defeat" as Stonewall, how could we have gone on to other victories? Though we disrupted some scenes, Friedkin finished filming in the Village, and *Cruising* is scheduled for distribution in February, 1980. A defeat? Only for those who imagined they could fight this skirmish with free enterprise as though it were the whole campaign.

Years ago, Hannah Arendt roused a storm of protest when she wrote of "the banality of evil" embodied in a man like the Nazi criminal Eichmann. Gay people on both sides of the barricades were called Nazis, the protesters for their tactics, the S/M extras for their lives. If we are to know our enemies, we'd better *not* make a Nazi of Friedkin. But Arendt's insight is useful in understanding him: he's an extremely banal man. Nothing "alien" is human to him. He's not greatly evil himself; he's just one of those people who makes great evil possible.

Will the film directly provoke murders, as some claimed, or was this simply "rousing" rhetoric? Direct cause and effect is usually hard to prove, but films like *Cruising* can charge an already stormy atmosphere so that lightning finally strikes "at random." And the messages such a film carries help to keep us fearful and in our "proper" place in the hierarchy of power.

We have already recognized that industry cannot be allowed to pollute our environment "freely," and anti-nuclear activists have already moved from symbolic action to actual obstruction. The cultural environment is also full of ideological radiation. We have good grounds for viewing the film industry as an abused public utility, good grounds for demanding resources to make our own films. With a budget of seventeen million dollars going for *Cruising*, pulling a production cable was little more than a symbolic act. But it was one way to say we won't let free enterprise monopolize free speech.

Defend free speech? To be sure. But often you must *create* it first. The surest defence of such rights as now exist will come from those working for *economic* democracy. The right to say what one wants means little to those who haven't got the bucks—and the power that comes from these bucks—to make themselves heard. Free speech costs. So far, most people can't afford it.

*

In one newspaper report, a frustrated protester at a film site was quoted as saying, "There's only one way to stop *Cruising*, and that's to stop cruising."

If we stop cruising, then *Cruising* will have stopped *us*. Is there any good reason why the streets and parks should not be safe for simple gay sociability? Even for sex? Women have long feared to walk the streets at night, knowing the risk of rape, knowing how cops and courts blame the victims. But now women are marching *en masse* to demonstrate that they will "Take Back the Night." Certainly gay people should respond with equal courage.

I remember the first time I visited the Anvil bar. A young man was bound on stage and was getting fist-fucked by a burly man in a leather hood. The young man couldn't take it; he said so, and the hooded man stopped, unbound him and took off his hood. They smiled at each other and then kissed.

Where are the films that show *this* reality? Where are the films that would explore the ambivalence about sexual submission and domination? Where are the films that might present the positive aspects of the rough-and-ready communalism of backroom bars, beaches, parks, instead of "documenting" such sexuality merely to shock a public which is fanatical about the "private nature" of sex? Such shocks are calculated to bring profit, for they confirm rather than challenge foolish and resentful morality.

That day in the Ramble I met a beautiful blond dancer, a boy from Texas. We sucked and fucked and did not castrate or knife each other. Friedkin has made two films about gay men focusing on physical and emotional wounds. He does not turn the camera on himself, on the weapons he wields against us. He doesn't care to show gay affirmation, gay resistance, the thousands of everyday acts by which we survive and love each other.

Of what *Cruising* shows, William Friedkin says, "It's there. It exists. It's the truth." But "It" is simply a pantheon of tired archetypes—doomed queens and sinister freaks. Such archetypes have shaped our lives. To recognize stereotypes is to demystify archetypes: it is to change our lives. If we must inevitably live by one mythology or another, let's at least have a choice in creating our own.

When we protested in the streets, that's what we were trying to say. We're here. We exist. We, too, are the truth.

Middle-class alarm
Vito Russo

Letter, Issue 59, December 1979/January 1980

What disturbed me greatly was the hostility of the "respectable" gay community—not to the film or United Artists—but to other gays who had made the free choice to cooperate in their own oppression. I think Scott Tucker's rhetorical question "Did we feel betrayed by these men being in leather in the film or did we feel betrayed by them being in leather at *all*?" is right on target.

I found that the majority of the gay sentiment against the people who frequent places like the Mineshaft was what stopped the *Cruising* demonstrations from becoming powerful and more effective. I know gay activists who stood in Sheridan Square at anti-*Cruising* rallies and listened to gay leaders say that they were against the film because it showed the type of gays who do dirty, disgusting things in the dark. A former officer of the Gay Activists Alliance turned to me and said "That's *me* they're talking about—I'm not joining this demo." I saw and heard gay activist Ron Alheim shout at the gay extras "Okay, you guys—you do what you want but remember you have to live in this community after this film is over and we'll get you for this." I thought of Carl Wittman's gay manifesto and how it said that no matter how bad things got our brothers were not the enemy and should not be attacked for what a sexist, corrupt society has turned them into.

Respectable middle-class gays can't have it both ways. They want the movies to reflect the private reality that they have always been unwilling to share publicly. They want most of all to be able to stay in the closets and not affiliate themselves openly as gay but at the same time they want nice middle-class motion pictures about two sleek, sophisticated lesbian lovers who own a townhouse in Boulder and do very well for themselves or two gay men who are account execs and are buying a co-op.

When Billy Friedkin decided to film what Hollywood has always decided to film—the visible gay ghetto—they freaked out. We don't want *those* people representing us on the screen while we're trying to tell the world we're just as All-American as everyone else. The pity of it is that they're right. Most gays, like most straights, would certainly be horrified at what goes on in the Mineshaft and really do want to be part of the heterosexual dream. The depiction of such things alarms them because it says there are gays who have no use for conventional sexual morality.

It can be said that Hollywood will learn a lesson from seeing how vocal gays are willing to be, but do we want Hollywood to change? They'll only begin to portray us all as they do everything else. Then we'll have to protest our being swallowed up in the industry meatgrinder of conformity. The answer, it seems, or one of them, is not to give a shit what Hollywood does, not care so much about our "image" and simply wait for the diversity of our experience to become a matter of public record. That will happen when the people who protested *Cruising* are as out of the closets as the leather men who participated in it.

Help them see *Cruising*
Ken Popert

Issue 60, February 1980.

Afterwards, as we lay in the almost dark bedroom, he lit a cigarette and casually exhaled:

"I saw a trailer last week for that movie, the one there's been so much fuss about, *Cruising*? It was just still shots, you know? Looks exciting, I want to see it."

I frown. "But that movie exploits ignorance. It exploits us."

Words fall into line, an army of paragraphs begins to march. Mere preaching to the unconverted?

But there's more than one unconverted here. I don't know what I want to say. The ranks of rhetoric waver and break. After a pause, I confess, just one faggot to another now: "I want to see it too." We smile.

If he wants to see it, if part of me wants to see it, how many other gay men want to see *Cruising*? What does this guilty desire mean for those, including me, who are concerned about this movie and its effects?

Cruising will open soon in Toronto. And the censors, among us and in us, are restless.

Some suggest a picket line in front of the theatre to express our anger that this movie is being shown. Others propose more direct action which will interfere with its screening.

We have to be very clear about the nature of these tactics. Any action which stops the film from being shown or prevents people from seeing it is an act of suppression. Any action which implies that it shouldn't be shown or that people shouldn't see it reveals the desire to suppress.

And behind this desire to suppress lurks the crude conviction that *Cruising* has just one message to deliver and that the effect of that message on the viewer is fully ascertainable. The protesters in New York who tried to stop the filming maintained (with variations) that the message of *Cruising* is this: violence and murder are in the nature of homosexuality. They speculated that the movie will augment a social ambience which promotes violence against gay men.

The neutral viewer may well take this meaning from *Cruising*. And the film could indeed be the drop which causes the bucket of hatred to overflow into violence in some homophobes. But there's more to it than that.

Don't gay demonstrations and marches add to the general store of homophobia? Of course they do. But we know that militance is the only way to defeat homophobia in the long term. So we accept a probable increase in homophobic violence in the short run.

Gay protest isn't peculiar in producing good and bad effects. Just about everything has its positives and negatives. We have to weigh them as best we can.

This goes for *Cruising* too. It probably carries many messages, good and bad. Which ones are received will depend on who's watching. Among the viewers will be some who watch for reasons which they don't quite acknowledge or understand. The movie will be important in leading some of them to define their repressed sexuality. Is that something we want to prevent? I don't think so.

If we assume that we can spot all the messages relevant to gay people in this or any other movie or book or song, then we are also assuming that we know all there is to know about gay people, about ourselves.

Are we prepared to suppress the positive messages in *Cruising* and potential new knowledge about ourselves in order to banish the evil it contains?

And, to be practical, we don't have the might to close down Friedkin's film. Only two groups in Toronto have that kind of muscle: the cops and the Mafia.

Any of us who try to stop *Cruising* permanently will certainly fail. And, in the process, like all leadership which urges the impossible, they will have robbed their followers of hope, while earning discredit for themselves among those who discerned the futility of their plans.

Further, any tactic which even implies that we would like to see the movie banned will rebound upon us, discrediting our fight against censorship. The news media and our opponents will sneer, with effect, that we oppose censorship only when it is aimed at us. That is the lesson of the New York protests.

Finally, the target of censorship and suppression is not the creator, but the creator's audience. Who will be the audience of *Cruising*?

We know the superstition freaks and, perhaps, the homophobes will be there. But there will also be: curious people with open minds; repressed homosexuals; gay men with a repressed interest in S/M; gay men who are into S/M; gay men looking for fantasy material; gay men drawn by the controversy about the movie; and who knows who else?

Is this a threatening rabble that we want to disperse? Are these people to whom we want to say: No, you shouldn't want to see this movie? No, you can't see this movie?

We should not suppress it. We cannot suppress it. But we cannot ignore it. So, what can we do about *Cruising*?

Of course, we must see it first. Then, even if it is as dangerous as its critics suggest, we must not greet it as an evil to be exorcised. We should look upon it as a spell to be conjured with, an opportunity to seize.

We should be present at every screening of the movie, unthreateningly, unreproachingly, to give people our view of *Cruising* before they see it.

That way, we can take *Cruising* away from Friedkin and make it serve us. By providing information, we can alter the meaning of *Cruising* for its viewers. They will not only see us through Friedkin's eyes, but also see his movie through our eyes.

So, the way to deal with *Cruising* is to help people see it. But help them to see it as it truly is, for what it is.

Through our eyes, in our lives.

Dangerous notions
Scott Tucker

Letter, Issue 62, April 1980

There are some vague and dangerous notions in Ken Popert's column which should be nailed down. Ken asks, "Don't gay demonstrations and marches add to the general store of homophobia? Of course they do." This is breathtakingly false. No, Ken, even though you go on to grant that "militance is the only way to defeat homophobia in the long term," you do gays no favour by implying that militance "adds" to homophobia even in the short term. Homophobia, like racism and sexism, is always with us; it permeates the social cloth like a deep dye. When we protest we do not create bigotry; rather, bigotry comes down on us and "comes out" as well.

It is really too fair-minded of Ken to write that *Cruising* "probably carries many messages, good and bad." Sure, and Mussolini kept the trains running on time. And but for the grace of the Third Reich, the world wouldn't have Volkswagens. And... but seriously, Ken, do we have to consume such poison to get any nourishment? The messages *Cruising* carries are, in fact, garbled and confused. Yet one thing is clear: this confusion serves reaction, not liberation. *Cruising* has a brief disclaimer tagged on now: throw *that* into the balance of a hundred and six minutes of menace and murder.

When I urged folks to use the force of Hollywood against it, to make their film our event, their lies our tools for education, I did not have in mind pretending that bigots and profiteers had done us a *favour*. Ken expresses concern for those who are just discovering their sexuality, or still defining it. He urges activists to be at every screening of the film to give patrons our view of it, to help people see it "through our eyes, in our lives." That's a pretty piece of poetry, but the reality is rather cruel. The fact is that *Cruising* will show at several hundred theatres, and that we can muster our forces only at a relative handful.

The great majority of folks who see *Cruising will* be seeing it through *their* eyes—the eyes of bigots, liars, and profiteers. It's tragic that some gay people are so starved for gay fare that they will pay for their own oppression. But instead of trying to extract some sweetness from cyanide pills like *Cruising*, we'd do better to fight for the resources to make our own films about our own lives.

Whose freedom and whose press?
Leo Casey and Gary Kinsman

Issue 63, May 1980

While the opponents of the anti-*Cruising* campaign claim to be defending free media and press, they use a particular and limited notion of freedom, a "free market" notion, to define those free media. This notion of freedom is given full expression in the view that those who own or control the press and media must be allowed to print or film what they wish. The content, and hence the social impact, of a movie or a news report must be left entirely to the discretion of the individuals who produce the movie or the journal; the sum total of their individual decisions will yield a pluralist world in which all views are freely expressed. To limit the discretion of those individuals is to "censor."

This "free market" notion of freedom is founded upon the idea of an individual's right to private property, a right which should not be restricted in any way or by anyone. The media are seen as the property of their corporate owners and their hired representatives, and the "common good" is served when they are free to use or dispose of their property as they see fit. The apparent exceptions to this unlimited freedom, such as the restrictions placed on the publication of libellous material, actually confirm the general rule: these exceptions concern the rights of other individual proprietors. Within this perspective, all rights belong to property-bearing individuals.

Those who support this commonly held notion of freedom assume that this is the only meaning that can be given to a free press. But there is an alternative notion of freedom which has been used by some of us who organized against *Cruising*. This view does not base itself on an individual's unrestricted right to private property; rather, it roots itself in the needs of communities of people. It begins with the understanding that open media are the primary means for a community to acquire a knowledge of itself. It is in such media that the various isolated parts of the community can find the tools of discussion and information.

In this alternative view, the content and social impact of the media are a matter of vital concern to the community they serve. Accordingly, it maintains that those who produce the press should do so in trust for the community, allowing for the widest possible community input and control.

Proponents of both of these views oppose governmental censorship, especially of community organs such as *The Body Politic*. But agreement on opposition to governmental censorship should not be allowed to mask more fundamental points of difference. The two views drastically diverge on the question of the media's relationship to the community they serve.

The first, orthodox view regards community input and control of the media as no different than governmental censorship: both restrict the property rights of the individual. It sees the community as a passive audience, and it limits the prerogative of the community to the right to purchase in the marketplace. An audience can choose as individuals to consume or not to consume, but it has no right—by this definition—to interfere collectively in the actual production of the journal or the film. It is from this viewpoint that gays and lesbians protesting against *Cruising* are equated with a board of censors, even when they suggest tactics no stronger than an organized consumer boycott.

In contrast, the second or alternative view argues that it is not possible to have real freedom in the media without community input and control. It is, or should be, obvious that a passive individual consumer has no meaningful choice in deciding whether to see *Cruising*, *Windows*, or *The Boys in the Band*. The privately owned and controlled media industries have not produced gay- or lesbian-positive images on their own initiative; the pluralist world—there is something for everyone—is a myth of "free market" ideology. Genuine pluralism exists only when oppressed groups develop the power to force access to the media. Yet the power to determine the alternatives from which a consumer can choose lies in the hands of these industries, for this power is the power *to produce and distribute* the film or journal.

In a society such as ours, this power rests almost exclusively in the hands of those who own the media; the fundamental issue is the identity of these owners. In the case of Hollywood film studios, this ownership is concentrated in multi-billion dollar conglomerates. The gay and lesbian communities, as well as other oppressed communities, cannot gain access to media industries by buying out some of these massive multinational corporations, nor by starting an alternative corporation with sufficient capital to compete with them. Such scenarios are utter foolishness that ignore the basic economic facts of life. Our political project is to transfer the power now concentrated in the corporate structures of the media to the communities they should be serving. And in our context, the alternative view of a free press necessarily assumes the form of an anti-corporate, broadly based movement for social change that includes many oppressed communities. The campaigns against *Cruising* and

Windows, and the campaign a few years back against *Snuff*, are a first step in that direction.

By raising the issue of the relationship of the major Hollywood film corporations to gays and lesbians, anti-*Cruising* activists have implicitly called into question the relationship of all media to the community they serve. The anti-*Cruising* campaign has, in part, indirectly challenged the relationship of the gay press to the gay and lesbian communities. While all of the gay press express some degree of concern for the issues that affect the gay and lesbian communities, many of these journals treat us as passive audiences with no rights but that of a consumer "choice."

The response of these members of the gay media to the anti-*Cruising* protests is not, therefore, simply the advocacy of an abstract notion of freedom as the right to unrestricted private property. It is also the defence of their limited social power, a social power acquired through the ownership of media in a society of private property. To the extent that they persist in viewing themselves and our communities in these terms, they will also continue to side with the major media and press in their confrontations with oppressed groups.

Chapter five
In the courts,
on the hustings, in the streets

"We retreat into a bar. Outside, a police car swoops down on a hapless demonstrator. He is dragged kicking and punching into the car, and it roars off. 'They'll come in here next,' says Bittor. The bar empties, and we run to the far end of the square."

*

"John Sewell conceded defeat to two hundred glum supporters at a community hall festively decorated for a victory party. 'Don't give up on the city,' he urged them. The stern-faced mayor wandered through the crowd, consoling his saddened workers. He worried to a *TBP* reporter that it might mean more difficulty for the gay community. Pressed by one reporter to explain his defeat, he laughed and replied, simply, 'We didn't have enough votes.' "

*

"It was the night Toronto came closer to a full-scale riot than it has in the last ten years. It was the night when three thousand people came within minutes of breaking down the doors of the Ontario legislature. It was the night the main street of Canada's largest city belonged to us, and nobody — not even the police — seemed able to do anything about it."

*

The Seventies

The gay liberation movement in Canada took shape in the early Seventies only after it had devised a strategy to reach out to gay people, had found a practical goal around which activists could organize.

For a brief period at the beginning, the movement was carried along by the radical impulse of the counterculture and American New Left political activism of the Sixties. Consequently, it was more defiant and rhetorically militant than it was self-consciously political. Early groups like the Vancouver Gay Liberation Front declared themselves to be part of a larger revolutionary struggle to change the economic and political structures of society. For these gay radicals, it was not sufficient to tinker with the present system, to work merely for law reform and equal treatment. Other gay leftists, while agreeing essentially with this analysis, saw that a practical interim strategy had to be devised which took into account both the apolitical nature of most homosexuals and the less polarized realities of Canadian political life in 1972.

Eventually, the human rights strategy became the dominant focus of gay movement political activity. It evolved into what was probably a characteristically Canadian blend: militant-sounding public demonstrations coupled with traditional lobbying for law reform and official recognition. The focus on human rights codes turned most of this lobbying attention from federal to provincial and municipal levels of government, governments comparatively more accessible to local gay groups. Despite years of pressure, however, by 1982 only Quebec and three Ontario cities had passed laws banning discrimination on the basis of sexual orientation.

After the Anita Bryant campaigns of 1977-78, resistance to the advances of the gay movement had hardened. Home-grown bigots and fundamentalists began to view homosexuals as dangerous, while right-wing journalists and politicians began to perceive the political utility of exploiting those fears. By 1979, the human rights crusade appeared to have reached a stalemate. The outburst of gay rage in San Francisco, following the announcement of the light sentence given the murderer of popular gay city supervisor Harvey Milk, struck a responsive chord with Canadian activists. Shortly thereafter, the first published expression of frustration with the ineffectual human rights strategy appeared in *The Body Politic*.

Nonetheless, the importance of a decade of token achievements, modest successes and quiet victories cannot be diminished. In ten short years, significant changes have come about slowly, almost imperceptibly. The human rights strategy is not dead in the Eighties, but it is no longer sufficient.

We demand
The August 28th Gay Day Committee

Issue 1, November/December 1971

The following brief was presented to the federal government in August 1971. Written and researched by Toronto Gay Action, the brief was supported by gay organizations across Canada, including: the Community Homophile Association of Toronto, Front de libération homosexuel (Montreal), Gay Alliance Toward Equality (Vancouver), Guelph University Homophile Association, University of Toronto Homophile Association, Vancouver Gay Activist Alliance, Vancouver Gay Liberation Front (GLF), Gay Sisters (Vancouver), Waterloo University's Gay Liberation Movement and York University Homophile Association.

On Saturday, August 28, over two hundred homosexual men and women rallied on Parliament Hill in Ottawa in support of the brief. The action was the first public demonstration of its kind in Canada.

In 1969 the Criminal Code was amended so as to make certain sexual acts between two consenting adults, in private, not illegal. This was widely misunderstood as "legalizing" homosexuality and thus putting homosexuals on an equal basis with other Canadians. In fact, this amendment was merely a recognition of the non-enforceable nature of the Criminal Code as it existed. Consequently, its effects have done but little to alleviate the oppression of homosexual men and women in Canada. In our daily lives we are still confronted with discrimination, police harassment, exploitation and pressures to conform which deny our sexuality. That prejudice against homosexual people pervades society is, in no small way, attributable to practices of the federal government. Therefore we, as homosexual citizens of Canada, present the following brief to our government as a means of redressing our grievances.

We demand:

1. *The removal of the nebulous terms "gross indecency" and "indecent act" from the Criminal Code and their replacement by a specific listing of offences, and the equalization of penalties for all remaining homosexual and heterosexual acts; and defining "in private" in the Criminal Code to mean "a condition of privacy."*

The terms "gross indecency" and "indecent act" in the Criminal Code remain largely undefined, thus leaving the degree of offensiveness of many sexual acts open to interpretation by enforcement officials according to their personal prejudices — which, by and large, are anti-homosexual. Therefore a specific listing of public offences is crucial in that only in this way can personal bias be eradicated and the legal intent of the law be preserved.

Sections 147 and 149 of the Criminal Code have been used to cover public homosexual acts, an offence which is punishable upon indictable conviction; similar public heterosexual acts have usually been dealt with under Section 158 of the Criminal Code, an offence which is punishable on summary conviction.

Moreover, indecent assault upon a female (Section 141) can result in a maximum penalty of five years imprisonment, while a person—in this case, always a male—convicted of indecent assault upon another male (Section 148) is liable to imprisonment for ten years. There is no reason for the continuation of this discrepancy in maximum penalties, since the relevant factor is assault, not the sex of the person assaulted.

"In private" when applied to homosexual acts means strictly in the confines of one's home or apartment. For heterosexual acts this interpretation of "in private" is less stringent, as the existence of "lovers' lanes" so well testifies. Persons engaged in sexual acts who have genuinely attempted to create a "condition of privacy" should not be arrested, but — as now happens with most heterosexuals — be told to "move along."

2. *Removal of "gross indecency" and "buggery" as grounds for indictment as a "dangerous sexual offender" and for vagrancy.*

Since persons convicted of homosexual acts are usually charged under Sections 147 and 149 of the Criminal Code, they are liable to be labeled as "dangerous sexual offenders" and sentenced to "preventative detention" for an indefinite period under Section 661 of the Criminal Code.

Section 164 of the Criminal Code labels an individual as vagrant and subject to summary conviction if, *inter alia*, he or she has been convicted of an offence such as "gross indecency." Denying the right of an individual to frequent specified places (school grounds, playgrounds, public parks or bathing areas) on the basis of having been convicted of "gross indecency" is excessive, especially when the specific offence for which the individual was convicted may have been merely an indiscretion and in no way a harmful act.

3. *A uniform age of consent for all female and male homosexual and heterosexual acts.*

Since the federal government of Canada does not recognize legal marriages between homosexual persons, the age of consent for their sexual contact, is twenty-one years of age. However, since heterosexual parties can be joined in a legally recognized marriage, their age of consent is dependent only upon the age at which they can legally enter a marriage contract. Further inequities result in that Sections 138, 143, and 144 of the Criminal Code specify various ages of consent for heterosexual acts between unmarried persons. We believe that the age of consent (twenty-one) for engaging in sexual acts is unrealistic and should be lowered. A number of provinces have reduced the age of majority. The effect of this is that individuals under the age of twenty-one can enter into contractual agreements, vote and drink alcoholic beverages, but cannot exercise their sexual preferences—no small part of one's life. The principle of maturity should be applied uniformly to all aspects of deciding individual prerogatives.

4. *The Immigration Act be amended so as to omit all references to homosexuals and "homosexualism."*

Denying immigration to Canada for any individual merely on the basis of his or her "homosexualism" is inconsistent with the Criminal Code. Since "homosexualism" is not, in itself, an illegal practice between consenting adults in private, the Immigration Act thus discriminates against a minority group.

5. *The right of equal employment and promotion at all government levels for homosexuals.*

The proposed implementation of Paragraph 100 of the Royal Commission on Security makes one's homosexuality an issue in the promotion and recruitment of civil servants. If an individual freely admits his or her homosexuality and is not afraid of disclosure and engages solely in legal acts, that person is hardly susceptible to blackmail. One cannot profitably threaten to broadcast to others what is already known. The effect of Paragraph 100 is to *force* homosexuals into a furtive situation in which they *might become* susceptible to coercion. Thus, Paragraph 100 becomes self-defeating.

If "homosexuals are special targets for attention from foreign intelligence services," this is evidently due to the threat of dismissal from employment, a situation which could be greatly improved by a more open policy on the part of the government.

6. *The Divorce Act be amended so as to omit sodomy and homosexual acts as grounds for divorce; moreover, in divorce cases homosexuality per se should not preclude the equal rights of child custody.*

7. *The right of homosexuals to serve in the Armed Forces and, therefore, the removal of provisions for convicting service personnel of conduct and/or acts legal under the Criminal Code; further, the rescinding of policy statements reflecting on the homosexual.*

Note (c) of Queen's Regulations and Orders (103.25: "Scandalous Conduct of Officers") and Note (b) of 103.26 ("Cruel or Disgraceful Conduct") both suggest that homosexual acts between consenting adults may be considered punishable offences in the military. This effectively contravenes the Criminal Code and, thereby, the principle that military law should be subordinate to civil law.

Paragraph 6 of Canadian Forces Administrative Order 19-20 ("Sexual Deviation—Investigation, Medical Examination, and Disposal") reads: "Service policy does not allow retention of sexual deviates in the Forces" and specifies the manner of discharging persons convicted of homosexual acts while in military service.

8. *To know if it is a policy of the Royal Canadian Mounted Police to identify homosexuals within any area of government service and then question them concerning their sexuality and the sexuality of others; and if this is the policy we demand its immediate cessation and destruction of all records so obtained.*

9. *All legal rights for homosexuals which currently exist for heterosexuals.*

Although numerous instances of the injustices and discrimination embodied by this demand could be cited, the following are indicative of the inequities with which homosexuals must contend:

(1) because homosexuals cannot legally marry, they face economic discrimination in that the benefits of filing joint income tax returns and conferring pension rights are denied to them;

(2) likewise, homosexuals are unable to partake of the benefits of public housing;

(3) they are brought up under an education system which either through commission or omission fosters both a narrow and prejudicial view of homosexuality;

(4) again, owing to the fact that homosexuals cannot enter into legally recognized marriages, they are not permitted to adopt children except under the most unusual circumstances. (Although we recognize that adoption is an area of provincial jurisdiction, we feel that this does not completely remove all responsibility from the federal government);

(5) too often in the private sector, once an individual's homosexuality has become known, he or she is discriminated against in employment, and exploited by unscrupulous landlords;

(6) in known places frequented by homosexuals or in places where they gather, both direct and subtle harassment by police officers is too often commonplace;

(7) since sexuality is not covered under the Canadian Bill of Rights, homosexuals are excluded from protections which are guaranteed to other minority groups such as those of race, religion, or national origin.

As a group, homosexuals are "second class citizens" in a democratic society which purports to recognize only one class of citizenship, based on equality.

10. *All public officials and law enforcement agents to employ the full force of their office to bring about changes in the negative attitudes and* de facto *expressions of discrimination and prejudice against homosexuals.*

The role of public officials must be twofold: (1) to serve as legislators formulating the letter of the law, and (2) to serve as representatives of the spirit of a system founded upon democratic principles. As such, holders of public office must transcend prejudicial attitudes (in this case against homosexuals) in favour of leading society to levels consistent with the principles of human rights.

We call upon government officials, as a show of good faith, to enter immediately into a dialogue with the various Canadian homophile groups regarding all the aforementioned demands and to respond publicly by supporting the purpose of this brief.

A strategy for gay liberation
Brian Waite

Issue 3, March/April 1972

The fight to include the term "sexual orientation" in the Ontario Human Rights Code is a fundamental one in the struggle for gay liberation and should be seen as an important priority for all Ontario homophile organizations.

Winning this demand, in itself, will not end our oppression, but in the process of fighting for it many gay men and women will develop a higher level of pride and consciousness. With a victory, thousands more will find it easier to come out and begin the task of educating their fellow workers, neighbours, families and friends about the nature of homosexuality, without fear of losing a job or apartment, being harassed at school, or facing discrimination in innumerable other ways because we have no rights guaranteed by law.

This campaign can give a focus for dealing with many other issues at the local level. Actions to protest police entrapment or conditions in the gay ghetto could also be used to publicize and build the campaign and the organizations that are leading it. Demonstrations don't have to be one-shot affairs aimed at one of a myriad of media establishments which constantly slander us. As well as demanding equal time or space to reply, we can point out the responsibility of the provincial government, which refuses to prosecute such blatant discrimination.

Such a campaign will necessarily be two-pronged, since a prior condition for winning is social recognition of homosexuals as a legitimate oppressed minority. We have a formidable task: to teach the truth about human sexuality to the people of Ontario and to oppose the powerful resources of the Ontario government's educational and legal systems. If they continue to refuse to recognize our legal rights, be assured that the miseducation mills will continue to grind out ignorant, guilt-ridden and sexually oppressed citizens.

This is an issue which will give us an opportunity to make links with the organized women's liberation movement. They have demonstrated in the past to demand the inclusion of the word "sex" in the Ontario Human Rights Code. Victory is due in some part to the demonstrations, but probably more to the general public discussion and awareness that has been generated by the activities of the women's movement on a whole range of issues during the past two years. It was the activist feminists who created a climate in which the Tory government would have found it very difficult to continue to ignore this elementary demand for women's equality.

Although both our demands relate directly to the Ontario Human Rights Code, our struggle will have a qualitatively different dynamic. Women have concentrated on the abortion campaign in the recent past because it is an issue which touches the widest layers of the female population, regardless of their economic position. Repeal of the abortion laws will give impetus to future campaigns by women. Any other possibilities for liberating themselves are inextricably tied to their right to chose whether or not they will bear children. This idea is summed up in one of their slogans—Control of Our Bodies, Control of Our Lives.

Most gays cannot be identified, and we leave ourselves open to economic discrimination only if we declare our homosexuality. This will often leave us feeling psychologically liberated, but jobless or red-circled.

Our "Human Rights" campaign is actually more closely paralleled in the women's abortion fight, rather than their demonstrations demanding inclusion of the word "sex." Winning our demand will give *us* the right to choose whether or not we tell our work-mates or fellow tenants of our sexuality — freely, without fear of reprisals from a bigoted boss or landlord. In the meantime, we must stress to those who support our aims that in our movement they can choose their own level of anonymity, taking into account their personal situation. This can range from marching in a demonstration to phoning people to involve them in a meeting or work party, both important activities.

Many feminists are aware of the common source of oppression in the socialization and education which take place in the traditional family structure and its continuation throughout the formal educational system. Those of us who dare to reject such distortions of our real sexuality and human potential face a material barricade of institutionalized discrimination and a lack of facilities which could permit us to gain control over our lives.

The foundations of this barricade are embodied in the governments at Queen's Park and Ottawa. As long as any laws discriminating directly or by omission against gays and women remain on the books, any chauvinist employer, educator, landlord, cop, doctor, psychiatrist or parent can trample on our rights and dignity with the tacit approval of these governments.

The effectiveness of the women's movement to date is partly due to their appreciation of the experiences of other movements for social change. They have learned from their own suffragists and the anti-war movement that along with petition campaigns, local demonstrations and actions, letter-writing and educational meetings, it is extremely important to organize large public demonstrations on as wide a basis as possible, whether provincial, national or bi-national.

Women activists have realized that this is the best way possible to show our common opponents and our supporters the power of our numbers, indicating most visibly that the demands we are putting forward represent the solutions to the problems faced by the overwhelming majority of women and gays. As the movement and the size of the demonstrations increase it will become clear that we are not a tiny, isolated minority, unable to relate to the rest of our brothers and sisters as implied by the media.

It is crucial that we assimilate various lessons of previous social movements:

• Oppression is not in one's head. There are powerful forces in this society which use and perpetuate ignorance, prejudice, hatred, and the divisions and alienation which these produce. If you care to believe this is merely the inertia of the status quo, fine. Nevertheless, this status quo is defended by traditional "natural" mores, social "norms" and laws, backed up by the confessional, psychiatrists' couches and the legal system's police force. This repressive power is generally efficient and well organized.

• Having none of the above apparatus at our disposal individually, we must realize the potential political strength of ourselves and our supporters numerically.

• We have to organize this strength in public actions, relying on the abilities of ourselves and our organizations, not on the good will of any individual, be he or she government official, party leader or movement hero.

• Our movement must devise a programme and strategy which will win full equality. The social activities which are necessary to maintain our morale and alleviate some of our daily stress are extremely important. But the aim of gay liberation is to root out the source of our oppression rather than apply bandaids to a never-ending stream of casualties.

• A conscientious organization recognizes the need for some parliamentary formalities, leadership and an active membership. The election of a leadership body, such as a steering committee, is not "elitist" as long as it reflects the varied composition and experience of the organization, and its power is delegated and controlled by membership meetings.

The vision of a future society free from sexism, which is one I feel we all share, can be turned into a reality sooner or later. Later, if we march haphazardly, ignoring the signposts of past experience; sooner, if we incorporate these experiences into the gay movement's arsenal of strategy and tactics. I am not suggesting that we adopt the programme or demands of other minorities and oppressed groups, for it is only by organizing around issues with which all gays can relate that we will realize our strength. Some individuals, no doubt, will be active in other movements or political parties, thereby raising consciousness about human sexuality in these groups.

I feel strongly that the movement in Ontario will greatly strengthen itself if we organize jointly to demand the inclusion of the term "sexual orientation" in the Ontario Human Rights Code.

Winning this demand will give life to the words "gay pride." It will impel and enable thousands more brothers and sisters to join us in future campaigns for the full sexual liberation of humankind — children, adolescents and adults, no matter what their position on the sexual continuum. *Homosexuality is a human right!*

Victories and defeats:
a gay and lesbian chronology 1964-1982

Every movement for social change leaves signposts of its progress. Some are major and some are modest, and it is easy for more recent travellers to forget that the road itself was barely passable a decade ago. A history of the first ten years of the Canadian gay movement will someday be written; the following selected chronology of significant events makes no attempt to perform that task. What it does offer is a preliminary map, an outline of the past. The compilation of the chronology has depended to a large extent upon the documentary news coverage provided by *The Body Politic*, beginning with its first issue in November 1971. As a magazine of continuous record of gay political activity in the Seventies, *TBP* is a valuable resource.

Certain threads of related events persist throughout this chronology, themes given priority by movement strategists and themes forced into prominence by religious or state opposition to demands for full emancipation by homosexuals. Among these themes: gay and lesbian visibility, the importance of organizing, the growth of a strong lesbian and gay community, the public struggle for gay civil rights, access to public services and to the mass media, law reform, right-wing reaction and police repression, gay resistance.

The perception of the necessity for gay and lesbian visibility as a precondition for further change has determined much of the gay movement's strategy. To emerge from the "twilight world," to come out of the closet, was an affirmation that gay is good. It was the proud assumption of a homosexual identity. It has been, in many ways, the gay movement's central political act and it led naturally to the formulation of a policy of public struggle for gay civil rights as an overriding priority. It accounts for the continuing significance of protest pickets and demonstrations during the Seventies. Although early gay demonstrations were small in number, they represented a unique declaration of visibility on the part of the individuals involved, a factor absent from comparable gatherings of political protest. For gay people, denied access to the mass media with its enormous powers of propaganda control, prevented from participating openly in the decision-making apparatus of the state, public demonstrations were the only way to be heard, the only way to be seen.

The pressure to include "sexual orientation" in provincial and federal human rights codes became the primary focus of activities for both provincial and national gay rights coalitions. The many manoeuvres, sideways shuffles and tiny steps forward in this tedious struggle dominate the following chronology, becoming increasingly half-hearted in the Eighties as more immediate issues loomed. To demonstrate the need for legal protection required proof that discrimination against homosexuals actually existed. *The Body Politic* played a key role in publicizing a number of job discrimination cases: John Damien, fired as a racing steward from the Ontario Racing Commission; Barbara Thornborrow and Gloria Cameron, dismissed from the Canadian Armed Forced for being "sexual deviates"; Doug Wilson, prevented from teaching by the University of Saskatchewan; Constable Paul Head, forced to resign from the Ontario Provincial Police. These were some of the individuals who chose to go public. It was anyone's guess how many more had quietly accepted their fate and did not fight back.

The understanding that the liberation of homosexuals would only come about through the efforts of homosexuals themselves fueled the growth of an autonomous gay movement, more slowly an autonomous lesbian movement and, eventually, a stronger, self-identified community. Although there had been a few earlier attempts at organization in the Sixties, the real flurry of gay organizing began after 1969. Year after year, organizations sprang up in each province until, by 1982, only Prince Edward Island was without a public gay presence. Year by year, gay and lesbian organizations have become more diverse: lesbian mothers, gay academics, gay and lesbian youth, gay fathers, gay counselling services, business councils, sports clubs, defence committees, support groups like parents of gays and spouses of gays, and many more.

In recent years the news pages of *The Body Politic* have become increasingly preoccupied with accounts of institutionalized reaction to the new visibility of lesbians and gay men. Attacks on the gay community first became an issue with the campaigns of born-again Christian Anita Bryant and with stepped-up police harassment in the watershed years of 1977-78. They were given a high media profile with the trial of *The Body Politic* in 1979 and the Toronto municipal election in 1980. Police raids on gay bars and baths, under the cover of the bawdyhouse laws, seized more and more attention in the first years of the Eighties.

The result of this police harassment has been a developing gay resistance. Nothing, in fact, has strengthened the gay and lesbian community more. Earlier police inroads into the lives and sexual practices of gay people had usually taken the form of arrests of individual men, often isolated, usually closeted. By contrast, the bawdyhouse laws, whose use was not even anticipated by the early movement, became an insidious weapon for interfering with the social spaces where gay men gathered. Attacks on the collective life of the community, however, made a genuine collective response possible, as the reaction to the February 1981 police raids on Toronto bathhouses amply demonstrated.

The list of events in the following chronology is selective. Frequently used abbreviations include: ADGQ—Association pour les droits de la communauté gaie du Québec, CGRO—Coalition for Gay Rights in Ontario, GATE—Gay Alliance Toward Equality, NDP—New Democratic Party, TBP—The Body Politic.

1964

1964   Toronto   Publication of Jane Rule's first novel, *Desert of the Heart* (Macmillan of Canada).

1964   Toronto   *Two* magazine published by Kamp Publishing Company. Name inspired by early American homophile magazine called *One*. Ceased publication in 1966.

February 22/March 7   Toronto   *Maclean's* magazine publishes two-part series by Sydney Katz called "The Homosexual Next Door: A Sober Appraisal of a New Social Phenomenon." Thought to be first positive article on homosexuality to appear in mass media in Canada.

March   Toronto   First issue of magazine *Gay* published. Later renamed *Gay International* and incorporated under name Gay Publishing Company. Ceased publication in 1966.

April   Vancouver   Formation of the Association for Social Knowledge (ASK), the oldest known homophile organization in Canada. Published *ASK Newsletter*, which ceased publication in February 1968.

1965

1965   Toronto   Publication of E A Lacey's *Forms of Loss*, first gay-identified book of poetry published in Canada.

May 26   Ottawa   Formation of Canadian Council on Religion and the Homosexual, concerned with "sympathetic understanding... of the problems faced by homosexuals in our society."

1966

December 31   Vancouver   Opening of ASK (Association of Social Knowledge) Community Centre at 1929 Kingsway, to "serve the homosexual community." First such centre in Canada.

1967

1967   Toronto   Publication of John Herbert's play *Fortune and Men's Eyes*, about homosexuality in Canadian prison system.

1967   Toronto   Publication of Scott Symons's novel *Place d'Armes* (McClelland and Stewart).

1969

June 27   New York   Gay customers fight back during police raid on Greenwich Village gay bar called Stonewall Inn. Symbolic beginning of contemporary gay liberation movement.

August   Ottawa   Amendments to Canadian Criminal Code come into effect, legalizing sexual acts between two consenting adults in private over the age of 21.

October 24   Toronto   First meeting of University of Toronto Homophile Association (UTHA). First gay liberation organization in Canada.

1970

1970   Toronto   Jane Rule's second novel, *This is Not For You*, published (Doubleday Canada).

Spring   Toronto   Catalyst Press launched as gay press by Ian Young. Publishes first book, *Cool Fire* by Ian Young and Richard Phelan.

November   Vancouver   Formation of Vancouver Gay Liberation Front.

1971

February 2   Toronto   First public meeting of Community Homophile Association of Toronto (CHAT).

Spring   Montreal   Formation of first francophone gay organization in Quebec: Front de libération homosexuel (FLH).

July   Vancouver   Founding meetings of the Gay Alliance Toward Equality (GATE), first Canadian group to talk about civil rights strategies.

August 21   Ottawa   "We demand," brief prepared by Toronto Gay Action and sponsored by Canadian gay groups, presented to federal government. Calls for law reform and changes in public policy relating to homosexuals.

August 28   Ottawa   First public gay demonstration in Canada assembles on Parliament Hill in support of brief "We demand."

September   Ottawa   Gays of Ottawa (GO) formed.

November 1   Toronto   Issue One (November/December 1971) of *The Body Politic* goes on sale.

Autumn   Saskatoon   Gay Students Alliance becomes first gay group in Saskatchewan.

1972

1972   Toronto   Publication of *A Not So Gay World: Homosexuality in Canada* by Marion Fraser and Kent Murray (McClelland and Stewart), first non-fiction book on homosexuality in Canada.

February   Winnipeg   Gays for Equality formed. First gay movement organization in Manitoba.

Spring   Edmonton   Formation of the first gay organization in Alberta, called Gay Alliance Toward Equality—Edmonton.

March   Saskatoon   Zodiac Friendship Society is registered as non-profit organization, becomes umbrella group for social and political activities in city.

April 15   Ottawa   Visible gay contingent joins Viet Nam Mobilization Committee demonstration protesting visit of US president Richard Nixon to Canada.

May   Toronto   First issue of *The Other Woman* produced. Combination of several feminist newspapers. Predominate input from lesbian feminists.

May 4   Toronto   Community forum ("Homosexuality: myth and reality") at St Lawrence Centre Town Hall disrupted by right-wing group Western Guard.

June 14   Montreal   FLH opens new gay centre with a dance. Police raid and charge forty people with being found in an establishment selling liquor without permit. Charges later dropped, but attendance falls at centre. Organization folds within a few months.

June 29   Toronto   Gays demonstrate at Queen's Park (site of Ontario legislature) to protest omission of sexual orientation from amendments to Ontario Human Rights Code then being considered by legislature. First public gay action around rights code reform.

August   National Gay Election Coalition formed by sixteen groups to intervene in October 30 federal election. Questionnaires sent to candidates.

August 19-27   Toronto   First Gay Pride Week organized by Toronto Gay Action.

August 23-28   Uproar in Toronto's dailies over the publication of Gerald Hannon article "Of men and little boys" in *The Body Politic*. Criminal charges threatened, but not laid.

Autumn   Montreal   Formation of first anglophone gay organization in Quebec: GAY, later Gay McGill.

Autumn   Toronto   First lesbian drop-ins organized at The Woman's Place at 31 Dupont Street.

October   Saskatoon   First annual Western Canadian Gay Clubs Conference. Representatives from private clubs in three prairie provinces meet to discuss ways to cooperate. Forerunner of gay political organizations.

1972

November 18   Montreal   Gay McGill holds first of what were to become the most successful community dances in the city. Ended in May 1975 by withdrawal of liquor licence by Quebec liquor board.

1973

1973   Montreal   Publication of first Canadian lesbian journal, *Long Time Coming*, by autonomous lesbian group, Montreal Gay Woman, originally women's committee of Gay McGill.

February 12   Toronto   *Globe and Mail* and *Toronto Star* refuse to publish classified ad soliciting subscriptions for *The Body Politic*.

Spring   Toronto   Formation of new gay rights group, Gay Alliance Toward Equality (GATE).

April 30   Toronto   Newsweb Enterprises, printing company controlled by *Toronto Star*, refuses to print Issue 8 of *TBP* following battle over classified ads.

June 30   Toronto   First lesbian conference in Canada held at YWCA (21 McGill Street).

Summer   Toronto   Metropolitan Community Church (MCC) given first mission status in Canada. Begins holding services at Holy Trinity Church under Rev Bob Wolfe.

Summer   Waterloo, Ontario   *Operation Socrates Handbook*, one of first education / information publications of gay movement, printed by Waterloo University's Gay Liberation Movement.

July 18   Windsor   Windsor Gay Unity tries to place classified ad for gay dance in *Windsor Star* and is refused.

August   Vancouver   First issue of *Gay Tide* published by GATE-Vancouver.

August   Toronto   Canadian Gay Archives founded by *The Body Politic*, with newspaper's back files as foundation.

August 17-26   Toronto, Vancouver, Montreal, Ottawa (Winnipeg: October 1-6)   Gay Pride Week becomes a national celebration. Political theme: sexual orientation in provincial human rights codes.

August 25   Toronto, Vancouver   Simultaneous demonstrations in both cities as part of Gay Pride Week.

September   Toronto   Club Baths open at 231 Mutual Street. First of modern gay-operated bathhouses in Canada.

September 27   Windsor   Windsor Press Council decides *Windsor Star* had unfairly discriminated against Windsor Gay Unity in refusing to publish classified ad (see July 18, 1973).

October   Montreal   Opening of gay bookstore, Androgyny.

October 6-7   Quebec City   First pan-Canadian conference of gay organizations, hosted by Centre humanitaire d'aide et de libération (CHAL).

October 10   Toronto   City council passes resolution banning discrimination in municipal hiring on basis of sexual orientation. First such legislation in Canada. Called "our first win" by *TBP*.

December 2   Vancouver   *Vancouver Sun* refuses classified subscription ad for *Gay Tide*. GATE organizes demo outside *Sun* building.

December 15   Washington, DC   American Psychiatric Association removes homosexuality from its official list of mental disorders, following three years of pressure from gay liberation movement.

1974

January 11   Montreal   L'Association homophile de Montréal / Gay Montreal Association holds first public meeting.

January 19-20   Montreal   Lesbian Conference, organized by Gay Women's Collective, held at Women's Centre, 3764, rue St-Laurent.

January 23   Quebec   First lobbying effort on part of alliance of Quebec gay groups, to include sexual orientation in a proposed provincial human rights charter, culminates in appearance before Justice Committee of National Assembly. First appearance of Canadian gay movement before legislative body.

February 11   Winnipeg   Richard North and Chris Vogel married by Unitarian-Universalist minister. First publicized gay "marriage" in Canada.

February 18   Toronto   GATE members picket Ontario Human Rights Commission offices on University Avenue.

March 1   Toronto   GATE representatives meet with full Ontario Human Rights Commission to discuss demands.

March   Milton, Ontario   Fundamentalist minister Ken Campbell, outraged by Hamilton-McMaster Homophile Association members addressing his daughter's high school class, forms Halton Renaissance Committee, forerunner of Renaissance Canada. Eventually becomes one of strongest opponents of gay rights movement.

May   St John's   Community Homophile Association of Newfoundland (CHAN) formed. First gay organization in province.

May 18-19   Saskatoon   First prairie conference of gay organizations, hosted by Saskatoon Gay Action.

July 2   Winnipeg   Derksen Printers refuse to print *Understanding Homosexuality*, educational publication of Gays for Equality. Group pickets printing plant.

July 7   Quebec   New Quebec Charter of Human Rights adopted by National Assembly without legal protection for gays.

August 17   Toronto   Gay Pride March converges on Queen's Park. First time dailies cover such a march.

August 30-September 1   Winnipeg   Second national gay conference.

August 30   Winnipeg   First public gay march in prairie provinces, part of national conference activities.

October   Fredericton   Gay Friends of Fredericton formed. First gay group in New Brunswick.

November   Vancouver   GATE-Vancouver files complaint against *Vancouver Sun* with BC Human Rights Commission regarding refusal to print classified ad for *Gay Tide*.

1975

January 18-19   Toronto   Founding conference of the Coalition for Gay Rights in Ontario (CGRO) at Don Vale Community Centre.

January 24-25   Montreal   Lesbian conference.

February 4   Montreal   Police raid Sauna Aquarius and arrest thirty-six people as found-ins in common bawdyhouse.

February 6   Toronto   John Damien fired from job as racing steward with Ontario Racing Commission "because he's a homosexual."

February 28   Vancouver   First public hearing of gay civil rights case under provincial human rights legislation: GATE vs *Vancouver Sun*.

Spring   Fredericton, New Brunswick   Five New Brunswick dailies refuse to carry classified ad for Gay Friends of Fredericton.

March   Toronto   Ontario Human Rights Code review committee established.

March 4-20   Ottawa   Eighteen gay men — owner and customers of modelling agency and dating service—arrested, charged with sexual offences in what became known as "Ottawa sex scandal." Names released by police and published by press day by day. Police allege "homosexual vice ring."

1975

March 18   Ottawa   Warren Zufelt, one of eighteen men arrested in "sex scandal," commits suicide by jumping from apartment building balcony after name published in press.

March 20   Gays of Ottawa (GO) pickets police station and office of *Ottawa Journal* to protest arrests and media coverage of arrests.

March 21   John Damien sues Ontario Racing Commission and individuals involved in his firing. Suit filed in Ontario Supreme Court.

April   Montreal   First issue of English-language news journal, *Gay Times*, published.

May   Toronto   Issue 18 of *The Body Politic* ordered off stands by Metro Toronto Police's Morality Squad because of a graphic cartoon called "Harold Hedd," depicting two men engaged in fellatio.

June 9   Toronto   GATE representatives appear before Parliamentary Committee on Green Paper on Immigration to call for dropping of all references to homosexuality in Immigration Act. Participate in demonstration outside Park Plaza Hotel. Gay groups make similar presentations across the country throughout year.

June 27-30   Ottawa   National Gay Rights Conference sees formation of National Gay Rights Coalition.

July 4-7   Winnipeg   Formation of New Democratic Party Gay Caucus at NDP national convention.

September   Saskatoon   Doug Wilson, graduate student in education at University of Saskatchewan, is prevented from practice teaching because he was publicly active in the gay movement. President of the university calls it a "managerial decision." Defence committee is set up to press for Wilson's reinstatement.

September 13   Toronto   Large gay rights march calls for reinstatement of John Damien and the inclusion of sexual orientation in human rights code. Sponsored by Coalition for Gay Rights in Ontario.

October   Toronto   First issue of *Esprit*, a gay publication for men and women.

October 17-18   Montreal   Five gay bars raided by police.

October 31   Montreal   Police raid two more bars, including Baby Face, popular lesbian bar.

November 6   Special Joint Committee on Immigration Policy recommends that homosexuals no longer be prohibited from entering Canada under revised Immigration Act.

November 9   Saskatoon   Saskatchewan Human Rights Commission rules that "sex" in Human Rights Act includes sexual orientation. Begins formal proceeding against University of Saskatchewan for discriminating against teacher Doug Wilson (see September 1975). University seeks court injunction to prevent inquiry.

November 11   Ottawa   Two members of Gays of Ottawa lay wreath at National War Memorial. First time gays allowed to participate in ceremony.

1976

January   Saskatoon   Saskatchewan Court of Queen's Bench rules that term "sex" in Saskatchewan Human Rights Act does not include sexual orientation. Legal action came as a result of Doug Wilson job discrimination case (see September, 1975). Wilson decides to abandon pursuit of legal redress.

January 12   Vancouver   British Columbia Board of Inquiry rules in *Gay Tide-Vancouver Sun* case that British Columbia human rights code provides protection for homosexuals.

January 23   Montreal   Club Baths of Montreal raided. Thirteen people arrested as found-ins in a common bawdyhouse.

Spring   Halifax   CBC Radio refuses to air a public service announcement from Gay Alliance for Equality for a Gayline and counselling service.

April 5   Ottawa   City council passes motion to prohibit discrimination in municipal hiring on basis of sexual orientation. Second city in Canada to do so.

April 21   Saskatoon   Board of Governors of University of Saskatchewan overturns recommendation of University Council that homosexuality should not be consideration in selection of dons of residence. It accepts that sexual orientation not be a factor in treatment of faculty or students in faculty positions. Decision result of Doug Wilson case (see September, 1975).

May 6   Toronto   Two MPPs—Margaret Campbell (Liberal—St George) and Ted Bounsell (NDP—Windsor)—introduce private member's bills to amend Ontario Human Rights Code to include sexual orientation. Bills are defeated.

May 14   Montreal   Police raid Neptune Sauna and arrest nineteen men, charging them with being found-ins in common bawdyhouse.

May 22   Montreal   Police raid Club Baths and charge twenty-seven men with being found-ins in a common bawdyhouse.

June 11-13   Kingston, Ontario   NDP convention calls for inclusion of sexual orientation in human rights codes. First time a major political party accepts gay movement demand.

June 17   Toronto   Coalition for Gay Rights in Ontario presents brief *The Homosexual Minority in Ontario* to the Ontario Human Rights Commission.

June 19   Montreal   Largest gay demonstration in Canada to date organized by Comité homosexuel anti-répression / Gay Coalition Against Repression to protest pre-Olympic "clean-up" raids on gay bars and baths.

June 24   Montreal   Gay activist Stuart Russell, along with four others, fired from COJO (Olympic organizing committee) for political activity and sexual orientation.

Summer   Toronto   *The Body Politic* receives $1,500 grant from Ontario Arts Council, the first of three such grants.

August   Vancouver   BC Supreme Court dismisses appeal of *Vancouver Sun* against pro-GATE decision of human rights commission's board of inquiry.

September 4-6   Toronto   Fourth Annual Gay Conference for Canada and Quebec. Includes a rally and march.

September 17   Toronto   Brian Mossop, gay activist, expelled from Communist Party of Canada for being openly gay and advocating homosexuality.

Autumn   Ottawa   Peter Maloney, former manager of Club Bath Ottawa, pleads guilty to keeping a common bawdyhouse and is fined $500; three others plead guilty to being inmates and are fined $100 each.

October 9-11   Ottawa   National Lesbian Conference hosted by Lesbian Organization of Ottawa.

October 30   Montreal   Formation of first gay civil rights group in Quebec, Association pour les droits de la communauté gaie du Québec (ADGQ).

November 7   Toronto   Founding of the Lesbian Organization of Toronto (LOOT) with first priority the setting up of lesbian centre.

December   Vancouver   Canadian University Press approves national boycott of CBC for refusing to air public service announcements for Halifax gay group.

1977

January   Winnipeg   First issue of *After Stonewall: A Critical Journal of Gay Liberation* published.

January   Toronto   Lesbian Organization of Toronto moves to new centre at 342 Jarvis Street, sharing with feminist publication *The Other Woman* and coffeehouse called Three of Cups.

January   Toronto   First issue of *Directions: For Gay Men* published.

January 7   Ottawa   CBC releases public policy on public service announcements: nothing controversial, and gay is controversial.

1977

January 28   Ottawa   Charges dismissed against 16 of 22 men arrested as found-ins in Club Ottawa.

February 17   Halifax   First public gay demonstration in Atlantic Canada. Part of nationally coordinated protest against CBC Radio's refusal to air gay public service announcements.

March 14   Windsor   Third Canadian city council to pass resolution banning discrimination against homosexual city employees.

Spring   Toronto   Feminist newspaper *The Other Woman* folds.

April 2   Argentia, Newfoundland   Master Corporal Gloria Cameron and eight other women are dismissed from the Canadian Armed Forces because they are lesbian.

April 28   Toronto   MPP Margaret Campbell's private member's bill, to include sexual orientation in Ontario Human Rights Code, introduced April 4, fails in legislature.

May 7   Winnipeg   Ten groups attend first Manitoba Gay Conference and form the Manitoba Gay Coalition.

May 9   Ottawa   Private Barbara Thornborrow confronted by officials in Canadian Armed Forces about her lesbianism. Decides to go public and fight before she is fired.

May 21   Toronto   Largest CGRO demonstration in Ontario to date converges on Queen's Park with civil rights demands.

June 2   Ottawa   Parliament passes Canadian Human Rights Act governing employment by federal government, but homosexuals are not protected.

June 7   Dade County, Florida   Referendum, forced by pressure from fundamentalist Christians Anita Bryant, husband Bob Green and their "Save Our Children" organization, repeals county ordinance prohibiting discrimination on basis of sexual orientation. First major battle—and defeat—in struggle for gay civil rights in United States. First successful use of "child molestation tactic" by anti-gay forces which sets pattern of attack for remainder of Seventies and into Eighties.

June 10   Vancouver   BC Court of Appeal reverses BC Supreme Court ruling favouring *Gay Tide* in complaint against *Vancouver Sun* classified ad refusal, by saying *Sun* had "reasonable cause" not to print ad.

June 20   Ottawa   Private Barbara Thornborrow given notice of discharge by Canadian Armed Forces as a "sexual deviate" who is "not advantageously employable."

June 25   Toronto   Newly formed Coalition to Stop Anita Bryant organizes demonstration. First of several coalitions and public actions across Canada reacting to Bryant's anti-gay crusade.

June 29   Ottawa   Gallup Poll shows that 52 percent of Canadians believe gay people should be protected against discrimination under new Canadian Human Rights Act.

June 29-July 5   Saskatoon   Fifth Annual National Gay Rights Conference sponsored by Saskatoon Gay Community Centre.

Summer   Toronto   Formation of Women's Archives.

July 21   Toronto   Ontario Human Rights Code Review Committee releases report *Life Together*, calling for major changes in code and commission, including strong support for inclusion of sexual orientation.

July 22   Toronto   Second march organized by the Coalition Against Anita Bryant.

August 1   Toronto   Emanuel Jaques, 12-year-old shoeshine boy, found sexually assaulted and murdered on roof of Yonge Street body-rub parlour. Four men later charged with murder. Begins huge media and public outcry which becomes focussed on entire gay community.

August 4   Toronto   Jaques buried. Large demonstration at city hall calls for return of capital punishment, more police power and elimination of gay people.

August 9   Toronto   Gay community leaders hold press conference to deplore press coverage of Jaques murder which implicates entire gay community.

October   Quebec   Association pour les droits de la communauté gaie du Québec (ADGQ) presents brief *The Homosexual Minority in Quebec and the Human Rights Charter* to National Assembly.

October 8-10   Halifax   First Atlantic Canada Gay Conference of groups in eastern provinces.

October 15-16   Montreal   First National Congress of Quebec Gays meets.

October 17   Ottawa   GATE-Vancouver's *Gay Tide* case heard before the Supreme Court of Canada. First time a gay civil rights case heard by Supreme Court.

October 21-22   Toronto, Halifax, Edmonton, Ottawa, Windsor, Vancouver   Damien Days of Protest. Rallies across Canada protesting job discrimination with focus on John Damien case.

October 22   Montreal   Police raid gay bar Truxx, charge 146 men with being found-ins in common bawdyhouse. Largest mass arrest since War Measures Act.

October 23   Montreal   Two thousand people demonstrate in downtown streets to protest raid on Truxx bar.

October 27   Montreal   Meeting between Quebec Human Rights Commission and representatives of ADGQ results in public recommendation that government amend Human Rights Charter to include sexual orientation.

October 31   Toronto   Halloween brings usual crowd of queer-bashers to Yonge Street looking for drag parade. Gay representatives meet with police beforehand to try to prevent crowds from gathering. Operation Jack-o'-Lantern, a gay street patrol, organized to monitor situation. Police do little to control crowd.

November 21   Toronto   Issue 39 of *The Body Politic* containing article "Men loving boys loving men" goes on sale.

December 15   Quebec   National Assembly, in quiet late-night session, amends Quebec Charter of Human Rights to include sexual orientation. Becomes first province and largest political jurisdiction in North America to provide legal protections for homosexuals.

December 22-27   Toronto   Series of articles and columns by Claire Hoy in *Toronto Sun* deplores "Men loving boys loving men" article in *The Body Politic*, calls on Ontario Arts Council grant ($1,500) to be returned and urges police to lay charges.

December 30   Toronto   Members of Operation P, joint Toronto-provincial pornography squad, raid offices of *The Body Politic*, stay over three hours and seize twelve packing crates of material, including subscription lists.

1978

January 5   Toronto   Charges laid by police against Pink Triangle Press and three officers under Criminal Code section 159 ("possession of obscene material for distribution") and section 164 ("use of the mails for purpose of transmitting anything that is indecent, immoral or scurrilous").

January 14   Toronto   Rally and march organized to protest visit of Anita Bryant to Toronto, sponsored by fundamentalist group Renaissance Canada.

January 15   Toronto   Anita Bryant speaks at People's Church in North York. Protest rally occurs outside.

February 3   Toronto   House of Bishops of Anglican Church of Canada affirms that gay people "are entitled to equal protection under the law with all other Canadian citizens."

March   Toronto   Incorporation of Toronto Lambda Business Council, first association of gay businesses in the country.

1978

March 6   Montreal   Montreal Catholic School Commission reverses January 25 decision to rent school space for an event sponsored by gay group ADGQ.

March 6   Hamilton   Ontario Provincial Police officer Paul Head arrested, charged with gross indecency and contributing to juvenile delinquency, for having sex with his under-age lover. He is forced to resign.

March 8   Toronto   Lesbian Mothers Defence Fund launched by Wages Due Lesbians.

March 12   Toronto   Jury finds three men guilty of murder of Emanuel Jaques. Fourth man is acquitted.

April 1   Ottawa   New Immigration Act goes into effect which removes prohibitions against homosexuals entering the country.

April 27   Toronto   John Argue, swimming instructor with Toronto Board of Education, a gay activist (later active in Metro NDP), is fired from his job at public school because he is gay.

April 29   Edmonton   Anita Bryant visit prompts demonstration organized by Coalition to Answer Anita Bryant.

April 30   Winnipeg   Bryant visit prompts gay protest demonstration.

May 3   Toronto   Coalition for Gay Rights in Ontario distributes brief *Discrimination and the Gay Minority* to Legislature. Liberal leader Stuart Smith supports inclusion of sexual orientation in human rights code.

May 8   Montreal   Trial begins of those in Truxx raid charged with being keepers in common bawdyhouse (see October 22, 1977).

May 17   Toronto   Board of Education committee rehires John Argue as swimming instructor, overruling principal of school.

May 18-21   Toronto   Second annual conference of MCC in Canada sees election of new Canadian coordinator and installation of Rev Brent Hawkes as pastor of MCC Toronto.

May 20-22   Toronto   First bi-national gay youth conference held.

June 28 - July 4   Halifax   Sixth National Gay Conference, hosted by Gay Alliance for Equality.

Summer   Kitchener-Waterloo, Ontario   Hour-long "Gay News and Views" begins on local station. First regularly scheduled gay radio programme in Canada.

Summer   Montreal   Quebec Human Rights Commission decides that Montreal Catholic School Commission's refusal to rent facilities to gay group is discriminatory. First such finding by commission since inclusion of "sexual orientation" in charter.

July 1   Moose Jaw, Saskatchewan   Gay protest rally responds to visit of Anita Bryant to province. First such rally in city.

August 15   Montreal   Quebec Human Rights Commission reconsiders earlier decision and now agrees Montreal Catholic School Commission could refuse to rent premises to gay group.

August 23-27   Toronto   Gaydays, popular gay festival, held in Toronto at Queen's Park.

September 10   London, Ontario   Anita Bryant visit sparks protest demonstration outside London Gardens Coliseum.

October 6-9   Quebec   Regroupement national des lesbiennes et gaies du Québec, Quebec-wide gay coalition, formed by groups meeting at Laval University.

September 29   Toronto   Ontario Arts Council gives *The Body Politic* its last grant ($1,650) following three-month delay and much backroom politicking. Uproar in press prompts minister responsible for OAC to publicly criticize the award.

November 7   California   Briggs Initiative or Proposition 6, a state-wide referendum calling for firing of gay or gay-positive teachers from public school system, is defeated. Broad-based grass roots movement to oppose right-wing offensive pol-

"Hi! Mind if we just browse for a while?"

Police raid The Body Politic *office: December 30, 1977*

Paul Aboud, Issue 40, February 1978

iticizes thousands of gay people. Major victory for gay movement in US.

November 13   Windsor   Gay activist Jim Monk loses in bid for school trustee in municipal elections.

November 27   San Francisco   Gay city supervisor Harvey Milk and pro-gay mayor George Moscone assassinated by ex-supervisor Dan White, who is charged with murder. Death of Milk, a symbol of ascendancy of openly gay men and women to public office, deals heavy blow to San Francisco gay community.

November 27   Toronto   Formation of first Parents of Gays group in Canada.

December 9   Toronto   Metro Toronto police raid the Barracks steambath and charge twenty-three men as found-ins, five as keepers of a common bawdyhouse.

December 18   Toronto   Metro Police sergeant calls three school boards in Toronto area and informs them six teachers in their employ were arrested in Barracks raid. Officer is given only internal departmental reprimand.

1979

January 2   Toronto   Trial of *The Body Politic* begins before Provincial Court Judge Sydney Harris (see January 5, 1978).

January 3   Toronto   Newly elected mayor John Sewell defends *The Body Politic* and calls for legal protection for gays in speech at a Body Politic Free the Press rally held during trial. Speech causes media uproar.

January 22   Toronto   Public meeting sets up a Barracks defence fund, the forerunner of the Right to Privacy Committee.

1979

February 14   Toronto   Judge Sydney Harris finds Pink Triangle Press and three officers not guilty (see January 5, 1978).

February 20   Seven men, including *Winnipeg Free Press* publisher Richard Malone, are charged with buggery and gross indecency and twelve boys are turned over to juvenile authorities after five-month investigation of "juvenile sex ring."

March 6   Toronto   Attorney General Roy McMurtry appeals Pink Triangle Press acquittal.

March 10   Toronto   International Women's Day includes call for end to harassment of lesbians as one of four demands. First time lesbian rights an upfront issue.

March 13   Toronto   Ontario Ministry of Community and Social Services refuses to grant licence to Tri-Aid to run gay group home.

March 28   Toronto   Metro Toronto police chief and police association president both issue statements of apology after anti-gay article "The homosexual fad" appears in police association newsletter.

April   Toronto   Provincial Council of the Ontario Secondary School Teachers' Federation (OSSTF) amends its anti-discrimination policy to include sexual orientation. Policy acts as directive to local bargaining units with school boards.

April 20   Regina   New legislation amending human rights code introduced in Saskatchewan legislature omits sexual orientation although provincial convention of government party, the NDP, called for its inclusion. Gay movement had mounted extensive lobbying campaign.

April 21   Edmonton   Alberta Lesbian and Gay Rights Association created during province-wide Alberta Gay Conference.

May 5   Saskatoon   Saskatchewan Division of Canadian Union of Public Employees (CUPE) at annual convention supports legislation banning discrimination on basis of sexual orientation.

May 13   London   Ontario Division of CUPE at annual conference opposes discrimination on basis of sexual orientation and urges local affiliates to include it in non-discrimination clauses of collective agreements.

May 15   Smeaton, Saskatchewan   Teacher Don Jones dismissed because of a complaint to school board that he is gay.

May 19-21   Toronto   Bi-national Lesbian Conference held at University of Toronto.

May 21   San Francisco   Near-riots occur outside San Francisco City Hall, as gay community reacts with anger after Dan White, murderer of gay city hall supervisor Harvey Milk, is given lenient sentence in jury trial (see November 27, 1978).

May 22   Ottawa   Supreme Court of Canada decides *Vancouver Sun* justified in refusing to print classified ad for *Gay Tide*, rules that it had "reasonable cause" to control content of advertising it accepted.

May 31   Toronto   Metro Toronto Police Commission responds to demands for disciplining of racist and homophobic officers by issuing a Declaration of Concern and Intent (Standing Order 25), which deals with discrimination and bigotry only in a general way.

June   Montreal   First issue of francophone journal *Le Berdache*, evolving out of a newsletter of Association pour les droits de la communauté gaie du Québec.

June   Toronto   Gay Liberation Union establishes first gay self-defence course in Canada. Grows out of experience of increasing anti-gay violence on streets.

June 6   Toronto   Teacher Don Franco, who made public issue of fact that a Metro Toronto police officer reported his arrest in Barracks raid December 8, 1978, charged with being keeper of a common bawdyhouse in his own home.

June 16-23   Montreal   Gay celebration, Gairilla Week, takes place.

"How sick!
How depraved!
How cru-ell!"

Item: Police astounded to find cell and handcuffs in raid on the Barracks steambath, Toronto, December 1978

Paul Aboud, Issue 50, February 1979

June 19   Toronto   Metro Council calls on police commission to answer specific demands of gay community. Toronto City Council makes same request June 25. Police commission does not act.

June 27-July 2   Ottawa   Celebration '79, seventh annual conference of lesbians and gay men. Officially opened by Ottawa Mayor Marian Dewar, who proclaims June 27 "Human Rights Day."

July 31   Vancouver   Public meeting of gay community discusses increasing violence against gay people on Vancouver streets, calls on police to take some action.

August 11   Vancouver   Public rally in Robson Square protests police inaction in dealing with street violence against gays.

August 12-16   Toronto   Ontario government administrative tribunal holds hearings to determine whether gay group home Tri-Aid should be licensed in order to qualify for government funding and referrals.

August 20-22   Toronto   Seven men stage Gay Sit-in for Justice in office of provincial Attorney General Roy McMurtry to demand meeting to talk about police and legal harassment of gay community.

August 20-24   Sarnia, Ontario/Port Huron, Michigan   Lesbians on way to Michigan Womyn's Music Festival harassed or turned back by US Immigration officials. Formal complaints are laid on behalf of Canadian women by American gay organization, the National Gay Task Force.

September 14   Smeaton, Saskatchewan   Education arbitration board orders teacher Don Jones reinstated to job from which he was fired for being gay.

September 27   Toronto   Provincial administrative tribunal refuses to grant registration to gay group home, Tri-Aid, ending its two-year struggle to be recognized.

1979

October 11   Toronto   Police raid gay bathhouse, the Hot Tub Club, charge forty men with bawdyhouse charges.

October 23   Winnipeg   Former *Winnipeg Free Press* publisher Richard Malone pleads guilty to charge of buggery and obstructing justice. Gets one-year sentence, following "juvenile sex ring" investigation in February 1979.

October 29   Toronto   Gay activists hold "mince-in" at Ontario legislature to draw attention to inaction on human rights protections for homosexuals.

November   Toronto   Delegates to province-wide annual convention of Ontario Federation of Labour (OFL) calls on provincial government to extend protection against discrimination to lesbians and gay men. Similar motion was defeated in 1978.

November 3   Toronto   Gus Harris, mayor of Toronto borough of Scarborough, calls for gay rights at Human Rights rally.

November 17   Vancouver   *Vancouver Sun* reverses stand, accepts ad from *Gay Tide* after five-year court battle. Supreme Court of Canada ruled *Sun* had "reasonable cause" to refuse advertising. First ad was submitted to *Sun* October 23, 1974.

November 22   Toronto   Ontario government tries to sidestep controversy over protecting homosexuals in human rights code by introducing Bill 188—Handicapped Persons Rights Act. Segregation attempt universally condemned.

November 29   Montreal   Quebec Superior Court judge rules that the Montreal Catholic School Commission did not have justifiable grounds to refuse to rent space to ADGQ, therefore was not exempt from the Charter of Human Rights and Freedoms. Overturns human rights commission's second opinion in 1978. First legal victory against discrimination since adoption of gay rights clause in charter in December 1977.

December   Toronto   Labour Minister Robert Elgie withdraws Handicapped Persons Rights Protection Act under pressure from handicapped, media and opposition parties.

December   Toronto   PLURA, an inter-church funding agency which supports projects for social change, gives $4,000 to CGRO to pay full-time grassroots organizer to establish gay political organizations in rural Ontario.

December   Montreal   Quebec Superior Court judge upholds Canada Customs ban on gay male pornography magazines, invokes "community standards" and defines "immoral" and "indecent." First judicial pronouncements in Canada on gay male pornography. Customs decision is appealed by Le Priape, Montreal gay sex shop.

December 27   Toronto   Provincial Court Judge Sydney Harris orders Crown to return material seized in December 30, 1977 raid on *The Body Politic* offices and to pay costs. Crown appeals decision.

1980

January 6   Toronto   Gay Community Appeal of Toronto is incorporated and begins plans to launch first United Way-type gay fund-raising drive in North America.

February 6   Toronto   Full-page ad in *Globe and Mail*, supported by over eight hundred individuals and groups, calls on Attorney General Roy McMurtry to drop appeal of acquittal of *The Body Politic*. First time an advocacy ad for a gay cause published in Canadian daily.

February 7-8   Toronto   County Court Judge George Ferguson hears Crown appeal of decision of Provincial Court judge acquitting *The Body Politic* of charges relating to using the mail to transmit immoral and indecent material.

February 29   Toronto   Judge George Ferguson orders *The Body Politic* back to Provincial Court to face a new trial. *TBP* decides to appeal.

*Ontario Attorney General
Roy McMurtry on* The Body
Politic *case: "Of course I
intend to follow the ruling
handed down by the court...
but not until the court hands
down a ruling I intend to
follow."*

Paul Aboud, Issue 60, February 1980

February   Kingston, Ontario   A Provincial Court judge awards sole custody of ten-year-old daughter to lesbian mother, concludes that proselytizing or copying of sexual patterns were not dangers. Third reported Canadian case of court awarding custody to homosexual parent.

March 13   Toronto   Association of Gay Electors chooses George Hislop as candidate for Ward 6 aldermanic race in November 1980.

March 21   Toronto   Three judges of Divisional Court order fired gay Ontario Provincial Police officer Paul Head reinstated as member in good standing of force (see March 7, 1978). OPP appeals decision.

March 31   Burlington, Ontario   OPP constable Paul Head is suspended from duty after court orders him reinstated. Given new charge of discreditable conduct.

April 2   Montreal   Municipal Court judge finds owner of Truxx bar guilty of keeping a common bawdyhouse and sentences him to ten days in jail and $5,000 fine (see October 22, 1977).

April 23   Montreal   Police raid Sauna David, gay bathhouse, and arrest sixty-one men on bawdyhouse charges.

April 26   Montreal   Large night demonstration takes over streets at Stanley and Ste-Catherine intersection to protest police raid on Sauna David.

April 30   Winnipeg   Two chain bookstores, Coles and Classics, remove copies of *Joy of Gay Sex* and *Joy of Lesbian Sex* from shelves following threats from police that they would lay obscenity charges.

June 2   Ottawa   Canadian Union of Postal Workers (CUPW) ratifies contract which includes non-discrimination clause protecting gay people. First time gay employees of federal government department awarded such protection.

June 21-July 3   Montreal   More than ten thousand gay men and lesbians participate in second annual Gairilla Week. Gay celebration awarded grant by organizing committee of Quebec's national holiday, la fête nationale des Québécois.

June 24   Vancouver   Gay Alliance Toward Equality (GATE), one of Canada's oldest and most active gay rights organizations, announces dissolution.

1980

June 27-July 1   Calgary   Celebration '80, eighth annual conference of lesbians and gay men, disbands the moribund Canadian Lesbian and Gay Rights Coalition. Proposals made to form more limited group aimed at lobbying federal government.

July 5   Winnipeg   National convention of Liberal Party of Canada adopts resolution to include sexual orientation in Canadian Human Rights Act.

July 31   Toronto   Toronto Board of Education votes to look into the possibility of setting up a permanent liaison committee between the board and the gay/lesbian community.

August   Halifax   General Council of United Church of Canada, largest Protestant denomination in country, gives approval to "In God's Image... Male and Female," study document which advocates acceptance of gays and lesbians into ministry and which says premarital and extramarital sex are acceptable under certain circumstances.

September 3   Toronto   Mayor John Sewell endorses George Hislop, gay candidate for alderman in November municipal election, and causes media uproar about "gay power politics" taking over city hall.

September 9   Toronto   Metro Council, governing body of greater Toronto area, refuses to pass Metro Bill of Rights which includes sexual orientation, and substitutes weaker declaration about being an equal opportunity employer (see October 10, 1973).

September 15   Toronto   Subcommittee to look into establishing liaison committee between Board of Education and gay/lesbian community caves into pressure from fundamentalist Christian groups, votes to disband at first meeting.

September 18   Toronto   Board of Education amends policy to ban discrimination on basis of sexual orientation, but adds clause forbidding "proselytizing of homosexuality in the schools."

October 31   Toronto   For the first time, police do not allow queer-bashers and spectators to congregate outside St Charles Tavern to wait for drag queens. Traffic and pedestrians are kept moving with help of large numbers of police officers. Not a single egg thrown.

November 10   Toronto   Municipal election sees defeat of first openly gay candidate to run for municipal office in Canada, George Hislop, and of gay-positive mayor, John Sewell. "Gay issue" figures prominently in campaign and brings out flood of anti-gay literature.

November 15   Vancouver   Michael Harcourt, an alderman consistently supportive of the gay community, is elected mayor. An organization called Gay People to Elect Mike Harcourt campaigned actively in gay community.

November 25   Toronto   Labour Minister Robert Elgie introduces Bill 209, an act to amend the Ontario Human Rights Code, in the Legislature. Sexual orientation is not included.

December 10   Toronto   NDP leader Michael Cassidy, despite years of lip-service paid to protections for gay people in legislation, says that issue of gay rights "is not a priority at this time." Provincial election in the offing March 19, 1981.

December 11   Ottawa   Representatives of the Canadian Association of Lesbians and Gay Men (CALGM) appear before Joint Senate/House Committee on the Constitution to argue for inclusion of "sexual orientation" in entrenched Charter of Human Rights and Freedoms.

December 19   Ottawa   Justice Minister Jean Chrétien announces proposals to revise Criminal Code to reduce age of consent to 18 years and make other changes in legislation related to sexual offences.

1981

January 29   Ottawa   Joint Senate/House of Commons Committee votes down amendment to add sexual orientation to Charter of Rights.

February 5   Toronto   Massive police raid carried out on four bathhouses, largest mass arrest in Canada since War Measures Act. Two hundred and eighty-six men charged as found-ins, and twenty as keepers of common bawdyhouse.

February 6   Toronto   Over three thousand people gather in downtown street in angry late-night protest against bath raids.

February 11   Toronto   Gay activist George Hislop announces plans to run as protest candidate in downtown St George riding in March 19 provincial election. Also running, Liberal candidate Rev Bruce McLeod, chosen over gay activist Peter Maloney, NDP candidate Dan Leckie, chosen over gay activist John Argue, and Conservative candidate Susan Fish.

February 20   Toronto   Over four thousand gays and supporters rally at Toronto Queen's Park and march to Metro Toronto Police's 52 Division to protest February 5 bathhouse raids and to call for independent inquiry.

March   Toronto   Founding meetings of Toronto Gay Community Council, first city-wide coordinating organization of gay and lesbian groups in Canada.

March 4   Toronto   Ontario Court of Appeal hears *The Body Politic*'s appeal of lower court order of a retrial (see February 29, 1980).

March 4   Toronto   *The Body Politic* attempts to cite Attorney General of Ontario and *Toronto Sun* for comments made in print a day before the appeal. Court of Appeal rejects attempt, orders *TBP* to pay costs.

March 6   Toronto   Gay Freedom Rally nears speakers including novelist Margaret Atwood and NDP MP Svend Robinson denounce bath raids.

March 12   Toronto   MCC pastor Brent Hawkes ends twenty-five day hunger fast when Toronto City Council decides to ask Daniel Hill to investigate police/gay relations. Hawkes began fast to create pressure for independent inquiry into bath raids.

March 19   Ontario   Provincial election sees return of Conservatives to power. NDP suffers losses, attributed in some parts of province to backtracking on gay issue. Conservative Susan Fish wins in Toronto riding of St George, defeating gay protest candidate George Hislop.

March 25   Toronto   Court of Appeal rejects appeal of *The Body Politic* to overturn order of retrial (see March 4). *TBP* decides to appeal to Supreme Court of Canada.

March 30   Toronto   Trial of alleged keepers of Barracks steambath begins. Includes gay activist George Hislop and four others. Charges arose from raid December 9, 1978.

April 21   Toronto   Six people, including activists George Hislop and Peter Maloney and head of Club Bath chain in US, Jack Campbell, charged with conspiracy to live off avails of crime. Final charges following February 5 bathhouse raids.

May 16-18   Vancouver   Fifth Binational Lesbian Conference draws women from across Canada, organizes first lesbian pride march.

May 30   Edmonton   Police raid on Pisces Spa results in sixty men being charged as keepers or found-ins in common bawdyhouse. Accused are questioned at specially arranged 5 am courtroom session permitted under little-used section of Criminal Code.

Late May   Calgary   Alberta Conference of United Church of Canada passes gay rights resolutions and votes to study possibility of ordination of gays.

June 2   Toronto   Standing committee of Ontario legislature begins hearings on Bill 7—Human Rights Bill. First to speak are *TBP*'s lawyer Clayton Ruby and the Coalition for Gay Rights in Ontario.

1981

June 5   Edmonton   Three keepers and five found-ins from Pisces Spa raid (see May 30) plead guilty in Provincial Court. Owners are heavily fined.

June 12   Toronto   Provincial Court judge finds two employees guilty and three owners not guilty of keeping common bawdyhouse. Charges relate to Barracks steambath, raided by police December 9, 1978.

June 16   Toronto   Police raid two more bathhouses, arresting twenty-one men on bawdyhouse charges.

June 20   Toronto   Gay demonstration, protesting bathhouse raids June 16, result in altercations with queer-bashers and police violence against demonstrators.

June 20-28   Montreal   Third annual Gay Pride Week (called "Gai-e lon la") draws nearly fifteen thousand lesbians and gay men. Coincides with La fête nationale.

June 30   Moncton, New Brunswick   City council passes last-minute amendment to bylaw to prevent a gay picnic from taking place in Centennial Park to celebrate Canada Day. Group of gay people hold picnic anyway.

July 3   Vancouver   Federal NDP convention calls for amendment of bawdyhouse section of Criminal Code.

July 8   Montreal   Owner of Sauna David is found guilty of keeping a common bawdyhouse. Charges resulting from police raid on bathhouse April 26, 1980.

July 13   Toronto   City council appoints Arnold Bruner to conduct study into police/gay community relations, five months after February 5 bathhouse raids.

August 1-7   Vancouver   Mayor Mike Harcourt, fulfilling election promise, proclaims Gay Unity Week. Parade is part of celebration for first time.

August 25   Ottawa   McDonald Commission on RCMP wrongdoings releases report after four years of hearings and research. Reveals that Security Service has long-established programme for collecting information on homosexuals.

August 30-September 5   Toronto   Cabbagetown Group Softball League hosts the fifth Gay Softball World Series. Players from eleven cities in US and Canada.

September 10   Ottawa   Gays of Ottawa (GO) celebrate tenth anniversary with official opening of community centre at 175 Lisgar Street. Reception attended by mayor Marion Dewar, Gordon Fairweather, head of Canadian Human Rights Commission, and MPP Michael Cassidy, leader of provincial NDP.

September 24   Toronto   Provincial Court judge acquits Don Franco of charge of keeping common bawdyhouse in own home (see June 6, 1979).

September 24   Toronto   *Out of the Closet: Study of Relations Between Homosexual Community and Police,* commissioned by city council, released by Arnold Bruner. Recognizes gay community as legitimate part of community and calls for permanent police/gay dialogue committee.

September 30   Toronto   Provincial Court judge acquits man of assaulting police officer during June 20, 1981 demonstration. She calls for investigation of police conduct during protest.

October 6   Ottawa   Supreme Court of Canada refuses to hear appeal of *The Body Politic.* Last resort of appeal exhausted; *TBP* back to retrial.

October 7   Toronto   Dykes in the Streets march, sponsored by Lesbians Against the Right, first lesbian pride march in Toronto.

October 14   Toronto   Ontario Court of Appeal overturns reinstatement of gay Ontario Provincial Police officer Paul Head (see March 21, 1980).

October 17-18   Fredericton   Third regional conference of Atlantic Lesbian and Gay Association brings together largest assembly of gays in New Brunswick.

October 19   Toronto   Former mayor John Sewell wins junior aldermanic seat in Ward 6 byelection without gay issue playing a role.

November 2   Toronto   First keeper trial following February 5 bath raids sees Romans II Sauna employee plead guilty, receive absolute discharge, while five others have charges withdrawn. Legal status of alleged found-ins ambiguous.

November 3   Toronto   Committee of city council considers Bruner Report on police/gay relations. Asks police chief to issue statement recognizing legitimacy of gay community and setting up gay awareness programme for police recruits.

November 18   Ottawa   Canadian Gay Archives wins appeal with Revenue Canada. Gets tax exempt status as registered charity.

November 20   Toronto   Club Bath chain head Jack Campbell, in surprise plea bargaining agreement, pleads guilty to conspiracy charges and is fined $40,000 (see April 21, 1981).

December 1   Toronto   Ontario legislature defeats amendment to include sexual orientation in human rights code. Five non-violent protesters handcuff themselves to railings in spectators' gallery. Legislature is disrupted briefly. Last chance to provide protection for gay people. Ends decade of protect and lobbying by gay movement (see June 29, 1972).

1982

January 11   Toronto   Owner of Richmond Street Health Emporium, one of four bathhouses raided by police February 5, 1981, pleads guilty to being keeper of common bawdyhouse (plea bargaining deal sees charges dropped against five others).

January 20   Toronto   Police chief Jack Ackroyd issues statement that members of gay community are entitled to "same rights, respect, service and protection as all citizens" and that gay people are "legitimate members of the community." Community leaders call statement evasive, claim it does not recognize legitimacy of the *community*.

February 6   Toronto   John Damien, racing steward fired from Ontario Racing Commission for being gay (see February 6, 1975), marks anniversary of fight to have case heard in court. Legal manoeuvres on part of racing commission officials Damien is suing have held off civil trial for seven years.

Frebrurary 6   Toronto   Anniversary demonstration commemorates police raids on bathhouses (see February 5, 1981), draws attention to Operation Soap, large-scale police investigation into "criminal activity in the gay community."

March 10   Edmonton   GATE representatives meet with full Alberta Human Rights Commission to ask for inclusion of sexual orientation in Alberta Human Rights Protection Act.

March 26   Toronto   Provincial court judge finds owner of Back Door Gym, raided by police June 16, 1981, guilty of keeping common bawdyhouse and fines him $3,000. Two others given conditional discharges.

April 21   Toronto   Metro Toronto Police Morality Squad officers seize two magazines, charge assistant manager Kevin Orr of Glad Day Bookshop with "possession of obscene material for purpose of resale."

May 7   Toronto   Morality Squad officers appear at *The Body Politic* office with search warrant, leave empty-handed after brief search (see December 30, 1977).

May 12   Toronto   Police charge all nine members of *TBP* editorial collective with publishing obscene material, related to "Lust with a very proper stranger," article on etiquette of fist-fucking in April issue.

May 31   Toronto   *The Body Politic* and three officers of Pink Triangle Press go on trial in Provincial Court a second time to face charges of using the mails to transmit immoral and indecent material (see January 5, 1978 and February 29, 1980).

June 2   Toronto   Full page advocacy ad, containing over 1,400 names in support of repeal of bawdyhouse laws, appears in *Globe and Mail*. Organized by Right to Privacy Committee.

June 15   Toronto   Provincial Court judge Thomas Mercer acquits Pink Triangle Press and its officers of immorality/indecency charges a second time (see February 14, 1979).

The end of the "human rights decade"
Michael Lynch

Issue 54, July 1979

A decade ends, who will sing its measure? From the Stonewall riot in New York in 1969 to the San Francisco riot in May 1979, gay rebellion burst from an east coast bar to a west coast civic centre, and in the intervening years altered millions of gay lives throughout the western world.

Stonewall defended a bar, San Francisco assaulted a city. From recalcitrant defence to enraged offence, the events are already mythic. San Francisco *must* make a difference. The burning police cars herald a new era in gay history, as dark and surpriseful as this one was in the first days of Stonewall. Their flames are a cadence to our decade, not a dying fall but a burning one.

What began with a Stonewall at Sheridan Square and cadenced with smouldering car seats has been a decade not of gay rage but of moderation, of what I'll call "the human rights strategy." Despite its violent extremes, the historian may well label this the "human rights decade."

The human rights goal is to win the same legal protections that are already enjoyed by others under existing human rights laws. Until those laws are actually amended to include "sexual orientation" as a protected category, that goal has not been reached. Of the eleven human rights acts in Canada, ten provincial and one federal, only one, the Quebec act, has been so amended. Elsewhere, according to the human rights goal, the gay movement has yet to be successful.

But if the political fight to achieve this amendment has not been won, it has provided a focus for other accomplishments. There is now a gay community that sees itself, and is seen by others, as a political "minority." Gay life has been brought to public consciousness; the facts of oppression, real and undeniable, have been made known. The strategy built to achieve human rights legislation may have failed in that one aim, but it has been wildly successful in fulfilling other, subsidiary goals which may finally prove more valuable than a few changes in law.

We sense failure, but the failure is in the goal, not the strategy. Looking back on ten years of Canadian gay politics, we can see the human rights strategy has, in fact, been *so successful that it is no longer necessary.* All along there has been an ambiguity as to whether this programme was a goal, or a strategy. The ambiguity has been instrumental in forming a gay minority. But we risk cynicism and disillusionment if we allow human rights to go on being vaguely understood as merely a goal. Reflecting now on the success and consequent demise of the strategy built around that goal, we must eliminate the ambiguity.

As a measure of the strategy's success, homosexuality is now a public issue, politicized even in the non-gay press, no longer clamped into the sin/sickness/deviance syndrome. The politicians have to face it, the public has to face it.

Another adjunct goal is proven successful by the multiform gay movement that has emerged since 1969. The human rights strategy gave a "respectable" political basis to gay groups of many kinds. The Metropolitan Community Church, which would not engage in politics at all five years ago (in Canada, that is), has become one of the more active forces in lobbying for the amendment.

Documenting and publicizing anti-gay discrimination was a third adjunct goal which has been accomplished. Although *Toronto Sun* columnist Claire Hoy can still pretend that this discrimination does not exist to any significant degree, as the Ontario Human Rights Commission itself pretended six years ago, the position is no longer tenable. Case files on persons such as John Damien and Lyn MacDonald in Ontario, Doug Wilson in Saskatchewan, Barbara Thornborrow and Gloria Cameron federally, are now part of the public record, and even the non-gay press has had to acknowledge them.

But looking at the human rights goal, we are easily disheartened. The Tory government in Ontario responded to the proposal from its own commission in 1977 by burying it and lopping away the commissioners who sought it. In Saskatchewan, the NDP adopted "sexual orientation" as party policy in November, 1978, but five months later the NDP government ignored its policy favouring the amendment. The October 1977 raid and mass arrests at the Truxx bar in Montreal provoked Canada's largest gay street protest and embarrassed the PQ government into amending, albeit as quietly as possible, the human rights act there.

"As quietly as possible"—this has become the theme song to human rights legislation tactics. The Quebec amendment was passed in a midnight session of the Assemblée Nationale, and hardly anyone knew about it. In many cities across North America, similar amendments have been coddled into law with much backstage lobbying and little public debate. Every time this happened, the adjunct goal of public discussion has been sacrificed to a dubious political "victory."

Stripped of the adjunct goals, the "sexual orientation" amendment must no longer be our priority. As the glass in the San Francisco Civic Centre is replaced and the cops collect insurance for the personal items burned in their cruisers, we have a major task before us: devising a strategy for the 1980s.

Now that we are a much larger and more complex movement, will we operate on many fronts at once without a central focus? Or will one issue draw to it a cluster of related ones and become the basis for a new strategy? Will 1979-89 be as easily nameable as was the human rights decade?

History not only chuckles, it will stick out a foot to trip you if you try to look too far into the future. But one issue, in Canada, seems to me a candidate for another strategy: containment of totalitarian power, particularly that of the police. Reports indicate that the RCMP have been beyond the control of any elected official. Canada, settled by the Mounties before it was settled by people, seems, to an American, a nation of schmoos when it comes to limiting police power. The cops are above the law, and no one seems to mind except the women, gays, non-whites and poor who are increasingly subject to police abuse.

Efforts are underway in Toronto to force the politicians to contain the police, and this may point the way towards a future strategy in other centres as well. But if it is to become our strategy, we must not see it merely as an issue of political containment. We must study carefully the experience of others who have suffered police abuse and begin to see police power as the strongest arm of racism and patriarchy. That study may lead us to strategic coalitions against those institutions and values, not just tinkering with the police bureaucracy.

But first, the choice must be made to relinquish the empty shell that remains of the human rights strategy. This may prove difficult. Many gays, particularly in the United States, are trying to prolong the human rights decade into this one. They are joining, and being swallowed up, by the Democratic—and even the Republican—Party; some are seeking to rehash gay rights plebiscites in cities where voters have already rejected them soundly. Energies that could be on the forefront are thus being sidelined.

In the terms of a decade ago, the "human rights strategy" has become the new "homophilism." It seeks assimilation, legislation, and isolation — the isolation of this one issue from all the rest that concern us. The pragmatic argument is that we can fight only one battle at a time, and so must shun the fight against sexism or racist or ageist issues in order to get these two words into the human rights acts. Code amendments risk becoming the "well-lit bars" that the publisher of *The Advocate* once saw as the high-water mark of gay liberation.

But the greatest danger in continuing to seek human rights above all is that we might get them. They are not much of a sop for a government to give, and the more we equate gay success with achieving them, the more we risk the fate of the abolitionist movement after the Emancipation, the feminist movement after the franchise, the black movement after the Civil Rights Act of 1964. To those American memories we may add the way the Quebec "sexual orientation" amendment lulled Quebec gays into a lethargy from which they have not yet fully recovered.

Will San Francisco be forgotten? That is, will our memory and scrutiny of what happened there on May 21, 1979, be eradicated, as so much gay history has been?

Some gay leaders want us to erase it, often in the service of the human rights lobby. Their argument: the riots were damaging to our "image" among straight politicians; they weren't really born of gay rage but were stoked by non-gay provocateurs.

The riots, we must say, are our own. Politicians and lobbyists will just have to cope. I'll argue with anyone who would deny the human rights strategy a death with dignity. Last decade's liberation can become this decade's leech.

In 1973, I lobbied Toronto City Council for human rights, and still believe the strategy was sound. In the last two years, I've slogged through the legal murks of the civil courts with the Damien case, and I know how badly we need "sexual orientation" in the human rights code in order to get redress without having to make that long, costly trek through the courts.

But I urge: let the human rights decade rest in peace in our memoirs, and in the archives.

We need another strategy now.

Into the Eighties

The decade of the Seventies witnessed the gradual spread of the gay liberation spirit beyond the North America of its origins. The Eighties promise to see that process quicken. As the gay movement takes root in other countries, it will inevitably assume new forms to help it survive in different social and political circumstances. Whereas the movement in Canada has operated largely as an autonomous pressure group, in countries like Spain, for example, it has surfaced as part of a larger progressive movement. Tim McCaskell's report on gay political activity in the Basque country takes us very far from the Greenwich Village gay bar of 1969 or the Parliament Hill of 1971.

Two recent events in Toronto have had a lasting impact on the gay and lesbian communities in that city. The first episode was the 1980 municipal election campaign, in which gay activist George Hislop ran, unsuccessfully, for alderman. The second was the 1981 police raid and mass arrests in four bathhouses, with the resulting deterioration in police/gay community relations. Each of these episodes helped to politicize gay people because the events touched their lives more directly than the symbolic battles of the "human rights decade." It is possible that one of the legacies of these two affairs—one, on the surface, a defeat, the other a frightening attack—will be the planting of the seeds of political stategies more relevant to the realities of a new decade.

Few people would care to predict what changes will have come about in the gay and lesbian communities in Canada by the end of the Eighties, but cartoonist Gary Ostrom, undaunted, has cast a jaundiced glance ahead. His futuristic fantasy, "Homos at war," ends this otherwise sober chronicle.

Out in the Basque country
Tim McCaskell

Issue 65, August 1980

Sunday, June 10, 1979, 3:30 am. The Apolo Bar was almost empty. Stale cigarette smoke hung in the air as a few clients nursed their drinks.

Vincente Vadillo sat alone at his table. No one remembers when Vadillo, an immigrant from Spain's rural south, had first arrived in Rentería, one of the towns making up the industrial belt that surrounds the Basque city of San Sebastian, a few miles from the French border.

In Rentería, Vincente Vadillo was better known as Francis the Queer. Francis was one of the thirty-two-year-old transvestite's stage names, and after a few years in the town, all Rentería had become his stage. He was a local character, treated with bemused tolerance, mixed perhaps with contempt. Everyone knew him.

The Apolo often featured transvestite shows, but Francis had not been working that night. He was dressed "normally" as a man.

Another man entered the bar. Witnesses said he had a wild look in his eyes, as if he were drunk or stoned. He asked for a drink. The bartender replied that it was too late. The bar was closed. The man was loud, aggressive. He said he was a member of the National Police. He demanded service. The bartender refused.

The policeman pulled out his pistol and began waving it around. "You Basques all hate us just because we belong to the Spanish Police," he shouted, "I've never killed anybody, but you look at me as if I were an invader or a murderer. I'm so sick of it tonight I *am* ready to kill one of you bastards."

"Well, if you need to kill someone so bad, here I am," said the sarcastic voice of the transvestite. The cop, his face distorted with rage, turned and fired his pistol at close range. The bullet entered Vadillo's left eye. Francis the Queer was dead before he hit the floor.

Rentería is a town of more than fifty thousand people. But, perhaps because they are squeezed so closely together in lumbering old apartments, or perhaps because the residents' common working-class background generates such a feeling of community, the place has a grapevine that functions better than that of most small villages. By Sunday afternoon, there were few who did not know that a Spanish cop had killed somebody in the Apolo the night before. A crowd of two hundred people gathered spontaneously in the town square. They decided to hold a public meeting the next day and fanned out to the bars and other public gathering places to pass the word.

There is a latent fury that runs through the people of the Basque country, a nationalistic fury against the Madrid government and its police force that trampled on Basque national rights, language and culture during the forty years of Franco's dictatorship. To the people of Rentería, this was simply one more victim, one more atrocity committed by an occupying army.

The morning paper, controlled by sympathizers of Franco's heirs and their police forces, reported the incident the following Monday. The headline read, "Man dressed as woman killed in bar." Obviously this was not something to get upset about—after all, it was just a faggot. But in spite of this attempt to defuse the issue, and despite the danger of police attack, more than four thousand people gathered in the town square Monday afternoon. They were angry and ready to hear and to shout back the familiar demands for regional autonomy, withdrawal of the National Police, and an end to the vestiges of Spain's years of Fascist dictatorship.

But then something happened that was not at all familiar in Basque nationalist or working-class politics. "Our next speaker is a representative of EHGAM, the Basque Gay Liberation Front." Interest gave way to astonishment as a familiar face took the stage. The young man was a lifelong resident of the town, a union militant and a well-known political activist. Mikel Conde, who had secretly joined EHGAM less than a year before, was coming out in style.

Conde read the communiqué prepared by his organization. He denounced the press for trying to manipulate public opinion and for using fag-baiting to divert public attention from the crimes of the National Police. He pointed out how sexual repression in general and the oppression of homosexuals in particular was part and parcel of the system that oppressed the Basque country and exploited its working-class citizens. He demanded that people have the freedom to dress however they wished without fear of ridicule or police harassment. He called on workers to organize a general strike and to discuss sexual liberation and oppression in their assemblies.

A few minutes later, police dispersed the crowd with tear gas, rubber bullets and clubs. The battle raged for hours. But the word was out. On Tuesday, the industrial suburb closed down in a general strike protesting the killing. Sexual liberation was a focus of discussion in dozens of workplaces. Two thousand people marched through San Sebastian under the banners of EHGAM in the group's first public demonstration in the city. In Rentería, the working people took up a collection to send the body of Francis back to his father in southern Spain.

*

The light of the late afternoon sun illuminated two massive faces of rock cleft by a canyon with almost perpendicular stone walls. "If this isn't the gateway to the Basque country, it should be," I thought. The road wound its way through the pass, solid rock on the right and a churning river on the left. The arid rolling country of Spain was transformed into a thousand shades of green. Euskadi, as the Basque country is called, appeared to be a cross between Ireland and the Swiss Alps—green forests studded with pastures and picturesque stone villages, and, when one least expected it, rocky crags that leapt into the sky.

The terrain helps explain why the Basques were able to maintain their independence and culture for so many years. Never conquered by the invading Moors, Euskadi was not even fully Christianized until the eleventh century. Euskera, the national language, is not related to Spanish or French. In fact, it is in a language group all its own, and its origins are shrouded in mystery and scientific dispute.

The Autonomous Basque Republic was a major centre of resistance to Franco's armies during the civil war. Gernika, the spiritual capital of the Basque people, was only subdued after massive Fascist bombing which left most of the town in ruins, an event immortalized in paint by Picasso. But neither military defeat nor the subsequent years of repression was able to extinguish Basque aspirations for national autonomy and social justice.

We descended from the pass toward San Sebastian, through quaint rural towns dominated by heavy old apartment buildings. In the late nineteenth century, the rich iron deposits here were the basis of Spain's first industrial revolution. The three Basque provinces of Araba, Bizkaia, and Gipuzkoa are still among the most industrialized and urbanized in Spain. San Sebastian, a slightly faded but still elegant seaside resort, is the capital of Gipuzkoa. An aristocratic promenade, ideal for cruising, overlooks the sweeping beach that once attracted the better families of Europe on their summer vacations. The water is still clean, since the city's industries are located in a belt of smaller, less "sophisticated" towns on the periphery — towns such as Rentería.

While the flavour of elegant leisure still lingers on in San Sebastian, Rentería has a different kind of class. It is dominated by chunky apartment buildings—workers' flats—and a sense of community that makes it impossible to walk two blocks without bumping into a neighbour or a workmate or a friend.

*

Mikel is unemployed. He was fired from his job over a year ago for union agitation. Like most unmarried young men in Rentería, he lives with his family. His mother is Basque, his father an immigrant labourer from the south who came looking for work after the civil war. Theirs is a tightly knit, fiercely protective family — republican, anti-fascist and anti-clerical. It is also a family that has learned to accept a faggot son and is learning to talk gay politics around the dinner table.

"It gave us a bit of a scare at first," said Mikel's mother as she dished another helping of food on my plate. "We didn't understand much about it. Now it's all right. We realize that everybody is different, that everybody has the right to live as they want to, as they need to."

"I'd never really hid the fact, but I hadn't actually come out to them either," Mikel explained later as we sipped soft drinks and ate olives in the community association bar. "But after I read the EHGAM communiqué to the demonstration, I knew I was going to have to talk to them, because they were going to read it in the papers anyway. So I explained that the cop had killed Francis and I had spoken as a member of EHGAM in the town square. I told them it wasn't just a matter of being able to love men, but that it was a political struggle. We had to struggle for our freedom the same way that the workers had to struggle against the capitalists—that helped them understand. My mother has always been pretty traditional in her beliefs. She began to cry. She said I should be really careful not to get beaten up by machos. My father was a bit uptight. He didn't want anyone to say he had a faggot son.

"Since then, they've understood a lot more. My relationship with them is more equal. I've met other people from the organization. But I want to teach them more than tolerance. I want them to take a part in the struggle against the repressive morality of this society." To go beyond tolerance was no personal ideal of Mikel's. As I was to find out later, it was of central importance to the organization to which he belonged.

Mikel's relationship to his community was even more remarkable. During my visit we never left the house without sporting pink triangles. Nor was it possible to walk two blocks without saying hello or stopping to chat with someone. It seemed as if he knew everyone in town and was on a first-name basis with all of them. And everyone knew that Mikel was a fag.

I was astonished at Mikel's integration into his community. I found myself asking him, "Was he gay? Is she a lesbian?" The answer was usually no. I began to realize how accustomed I was to neat categories, to a world cleanly divided into gay and straight continents. Not knowing people's sexual orientation was a little disturbing.

The Basques, in spite of their streak of political radicalism, have always been reputed to be one of the most conservative and traditional of the Spanish minorities. Yet Mikel had managed to come out and link his personal struggle with the broader struggle of his community, and therefore found himself neither isolated nor exiled to the ghetto.

Almost as surprising for me as his integration into a straight, working-class world was Mikel's deep relationship with lesbian friends. A lesbian couple who lived a few blocks away were just breaking up after a seven-year relationship. It was a painful time for a wide circle of friends, straight and gay, which included Mikel's family. The problem worried everybody. The chasms between lesbians and gay men, or between gay people and straight, that I knew in North America seemed insignificant here. Advice, support and sympathy were offered from all sides.

This personal integration was not, however, reflected in EHGAM's organization. The San Sebastian group has been all-male from the beginning. When I asked him, Mikel felt it was obvious that lesbians were oppressed both for their sex and their sexuality. When they were ready, they would organize themselves independently within the women's movement. As I travelled on, I found there was little consensus on the best political relationship between gay men and lesbians in Euskadi. But whether lesbians remained unorganized, as in San Sebastian, or organized separately, as in Bilbao, or belonged to EHGAM, as in Vitoria, the pattern of personal interaction and warm friendships between gay women and men was the same.

*

It was a cool, wet afternoon as I hitchhiked to Bilbao. The peaks of the mountains lost themselves in a heavy sky. "Typical Basque weather," I was told.

While I waited to meet my contact from EHGAM, I walked through the winding stone streets of the old city centre, alive with bars, cafés and restaurants. I was surprised to find walls and hoardings papered with purple and white posters. "Lesbian," they said, "reconquer your identity." In a central square, I found a large poster advertising an educational forum organized by EHGAM.

Bilbao, the capital of Bizkaia, is the industrial heart of Euskadi. With its surrounding towns, the metropolitan area reaches a population of two million. It was here that EHGAM was first organized in 1976.

José Mari Gil has been working with EHGAM in Bilbao for the last two and a half years and does much of the art work for their magazine *Gay Hotsa*. He is one of the lucky few who do not live at home. His father is a custodian in a local school and has also built up a small business as a travelling salesman. José supports himself selling woolen goods in the markets of the small towns surrounding Bilbao. His apartment is half full of boxes of sweaters and socks.

"I came out to my parents a couple of years ago," he told me. "I think our relationship has been much more honest since." The two friends who share his apartment weren't so lucky. They were both thrown out of their homes when they came out. "That's pretty much the norm here," says Jon, who has been working with EHGAM for only two months. "If my parents found out, I'm sure I'd be out on the street."

Unlike Mikel, who decided he was gay after reading an EHGAM manifesto in a left-wing magazine, neither José Mari nor Jon have had experience working with the parties of the political left.

José Mari had been suspicious of politics, but came to his first EHGAM meeting after he was fed up with the "superficial" life he had found in Bilbao's rather closety ghetto. Jon decided he had to get involved when he returned from military service. Both found the organization offered them satisfaction and personal relationships which they were unable to find elsewhere, and were swept up in its ongoing work. "When I started to help out two months ago, I said I couldn't do any public work," Jon told me. "But after a few days, I sort of got carried away. I was out on the street putting up posters and going to political meetings. We were really involved in this last election campaign. We put up literature tables at the meetings of the left-wing parties and often would read a communiqué. Although we are nonpartisan, we supported the left. Our slogan was, 'Gays, don't vote for those who oppress you.' "

*

April 14—the anniversary of the founding of the Spanish republic—a subversive anniversary. Spain is officially a monarchy—part of the Franco heritage. In Rentería, a grotesque dummy of His Royal Highness Juan Carlos I was hanged by the neck from a pavilion in the central square. Groups of townspeople stood around and clapped with delight.

I attended a semi-clandestine meeting organized by the EMK, the Basque Communist Movement, to celebrate the founding of Republican Spain in the 1930s. From the faces and hands and clothes of the people around me, I could see I was in a room of working people; there was also a small number of students. The EMK is part of the Spanish Communist Movement—the largest Marxist-Leninist group to the left of the officially Eurocommunist Spanish Communist Party.

Marxist-Leninists in Canada do not have a very inspiring record when it comes to supporting gay people. Yet here, when it was announced that I and a Dutch lesbian also visiting Mikel had been delegates to the International Gay Association Conference in Barcelona, there was thunderous applause.

Mikel has been a member of the EMK since he was sixteen. He is obviously out, well known and well liked. When I told him about the attitude of some Marxist-Leninists in Canada, he frowned. "The party never discouraged me from speaking for EHGAM. The attitude at first was that we didn't know much about gay liberation, but that didn't mean we should be against it. So lesbian and gay party militants were encouraged to work to educate the party in this respect. The party has become conscious that machismo is a problem even for its own members.

"My comrades really helped me a lot. Since there is such sexual repression in Spain, people who aren't married have a hard time finding a place to sleep together—for two men it's even worse. So anybody in the party who has a private place makes it available. I've often been lent places to be with a friend to have sex."

Josetxu, another acquaintance, told me he is a militant in the PTE—the Spanish Workers' Party. I am quite surprised. The PTE is the pro-Chinese party in Spain. Militants of its sister party in Canada, the Worker's Communist Party, have explained to me on various occasions that homosexuality is a symptom of bourgeois decadence. With a naïveté that would make Anita Bryant blush, they have described how former homosexuals inspired by Marxism-Leninism-Mao Zedong-Thought have, upon joining the party, left their wanton ways, and now lead perfectly happy heterosexual lives. Yet in Spain Josetxu works openly for EHGAM and is preparing papers for an internal party discussion to develop a position on the gay question. Ana, organizing lesbians in Bilbao, tells me that the Spanish Communist Party has been very helpful in lending her rooms at their headquarters for meetings.

*

The men who make up the vast majority of EHGAM find their personal and political lives far more intertwined with lesbians and with straight people of both sexes than gay men are apt to in North America. The common understanding of the goals of sexual liberation helps bridge the gaps even when familiar kinds of divisions do assert themselves.

I met with Ana Urkijo and Fabiola Alberdi in Lamiak, a coffeeshop-cum-bar in the old part of Bilbao. In Basque mythology, the Lamiak were the good witches. The place, owned by four women who belong to the Bilbao Women's Assembly, is referred to as a "feminist" bar. It is a huge old building with heavy stone walls and massive black beams in the ceiling. Flowered tablecloths, warm lighting, and gentle Basque folk music produce a friendly, relaxed atmosphere. People play dice games and no one is pushed to consume. It is a favourite haunt of Bilbao's young progressives. As I talk to the two women, a group of ten men from EHGAM is having a committee meeting at the next table.

"It has been a year since the four of us left EHGAM," says Ana as she begins to describe the formation of the Basque country's first lesbian organization, ESAM. "Personally I never felt any trauma about loving women, but I learned early that I had to keep quiet about it. It's really difficult for a lesbian to come out. There isn't any ghetto here for us. When a friend told me about EHGAM several years ago, I went to a meeting. It was an incredible liberation for me."

"It was really good to meet other women," says Fabiola, who had stumbled across EHGAM's address and written the group. "Two other women had joined, so there were four of us. But after a while we all began to feel that work around lesbian issues was not being carried out in EHGAM. The men just weren't interested enough. We found ourselves absorbed by the work of the organization — work around male homosexuality. We weren't attracting more women. They just weren't interested in an organization which they saw was mostly concerned with men.

"The same kind of thing was happening in the Women's Assembly, the coalition of women's groups and feminists here. Only there, lesbian issues weren't being taken up because there was a fear that the organization would be labelled as lesbian. So the four of us began to meet separately. We decided that we need an autonomous group. I guess it was the right decision: in less than a year, we now have twenty-two new members.

"We don't automatically reject men. In fact, we're working with EHGAM right now on the June gay pride festival. Last year, for the first time, we had a pretty strong lesbian contingent in the gay pride march. Our banner read: 'Women's Sexuality is Also Sexuality Between Women.' The reaction of a lot of the bystanders was really funny. They were saying, 'Look at those women. What are they doing there? They must be sympathizers marching with the queers to show their solidarity.' It never occurred to them that we might be dykes. They didn't know such a thing existed. There's really a huge ignorance about women's sexuality. Sexuality is so bound up with the idea of penetration that many people think where there's no penetration there's no sexuality."

"We've made a lot of headway in the Women's Assembly too," added Ana. "We've been working there as an independent lesbian group and we've participated in all the campaigns for divorce and abortion reform and the rest. We got them to take up lesbian issues last International Women's Day. Now we're working to open up a real debate on the question of lesbian sexuality. But there are still a lot of lesbians in the assembly who don't work with ESAM because they feel the feminist movement can only advance through the general women's movement."

In a year's steady growth and exploration, ESAM has begun to map out the topography of a lesbian world which few suspected existed. "Before we began, we really idealized lesbians," says Ana. "The only ones we knew were younger progressive people like ourselves. But we've stumbled across a whole new world. There are women who have been living in couples for years with all the traditional roles, possessiveness, jealousy, and domination of straight relationships. We found other groups of ten to fifteen women who know each other but are completely isolated from the women's movement. Many of these people are quite anti-feminist. Others are living with their parents or are married and don't know anyone. We are realizing that we were missing a lot of the reality of lesbian life. One of our struggles is going to be to contact these groups and learn how we can work with them."

The women who make up ESAM are mostly in their twenties. Only three are university graduates. The rest are office workers or are unemployed. Most have little political experience. About ten have left their parents' homes, but the economic problems that most Spanish young people must face make it difficult for most to set up an independent life. Many of the weekly meetings of ESAM's first year have been spent in the reading and discussion of feminist literature to raise the group's political level. A dossier has been prepared based on this work and the personal experiences of the women involved, which is now ready to go to press.

But ESAM's work has been far from completely internal. The posters that plaster downtown Bilbao testify to that. Three pamphlets have been issued— one directed at lesbians for distribution at women's meetings and the other two aimed at educating a more general audience.

Work was underway to prepare for the first meeting of lesbians from across Spain to take place in Madrid in June. "It will be our first contact on a national level," says Fabiola. "We may even be able to set up a coordinating committee."

One can sense the growing confidence the group has produced. "In the beginning, we didn't want to call ourselves a group of lesbians. That's why we chose the name ESAM, which means Women's Sexual Liberation Movement. Now we understand it is necessary to identify ourselves as lesbians. But we don't just want rights for lesbians—we want a total sexual liberation that will allow everyone to realize the plurality of her sexuality. We want to be recognized as lesbians and women. Our group is a feminist group, and we have a sense of feminist struggle as valid as anyone's. The ideal would be for all the sexual liberation groups—lesbians, straight women and gay men—to be together, but that's still a long way off."

*

It was still raining when I arrived in Vitoria at 3 am and was deposited at the apartment that an EHGAM member shares with a straight couple. I had been given a lift by several members of the group who had come down to Bilbao to enjoy the ghetto. Vitoria's magnificent cathedral and ancient architecture may attract tourists like pigeons, but gay life is subdued in this, the smallest and poorest of the Basque capitals. I was given a guided tour of the city the next day, beginning with the principal monuments and going on to the principal cruising grounds, the La Florida park and the railway station. The station was the most interesting: one simply waits for a train, and in the early evening there are lots of commuter trains to choose from. A middle-aged man walking two dogs approached us. He turned out to be the friend of one of the young EHGAM militants showing me the town. We chatted as we watched the men watching the men getting on and off the train.

The economic situation and more conservative family life make it more difficult for people to come out in Vitoria. Many young gays leave the city to go to Bilboa or Barcelona, where work and the ghetto provide greater possibilities. EHGAM is relatively new here. Its members are working hard just to keep the organization alive. But the emergence of the Vitoria group meant that EHGAM's claim to represent all Basque gays was becoming a reality.

I was invited to go to a disco with Josetxu and several other friends. "A gay disco?" I asked.

"No, there aren't any gay spots here in Vitoria," I was told. Once again, I found it hardly mattered. We arrived early, and I danced with my friend from EHGAM on a nearly empty dance floor. No one seemed to notice. As the place filled up, most of the couples did seem to be heterosexual, but there was no pressure to be closeted. Our group left in the small hours of the morning without incident. I can't imagine such a place in Toronto.

*

We pulled out onto the freeway in the little pickup José Mari uses to carry his woolen goods to the different markets. The previous day, the newspapers had reported that a member of the National Police had raped a young Basque girl in the fishing town of Bermeo. The Women's Assembly in the town and the left and nationalist parties had called a demonstration in protest. I decided to see firsthand how sexual, social and nationalist politics mix.

We stop in Gernika to pick up more members of EHGAM. I'm given a quick tour of the most revered sites of the Basque nation—the National Assembly and the Great Tree, under which Basque elders have held their traditional councils for centuries.

We are packed like sardines in the pickup as we bounce along the winding road to Bermeo. "If you see a police block, pull over quick. They'll use the fact that we're overloaded to arrest us if they think we're going to the demonstration." Luckily there is no roadblock. We park in the main square, which overlooks a picturesque harbour. The square is already filled with people, the majority women—housewives or workers. My friends are hastily preparing signs identifying themselves as members of EHGAM. We all wear pink triangles.

I've been warned to leave my camera at home in case the police attack. "They really go after cameras," says José Mari. As we march off through the drizzle, five thousand strong, there is no sign of police.

We wind through the narrow streets, calling for justice for rapists and the disbanding of the repressive forces of the National Police. The marchers are militant but peaceful. We loop through the town and are almost back to the square again, where the crowd will disperse. All of a sudden, I notice men with rifles to my right. "That's the barracks of the National Police," says Bittor, as we walk hand in hand. Bittor is a sailor on shore leave who is just coming out. "It doesn't look like we'll get any action today," I say. "I should have brought my camera. There's nothing to provoke them."

"They don't need any provocation," he replies.

The crowd roars out its condemnation as it passes the building in the narrow street. I can see two parade marshals in a heated conversation with the head of the police. Other marshals are trying to hurry us on. I overhear the cop say, "You've got two minutes to disperse. This is an illegal demonstration."

"Two minutes, that's impossible," says the marshal. "Look, people are still coming down the street. There's no place for them to go."

"Two minutes," says the cop.

I am swept onward by the crowd. We reach the square and stop to watch what will happen as the people continue to spill out of the narrow street. Suddenly we hear the explosions—rifles firing.

"It's crazy," I say to Bittor. "People were dispersing. There's no need for them to do anything now."

"Run," he says.

Tear gas canisters are arcing through the air and bouncing along the pavement. Brave souls pick them up and hurl them into the harbour. People are dashing in all directions. "Are they using rubber bullets?"

There is a brief pause in the firing. Now it's the turn of the enraged townspeople. They run back towards the barracks and start to throw anything they can get their hands on. The police charge the crowd again. More gas, and sirens.

Sirens, I learn, are a bad sign. They mean the police are coming out to get us. We retreat into a bar. Outside, a police car swoops down on a hapless demonstrator. He is dragged kicking and punching into the car, and it roars off. "They'll come in here next," says Bittor. The bar empties, and we run to the far end of the square. A volley of tear gas can be heard exploding in the town above us. "They must be circling around through the back streets." A knot of us stand at a corner, not sure which way to go. "If they get too close, come up here," shouts someone from a window above us. "The fourth floor."

We hear a siren coming down the street. "Let's go."

We scramble up four flights of stairs. The apartment seems to be owned by some elderly women, but soon it is full of demonstrators. We crowd the window to watch the action on the square. The police car screams past below us, its blue flashing light reflecting off the buildings. Small groups of demonstrators are still running around in a serious game of cat and mouse with the forces of order. It begins to get dark. A half hour later, we are ready to venture downstairs. We scurry into a bar. Whenever a police siren gets too close, the bartender locks the door and pulls down the blind. The regulars continue watching the soccer game on television. An hour later, it seems safe to cross the square to the car.

I understand a little better the coalition of sexual, leftist and nationalist politics that has marked the development of Basque gay liberation. The common enemy is obvious.

We rumble back to Gernika and spend the night in the apartment of some women friends of José Mari's. The place soon fills up with people eager to discuss the demonstration. The politics is contagious. I forget to ask who's gay and who's straight.

It doesn't seem to make so much difference when we're all running in the same direction.

Close but not enough:
the 1980 Toronto municipal election
Ed Jackson

"Window on Sewell," Chris Bearchell and Ed Jackson, Issue 60, February 1980; "Ward Healer," Ed Jackson, Issue 64, June/July 1980; News, Issue 67, October 1980; "The time, the place and the person," Val Edwards and "The hot little issue that grew," Ed Jackson, Issue 68, November 1980; "Close but not enough," Ed Jackson, Issue 69, December 1980/January 1981

The November 1980 Toronto civic election will be remembered as the election in which the "gay issue" dominated all other concerns, although no one could seem to agree on what the "gay issue" really was. Spawning an unprecedented flood of anti-gay hate literature, the election campaign was the first in Canada to frighten voters by raising the spectre of "gay power politics." It was also the election that witnessed the defeat of the city's outspoken gay-positive mayor, as well as the defeat of the first openly gay candidate to run for municipal office. Beginning with the events during our own trial almost two years earlier, The Body Politic *published a series of news features documenting and analyzing the significance of this chapter in the history of the gay community's involvement in electoral politics. The following article is an edited version of this coverage.*

January 3, 1979
The man on stage had been in office for little over a month and he was making his first important speech as the mayor of one of Canada's largest cities.

"I recognize that the gay community feels that it is under attack from a number of sources," he was saying to the packed auditorium. "I'm here this evening to try to help calm the political atmosphere so that issues can be clarified."

It was January 3, 1979 and the Body Politic Free the Press Rally was under way. It was the evening of the second day of the most controversial event ever to hit Toronto's gay community. In a courtroom in Old City Hall, *The Body Politic* and three officers of Pink Triangle Press were on trial on a charge of mailing immoral, indecent and scurrilous literature.

While TV lights blazed and flash bulbs popped, the man at the bright centre continued, "It would be extremely helpful at this point if the provincial government were to amend the provincial human rights code to prohibit discrimination on the basis of sexual orientation across the province.

"We know it's not illegal to be gay. We should take the next step and make it clearly legitimate to be gay."

The crowd went wild.

John Sewell, his five-minute speech finished, was already hurrying down the aisle. He disappeared from the auditorium even before the cheers and echoing applause had finally died away. But the swarm of reporters knew they had a great story. It was a story that would create a bigger media uproar than the mayor's office had ever before known.

Next day, city hall switchboard was flooded with hundreds of angry phone-calls. All three dailies editorialized their disapproval and for days the letters pages were filled with cries of outrage alternating with messages of support. The *Toronto Sun* declared that Sewell had lent "an authority to the radical homosexual movement which is wrong." Ward Six alderman Dan Heap said, "The time to defend freedom of the press is when it's under attack," while veteran conservative alderman and interim mayor Fred Beavis snorted, "The chain of office for mayor is becoming a daisy chain." A typical letter to the editor concluded, "Though I have this garbage thrown on my plate I certainly do not have to eat it."

January 9, 1980

We are sitting in the reception area of the mayor's office. *The Body Politic* has come to find out what John Sewell has to say to the gay community now that he has spent a year in office.

His Worship, Mayor Sewell is surprisingly informal, the sort of person who puts you at your ease at once. We are soon settled into the roomy wingbacked chairs that occupy one corner of the large modern office.

We ask the obvious question.

"I made the speech because I thought it was the only reasonable thing to do. There was a large community of people who felt very much that the world was after them. I though that the appropriate thing for the mayor to do was to say: 'all that is crazy.' If people are under attack you go and try and get them some protection."

Sewell also admits, "I was absolutely amazed that the thing blew up in the way that it did."

A *Globe and Mail* editorial awarded Sewell the "ill-timing award of 1979." Art Eggleton, senior alderman and one of Sewell's most likely opponents in the November municipal elections, also thinks it was bad timing. "By making that speech in the context of a court case," he says, "Sewell exercised poor judgment."

Sewell admits that he has had a few doubts himself. "Thinking about it, the general impression I have is that it would have been much better if I had had a slightly different forum in a slightly different place." But he quickly adds, "When it comes down to it, politicians don't get the opportunity to choose the exact time or the right place to say what has to be said. I'm not interested in backing down on issues that some people find offensive."

We ask Sewell if his stand has jeopardized his reputation or his effectiveness as mayor. "I confirmed both of them," he answers without hesitation. "I confirmed my reputation and I confirmed whatever clout I can wield from this office."

One of the first steps taken by the gay movement in this city was to lobby in 1973 for the passage of a resolution prohibiting discrimination on the basis of sexual orientation in city hiring. The resolution passed through city council with almost no mention in the mainstream media. At that time, John Sewell was an alderman, and he did not think gay rights was an important issue at all. What happened between then and now?

"Two things happened," he explains. "One, obviously I changed in my thinking and became more liberal in regard to the issue. I loosened up a bit. Secondly, I made a distinction between the politics of certain members of the community and the interests of that whole community. I'm rather discouraged about some of the underlying political arguments made about the breakup of capitalist society that's going to come about because of gay rights. I thought those arguments were generally foolish and didn't make any sense to me. And I think that still, basically. But I managed to recognize that it's just an argument some people are making which has nothing to do with the other question involved."

Sewell thinks his speech made an impact on attitudes toward gay people at city hall. "I sense there's a great loosening of the whole thing. Finally people are saying, 'We can talk about it; we can relax about it.' "

Ward Six alderman Allan Sparrow is more cautious about the mayor's effect on Toronto City Council. "Council is split along predetermined lines and the mayor's vote is only one out of twenty-three. Unlike American cities, we have a 'weak mayor' system. What his speech did was highlight the issue."

Observers generally feel that in the last year gays and gay issues have acquired a higher profile at city hall, but it would be simplistic to attribute it all to a five-minute speech. The most recent event was the December 10, 1979 election of long-time gay community leader George Hislop to the City Planning Board.

Sewell says he approves of the increased interest of gays in city politics, although Hislop's election focussed some of his earlier doubts.

"The concern I originally had was that we'd be getting into one-issue people. I'm very worried about that. We've seen it happen in the States: the anti-abortion crowd is into that, the anti-gay rights crowd is into that. I'm interested in real individuals who've got good stands on a number of issues. The key argument that Hislop made to me—and I found it impressive—was this: if you're not interested in me being a one-issue person, then get me into a position where I can figure out how all that other stuff works. Then I can take good and solid positions on other issues."

Sewell is adamant on one point. "Sexual orientation is not the question. The fact that a person is gay should be no bar at all in consideration of that person for appointment or election to a position. The real question is their politics and what it is they're doing, and what it is they're not doing."

Sewell has always been identified with the preservation of downtown neighbourhoods and with the support of smaller communities within the city. His January 1979 speech was the first by a straight politician to place the gay community in this context.

"There are a variety of types of communities," he said. "Some are geographical, some are ethnic—and all of them contribute significantly to the vitality and versatility of the city. They can be called neighbourhoods, or they can be called communities, but they are elements that many of us on city council have struggled long and hard to protect."

He elaborates a year later: "Gays represent a community of interest in the same way that people interested in non-profit housing represent a community of interest, or people interested in historic buildings. That's the type of community I think we're talking about."

The public's perception of him continually disturbs Sewell. "I sense there's a real gulf between the way the media portrays me and what I am," he says. His public call for reforms in the police department, for example, was sabotaged by inadequate media coverage. His criticism of the police commission was converted by the media into an attack on the cop on the beat.

The public may have been confused, but Sewell has never had any doubts about where the changes have to come in the police department. "The cop on the beat has very little flexibility. He knows what to do to make his superiors happy, so he does it. If we had different management policies, even in regard to how people should act as policemen, we'd have different cops on the beat. They are the guys at the bottom who are really getting hit."

Unfortunately, most people's experiences of police homophobia and racism come in encounters with the cop on the beat. We ask if a change in management policies could really control a bigoted cop.

"With the bigoted cop, you have to say: 'No, you can't harass gays. you're not allowed to do that.' I think most cops would say: 'Okay, I can't do it. Maybe I'd like to, but....' or 'Thank God I don't have to.' And the world would change."

Sewell adds that change will also come about through getting more varied personnel in the police department. When more blacks, for example, start working on the force, familiarity will make other cops less racist. Does Sewell then think there should be more openly gay cops hired by the police force?

There is a long pause. "That's really a difficult one," he begins. "Sure, I would hope that we'd be in that position. But it's difficult enough in most branches of society without getting into delicate areas like the police."

He elaborates. "The gay movement obviously is trying to find its feet politically because it has been discriminated against for so long. Being openly gay usually means you are politically proselytizing people and that might be a worry to some. What they would prefer is not to have people who are too political, and 'openly gay' means you're being 'too political.' "

John Sewell has understood the need to legitimize the gay struggle and he has done his part to help the process along. But he sees sexual orientation primarily as something that limits, something that can be used to keep gays apart from the mainstream, or else as a purely private matter. He says sexual orientation is for individuals to figure out, that the real question is their politics. It is clear that he does not think sexual orientation will have an effect on those politics.

The fact is that once gay people are recognized as "legitimate," we will continue to live our lives from day to day *as gay people*. We won't suddenly disappear back into the general populace. We will still go on seeing and interpreting the world filtered through our experiences as gay people. And it will not be a monolithic experience, since there are many ways of living as lesbians and gay men.

In short, we will continue to grow into a stronger and more visible community, held together as much by common experience as by an idea. Sewell's analogy to non-profit housing advocates or promoters of architectural conservation does not illuminate what we are, it diminishes it.

We should not be surprised that a straight politician is still struggling to understand what we are all about. We are only just beginning to enter the public arena. We will have to be out there—visible and active—in much greater numbers before we can expect to see significant changes.

It seems that the next step in Toronto may be the election of an openly gay alderman at city hall. "The climate is one of acceptance for that to happen now," observes Ward Seven alderman Gordon Cressy. No one we spoke to at city hall would admit being opposed to such a development.

April 26, 1980

Two men kissed recently on the floor of Toronto's city hall council chamber. No outraged policemen came to take them away. Instead, the overflow audience erupted in approving applause while inquisitive TV cameras recorded the moment.

The two men were George Hislop and his lover Ron Shearer and, by a vote of one hundred and ninety-nine to one hundred and sixty-one, members of the Ward Six Community Organization had just given Hislop the nod as their choice for alderman in the November civic elections. It meant that not only had Hislop become the first openly gay candidate to run for civic office in Toronto, he had also gained the backing of an established community organization in the process.

With this vote the political chemistry of Ward Six has been decisively altered and a major new force—the emergent gay community—has entered Toronto city politics. And because of the particular nature of the Ward Six political scene—called "byzantine" by one observer—Hislop has suddenly come to be seen as a credible, even desirable, candidate.

Hislop's success at the April 26 nomination meeting was the culmination of a process set in motion in the summer of 1979. And now, on this night in April, it was no longer a wild idea.

"Hislop's nomination," says campaign manager Peter Maloney, "demonstrated that gay people are the best organized political group in downtown Toronto these days." And so it seemed to other observers as well. A phalanx of scrutineers to greet voters as they arrived in the city hall rotunda, carefully compiled supporter lists, hurrying messengers, phone workers calling the forgetful, six cars shuttling voters from home and work and back again—it was the kind of campaign machine they usually call "well-oiled."

Two other factors were important in bringing Hislop to that moment on the floor of the council chamber. One is the history of distrust between the Ward Six New Democratic Party (NDP) and the Ward Six Community Organization, a distrust based partly on the estrangement of the present aldermen, Allan Sparrow and Dan Heap, and partly on strategy and policy differences within the NDP itself. The other factor is the ever-present danger of a developer-backed candidate and the fear that he could capitalize on dissension between progressive candidates.

For a significant number of urban reformers, Hislop's candidacy was seen as a chance to introduce a healthy new political element into the ward. It was seized upon as an opportunity to heal old wounds that have drained the ward's political energies. With the retirement of Ward Six CO incumbent Allan Sparrow, the way seemed suddenly clear.

The outspoken Allan Sparrow, a former systems analyst, has always been associated with the Ward Six CO and that organization has always been linked to urban reform politics and neighbourhood preservation. It was founded in 1973 as a coalition of community groups to defend their neighbourhoods against destruction by demolition-hungry developers, short-sighted planners and university sprawl. In 1974, Ward Six CO ran a successful campaign for alderman Allan Sparrow. In 1976 it helped elect Dan Heap and Allan Sparrow, and in 1978 it elected Allan Sparrow and two school board trustees.

It has long been a truism in Canada that party politics do not work at the municipal level. But in 1978 the democratic socialist NDP decided it was time to unfurl its party umbrella and launch selected candidates across Metro Toronto. Dan Heap, who had tried many times before to get elected to various offices as an NDPer, was more than ready to try again. Sparrow, however, could not be persuaded to join the NDP team, to the disillusionment of some of his supporters. In 1978 Ward Six NDP and Ward Six CO agreed on a joint campaign, which involved mutual endorsement and sharing of literature. The NDP later felt that Ward Six CO betrayed this cooperative agreement by producing literature which relegated Heap's name to small print at the bottom.

Whatever finally influenced their decisions that year, eighty-five hundred voters chose Sparrow, seventy-five hundred chose Heap and sixty-five hundred votes went to Dan Richards, the business candidate.

A second truism in Ward Six is that only two progressive candidates can run. The fact that Dan Richards got only one thou: and fewer votes than Dan

Heap in 1978 is an uncomfortable reminder of that reality. As a result, two currents of thought contend within the NDP. One group has always wanted to run a complete slate of party-identified candidates—two alderman and two school trustees. They see reform politics as a dead end, and the promotion of socialist policies and of party discipline impossible within creaky alliances of convenience. The second group claims that the time is not yet right for a full party slate. A developer candidate, they argue, would steamroller divided progressives. Building a broad base of support for a social democratic party at the municipal level is a long process; the truce between the NDP and Ward Six CO must continue for the present.

The support of one such NDPer was pivotal in giving Hislop credibility as a progressive candidate. Phil Biggin, head of the Union of Injured Workers, nominated Hislop not because he sees a particular need for a visible gay presence at city hall, but because he believes that, at this juncture, Hislop is the most effective candidate to work with Dan Heap in the interests of Ward Six. He professes to being comfortable with Hislop's non-aligned stance.

"Organizations that have grown out of community struggles should have representatives from that community," Biggin says. "Hislop has an effective mass base in the community and it is one that can be mobilized."

Dan Heap will be seeking the NDP nomination in Ward Six again, and no one is expected to contest him. A few NDP members will express private reservations about his old-fashioned image, plodding manner and tireless single-mindedness. His defenders say that he is merely misunderstood. Anglican priest, factory worker, long-time union man, dedicated socialist—Heap is a minor city hall institution.

I asked Heap to comment on Hislop's nomination. Reluctantly, he said, "From what I know of George, I respect him. His policy letter, so far as it goes, is in agreement with some NDP policies, for which I am glad."

Asked if he thought it important to have an openly gay presence at city hall, he referred me to the NDP's provincial and federal assertions on gay rights. "I see that item as a positive part of the NDP's political programme. But I don't find the issue of being gay or non-gay a major political issue at city hall. Most of the work there does not relate to sexual orientation."

Heap finds that he can focus on a phenomenon comfortably only after threading it through a class analysis sprocket. "I don't regard the sexual relationship as primary," he said, "I regard the productive relationship as primary. You have to eat before you have to make love. I don't see gay rights issues related to the general concerns of the working class, nor do I find gays as a group supporting the working class. Some do, I'm happy to see."

The NDP has already decided to run an independent campaign, which means it will not endorse candidates from or coordinate campaigns with any non-NDP-identified organizations.

To date, there has been no attempt by Hislop's Ward Six opponents to resort to anti-gay slurs. In fact, a great deal of care has been taken to avoid even a hint of such tactics. But many people active in progressive politics have expressed doubts about Hislop's true political allegiances. "Hislop in the long run is a complete dead-end issue," said NDPer Ellie Kirzner at a recent meeting. "In the short run he may be a novelty, but experiences in the US have shown that a gay candidate pure and simple is not enough. Hislop is either a Red Tory or a closet liberal. We will see that he will give no real support to working people. This is death for us. It should not be an issue here."

Hislop, however, has expressed support for the Ward Six CO platform, a comprehensive policy statement on a number of urban issues from land use and public transit to tenants' rights and social services. As a Ward Six CO candidate, he has agreed to full accountability to that organization. And, since he has sought his political base in a progressive organization, his politics will in all likelihood begin to be shaped by that mold.

It is one of the ironies of the Hislop nomination that, almost at the very hour Ward Six CO members were casting the decisive vote, "Gay Power, Gay Politics," a CBS-TV documentary on gay political clout in San Francisco, was setting out to show that gays wield excessive power in that city and were forcing Horrible Things on innocent straights. Local commentators, having apparently accepted the message of the programme without question, are already asking: could it happen here?

One of those commentators, an editorialist for CKEY Radio, is a man whose experience should have taught him to be more skeptical of what the media says about social movements. It is doubly ironic, given the NDP's role in Ward Six, that that man should be Stephen Lewis, former leader of the provincial NDP.

September 4, 1980

The support of Mayor John Sewell has given an early boost to George Hislop's campaign. Sewell's critics, meanwhile, hopeful that his courting of the gay vote will hurt his own chances in the November 10 election, have created a media uproar around the spectre of "gay power politics" taking over city hall.

The storm erupted when the media learned Sewell had agreed to attend the opening of Hislop's campaign office on September 3. There were as many reporters and cameramen as Hislop supporters present at the office launching, all clamouring to ask Sewell why he was willing to risk endorsing an openly gay candidate.

Sewell explained that he was supporting Hislop both "as a reformer and as a representative of a minority group that is making a contribution to the city."

"We are on the same wavelength" on the meat-and-potatoes issues of reform politics, he said, citing such issues as police review, the Toronto Island homes, public transit and the preservation of neighbourhoods.

"This city has to begin changing," Sewell said, introducing a major theme that will be running through his election speeches in the coming weeks. "We have to find institutions and policies that help us live together in harmony, to make sure this is a city where everybody is getting a fair share.

"This city has lots of minorities," he said, "and city council had to reflect those minorities. I hope Hislop will be elected and become a real contributor to council."

In their reporting of the Sewell-Hislop alliance, the media did not mention the issues upon which the two campaigns agree, nor did they mention that such an arrangement had also been made with the Ward Six Community Organization candidate in the last election.

Sewell's opponents at city hall wasted no time in criticizing his cooperative arrangements with Hislop. Mayoral hopeful Art Eggleton led the attack with a series of contradictory statements about the gay issue. Tony O'Donohue, the right-wing Ward Four alderman, called it a "desperate bid to hold onto the mayor's chair. I can see no good coming through this gay alliance."

October 20, 1980

In Ward Six George Hislop finds himself in the thick of an election campaign. Why? "I'm running because enough people argued that this is the time, Toronto's the place, and I'm the person."

"I'm the most interesting thing happening in this campaign," Hislop proudly confesses, and so he is, at least to date. And for better or for worse, Hislop's campaign has thrust Toronto's gay community onto centre stage.

"I don't think there is such a thing as gay issues," says Hislop, referring to the municipal level of politics. Then what's the point of having a gay alderman? "Visibility," he responds. "Since day one of the current era of gay liberation, we've stressed the need to come out of the closet, to be visible. By being out, we are no longer perceived as a mystery or a threat. By not being judged solely in terms of our sexuality, we regain our humanity."

Which isn't to say, however, that there aren't issues here that touch the lives of lesbians and gay men. City Hall is responsible for the administration of welfare, for instance, as well as non-profit housing and daycare. Hislop believes that lesbian mothers are being discriminated against in public housing developments, as are single mothers generally. Police relations are another big issue. Hislop points out that seven of the nine people killed by policemen in the last two years were members of minority groups. He feels that gay people — gay men in particular — are being singled out for special treatment.

Hislop doesn't view himself as a representative of the gay community — notwithstanding that a columnist in the *Toronto Star* once referred to him as "the unofficial mayor of Toronto's gay community."

"I've always maintained that I represent myself — and anyone else who wants to jump on the bandwagon. No one can fairly represent the entire community."

If George Hislop finds the "unofficial mayor" label irritating, so do a lot of politically active lesbians and gay men who think Hislop is too conservative, business-oriented or non-feminist. Lesbian feminists have expressed reservations about his campaign, and some have cited his association with the Barracks—a gay men's bath—as a reason for not supporting him in this election. To feminists, presumably, gay baths epitomize non-feminist objectification of sex.

Hislop, who with his lover Ron Shearer owns fifteen percent of Crispin's Restaurant and Buddy's Backroom Bar, resents the implication that, as a small businessman, he must by definition be a conservative. "Some people talk about gay business as if it were General Motors, for Christ's sake. Crispin's is the culmination of a lot of people's life savings. A lot of money was put into it, but that doesn't mean we're making money. As a matter of fact, we're not."

Hislop's dilemma—being perceived on the one hand as a faggot radical by straights (and as a radical, period, by most gays), and on the other hand as a conservative by more political gay people—really has little to do with Hislop himself. Rather, it is the dilemma of everyone who has a high profile in a "protest" movement. "It amuses me when gay people talk about me as that wild-eyed, radical man who's rocking their boat," says Hislop. "And the political gays view me as a reformist. I've lived with this for ten years. But, basically, I think I have the support of a wider section of the gay community than in the early Seventies, when the most timid and conservative thought I was dangerous. And the political gays aren't as hostile as they used to be.

"Still, there's someone who writes 'Vote Hislop' on the blackboard at Buddy's and someone else who scribbles in 'Opportunist' beside it. It happens just about every day."

Having sat as a member of the City Planning Board, Hislop knows how dreary committees and meetings can be. "I thought to myself, do I really want to spend my days doing this? But we have such a heavy investment in the movement. I've become a prisoner of it; I've spent so much time working for it and the work's not finished yet. I can't walk away from it now."

Hislop views this election as the culmination of years of work—his work and that of others—in the gay movement. Hislop has been there since the beginning and he is, for lack of a better phrase, the perennial optimist. He believes that life for gay people cannot help but get better, that we are not simply on the upward swing of the pendulum.

The young George Hislop who, thirty years ago, sat around in people's kitchens and talked about the need to organize, the need to come out, envisaged the day when he could say "I'm gay," and people would respond, "So what?" That day is not here yet, but Hislop is confident that we will live to see it. The same young man could never have anticipated that, in 1980, he would be running for alderman and knocking on strangers' doors—that he would have become, in his own words, a prisoner of the movement he helped create.

And yet, when I heard Hislop talk about daycare and public housing, I couldn't help but feel that he is not the prisoner he thinks he is. Whatever gay spirit that initially motivated him to seek public office has been tempered, in the long months of campaigning, with a broader concern for the residents of downtown Toronto.

November 10, 1980

The polls had just closed on another Toronto municipal election—the first in the city's history in which the gay community had played a central and visible role.

The huge circular foyer of city hall was a crazy forest of cables, wires, lights, cameras, newsdesk sets and bustling technicians. All the local radio and TV stations had set up operations at city hall to cover the election returns as they flowed in on computer terminals dotted about the floor.

Expectations were high. At 8:01 pm an over-confident CBC Television had declared John Sewell mayor of Toronto for another two years. But the expectations were soon dashed as returns began to trickle in. The first reports from Ward Six, where George Hislop was running as the "candidate who, among other things, happens to be gay," came from the business polls. Art Eggleton, the accountant contender for mayor, and Gordon Chong, the conservative newcomer to the aldermanic race, were ahead.

Fuller returns never really changed that initial picture. Chong and Dan Heap, the NDP incumbent, maintained healthy leads in Ward Six. Hislop was never to get beyond third place. For a while it was a real cliffhanger in the Sewell/Eggleton race, with the popular vote percentages leapfrogging over each other minute by minute. By 10 pm, however, Eggleton had widened his lead; by 10:30 it was decided.

Art Eggleton, the nondescript alderman who had used a pricey TV advertising campaign to construct his image, was the new mayor of Toronto. John Sewell had been defeated by just over two thousand votes. The final count gave Eggleton eighty-nine thousand votes and Sewell eighty-seven thousand. Gordon Chong led the polls in Ward Six with ninety-six hundred votes, while Dan Heap remained as junior alderman with ninety-three hundred votes. George Hislop had lost his first bid for a seat on city council, but came a creditable third with seventy-four hundred votes.

Beyond Ward Six, Toronto voters indicated that they wanted city council to take a clear although not overwhelming shift to the Right. In addition to a more conservative mayor, the voters elected only nine left-leaning aldermen to the twenty-three-member body, now dominated by the thirteen moderate and right-wing aldermen.

John Sewell conceded defeat to two hundred glum supporters at a community hall festively decorated for a victory party. "Don't give up on the city," he urged them, and defended his stands on "good and valid issues." The stern-faced mayor wandered through the crowd, consoling his saddened workers. Characteristically, he turned discussion away from his own defeat and speculated on the impact of the new conservative city council. He worried to a *TBP* reporter that it might mean more difficulty for the gay community. Pressed by one reporter to explain his defeat, he first laughed and then replied, simply, "We didn't have enough votes."

Dentist Gordon Chong, a newcomer to city politics, came from relative obscurity to take the Metro Council seat in Ward Six—to everyone's surprise, including his own. "Winning the top spot was a surprise to me," he later admitted. The campaign of veteran NDP alderman Dan Heap tried a variety of tactics to secure the Metro seat and, although this failed, Heap's support in the ward remained solid. There was never any doubt that he would win.

At the St Lawrence Market North, in what was to have been the victory party to end all victory parties, Hislop supporters, mostly gay, stood around in small groups, still not fully comprehending the defeat. Finally, Hislop made his entrance in a jostling crowd of TV cameras and microphones.

Amidst applause and cries of "George! George!" and "Next time!", Hislop told the emotional crowd "The amount of love that has been shown toward me and towards our community in Ward Six has vastly outweighed the hate we have seen demonstrated."

He was referring to the volume of hate literature distributed throughout the city in the weeks preceding election day, literature from groups with names like the League Against Homosexuals, Renaissance International and Positive Parents.

Hislop paid special tribute to Sue Sparrow, whom he once called his "tiny perfect campaign manager." As warm applause enveloped her, the steely calm and quiet confidence which had inspired campaign workers for weeks finally deserted Sparrow. She sobbed convulsively on Hislop's shoulder while stricken workers watched.

But the tears and the mourning were short-lived. Next day, we all began to look at the returns more closely. Slowly, it began to dawn: we had lost, yes, but this was no resounding defeat. In fact, there was much to feel good about. John Sewell, despite two years of taking uncompromising stands on a number of difficult issues, had increased his popular vote substantially, to forty-seven percent, up from the thirty-nine percent he won in 1978.

"I got eighty-seven thousand votes," observed Sewell himself. "That's a lot of votes for someone taking such tough positions." It was an increase of thirteen thousand votes over the last race. In 1978, Sewell was running against two conservative candidates, whose combined strength would have trounced him. This time, however, it was a two-way fight and, although he still lost in areas outside the downtown core, he picked up votes in every one of the eleven wards.

Although it became a commentator's phrase to say that "voters were tired of confrontation politics," the final result seemed to show that the city was rather evenly divided in its reaction to Sewell's style and policies. And, of course, it's always easier to sell a reassuring, don't-rock-the-boat approach. Art Eggleton and his image-maker, film producer Bill Marshall, picked it as the gimmick to win. As Ontario premier Bill Davis has remarked, "Bland works." He ought to know.

One columnist said that this was a municipal election that turned into a referendum on tolerance. If this is true, then it was a referendum which was only narrowly defeated. The hard-core bigot vote, as indicated by the thirty-five hundred votes that went to fundamentalist Christian mayoral candidate Ann McBride, represented about two percent of voters.

Toronto under Art Eggleton will probably not be immediately or noticeably worse for gay people. His predictable caution and silence on this and other issues, however, will have a chilling effect on the process of change. The police expect to feel more comfortable with Eggleton in office, and this could result in increased harassment of gays and other minorities.

Toronto has a weak mayoral system of government. John Sewell's unique contribution was his use of the limited powers of the mayor's office to concentrate attention on issues that he perceived could not be solved by other methods. Eggleton will never use this approach. More significant, however, is that Eggleton's compatibility with a more conservative city council and with Metro chairman Paul Godfrey, the Tory party's unelected power broker in the city, will help to encourage business interests over social services and minority rights.

In Ward Six, George Hislop's seventy-four hundred votes represent two kinds of people: gays politicized to the extent that they will vote for a gay voice at city hall, and non-gays who are not frightened by a candidate's gayness and have sufficient trust in his abilities to represent other interests in the the ward as well. It is now much more difficult to to claim that being openly gay is a political albatross.

"It was the first time," said Hislop. "Someone had to put his big toe in the pond, so I did and a big crab got me." Changing the political consciousness of both the gay community and the wider voting public is no short-term project to be achieved by a couple of months of media attention-grabbing.

It's heartening that Hislop got as many votes as he did. The question is: why didn't he get more?

"I was very worried about complacency," says Hislop. "The belief that we were a shoo-in really harmed me." Hislop was given a high public profile by the media early on in the campaign and things seemed to be going deceptively well. It seemed inevitable, so inevitable that many people did not bother getting out to vote. Hislop reports a common reaction from people after the election: "I didn't vote because I didn't think it was necessary. I'm really sorry. I will next time."

The closet bigots seem to have been another significant factor. These were the people who smiled politely at Hislop canvassers at the door, but harboured too many reservations to vote for him. Bigot may be too strong a word; misinformed and fearful may be more accurate. They did not have the language or the understanding to discuss sexuality easily.

A fundamental problem in the election, in fact, was the failure to define the "gay issue." People spent most of their time saying it wasn't a real issue.

The major strategy of the Hislop campaign was to show that Hislop was not a one-issue candidate. It assumed that everyone had a clear idea of what the single issue was, and its efforts in literature and canvassing were spent in proving that he was a credible candidate on a variety of other issues. Obviously, this was important to do, but the singlemindedness of the strategy made it impossible for the campaign to respond quickly to the misinformation contained in the hate literature being distributed.

"It was a mistake," admits Hislop. "Next time we will know better what to do."

Although it was the media that first focussed attention on Hislop's campaign, they did so mainly because of its novelty value. The media incessantly played the numbers game: How many homosexuals were crammed into Ward Six? Were there ten thousand? Did they represent a block vote? This approach put the matter purely in terms of gay clout. It assumed that homosexuals didn't live anywhere else in the city, that the gay community was clearly defined socially and physically, with all of its members politicized at exactly the same level, and ready to be mobilized at the drop of an election. It is a completely static view of community and of the process of politicization.

And finally, the Sewell campaign, irretrievably embroiled though it was in the controversy, did not know what the gay issue was about—and didn't want to know. The mayor, at least, was able to find a framework of analysis that allowed him to comprehend the gay community as integral to the social life of the city, and to recognize the importance of minority voices in its political arenas. His principles made him stick to this line despite the clamour of advisors to cool it.

John Piper, Sewell's campaign manager, championed the cautious approach. His aim, of course, was to get Sewell re-elected, and anything which might undermine that goal had to be avoided. From the beginning, the gay issue spelled one thing only to Piper and his fellow strategists: trouble.

"It was amazing to me," said one source close to the centre of the Sewell campaign, "that the Sewell people had not thought through the gay issue beyond realizing that it was not proper to make disparaging remarks about gays. It was seen as a nuisance, not as a political issue."

Not surprisingly, in the immediate aftermath of Eggleton's win, one of the first people to publicly attribute Sewell's defeat to the gay issue was John Piper. "1980 was a bit too early in the twentieth century for that issue," he said. "People just couldn't buy it. It tipped the balance in Wards One and Nine."

In Ward Nine, Sheila Meagher, a defeated NDP school trustee who had been identified by opponents as a supporter of a gay/lesbian liaison committee with the Toronto Board of Education, also said bitterly: "The homosexual thing did it. I was defeated on the homosexual issue and not on educational issues such as lowering class size, which I helped accomplish."

In these remarks, uttered in the emotion of the moment, one message is clear: defending the gay community and facilitating its genuine integration into the public life of the city is perceived neither as a political issue nor as an educational issue. It is a red herring, certainly not a worthy enough issue to be defeated on.

One factor influencing voting patterns was the decision of the NDP to run an independent campaign.

In Ward Six, the strategies of the NDP served not only to put the Sewell canvassing in disarray but also to undermine the strength of the Hislop campaign. Sewell relied on both Ward Six candidates—Heap and Hislop—to distribute his literature and to canvass for him. Since the NDP would not cooperate with the Ward Six CO, the canvassing had to be arbitrarily divided into east and west sections, Hislop being assigned the east, where association with his name would likely do the least damage. The result was uneven canvassing and a legacy of distrust and misunderstanding between groups who should have been working together.

The final piece of Heap literature revealed the NDP strategy: it was more important to get Heap to Metro Council than it was to make any distinctions between the other serious candidates. Since Hislop and Chong were relatively unknown quantities in the ward, this distinction was crucial. On a superficial level, Chong and Hislop appeared to be similar kinds of moderate candidates. As a candidate of the Ward Six CO, however, Hislop was committed to a progressive programme which differed only in detail from NDP policies. Chong, on the other hand, although he did not appear to be the business candidate, was busy courting the business vote. In addition, he never rejected the help of off-duty police sworn to defeat Hislop.

There were, therefore, important distinctions to be made, but the NDP did not make them. Their strategy ultimately backfired because it did not get Heap the top seat, it allowed Chong to sweep ahead and it lost Hislop votes.

The 1980 municipal election in Toronto taught the gay community a great deal about itself and its potential. We learned that it is possible to make gay people think about electoral issues *as gay people*—once those issues appear to have some connection to our own lives. We learned that many people can become involved in a political process—nearly three hundred were working regularly in the Hislop campaign alone.

And we learned valuable new information about the diversity of lives and opinions within a largely uncharted gay community. The response, for example, to an election leaflet distributed in the bars and baths indicated that many downtown bar patrons do not live in Ward Six, but come from the boroughs and suburbs outside the city itself. The election marks the beginning of the end of the myth of the exclusive Ward Six gay ghetto.

Observers of the emotional scene at St Lawrence Market North on election night were aware that they were witnessing more than the defeat of an individual candidate. In a sense, the entire gay community had had a stake in the election, and this defeat was a collective rite of passage.

Peter Maloney, Hislop's assistant campaign manager, speaking from the stage that night, summed up the new spirit of anger, hope and determination which was emerging even at the moment of defeat: "We'll be back—again and again and again. This city has just begun to know about us."

Postscript on Ward Six
NDP alderman Dan Heap, running in an August 17, 1981 federal by-election in downtown Toronto, defeated the well-financed Liberal candidate to become member of parliament for Spadina. A municipal by-election was then called to fill the vacancy left by Heap's move to Ottawa. On October 19, 1981 former mayor John Sewell was returned to Toronto city council as the junior alderman for Ward Six.

Raids, rage and bawdyhouses
Gerald Hannon

"Taking it to the streets," Issue 71, March 1981; "Who is the next? Me?"
and "Uncovering the enemy within," Issue 72, April 1981; "Putting on
the pressure," Issue 74, June 1981; "Judge finds group sex indecent,"
Issue 75, July/August 1981; "Our anger, their violence," *TBP
Newsbreak*, July/August 1981; "Police and gays: study calls for
dialogue," Ed Jackson, Issue 78, November 1981

*It may be that the police raids and mass arrests in four Toronto bathhouses in
February 1981 will one day be seen as a crucial turning point in the growth of
the city's gay community. The raids were like an electric jolt. They set off immediate explosions and sparked social and political fuses that will take much
longer to detonate. No previous intrusion by the police had startled so many
men into defiant anger. In the past, the police have often charged isolated individuals with sex-related offences. Those individuals have recoiled at the
direct intrusion into their private lives, the threat to their sexual practices, but
have been powerless to fight back. This time there was a difference. This time
the police attacked a popular social institution, and the legacy was hundreds
of gay men with a common experience of police repression. The result was an
unprecedented series of large and militant demonstrations and a revitalized
defence organization strengthened by an influx of completely new and highly
skilled members. Indirectly, this new political consciousness also inspired the
launching of a variety of other community groups and organizations. Perhaps most significantly, the raids hastened the establishment of a democratic-
ally constituted Gay Community Council with the potential for responding
more effectively to attacks. Where once there had been merely hazy outlines,
there were now visible contours of a self-conscious and self-confident gay
community.*

*Tremors from the raids continued to be felt throughout the year and the
news pages of* The Body Politic *were filled with accounts of related events.
The following edited extracts record highlights of an exciting and decisive
year for gay people in Toronto.*

Rage: February 6, 1981
It was the night Toronto came closer to a full-scale riot than it has in the last ten
years. It was the night when three thousand people came within minutes of
breaking down the doors of the Ontario legislature. It was the night the main
street of Canada's largest city belonged to us, and nobody—not even the police—seemed to be able to do anything about it.

It was midnight, February 6—just twenty-four hours after the largest mass
arrest since the 1970 invocation of the War Measures Act.

It was midnight, February 6—just twenty-four hours after what George

Hislop has called the gay equivalent of "Crystal Night in Nazi Germany—when the Jews found out where they were really at."

At approximately 11 pm on Thursday, February 5, one hundred and fifty police officers coordinated by police intelligence descended on four Toronto steambaths, arresting two hundred and eighty-six men as found-ins in a common bawdyhouse, and twenty men as keepers. In law, a common bawdyhouse can be any place "resorted to for the purposes of prostitution or the practice of acts of indecency"—and cops have been using the vaguely worded statute to arrest gay men in bars, baths and private homes. But this was a premeditated attack of such violence and scope that the community is still seething with anger.

The anger paid off early. By noon on Friday, a hastily arranged meeting at *The Body Politic*'s office brought together representatives from the Coalition for Gay Rights in Ontario (CGRO), the Right to Privacy Committee (RTPC), the Metropolitan Community Church—and some people who just turned up because they wanted to do something. By 4 pm the organization was in place—there was a sound truck, marshals were recruited from graduates of the gay self-defence course and four thousand leaflets were ready for distribution.

"Enough is Enough," they said. "Protest. Yonge and Wellesley. Midnight tonight."

Yonge and Wellesley is an intersection at the heart of what has come to be known as Toronto's gay ghetto. It is also one of the busiest intersections downtown. By midnight there were probably three hundred people there, blowing whistles, brandishing homemade signs, chanting "No more raids!" and "Stop the cops!" Half an hour later that number had swollen to fifteen hundred, and with the first illegal step in the intersection, the street was ours. The police, undermanned and apparently unprepared, could do little but reroute traffic.

Civil disobedience was in the air, people were drunk on the prospect of it, on the prospect of power over turf we've liked to say belongs to us, but realize is really ours only grudgingly, and on loan.

Civil disobedience was in the air, and speaker Brent Hawkes of the MCC said it was the time for it, this was the night when, legal or not, we'd take over the streets. *TBP*'s Chris Bearchell hit the crowd with the slogan that would be taken up over and over again: "No more shit! No more shit!"

CGRO coordinator Jim Monk says it: we're going to march. South. Into the heart of the city, and towards police 52 Division—the concrete and glass fortress that only hours before held hundreds of frightened and angry men.

The scene is surreal. Yonge Street, usually a river of bumper-to-bumper traffic, is an empty canyon echoing to the shouts, screams and whistles of an advancing crowd the full width of the street. The occasional car the police haven't stopped somehow makes it onto the street, stops, can't turn around, gets swallowed up. A man jumps onto the roof of one of them and does a disco turn before leaping back into the crowd.

The first signs of trouble come just north of Dundas Street.

Cop cars are parked in the middle of the street, angled to form a kind of barricade. It doesn't work. A few sharp blows and a windshield cracks. Two men stand and piss on one of the cars. Suddenly there is a scuffle beside Cinema 2000—it's unclear what happened but it seems a straight man has attacked one of the marchers. A cop intervenes and all hell breaks loose—the crowd apparently thinks the cop is the attacker and surges at him, fists flying. Three other cops try to force themselves through the crowd but simply end up being trapped with the first one, pinned against a store wall, hopelessly outnumbered but fighting back, and it looks like the first blood of the evening will flow here—until enough marshals force their way in and break it up.

The atmosphere gets uglier—by this time the march has attracted a peripheral crowd of twenty to thirty straight men. As the crowd surges towards 52 Division chanting "Fuck you, 52! Fuck you, 52!"; they counter with "Fuck the queers! Fuck the queers!" In a final desperate and quixotic gesture they link arms and try to block University Avenue. By that time it's thirty against three thousand and it's no contest—a short scuffle, and they scatter.

We reach 52. The stabbing lights of the TV cameras pick out an astounding sight — cops, one hundred and ninety-five of them, standing shoulder to shoulder completely surrounding the front of the building. Our line surges up and slaps against theirs but theirs doesn't break—even when the crowd gives them the Nazi salute, even when the crowd spits in their faces.

There is only one target left and someone has only to suggest it. The name comes booming over the sound system: Queen's Park.

The Ontario legislature is a scant ten minutes away, and the focus of a particular hatred in the last six weeks since all three political parties backed away from an opportunity to legislate human rights for gay people.

The crowd seethes up University Avenue, and the front line of marshals is having more and more difficulty trying to contain it. They link arms, stretching themselves across the front, but as the thousands of marchers take their first step onto the vast expanse of lawn that sweeps up to the legislature, the front line crumbles and nothing can hold people back. They run, hundreds of black figures against the snow, heading for the massive oak doors of our legislative assembly.

They get there before the cops do and for a few thrilling minutes dozens of bodies throw themselves repeatedly against the doors, and even people halfway back in the crowd report seeing the doors vibrating in the probing light of the television cameras, and hearing the hollow booming of bodies thudding against the barriers.

But that sound is the signal for the cops to come down with a viciousness they'd kept in check till then. A wedge of some twenty officers forces its way through the crowd, and punching, kicking and shoving they beat the crowd back. One man's face is bloodied. Another man is shouting that his sister has been hit over and over again by a cop. But somehow the clash has left both sides stunned, and organizers take the opportunity to encourage people to leave—in groups, for their own safety.

Although numbers are dwindling rapidly, there are still enough people together at Yonge Street to tie up traffic. But the ugliest scenes of the night are reserved for Yonge and Bloor — by that time, cops and straight thugs far outnumber what few marchers are left. The straights are shouting insults, and I watch as half a dozen cops completely surround a man, drag him to the ground and begin kicking and punching. A *TBP* photographer who tries to photograph the scene is hauled to the ground by his hair, his flash attachment smashed, his glasses broken. He is later charged with breach of the peace. It turns out the man being beaten was one of the found-ins.

It was about 2:20 am, Saturday, February 7. Eleven people had been arrested during the preceding two and a half hours—two for assaulting a police officer, one for damage to public property, one on a drug charge and seven with breach of the peace. One policeman was slightly injured. At least one cop car had its windsheild cracked and its headlights kicked in. A streetcar had four of its windows smashed. But most of the damage was on the other side.

Complaints about police brutality will probably go nowhere, however, largely because most cops rendered themselves unidentifiable by removing badges and flash numbers. Although photographs of the events show officers with neither badges nor flash numbers, Deputy Chief Jack Marks says his investigations have satisfied him that all officers were wearing one or the other. The investigation seems to have taken less than a day.

Raids: February 5, 1981

"About 11 o'clock these two guys come to the door and asked for a room and a locker. They paid, and I gave them their change, and since we were full I gave locker twenty-five to the guy wanting the room and put him on the waiting list, and I went on to the next customer.

"A few minutes later both guys came right into the kitchen and asked for their money back. I suspected a robbery and called for Tony, the supervisor, and then they grabbed me and told me to stay where I was. When Tony came in they grabbed him too and he shouted out to call the police. I looked out the window and saw all these men pouring in through the door and some of them were in uniform, and I said 'I don't think that'll be necessary.'"

Cashier at the Richmond Street Health Emporium, recalling the events of February 5.

"I was in a room with someone and I heard a noise. I got up to open the door but it burst open and a guy in plain clothes pushed in and shoved me up against the wall, my face pushed hard into the wall. My nose was lacerated and bloodied. The cop kept punching me in the lower back and pulling my hair and saying 'You're disgusting, faggot. Look at this dirty place.'

"I was choked, and something was jabbed into my neck. Before they took us out of the room, they used a pen to gouge the room number into the backs of our hands.

"I was naked. They herded me into the shower room with about eight other men and we had to stand against the wall with both hands up against the wall. I couldn't see anything but I could hear a guy choking, and then a cop said, 'If you're having trouble breathing we can give you trouble with your spleen or kidneys.'

"I could hear them moving around, kicking things, overturning things. Someone said 'Too bad the place doesn't catch fire, we'd have to catch them escaping custody.' Somebody else said, 'Too bad the showers aren't hooked up to gas.'

"I was finally called to face a guy sitting in the locker room. I was still nude. He looked at the blood on my face and said, 'Get that man washed up.' After I showered, he said 'Add obstruct police and assault police to that guy.' They did that. But he never identified himself as a cop. I was never told I was under arrest."

Testimony of one found-in at the Barracks, describing the February 5 raid.

It was, of course, also happening at the Club and the Roman. Four of Toronto's five gay baths were pillaged in about three hours—the climax, according to police, of six months of investigations which led them to conclude that "acts of prostitution and indecent acts" had taken place.

It was a pillage. The damage to the premises is now estimated at thirty-five thousand dollars. Photographs taken within hours of the raids vividly corroborate the testimony of men who say plainclothes cops identified only by red dots somewhere on their clothing used hammers, crowbars and shears to smash through doors, shatter mirrors, rip apart mattresses and wrench the doors off lockers. Cops kicked holes in corridor walls.

It was a pillage authorized from the top. Police chief Jack Ackroyd says he approved both the investigation and the raids—and in one swift stroke destroyed whatever credibility he had as the "liberal friend to minorities" chosen to replace former chief Harold Adamson. As well, the rumour is afoot that approval for the raids came finally from Attorney General Roy McMurtry himself.

Whatever the level of authorization, the cops seemed to feel they were operating with a virtual carte blanche. Verbal harassment was common — men were called faggots, Vaseline jokes were made, a couple of officers joked about being sure they'd find a teacher and when they did they'd spread the word around.

Robert Trow, a paramedic with Hassle Free Clinic, was arrested and charged even though he was on duty as a Hassle Free employee giving free VD checks to anyone who wanted them. He has since been informed that the city's health department will require the alleged keepers to undergo compulsory VD checks, and that Hassle Free should prepare itself for a few days of increased business. As well, the found-ins will be served with notices recommending VD tests, but they are not compulsory. "The caller was a little nonplussed," he reports, "when I told her I'd be among the people getting a notice to have a test."

Another disturbing allegation comes from employees at both the Club and the Richmond. They say that though the police claimed to have search warrants with them—in neither case were they shown when requested. As well, at the Richmond, the cops began answering phone calls after the raid, telling callers things like, "Michael's all tied up right now. Want to come down and see his rope burns?" or "Larry's around the corner with a rat in his mouth."

There are also allegations that some of the police investigation that preceded the raid consisted of illegal police tampering with the mail. Peter Maloney, an executive member of the Coalition for Gay Rights in Ontario and a vocal police critic, says he was tipped off by a post-office employee that mail addressed to him and three gay baths was being intercepted and routed to the employee's supervisor. Since the tip-off, Maloney says, mail addressed to him has arrived pre-opened, and some of his mail has arrived at the Club Bath's business office.

Maloney complained to federal Solicitor General Robert Kaplan, who has since said that neither the RCMP nor any federal government agency is examining Maloney's mail—but admitted that his office did not look into the activities of any other police force. It would presumably be the Toronto police who are intercepting Maloney's mail.

It is possible the police were after mail that would provide links between baths here and in the United States—the original police press release makes reference to "club records showing an association to persons in the USA."

Police have been eager to discover a link to organized crime in the States—though so far they've had to admit only that they've found evidence linking "these clubs to international clubs that are in the States." Presumably a link to "organized crime" would provide a reason scary enough to justify the scope of the raids.

It is no secret, however, that the Club Toronto is part of the Club Bath Chain. The American enterprise has headquarters in Miami, and baths in most major American cities, as well as Toronto, London and Vancouver. As one local activist put it, "It's like 'discovering' that Colonel Sanders restaurants have connections in the US. The whole thing looks like a desperate ploy to justify something that can't be justified."

Support: solid to surreal

Although the Friday night march down Yonge Street was the most dramatic example of community solidarity with the three hundred and six men charged in the raids, subsequent events seem to indicate a developing and impressive coalition of both gays and straights shocked by the abuse of police power.

However, the many individuals and organizations demanding an inquiry into the raids have been disregarded by officials.

Attorney General Roy McMurtry's response to a Canadian Civil Liberties Association request for an independent inquiry was made public during a heated and acrimonious police commission meeting February 12. The answer, coming at the end of a seven-page letter full of outright lies, was no. Since one speaker after another had called for such an independent inquiry, there were shocked cries of "Shame! Shame!" and "Resign!" after the announcement was made.

Writing that he was not "satisfied that there has been an accurate reporting of these events by the media," McMurtry went on to say that "at one of the four premises in question one police officer took a hammer into the place with him but it was not used. At another establishment one crowbar was taken and was used to open three lockers. This is the total evidence available with respect to crowbars and hammers."

Since the raids, there have been several media visits to the baths, all of whom have recorded extensive damage, estimated by the owners at about thirty-five thousand dollars.

McMurtry also claimed there was only one report of police using abusive language, and "no evidence of anyone being injured"—though as the CCLA's Alan Borovoy said, "It is easy to understand why no one would complain when the only body they have to complain to is the police themselves."

The afternoon police commission meeting attracted more than a hundred people—although almost all of them were forced to stand outside in freezing weather for all but the last half hour or so. Only the press, official delegations and a few early-birds were allowed inside—and the police reneged on a promise to allow everyone access to the first-floor cafeteria.

Inside, speaker after speaker demanded an independent inquiry. There was a delegation led by alderman Gordon Cressy, representing a majority of city council, there was journalist June Callwood, retiring MLA Margaret Campbell, St George hopeful Bruce McLeod, St George NDP candidate Dan Leckie, the CCLA's Alan Borovoy, Allan Strader and Mary Eberts, Jack Layton from the Working Group on Minority-Police Relations, a representative from several downtown United Churches, and several gay speakers.

Outside, protesters faced a wall of police security that included a mounted detachment on the ready in a nearby side street. Demonstrators chanted "Sack Jack, Dump Phil"—referring to police chief Jack Ackroyd and police commission chairman Phil Givens. One man, finally succumbing to an impulse everyone was feeling, grabbed a brick—but cops had him under arrest before he could throw it.

The noise from the protest carried up into the second floor meeting room where Givens, Ackroyd and several police commissioners heard MCC's Brent Hawkes say, "Get out of our clubs, get out of our baths, get out of our homes and get back to fighting crime. Stop killing my city."

They heard Jack Layton call for the firing of Ackroyd and the head of the Intelligence Bureau, and the resignation of the entire police commission.

They heard George Hislop talk about the suicide of a twenty-year-old found-in of last year's Hot Tub Club raids. "May his death be on your consciences," he told them.

During many of the presentations, commissioner Winfield McKay smirked, or conspicuously yawned. Other commissioners talked among themselves, or stared impassively as Brent Hawkes referred them to a *Toronto Star* story that day revealing that the police operating budget for 1981 is requesting a total of seven and a half million dollars for the intelligence and morality bureaus together, while asking for a scant one million dollars for homicide investigation.

The meeting finally dissolved in hoots and jeers as Givens told the crowd,

"We deny any allegations of police harassment," and said there was no need for an inquiry and there would be no inquiry.

Despite the commission's dogged intransigence, there was no doubt gay people found heartening the wide range of support they were hearing. It had begun in earnest two days earlier when more than a thousand people packed the auditorium of Jarvis Collegiate. Though most of them were gay, they were hearing echoes of their own outrage from straight supporters like Fran Endicott, a black Toronto school board trustee who spoke eloquently of the need for links with all minorities. They heard Menno Vorster, president of the Toronto Teachers' Federation, remind them that the Toronto board had sexual orientation protection on the books, "and now's the time to do something about it. It's none of anyone's business what happens outside the classroom."

It was a foot-stomping, turbulent, militant crowd that bounced a *Toronto Sun* reporter out of the meeting, called for another, larger demonstration, and arranged for subcommittees to coordinate everything from fund-raising to counselling of found-ins.

Support had also surfaced that morning when about twenty-five city aldermen, writers, and civil libertarians were brought together by alderman Gordon Cressy to demand "some speedy explanations," and to extend "their deepest concern" to the men affected.

"Please be assured," the statement read, "that there are many in Toronto, among whom we are but a few, who will stand behind you."

Among the endorsers of the statement of concern were writers Margaret Atwood and June Callwood, retiring St George MLA Margaret Campbell, Robert Fulford of *Saturday Night*, lawyer Morris Manning, former NDP leader Stephen Lewis, Clifford Elliot of Bloor Street United Church, and ten city aldermen.

Notable no-shows on the support list: Toronto mayor Art Eggleton, the members of Metro Council except for Scarborough mayor Gus Harris and alderman Gordon Cressy, and the leaders of the three major provincial parties.

The *Globe and Mail* editorialized on the issue, calling the police action "ugly," and saying it was "more like the bully-boy tactics of a Latin American republic... than of anything that has a place in Canada."

Support even had its surreal side. Ken Campbell of the vehemently anti-gay Renaissance International denounced the raid—though he clarified his stand in a letter to the *Globe* February 12 which ended "God bless 'the boys in blue' and God have mercy on... that 'bath-house crowd.' "

Demonstration: February 20, 1981

"It looks like we finally may be getting something we've been saying we've had for the last ten years—a gay community." Fellow journalist Chris Bearchell told me that and, though she wasn't exactly saying the city had been a collection of gay solitudes for the last decade, it almost seemed so in comparison to the uncontrollable bubbling up of energies, determination and a collective will for justice that has exhilarated the gay community in Toronto since February 5.

It can be sensed even at the street level. Gay people smile at each other when they pass, a quick acknowledgement that each is wearing a "No more shit!" button. It seems that every second Tory election poster has a "No more shit—Gays fight back" sticker slapped over Premier Bill Davis's mouth. Some of the smaller *sub*committees within the Right to Privacy Committee—the organization coordinating gay community response to the bath raids—have upwards of a hundred members.

"We're suddenly the largest grassroots gay organization in Canada," says RTPC chairperson George Smith. "We've got more than seven hundred members now—and we're still growing."

The sense that Toronto's gay community has passed through its tentative political adolescence came the night of February 20. It was exactly two weeks since three thousand angry people had virtually taken over downtown Toronto in a turbulent protest against police raids. No one was certain the community would match either those numbers or that spirit again.

It did. That night, almost four thousand gay people and their supporters among women, labour, straight people and ethnic communities turned up at Queen's Park to march one more time to 52 Division.

The spirit was there, a spirit growing from a sense of unity and determination. *TBP*'s Tim McCaskell told the wildly cheering crowd, "We've shown Roy McMurtry, Jack Ackroyd—and the gang of hacks that presently masquerade as a police commission in this city—something I think they're even more afraid of than gay rage—and that's unity. Unity with all minority groups in this city. Tonight, citizens of Toronto, straight and gay, black and white, immigrant and Canadian-born, have come out to stand beside a gay community under attack."

Only moments before, McCaskell had introduced Lemona Johnson, widow of a black new Canadian shot to death in his own home by two Toronto police officers. "The murder of Albert, my husband, was one of the most brutal and senseless killings of any innocent man that has ever taken place in this city," she told the hushed crowd. "The raids and arrests of members of the Toronto gay community are further indications that the police force is lacking in discipline and proper supervision. I have a responsibility to my children, myself and my community to speak out...."

Earlier, Josephine Godlewski had stepped firmly to the microphone and though a little dazzled by the television lights, said "I'm a housewife and I'm not gay, but the people who were arrested... were minding their own business in a place of their own choosing. First there was the blacks. Now the gay people. Who is next? Me?" When she finished, a gay man suddenly leapt forward, bussed her on the cheek—and presented her with a dozen daffodils.

It was a stunning display of strength, unity and determination. Tightly organized, and controlled by a crack marshalling team, it was a demonstration in which there should have been no "incidents"— but there were. Six people were arrested — some of them under decidedly suspicious circumstances.

Four of the people carrying the banner that headed the largest gay demonstration in Canadian history were plainclothes police officers. And several more were photographed carrying placards.

Since the publication of revealing photographs in two Toronto dailies, police commission chairman Phil Givens has said that, while he won't ask for a formal investigation, he will ask police chief Jack Ackroyd to "enlighten" him on the matter. Ackroyd concedes that it is improper for police to carry signs during demonstrations. Yet we have police superintendent David Sproule telling the press that such activities are "absolutely routine."

And there is more. Plainclothes officers have been spotted at a February 12 police commission meeting, at a city council debate over a public inquiry into police actions, and at a March 7 picket protesting the right-wing Canada in Crisis rally.

"The effect," according to one civil rights lawyer, "is to put a distinct chill over the right to freedom of assembly. People should have that right without having to fear they are under surreptitious surveillance, without having to worry about the person next to them."

Ackroyd told the press these undercover cops are community relations officers, well known in the gay community, thereby adding yet one more fabrication to the self-serving fictions which have issued from the police force, the police commission and the office of the attorney general since the February 5 assault on the gay community. Two community relations officers *are* known to gay activists. But they were not among the plainclothes cops photographed at the February 20 demonstration, who seem to have been there in the role of secret police.

Some witnesses, including several demonstration marshals, reported incidents which indicate that the altercations which led to the six arrests took place at the provocation of undercover cops. It is reported that they ripped the leading banner almost in half, spat in people's faces and finally provoked fights resulting in the arrest of three marshals who attempted to stop the fighting. At least one of the marshals under arrest was manhandled, kicked and abused.

A report submitted to Toronto City Council February 26 by aldermen David White and Pat Sheppard has begun to expose to public scrutiny some of what happened the night of February 5.

The report includes about seventy-five excerpts from statements by gay people swept up in the bath raids. The document makes for chilling reading. Some examples:

• "Patrons were made to stand facing the wall. After forty-five minutes one man turned green and asked if he could sit down. The police wouldn't allow him to. A few minutes later he fainted and fell to the floor."

• "The preliminary officers scrutinized the genitalia of each person. Everyone was made to turn around and bend over and spread their cheeks, for no apparent reason."

• "One officer went along the line asking 'Are you married?' If people said yes or he saw a wedding band he said stuff like 'You'll wish you had stayed at home with your wife tonight, you fucking queer.' "

• "I witnessed one officer wielding his sledgehammer with abandon and then saying, and I quote, 'Boy, I must be getting old, that took two whacks!' I also saw another officer pull an undamaged door shut and then smash it with his hammer."

The report included photographs of the damage and photographs of police officers without their badges, in direct violation of police policy. The report concluded by recommending that "the attorney general initiate an impartial public inquiry as soon as possible."

Although Toronto City Council passed the motion eleven to nine (with a surprise swing vote from the usually conservative Ying Hope), Metro Council has refused to do so, and Metro chairman Paul Godfrey says bluntly, "For my part, I support the police position. It's against the law to operate a brothel in Canada, no matter what your sexual persuasion...."

Despite the stonewalling by people like Godfrey and the police commission (commissioner Winfield McKay said on television that the gay community "squealed like a collection of stuck pigs," and that the cost of an inquiry couldn't be justified), there is a new tone to gay life in Toronto—and much of the energy for it flows from the Right to Privacy Committee. Before the February 5 bath raids, it was just one more gay organization in Toronto plodding through the necessary work of coordinating the defence of those charged in previous bath raids in the city. Since that time, there has been an "enormous transformation," according to chairperson George Smith. "There's a constant flow of resources and energy. We have skilled people to tap—media people, professional writers, legal people—and when this is over we should have a whole new group who can arrange demonstrations, chair meetings, get out press releases and handle the media."

No issue has ever drawn such a wide range of support to the gay community. No issue has ever radicalized so many gay people. The baths are still open and busy — with the notable exception of the Richmond Street Health Emporium, which closed February 17 because the management felt it could not afford to both cover repairs and hold on while business slowly built up again. In a particularly grotesque finale to its five years on the gay scene, someone broke into the premises the night it closed, and did about three thousand dollars worth of additional damage.

That "radicalization" of the gay community has made it noisy and impatient, and has pulled it out in hundreds and sometimes thousands to more than a half-dozen events in the last month alone. Mariana Valverde, speaking for the International Women's Day Committee February 20, said what most people listening had been feeling in the gut of their daily lives since February 5.

"As women," she said, "we did not get the vote by writing polite letters. We got the vote by demonstrating, by going on hunger strikes, by chaining ourselves to railings, and all kinds of other very unladylike behaviour. As gay people, we will not win our rights by getting up in our Sunday best and going to knock on politicians' doors. We will not gain our rights by being deferential and nice, and saying please and thank you.

"Gay people cannot afford to be polite. We have to fight back."

Conspiracy charges: April 21, 1981

About 10:15 pm April 21 I got a call from George Hislop. "They've dropped the other shoe," he said. He'd been told to present himself, along with fellow businessmen Rick Stenhouse and Jerry Levy, and gay activist Peter Maloney, at 52 Division at noon the following day to be taken into custody and charged.

The "other shoe" proved to be a bewildering array of new charges, the most serious relating to conspiracy, against six individuals, three of whom were already on trial on charges arising out of the first raid on the Barracks two and a half years ago.

This is where it gets complicated. Hislop, Levy and Stenhouse (along with two others) are awaiting judgment from a recent trial from the "old" Barracks raid. In the middle of *that* comes this series of new charges from the February 5 raid this year. However, this second round of charges includes three new faces: John Willard (Jack) Campbell and Raymond Diemer, two American investors in the Club Baths and the Barracks and, inexplicably, gay activist Peter Maloney.

The charges against all six men include:
• conspiracy to possess proceeds obtained by crime;
• conspiracy to keep a common bawdyhouse; conspiracy to publish, distribute, or circulate obscene matter, and conspiracy to sell obscene matter.

Charges against Hislop, Levy and Stenhouse only:
• keeping a common bawdyhouse at the Barracks;
• selling, exposing to public view and possessing for such purposes obscene matter.

Further charges against Levy and Stenhouse only:
• keeping a common bawdyhouse at the Club Baths;
• possessing obscene matter for the purposes of publication, distribution or circulation.

And that obscene matter? A fine spluttering list of things that went entirely unreported in the "family" press: butt plugs, ass spreaders, ball stretchers, cock rings, tit clamps, hoods, gags, enema bags, and so on.

The new charges brought the total of those charged in the bath raids up to three hundred and fifteen. And the choice of Howard Morton, director of the Crown Law Office (Criminal), to prosecute the case, meant that one of Attorney General Roy McMurtry's top honchos was in charge. Morton told me that though he hadn't consulted with McMurtry before laying charges, he had "advised" him that charges would be laid. And McMurtry is taking the whole sorry business seriously enough to begin extradition proceedings against both Campbell and Diemer.

Community response was swift. A press conference April 23, the day following the charges, brought together men and women from nearly three dozen gay organizations to label the charges "an attempt to characterize our leaders, and by implication the gay community, as criminal."

On behalf of the groups, Gays at the University of Toronto chairperson Dan Healey called the charges "a deliberate police attack," and pointed out that both Hislop and Maloney have been long-time critics of the Toronto police force. Maloney had been responsible for forcing the police to present a more detailed budget to Metro Council. The vague, rarely used, but serious charges of conspiracy (which carry a maximum sentence of ten years) seemed designed to get the "cop-bashers" off the police's backs.

The charge against Maloney seemed particularly gratuitous. He is the only one of the six charged who is not a director of either the Club or the Barracks. In fact, he appears not to have been a director during the period of the indictment (January 1, 1978 to February 28, 1981). His last appearance on the corporate papers as a director is in a filing of February 1977 where he appears as a director of the Barracks with no share interest. As well, at that point he appears simply as a ten percent shareholder in the Club Toronto—but not a director.

It appears Maloney will be prosecuted simply for owning shares in a Canadian corporation—rather like prosecuting every small shareholder in the major oil companies after they were charged with conspiring to set oil prices.

Community response continued with a picket of police headquarters May 2. A hundred and fifty people turned out to hear *TBP*'s Tim McCaskell charge police chief Jack Ackroyd with several "conspiracy" charges, including "conspiracy to politically manipulate the legal system" and "conspiracy to cover up wrongdoings by undercover cops."

So far it is people like Hislop, Maloney and the others who are bearing the brunt of the new police initiatives. But there is a filter-down effect which ranges from the simple deterioration of our social lives to the grossest kind of police abuse.

Two of the baths—the Club and the Barracks—have suddenly gone all "respectable." Those deliciously dark second-floor rooms at the Barracks have simply been boarded up, and those "waist-high holes between rooms" (as they were described in court) have been sealed. At the Club, regular announcements come over the PA system asking patrons to keep covered both in and out of their rooms, to keep their room light on at all times, to close room doors if more than one patron is in the room. A light has been installed in the wet sauna.

One can hardly blame the management, who must be at their wits' end trying to guess what "indecency" means in the context of a gay bath where everyone turns up knowing what to expect and what he wants.

The subtle terrorizing continues too. I spoke with a guy on the door at the Club recently. He told me that there have been rumours from authoritative sources that another raid was on the way—"It's been really uncomfortable working here," he told me, "you never know when it's going to happen."

The Barracks verdict: June 12, 1981

A decision by a provincial court judge June 12 concluded that buggery, fellatio and other gay sex acts are not in themselves indecent. However, in finding two men guilty of keeping a common bawdyhouse at the Barracks, Provincial Court Judge Harold Rice concluded that such sex acts, when performed so that others may see them, are not within the community standards of tolerance.

Rice found Barracks employees Andy Fabo, 28, and Paul Gaudet, 33, guilty as charged. To the surprise of almost everyone in the packed courtroom, Rice then went on to acquit Barracks owners George Hislop, Rick Stenhouse and Jerry Levy.

Although Rice said that, as officers of The Barracks Ltd, it was "inconceivable that they did not have knowledge of the acts of indecency going on at 56 Widmer," the Crown had not proved without a reasonable doubt "what active participation they took, if any, with regards to the acts of indecency" going on there.

The judgment brings to a conclusion a legal battle that began December 9, 1978, when police raided the gay bathhouse and charged twenty-three men as found-ins and five as keepers.

Rice devoted much of his judgment to a review of police testimony, and descriptions of the kinds of sexual acts that took place at the Barracks. He went on to say that the court must consider all the circumstances surrounding the charged acts—they may be within community standards of tolerances under some circumstances, and not others.

However, in the case of the Barracks, Rice felt that the orgy rooms, rooms with windows and two-way mirrors, and rooms with peep-holes encouraged public sex. "Patrons attending," he said, "did so with the knowledge that their acts would be observed and in the hope and expectation that others would join them."

He went on to say that, in those circumstances, such sexual acts did not fall within the community standards of tolerance.

In an interview after the verdict, Crown Attorney Paul Culver said that the city could now serve notice under the Municipal Act to close the Barracks. He said the same procedure used to close bodyrub parlours on Yonge Street could be used against any bath convicted of being a common bawdyhouse.

At 10 pm on the night of the verdict, a protest organized by the Right to Privacy Committee drew two thousand people to the corner of Yonge and Wellesley to protest the decision.

Marchers created a deafening roar with whistles, noisemakers and cheers as speaker after speaker denounced the bawdyhouse laws and the invasion of privacy which they legitimize. As the crowd grew and movement on the sidewalk became almost impossible, tempers frayed. An altercation between one man and a police officer developed into a serious situation after someone knocked off the officer's hat. Police waded into the crowd with billy clubs in hand, and observers generally agree that a riot might have followed had quick action by the marshals and the density of the crowd not prevented it.

Police charged one man with breach of the peace, and another with assault and theft (the officer's hat).

More police raids: June 16, 1981

The police putsch against Toronto gay baths have come full circle June 16, as members of the Metropolitan Toronto Police Intelligence Bureau raided the only two gay-identified bathhouses not swept up in the February 5 raids.

Twenty-one men were arrested, bringing to three hundred and thirty-seven the total number of men facing bawdyhouse charges since the February raids.

Plainclothes officers entered the Back Door Gym and the International Steam Bath at about three o'clock in the afternoon, a marked change from the late-night raids which swept up so many men four months before. Intelligence Staff Sergeant Dennis Robinson has been quoted as saying the police chose that hour because "we certainly don't want to aggravate the gay community at large"—a clear indication of the impact of the increasingly militant demonstrations over the past four months. As well, reports from at least the Back Door Gym indicate the raiding officers were neither abusive nor destructive.

At the International one man was charged as a keeper and nine were charged as found-ins. Further charges are pending against the owner, who was out of the country at the time of the raid. At the Back Door, three men were charged as keepers and eight as found-ins.

According to one of the alleged keepers at the Back Door, one of the men charged as a found-in was simply on the premises to do some electrical wiring.

Officers spent about three hours there — customers arriving during that period were told the premises were temporarily closed for renovations. Officers seized cash receipts, office records, lubricant, bottles of poppers—and were particularly delighted to find some condoms, according to one observer.

The police say both baths have been under observation since August 1980, and that undercover officers "observed acts of group sex, indecent acts and buggery taking place.... The officers were also solicited by male prostitutes making use of the premises to engage in the acts of sex for a fee."

Staff Inspector Donald Banks denied the raids had anything to do with the recent decision by Judge Harold Rice that the Barracks is a common bawdyhouse—though immediately after that decision Crown Attorney Paul Culver answered a question about future raids by saying, "the police have a precedent now, and it wouldn't surprise me."

It probably surprised both the Back Door and the International—though activist Peter Maloney has pointed out that the International has twice been acquitted of being a common bawdyhouse. Police raided it in the 1960s and 1970s, he says, and failed to get a conviction both times. The International has been operating for about twenty years. The Back Door has been in business for only about two years.

Demonstration: June 20, 1981

Four days later, two thousand demonstrators hit the streets more angry and more defiant than ever before.

Yonge and Wellesley at 10 pm: the starting time and location were quite familiar by the night of June 20. By 10:30 the crowded sidewalks were overflowing with expectant demonstrators and bystanders, and anxious cops appeared on the scene to keep the streets free of congestion.

"Blow the whistle on the cops," the leaflet calling for the action had read, and the din from the scores of gay self-defence whistles, mixed together with now familiar chants against police harassment, could be heard for a radius of four city blocks. The rally was opened by RTPC spokesperson Dan Healey, who asked the crowd to step back in order to relieve the crush on the speakers' area. Before the surprised line of fifty police surrounding the sidewalks could react, the demonstrators had taken more than a few steps and the street was ours. The isolated cops moved off to the side. Healey expressed the mood of the moment when he responded to a police claim published in the press that the latest bath raids had been scheduled so as not "to aggravate the gay community."

"We're not aggravated, we're fucking angry!" he declared to an approving chorus of shouts and whistles.

At a few minutes past 11, the demonstration moved up Yonge on a march to the Jarvis Street headquarters of the Metropolitan Toronto police. The long line of march was led by two large pink triangles hoisted on poles and emblazoned with the words "Resist" and "Defend," together with effigies of Toronto police chief Jack Ackroyd and Attorney General Roy McMurtry.

As the head of the march reached the major downtown intersection of Yonge and Bloor Streets, individuals within the crowd began an apparently spontaneous sit-down which occupied the streets for five minutes. It was a statement of civil disobedience.

Taken unawares by the unexpected sit-down, the marshals reacted with momentary confusion. Some urged the entire line of demonstrators to sit down while others attempted to restart the march. After the point of the sit-down had been made and the marshals had regrouped, the march proceeded.

The procession had attracted a small band of thirty queer-bashers who had left a Yonge Street bar to run along the edge of the protest, taunting the demonstrators. This group of teenage thugs followed all the way to the rally site at the Jarvis Street police headquarters.

"The people of Toronto do not fear the gay community," declared the first speaker, Ward Six alderman Dan Heap. "But when extreme right-wing groups target the gay community and the police then attack it, the people of Toronto have good cause to fear the actions of the police."

Heap's speech was interrupted at one point when a woman protestor ran up to the effigies of Ackroyd and McMurtry and set them afire. A chant of "Burn, burn," was taken up by the approving rally.

Violence

Although the demonstration of June 20 was peaceful, the events which came after it were not.

As the demonstration broke up, about five hundred people walked west along Charles Street. Head marshal Bob Gallagher was worried. He had seen how the cops who were keeping an eye on the knot of queerbashers at the north end of the rally had let them go into the night just before the rally ended. He urged a police supervisor to make sure that the length of Charles between Jarvis and Yonge Streets was patrolled to minimize the likelihood of violence. The supervisor assured him that the situation was under control.

Part of the crowd had already passed the intersection of Charles and Church at about 12:10 am when a squad of about ten queerbashers emerged from Hayden Street. They ran south on Church toward the crowd, swinging lengths of wood and shouting obscenities. Marshals and others quickly linked arms between the bashers and their targets. After several feints, one of the thugs struck a man with his weapon. Another hurled a piece of lumber into the crowd.

Furious, the dispersing demonstrators began to chant "Kill them, kill them." Outflanking the marshalling line, they moved to surround their attackers.

The would-be queerbashers turned and fled north on Church, most of them abandoning their weapons as they went. About fifty pursuers went after them. And at about the same time the cops, who were just a block away at police headquarters, began to show up. They ran up Church, pursuing the pursuers.

What happened next is somewhat clouded. There seems to have been a scuffle halfway up Church to Bloor Street, involving at least one queerbasher, one gay man and several cops. The body of the crowd had begun to advance to the scene and shouts of "Bust him, bust him" filled the night air. Along the north perimeter of the crowd a new marshalling line quicky formed, again made up partly of marshals from the demonstration and partly from other demo participants. As the line was hardening and arms began to interlink, more police police arrived from the south, pushing through the line. They formed their own line, shoulder-to-shoulder and face-to-face with the angry crowd, about a metre from its northern edge.

An angry voice screamed "Where were you?", underlining the fact that the police had been ostentatiously absent while gays were being attacked but were able to muster in strength in a few seconds in order to rescue the attackers from the revenge of their victims. Instantly it became an accusing chant: "Where were you? Where were you?"

The police began to inch south, pushing back the seething crowd. The billy-clubs were out and the cop in charge of the advance swung his club in the air in front of the marshalling line.

Rising to fury, some people behind the line began to rock and bang on an empty police cruiser, a supervisor's car, which must have been left in the middle of the road before the marshalling line sprang up between it and the cops.

For whatever reason, the police went berserk and broke through the line, shoving and clubbing. Tim McCaskell, a member of the RTPC executive and of the Body Politic collective, went down with a gash to the head which would later require six stitches to close.

The police continued to advance as they knocked people to the ground, piling fresh victims on top of the already fallen. A woman apparently had her leg broken. Others were pinned against the car and beaten. MCC pastor Brent Hawkes, going to the rescue of an older man who was being kicked as he lay on the pavement, was seized and held by two cops as a third punched him. Another victim was pinned down by three police officers while a fourth attacked her crotch with his billyclub. Later she kicked the police supervisor in the shoulder, dislocating it.

All the while, the cops continued their push south. The marshalling line tried to re-form south of the captured cruiser, but was in disarray.

It was at this point that police car 5210, with one police officer at the wheel and another in the passenger seat, suddenly turned onto Church and headed for the dwindling army of demonstrators. According to one witness, the cruiser slowed almost to a stop and then accelerated into the backs of those who still gathered in the middle of the street.

People scattered gingerly to either side and the tattered remains of the marshalling line collapsed on the north edge of the assembly. Ken Popert, a marshal and a member of the Body Politic collective, was struck down as he tried to move out of the path of the car, bouncing off the passenger side of the hood and hitting the pavement to one side of the car, which did not stop.

The police continued to harry what was left of the crowd, driving it to the sidewalks, from which it began to melt away.

Three people were sufficiently injured to require treatment at the emergency ward of Wellesley Hospital; in addition to McCaskell and Popert, a woman demonstrator was treated for her leg injury.

Police reported to the press that, of the six people arrested and charged with assaulting police or obstructing police, all but one were agitators who attempted to disrupt the demonstration.

An investigation by *The Body Politic*, however, has revealed that three of the accused had taken part in the demonstration, one was a passer-by arrested while trying to help a woman being attacked by the police, and the remaining two — an eighteen-year-old woman and a forty-two-year-old man — clearly were not among the troublemakers captured in photographs.

Police claims to the contrary, not a single person who attacked the demonstration was charged.

Attempts to take action against the police after the June 20 demonstration proved futile. Brent Hawkes, acting as a private citizen, tried to launch common assault charges against the policeman who is alleged to have punched him. The Crown intervened in court to prevent him from conducting his own

suit, then eventually refused to proceed, claiming lack of necessary informa-
tion. Ken Popert made attempts to lay a complaint and criminal charges
against the policeman responsible for his injuries. The police claimed they
couldn't discover who was driving the patrol car that night. A justice of the
peace refused to accept the charge because Popert was unable to identify the
driver.

The Bruner Report: September 24, 1981
A strongly worded report commissioned by Toronto City Council has called
for the establishment of a permanent gay/police dialogue committee, an end
to police entrapment and undercover surveillance of gays, and the recognition of gays as a legitimate minority entitled to legal protection against discrimination.

Law student and journalist Arnold Bruner, who researched and wrote the
report in two months, was directed by council July 13 to look into the "disagreement and difficulties surrounding the police and the homosexual community."

City council appropriated twenty-two thousand dollars for the study, to include a stipend of two hundred and fifty dollars a day, a research assistant and
visits to San Francisco and Vancouver. The study was the city's compromise
response to five months of pressure and agitation for a public inquiry into
police raids and mass arrests in four Toronto bathhouses in February.

Released September 24, Bruner's report, entitled *Out of the Closet*, makes
sixteen recommendations. Among them:

• The establishment of a police/gay dialogue committee to meet on a regular
basis and to be composed of at least two police officers, at least two gay people
selected by the community, and an impartial chairperson appointed by the
city.

• That the chief of police clarify to the force and to the public that the gay
community (a) constitutes a legitimate minority, entitled to the same rights
and the same respect, service and protection as all other law-abiding citizens,
and (b) is not to be singled out for special attention by police, uniformed or
plainclothes.

• That the chief of police issue a new directive on the use of abusive language,
ordering supervisors to discourage its use by police personnel in the station as
well as in public, and making it clear that infractions will result in disciplinary
action.

• That undercover surveillance of public washrooms be discontinued and
that the arrest of persons suspected of engaging in sex in public parks also be
discontinued while the dialogue committee finds a solution to these "problem areas."

• That the police guidelines on law enforcement give lower priority to cases of
sexual practices among adults where there are no observers, minors or unwilling participants.

• That lower priority also be given to entrapment in cases involving participants in sex acts in private.

• That leaders of gay community organizations, in a spirit of dialogue, urge on the gay community the value of a moderate stance toward police, law officials and government.

• That a gay awareness programme be established as a regular part of trainee curriculum for recruits of the Metro police force. The programme should consult qualified members of the gay community, gay police officers and include a guided tour of gay establishments.

• That the Toronto police force establish a long-range programme to raise the educational levels of the force, expecially in the middle and senior ranks.

• That the provincial government change the makeup of the police commission to make it more representative of the community by allowing for a woman member and for representation of ethnic and cultural groups, including the gay community from time to time.

• That Metro Council prohibit discrimination in hiring of its employees on the grounds of sexual orientation.

• That the provincial government amend its human rights legislation to prohibit discrimination on the grounds of sexual orientation.

Following the release of the report, the recently formed Toronto Gay Community Council, at a press conference representing about twelve groups, gave cautious approval to most of the recommendations.

The community council was responsible for organizing the closest thing Bruner got to a public hearing into the question of gay/police relations. The meeting, which took place August 18 at Jarvis Collegiate, heard bitter testimony of police harassment from individuals, and briefs and recommendations from nine gay, lesbian and feminist organizations.

Chris Bearchell, speaking for the council, disputed Bruner's perception that lack of communication between gays and the police was the basic problem, to be solved merely by sitting down and talking. Right to Privacy Committee chairperson George Smith said, "The report's major deficiency is that it doesn't look adequately at the management of the police. The real question is how the police force is run and how it's going to be run." MCC pastor Brent Hawkes, whose hunger strike last spring helped launch the study, said he was "ecstatic" about the positive content of Bruner's findings.

(Hawkes began his protest in late February. He remained on a hunger strike for twenty-five days, pledging not to eat until an independent inquiry was launched. His tactic worked in part. He ended his fast March 12 after Toronto City Council called on Dan Hill, the mayor's advisor on race relations, to conduct a limited study into "disagreements and difficulties." Hill hedged on accepting the offer and delayed several months before finally refusing It was not until July 13 that Arnold Bruner was selected to take Hill's place.)

The report ran into heavier fire from politicians and distorted coverage from the media. Much of the criticism seemed to result from a failure to read the entire report carefully, and from misinterpretation of ambiguous wording in two of the recommendations—the call for a "moratorium" on park and washroom arrests, and the proposal for "recruitment" of gays and lesbians into the police force.

Mayor Art Eggleton worried that the recommendations would "give special status to the gay community." He said, "It's wrong for the police department to be asking anyone what their sexual orientation is."

In an attempt to counter the effects of this initial media distortion, Bruner clarified the wording of some of his recommendations in a letter to city council.

"Nowhere in the report is there any recommendation, proposal or suggestion concerning a quota system, nor the slightest allusion to preferential treatment for the gay community or any other community," he said. He repeated the report's wording: "I propose a joint community programme which would basically be an 'outreach' programme operated by the gay community."

Bruner also clarified his remark about the police control of sexual activity in washrooms and parks. "The report does not call for an end to surveillance —but for an end to *hidden* surveillance, which in a public washroom is a general invasion of privacy, and for an end to entrapment techniques," he said. "The report calls for well-publicized patrolling by police as a way of crime prevention. There was no intention to suggest that the police should ignore public complaints in these areas, or that they should refrain from arresting offenders in response to public complaints."

Bruner claimed he was not calling for special status for the gay community, merely asking that all members of the public be treated equally. "This recommendation goes to the heart of the problem between the police and the homosexual community," he said. "The high priority given to (law enforcement in the area of) consensual sexual activity led to the bathhouse raids and mass arrests."

One section of the report documents attitudes of both senior police officials and members of the Metro Toronto Police Association, which represents officers below the rank of staff sergeant. Bruner paraphrases the reasons which association president Paul Walter gave for his membership being opposed to the hiring of gay policemen: they would be "prone to engage in overt sex acts with each other in inappropriate places," they "might slip away to have sex" if placed on duty together, and they "would attempt to seduce heterosexual policemen—particularly young ones."

Following the release of the report, Walter took the unusual step of writing a letter to the mayor and city council challenging Bruner's reporting of their conversation. He said that the statements were a "severe distortion of my point of view," but did not deny that he had made them. He claimed that the remarks were "clearly jocular and made in a light-hearted vein."

Bruner said that he had taken Walter's remarks seriously, and as representative of the homophobic view of many members of the police association.

Although not an inquiry into the bathhouse raids, Bruner states that "it would be sticking one's head in the sand to ignore that (it) is a direct result of events precipitated by those raids." In order to get beyond the official excuse that nothing could be said because the matter was "before the courts," Bruner attempted to obtain direct authorization to comment from Attorney General

Roy McMurtry. He submitted a list of questions to McMurtry—including one which asked "What officials knew of the raids before they were carried out?" A reply was sent back with only one answer, according to Bruner: "Neither McMurtry nor any official in his ministry knew of the raids before they were carried out." All other questions, writes Bruner, either "touched on evidence, were a 'post-mortem of the raid' or were outside the scope of the study and therefore were not answered."

One of the key conclusions of the Bruner report is that "Toronto's gay community is a community in fact." Bruner felt that a large section describing the customs and culture of the gay community was essential for its educational value. He called it "a major part of the report—second only to the recommendations."

"The gay community is the community that is misunderstood," he said. "Knowledge of it is obscured by myth, stereotyping, prejudices and fear. That's where the exposition was needed. The same thing was not possible with the police without doing a deep sociological probe."

"This report says things people don't want to hear," Bruner commented weeks after its release, "and that may be used to discredit it. But we can't go backwards now."

"In my view," he writes, "the issue of dealing with the gay fact in our community emerges fully 'out of the closet' with this study and this report."

Major developments after this date centred on reaction to the Bruner Report and the slow passage of the many cases through the court system. In November, Toronto City Council called on police chief Jack Ackroyd to act on two recommendations of the Bruner Report—to acknowledge the gay community as legitimate and to approve a gay awareness programme for police recruits. Ackroyd issued a statement in response January 20, 1982 which was too equivocal to satisfy most people in the gay community. As of March 1982, there was no discernable pattern in the disposition in the courts of the three hundred and forty-four bawdyhouse or conspiracy-related charges. One "conspirator" (Jack Campbell, American head of the Club Bath Chain) pleaded guilty and was heavily fined. One keeper at each of two baths was bargained into a guilty plea in return for charges being withdrawn against the other keepers. Few alleged found-ins had pleaded guilty, but several were found guilty. Proportionately more were acquitted or had their charges withdrawn. Meanwhile, estimates of the total cost to the taxpayers of police operations and court proceedings ranged as high as ten million dollars.

Homos at war
Gary Ostrom

Issue 43, May 1978; Issue 59, December 1979/January 1980

A "Gay Watch" tartan is created for the popular kilted divisions…

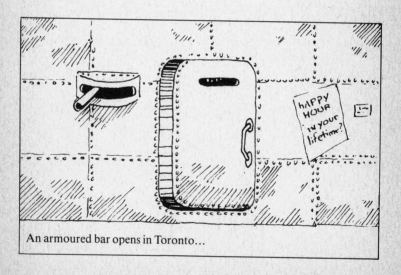

An armoured bar opens in Toronto…

A general strike cripples the nation…

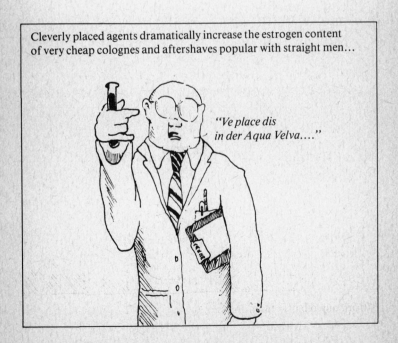

Suicide squads of Cockettes
fiendishly disguised
in leisure suits
hijack singles bars
and hold them
for ransom...

*"Alright,
everybody strip!
These nails are
poison!"*

Dykes on Bikes terrorize tourists by riding
through the halls of Holiday Inns at 3 am...

The MCC simultaneously immolate
themselves in washrooms across the nation…

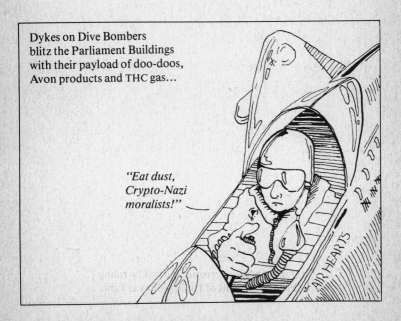

Dykes on Dive Bombers
blitz the Parliament Buildings
with their payload of doo-doos,
Avon products and THC gas…

*"Eat dust,
Crypto-Nazi
moralists!"*

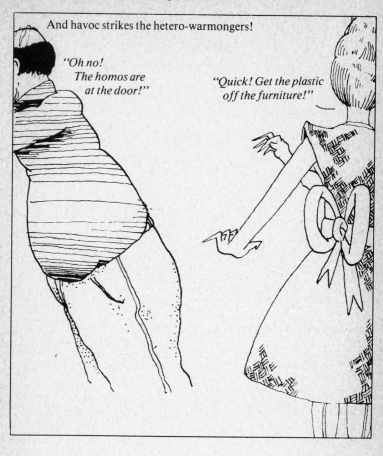

Contributors

Paul Aboud's "claims to fame" are: his *Body Politic* cartoons, being an alleged keeper of a Toronto bathhouse, and two cats who eat on command... though not necessarily in that order.

Beatrice Baker is an Ottawa lesbian gay liberation activist, currently on maternity leave.

Chris Bearchell was born in Edmonton, Alberta in 1953. She began writing for *TBP* in February 1976, became a director of the Body Politic Free the Press Fund in February 1978 and joined the editorial collective for Issue 49 in December 1978.

Rick Bébout was born in Massachusetts in 1950 and immigrated to Canada in 1969. He has been doing editorial, administrative and design work for *TBP* for the past five years.

Andrew Britton lives in London, England and teaches film studies at Essex University. He has written on film for *Movie* and *Framework*, has contributed articles to *Gay Left*, and is currently working on a book on gays and the law.

Walter Bruno, since leaving *TBP* in 1974, has earned a couple of masters degrees, spent two years in France, made two short films, and is now involved in theatre. He has had one play produced professionally.

Leo Casey is a politically incorrect and generally irreverent faggot who will admit to being a democratic socialist and an heretical Marxist in his more sober moments. He is on the verge of escaping from graduate school with a degree in political theory, with which he will return to his native land south of the forty-ninth parallel. His Canadian interregnum has included stints on the Ontario Federation of Students executive and the Body Politic collective.

John D'Emilio is a writer, activist and historian living in New York City. An expanded and substantially revised version of "Dreams deferred" will appear in *Out of the Closets: The Homosexual Emancipation Movement in the United States, 1940-1970 (Chicago: University of Chicago Press, 1983)*.

Val Edwards, born in Sarnia, Ontario, has been active in the gay movement since January 1, 1978 (a New Year's resolution). However, she is currently pursuing a Bay Street legal career, but she assures us that it's only a phase.

Lilith Finkler, now twenty-three, is a Toronto activist organizing in various social change movements. Her present work involves creating links between women and other oppressed groups in order to overthrow patriarchy. She is not ambitious!

Gerald Hannon has been a collective member of *The Body Politic* since its second issue. He enjoys homosexuality, opera, homosexuality, travel and homosexuality, in that order.

Robin Hardy was born in Yarmouth, Nova Scotia, grew up in Winnipeg and Ottawa, attended the University of Alberta in Edmonton, graduated from Dalhousie Law School in Halifax, and is now a freelance writer living in Toronto. Reaching no absolute in which to rest, he fools himself that he is always nearer by never keeping still.

Andrew Hodges, who lives in London, England, is co-author of *With Downcast Gays*, published in 1977 by Pink Triangle Press. Due soon is his biography of Alan Turing — a chief World War II cryptanalyst, inventor of the computer, and gay man who flaunted it.

Ed Jackson, born in New Brunswick in 1945, has been involved with *The Body Politic* since its second issue. He wouldn't have missed any of it.

Gary Kinsman, of Toronto, is currently a sociology student at the Ontario Institute for Studies in Education. He describes himself as a gay feminist socialist, and is a member of Gay Liberation Against the Right Everywhere.

Michael Lynch, a movement activist through the Seventies, has turned "typewriter activist" in the Eighties. Involved with *TBP* since 1973, he now indulges in full-time fathering, gay studies, and his first novel, *The Very Man*.

Tim McCaskell was the Canadian representative at the Second Annual International Gay Association in Barcelona in 1980 and spent time in the Basque country while in Spain. McCaskell has been a member of the Body Politic collective since 1975.

David Mole lives with his lover in Winnipeg where he teaches economics at the University of Manitoba. His economic journalism and reviews also appear in *Fuse* magazine, in *Canada Dance News* and on CBC radio and television.

Gordon Montador is currently writing fiction and living in Toronto.

Brian Mossop. Born London, England 1946. Last thirty-one years in Toronto. Occupation: translater. Avocation: activist in student and trade union movements before coming out in 1974, in gay movement thereafter. Expelled from Communist Party of Canada in 1976 for gay activism. Has been president of Toronto Gay Alliance Toward Equality and coordinator of Coalition of Gay Rights in Ontario. Currently dabbling in various gay community activities.

Gary ("Whom the hive doesn't cherish, it eats") *Ostrom* was found on a hillside wrapped in old *New Yorker* magazines. His work has appeared in *TBP* since 1972. He is obviously self-taught. There is an institution at the end of his rainbow.

Stan Persky teaches sociology and political science at Northwest College in Terrace, BC. He is the author of *At the Lenin Shipyard: Poland and the Solidarity Trade Union Movement* (New Star, 1981) and two books on BC politics.

Ken Popert is a *TBP* bureaucrat who likes to see himself as a radical democrat, gay activist and socialist. He once thought that his politics should guide his sex life, but has since found that both work better if his sex life guides his politics.

Jeff Richardson: G/M, 24, 150, 5'7" brown, brown. Insincere, hates meaningful relationships, loathes sharing/caring. Sleeps through sex. Interests: toaster-ovens. Photo and phone get nothing.

Michael Riordon. "I've learned I fear women even more than men. But am coming to know some of each, gingerly. I'm absorbed with Latin American struggles; the distance is maddening. The agitprop street-theatre group I've started may... I'm allowed forty words!"

Marie Robertson lives in Ottawa, where she spends her time writing, lusting after Christie, polishing her tap shoes, programming computers and feeling incredibly guilty and unproductive since her "retirement" from the political scene. Fortunately, these feelings don't last long.

Jane Rule, born in 1931, is the author of *Desert of the Heart, This Is Not For You, Theme for Diverse Instruments, Lesbian Images, Against the Season, The Young in One Another's Arms, Contract with the World* and *Outlander.*

Vito Russo is a freelance writer and the author of *The Celluloid Closet.* He lives in New York City and is not affiliated with any organization. He abhors political correctness.

James Steakley is an assistant professor in the Department of German at the University of Wisconsin in Madison. His book, *The Homosexual Emancipation Movement in Germany* (New York: Arno Press, 1975), is an expanded treatment of a series of articles that appeared in *The Body Politic* in 1973-74.

Scott Tucker (Philadelphia, Pennsylvania, USA): "I salivate at the sight of black basketball sneakers, what else do you need to know? If you *insist* on politics, my main concern is International Terrorists, like Reagan, Brezhnev and John Paul II."

Brian Waite. A lapsed Trotskyist, Brian has not been politically active for some years now. But like an old fire-horse that smells smoke and still a firm believer in broadly based mass action in the streets, he can be found at such actions as demos and rallies against the bath raids. Who was it that said, "Being creates consciousness" or "If the towel fits, wear it"?

Irene Warner is the pseudonym for a thirty-seven-year-old Toronto single parent and teacher whose most important relationships have been with women.

Lorna Weir has been an activist in feminist, lesbian and gay politics. She is currently hoping to find the time to complete a thesis in political theory.

Alexander Wilson is a former member of the Body Politic collective. He has taught literature, history and science fiction at the University of Toronto. His writing on culture has appeared in *Gay Community News*, *Fuse* and *Social Text.*

Mariana Valverde has been living in Toronto for the past five years, and is active in socialist-feminist and lesbian politics in the city. She has just completed a PhD in Social and Political Thought and is now living in the twilight zone of underemployment.

Ian Young is a poet, editor and bibliographer. His books include *Common-Or-Garden Gods*, *The Male Muse: A Gay Anthology*, *On the Line: The New Gay Fiction*, and *The Male Homosexual in Literature: A Bibliography*. His latest book is *Overlooked and Underrated: Essays on Some 20th Century Writers*, an anthology published as a special issue of *Little Caesar* magazine. He writes regularly for several gay periodicals in Great Britain, the US and Sweden. His column, The Ivory Tunnel, appears monthly in *The Body Politic*.

Eve Zaremba lives in Toronto, works on *Broadside*, a feminist review. She has published *Reason to Kill*, a thriller with a dyke detective, *Privilege of Sex: A Century of Canadian Women*, and numerous articles on feminist and lesbian issues. She is presently working on a book on sociobiology.

Index

Index 307

"lesbian," as adjectival qualifier 100, 101
oppression 91-94, 98-100
promiscuous/effeminate/deviant notions 95-96
Labonté, Richard 112, 117
L'Association homophile de Montréal /Gay Montreal Association 228
Le Berdache 236
Leckie, Dan 279
Lee, John 58, 61
lesbians/lesbianism 42-43
civil rights of 184
critique of pedophilia by 168-69
feminism and 175-76, 177-78, 181-82, 186, 195-96
gay males in Basque and 253-54
gay men, working with 175-76
gender of women and 179
"lesbian," as adjective 100-01
male chauvinism and 179-80, 183, 195
motherhood case 239
as mothers 58, 59, 60-64
recognition of 20-24
Robin Tyler's view of 106-07
separatism and 176, 178, 179
sexual freedom of men, as issue 181
sexuality of 254
sexual liberation 178-79, 181
sexual objectification 179-81
stereotypes and realities of 101, 102, 192-93
"unity" with gay movement 179-80, 181, 182, 184-86
visibility of 183, 186
Lesbian Mothers Defence Fund 234
Lesbian Organization of Toronto (LOOT) 231
Levy, Jerry 284, 286
Lewis, Stephen 265, 280
lover/friend dichotomy 96-98
Lynch, Michael 168

McArthur, Scott 64, 65, 70, 72
McCarthy, Senator Joseph 127, 158
McCaskell, Tim 247, 281, 285, 290
McKay, Winfield 279, 283
McLeod, Bruce 279
McMurray, Alan 27, 29, 30, 31, 32
McMurtry, Attorney General Roy 277, 278, 279, 281, 284, 288, 294
Mager, Don 57, 58
male chauvinism 179-80, 183, 195

Maloney, Peter 231, 241, 263, 272, 278, 284, 285, 287
"Man, being a" 190-91
Manitoba Gay Coalition 232
Marks, Deputy Police Chief 276
marriage, first gay (Canada) 229
masturbation:
by children 164
myths about 163
Mattachine Review 137
Mattachine Society 127-38
Bachelors for Wallace 129
communism and 127, 128-29, 130, 132, 136, 137
conservatism within 135-37
conventions 135
discussion group 135
early organizational structure 131-32
founding of 131
Henry Hay's leadership 128-33
homosexuals as minority, idea of 134
ideology of 133
lessons of 137
mass action 135
Mattachine Review 137
ONE 135
personal histories of founders, as theoretical base of 133-34
repressive climate in Fifties, 131-33
structure of 133
media:
community right to 211-13
violence against gays and 204
See also Cruising; Sharing the Secret
"Men loving boys loving men" 5, 146-47, 161-62, 167-74, 195, 233
Mercer, Judge Thomas 30, 243
Metropolitan Community Church (MCC) 116, 228, 245, 274
Milk, Harvey 216, 235, 236
Miller, Brian 56
Mineshaft 200, 201
minority, gays as 138-39, 244
molestation, child 147-39, 150, 158, 159, 161, 166, 167
Monk, Jim 235, 274
Montreal Gay Woman 228
Morton, Howard 284
Moscone, Mayor George 235
Mossop, Brian 231

National Council for Civil Liberties (Britain) 27